ONE STEP-

"You're like me, L[...] [...]nd, the rain, the sun, the moon, clean air."

I'm not like you at all, she thought fiercely. *I have plans for my life, places to go, things to learn, security to gain for my mother and sister.* But she remembered the way his music had called to her, an invitation to the wind, a summoning to be free, and she was suddenly nervous.

"What are you doing at Ruby's anyway?" she asked.

He stepped into the light and smiled a slow, lazy smile. "I wanted to dance with you."

Ivory Joe Hunter's "Since I Met You, Baby" came from the speakers hanging in the eaves of Ruby's roof. Black came toward her, into the wavering neon light.

"Here?" she questioned, her heart beating wildly. "Here in the parking lot?"

He put his arms around her. Heart in her throat now, and with the brief sensation that this was the beginning of something that couldn't be finished, she drifted naturally into his body, and they began to dance. . . .

Linda Anderson

OVER THE MOON

A SIGNET BOOK

SIGNET
Published by the Penguin Group
Penguin Books USA Inc., 375 Hudson Street,
New York, New York 10014, U.S.A.
Penguin Books Ltd, 27 Wrights Lane,
London W8 5TZ, England
Penguin Books Australia Ltd, Ringwood,
Victoria, Australia
Penguin Books Canada Ltd, 10 Alcorn Avenue,
Toronto, Ontario, Canada M4V 3B2
Penguin Books (N.Z.) Ltd, 182–190 Wairau Road,
Auckland 10, New Zealand

Penguin Books Ltd, Registered Offices:
Harmondsworth, Middlesex, England

First published by Signet, an imprint of Dutton Signet,
a division of Penguin Books USA Inc.

First Printing, February, 1995
10 9 8 7 6 5 4 3 2 1

PUBLISHER'S NOTE
This is a work of fiction. Names, characters, places, and incidents either are the product of the author's imagination or are used fictitiously, and any resemblance to actual persons, living or dead, events, or locales is entirely coincidental.

Dedicated to my mother,
Irene Berry Kirchman,
who would have been so proud.

ACKNOWLEDGMENTS

Love and thank you to Hugh, Kris, Karin, Melissa, Alec, and Duffy Anderson for their faith in me. A particular thank-you to Linda Parr who did much of the drudgery.

Acknowledgments to Sue Yuen for believing in me, to Jennifer Enderlin for taking the gamble, and to Jeanmarie LeMense who shepherded this book to its final berth. Deep gratitude to Pam Amerine, Sandy Coakley, Pam Mantovani, and Debbie St. Amand. I couldn't have done it without you.

Finally, thank you to my friends and relatives in West Virginia who drew me into their hearts again, as they always have and always will.

Part One

Summer 1950

Chapter 1

The three loutish young men had hidden themselves well in the thick-forested mountainside. While they waited, one whittled a rhododendron stick, one examined his navel, and the other stared dully into space. The lush signs of spring erupting around them were ignored and unappreciated. The one who whittled stopped for a moment to peer through the bushes. He folded his pocket knife and shoved it in the pocket of his soiled overalls as he turned to motion to the others.

"She's comin'."

Lilibet Springer climbed the steep, narrow, barely discernible mountain path with sureness. The evergreens grew taller and thicker as she went, the bottom branches easily accessible with a stretch of the hand. She reached to touch one spiny branch and then held her finger beneath her nose to inhale the sticky, piney residue.

Her skin crawled with the sensation that someone watched her. The glorious day she'd planned alone on the mountain had soured, but she kept moving, assuring herself it was her imagination. No one else knew this area or had the ambition to venture this far from the mining camp.

A Cincinnati Reds baseball cap, its bill turned backward, hid her hair. Covering her slight form, a denim-blue shirt billowed over old patched jeans. A strip of fair, white skin gleamed between outgrown jeans and high-top hiking boots.

She'd turned eighteen yesterday. Marm had scraped together enough money to buy her a simple white dress for graduation, but today she was giving herself the best birthday present. She was going to her secret place. Determined to enjoy the time to herself, she threw off her uneasiness and moved eagerly away from the screeching sound of coal cars traveling on the tipple down the mountain. As she moved deeper into the wilderness, the noise faded then disappeared.

With growing excitement she searched for the first signs of spring. She grinned at every white bloodroot and said hello to the diminutive dogtooth violets. Every step upward took her to where the air was clean, the trillium grew pure white and free of coal dust, and the only sounds heard were those of a warbler or the buzzing of an industrious bee.

A pungent odor intruded rudely upon the fresh, woodsy air about her. Her heart jumped and she quickened her pace.

They couldn't have followed her. She'd been careful to elude her snake of a brother Eugene and his buddies, the MacDonald boys. Evidently, not careful enough. Angry with herself for not using the tracking skills she'd been taught, she began to run. They must have been downwind, dammit.

A grimy hand shot out from a purple laurel bush and clasped around her ankle, bringing her down with a painful thud. Knocked breathless, Lilibet fought gamely to gather her wits about her. She gulped and released a scream of outrage that rent the quiet mountain air.

Virgil MacDonald flipped her over on her back, sat on top of her, and ran his hands roughly over her chest. Through the strings of greasy red hair hanging lank to his gap-toothed mouth, she could see his eyes were feverish with excitement.

"Gawd Almighty, Lilibet! You sure took long enough to come full-growed," he whined.

"Atta boy, Virgil. Uncover them titties Hee, heeee . . . thought I didn't know you had 'em, did you? Been tryin' to hide 'em, ain't you? Well, I seen plenty through the crack in the outhouse door."

"Get him off me, Eugene!"

Desperately, she fought the searching hands.

"Hell no. Jest because I'm your brother don't mean that I don't want to see 'em, too. Hee, hee, heeee . . .

looka there, Jud, your brother sure knows how to handle a girl, don't he?" Eugene Springer snickered as he punched Jud MacDonald in the side with his elbow. Jud's eyes held the same animal fever as Virgil's as he watched him maul the struggling girl.

Anger fueled Lilibet and she raised up as far as she could and sank her even white teeth into Virgil's arm, drawing blood. He yelped and drew back to hit her, but Eugene caught the fist before it could connect with her chin.

"Nope. None of that, Virg. My pa's gonna be mad if he finds out. If you mark her, he'll know and he'll sure as hell kill me. Jud, you get down there and hold her arms while Virgil does his explorin' and then you can have a turn at feelin' them beauts. And, if you all promise me more of your best moonshine, I'll even let you take down them panties for a real feel."

Jud, dropping to his knees, caught Lilibet's pummeling arms and pinned them to the ground. His oily, pimpled face hung over Lilibet's. From his slack mouth came the smell of stale whiskey and rotting teeth. His brother, Virgil, as always, smelled of urine. Their rancid body odor was sickening.

She knew Eugene wouldn't let them really harm her—or hadn't intended to—but she saw the lust mounting in their twenty-year-old eyes. Eugene wouldn't have much to say about what they did to her. Fingers of fear twisted through Lilibet's anger. With determination she fought off the fear and stoked the anger. She would not be defeated, never, and certainly not by this low-life scum.

Jerking her body hard, again and again, she tried to throw Virgil off. Rocks and prickly pinecones on the path cut painfully into the tender skin on her back. She bucked and squirmed desperately, anything to keep his dirty hands from her.

"Get off me this instant!" she ordered. It took every ounce of control she possessed to keep her voice from shaking. "If you don't stop this, I'll tell Deputy Hager where your still is."

"My, my, don't she talk so proper since she's been

goin' to county high school. Maybe you shoulda gone to school, too, Eugene," said Virgil with a laugh.

She brought her knee up and jabbed Virgil hard in the small of his back. He grunted and slid backward to sit on her thighs.

"Hold still, Lilibet, this won't hurt, an' I been waitin' to see these tits since we first seen 'em start to grow: This here's worth goin' to jail for. Besides, you ain't goin' to tell Hager, cause if you do I'll tell him about Eugene's runnin' shine for us. Your pa wouldn't like that, now, would he?"

Despite her frantic movements, Virgil managed to bunch her shirt under her chin and pull up her bra. Her breasts were now exposed, the breasts she'd meant for only one person to see. She sucked in her breath to keep from crying as she felt the clean air hit them and the dirty eyes looking at them. She bit her lip as he pinched a nipple with his gritty fingers and laughed, and she felt the hardness of him biting into her jeans. Her stomach turned over and bile filled her throat.

"Hoo, eeee ... wouldn't Cledith Hutton like to get a good look-see at those, now wouldn't he, Lilibet?" asked Jud, leering down at her from above. "He's your boyfriend, ain't he?"

Keep them talking, she told herself.

"No, he isn't." Her tone low and fierce, she choked back the urge to vomit.

"No, but you'd sure like for him to be, wouldn't you? Ever since you first saw him in ninth grade, you've had a strong hankerin' for him." Virgil sneered, his hand rubbing her breast. "Honey, he don't know you're alive."

Don't panic. Keep them talking, she reminded herself, keep them talking. They'd been playing around with her until now, but she sensed that the cruel mauling had turned to lust. Virgil was panting, his eyes hazed with heat, and Jud's hot spittle drooled onto her cheek.

"He spoke to me at school yesterday," she insisted through clenched teeth.

"Honey, them rich town folks ain't for the likes of us mountain people ... especially you. ... Your pa works in Pappy Hutton's mines," Virgil sneered, his chest heaving as he ground himself against her. He lowered his head to fasten his slobbering mouth onto her pink nipple.

Suddenly, a tanned hand caught Virgil's shirt collar and jerked him cruelly to his feet. Lilibet tried to roll away, but Jud quickly took Virgil's place on top of her.

"Hey, what the hell's goin' on?" Virgil yelled. He dangled in the air, his booted toes searching frantically for the ground.

"Tell your brother to let the young lady go." The threatening demand was enunciated directly into Virgil's ear.

"Hell, no! Jud, don't let her up. I don't know who you are, mister, but you're fuckin' with the wrong people."

Lilibet, busily battling Jud's dirty hands, caught a brief glimpse of the man who held Virgil. This nightmare is getting worse, she thought, for she could swear it was an Indian who blocked the sun as he dangled the furious, cursing, red-faced Virgil. With a frightened squeak Virgil abruptly stopped struggling, and Lilibet realized the stranger had brought a knife tight under Virgil's chin.

"Jud MacDonald, I'll give you five seconds to get off the young lady or I'll gladly slit Virgil's filthy throat," warned the cold voice.

Stunned, Jud twisted his head to look up at the tall, bronzed, half-naked figure who held a knife at his brother's throat. The mercilessness in the eyes of the grim-visaged man convinced Jud that he meant exactly what he said. A drop of Virgil's blood already trickled down the mirror-shiny surface of the lethal knife.

Eugene Springer, backing away, said, "J-J-Jud, if I was you I'd do what he says. I think it's Black Brady, and he means what he says."

Jud leaped off of Lilibet.

Pulling her bra into place with an angry yank, she jumped up, allowing her shirt to fall back around her slim hips. The baseball cap fell off as she stood and a glorious mane of silvery-gold hair tumbled forth and lay in wavy disarray over her shoulders. With a furious swipe of her hand, she wiped Jud's spittle from her cheek.

Eugene was long gone, but Lilibet charged for the nearest target, which was bandy-legged Jud MacDonald.

Breathless with fury and embarrassment, her face a mask
of icy resolve, she attacked him. She kicked his shins and
swung her small fists, punching ferociously at his shoulders, his chest, and anywhere she could reach.

The stranger gave Virgil a vicious shake, then dropped
him on the path like a piece of maggoty meat.

"If I were you boys, I'd take off and not come back,
because it looks like if I don't finish you off, Miss Hell-
cat here will."

Jud and Virgil MacDonald backed away carefully.
Lilibet, breathing hard after her attack on Jud, saw the
calculation in their eyes as they estimated their chances
of rushing the man who stood before them. There were
two of them but he was twice their size and he was quick
with his knife. He slipped the knife back into its sheath
and stared back at them, almost daring them to come at
him.

"I mean it," he cautioned, venom dripping from his
voice. "Touch her again and I'll slice off your ears faster
than fat on a side of pork."

"You ain't seen the last of us, mister," muttered Virgil.
The brothers gave the man and Lilibet one last murderous
look and slunk away.

Lilibet brushed herself off and tried to tuck her hair
back into the baseball cap. Glistening curls escaped and
framed her heart-shaped face, wisps of it falling into her
violet eyes.

"Are you all right? Did they hurt you?" he asked.

"I'm just dandy, and I could have taken care of them
myself," she replied angrily.

"Didn't look like it to me, missy," he said and stepped
closer to stare at her.

Lilibet stared back at him, carefully concealing her as-
tonishment at the apparition before her. Old man mountain had reached into the bowels of the earth and brought
forth an Indian savage from a century ago. He stood well
over six feet tall, naked and bronzed to the waist where
a loincloth tied with leather thongs covered his private
parts. A sheathed knife hugged his lean hips. Long, muscular legs stretched below the loincloth to feet covered
with well-worn moccasins.

She raised her head to look full into his face. The harsh planes of his square jaws and high cheekbones gave it an imperious look. Black hair fell across his smooth forehead and into crystal-clear, green eyes. They were, she thought fleetingly, the eyes of a mystic, and a feathery tingle ran up her spine. They looked vaguely familiar, but how could there be two such pairs of eyes in this world?

For a brief moment she wondered if she should be afraid. After all, they were alone and he looked pretty fierce. She saw amusement crystallize in his amazing eyes and her fear turned to curiosity. An odd urge to touch him shook her. She wanted to reach out and feel the tanned skin on his arm. It looked ... pleasantly warm, healthy, vibrant. A tremor leaped from her toes to her tummy. *You're crazy, Lilibet Springer.*

"Seen enough?" he asked with amusement.

"And you, have you seen enough?" she asked, trying to mask her embarrassment at the emotion her voice betrayed. A belligerent lip poked out and she placed her fists on her hips.

The attack had left her shaking inside, but she'd be damned if she'd reveal any emotion to this arrogant person standing tall in front of her.

"Enough to know that if you have any manners, you've forgotten to say 'thank you', and enough to wonder what you're doing up here in the first place."

His voice intrigued her. It was husky, smoky.

Grudgingly, she said, "Thank you. I was about to ask *you* what *you* were doing here. The boys must have been following me because no one knows about this path but me and Uncle East."

"Wasn't one of those trolls your brother?"

"Yes."

"If I had a sister, I wouldn't treat her like that."

"My brother's run wild since he was little. He's never been to school ..." She stopped abruptly. This stranger had probably saved her from rape, but she owed him no details of her personal life. She had no desire to tell anyone how she'd had to beg to go to school herself. "I asked you what *you* were doing up here."

He hesitated before replying, carefully surveying her

face again, then seemed to come to a decision and answered her. "I broke this path years ago, but I haven't been on this side of Catawba for a long time. I was getting reacquainted with it when I heard your scream."

"That's impossible. Uncle East said his grandson found the way through the gorge. You can't be his grandson— you're an Indian!"

The skin over his cheekbones tightened imperceptibly and his full mouth flattened cruelly.

"You have something against Indians?" His voice was hard and the coldness had returned to his eyes.

"No. But you'll have to admit that it's a bit unusual to find an Indian running around the mountains in this day and age. I mean, this is 1950, for heaven's sakes."

"Then I must be a figment of your imagination, or perhaps I've been reincarnated just to rescue you today," he said, the amusement back in his voice.

She shivered as she looked at him. This was no figment of her imagination. The savage energy that emanated from him was real, as was the pleasant musky scent of him, and the sheen of perspiration that covered his sleek muscles.

He reached over and tweaked her baseball cap, turning it so the bill now stuck out to one side. "The Reds haven't won a series since 1940. You need a new cap," he said teasingly.

Lilibet twisted the cap back to its original position and stood defiantly with her hands on her hips. "I listen to them every Saturday on the radio. They're doing okay."

"The Phillies will win the pennant." He smiled. "Since you seem to feel you own this path, perhaps I'd better let you be on your way to your 'secret place.' "

He slipped swiftly into the forest line without leaving a trace. Not a leaf shimmered or shook. It was as though he'd never been there.

Lilibet shook her head, bewildered and frightened by the turn of events in the past hour. She was stupid to have let the boys get that close to her . . . and how did the Indian know about her secret place? She looked up at the sun. She'd started late anyway. Now she would have to return home. There was homework to do and chores left from this morning. Ordinarily, she hated the trip back down the mountain toward the mining camp, but this time she turned down the path toward home gratefully.

The Indian watched as she made her way down the mountain. Silently, he tracked her progress, making sure no one followed her but himself. He smiled as he remembered the faint trembling of her sweet, lower lip that had betrayed her pretense of bravery. A virgin face, he decided, made by the angels for a man to cover with kisses. Surprise filled him as he realized he wanted to be that man. The tiny brown beauty mark near the corner of her mouth had been particularly enticing. He'd admired her courage under fire and been amused at her attack on Jud MacDonald. But admiration and amusement weren't reason enough for the lurch his heart had just experienced.

An hour later, he saw the dirty yellow-gray haze hovering in the air over Big Ugly Creek mining community and knew civilization was near. With a twinge of disappointment, he stopped and watched until Lilibet disappeared around a hillock, then he turned and ran back up the mountain.

Lilibet rounded the bend at Big Ugly and stopped at a small stream not far from the camp. She removed her hiking boots, hid them in a log, then fished out the school shoes she'd placed there earlier and slipped them on.

Coal dust coated everything she passed. Leaves, pale green at their birth a few weeks ago, hung heavy with black grit from the mines. A few of the dejected houses she passed boasted carefully tended lawns, but the grass was gray-green and struggled to survive. It looked as if a cheerless painter had come through and painted everything gray: houses, old cars, new cars, toys piled up in the yards, sheets hung on the line to dry. An invasive grit, it sifted through windows and vents, coating chairs, refrigerators, drawers, carpets, and clothes. Lilibet hated it. Marm said she'd grow used to it, but Lilibet hadn't and knew she never would.

Lilibet walked through the camp, head high and eyes straight ahead. She detested the whole look of it. The dingy houses, all in need of fresh paint, sat too close to one another, their porches and steps sagging with dejection. Leaky roofs hung over the rotting board and batten houses, and rubbish was strewn throughout the overgrown lawns.

Because Marm was a strong, determined woman, the Springer house sat back from the others. Her mother had begged, pleaded, wheedled, and generally made a pest of herself until management had said they could have the old house that sat by itself. At one time it had been the mine manager's house but now he lived in town with the rest of the higher-ups. Their house was larger than the others, with an extra bedroom and room for gardens in back and front.

Lilibet skirted the junk that kept piling up in the front yard. Marm had given up on her front garden, keeping only the small struggling patch in the rear. The junkyard began with a couple of derelict cars deserted by Lilibet's father, Roy. Rather than repair the cars or pay to have them hauled away, Roy simply left them in the yard, where they were soon joined by a broken porch swing, an old refrigerator, a battered washtub, and other odds and ends.

Her father had found a way to make a little money without working too hard. The coal mines had beaten all the ambition out of him. Roy discovered that people wanted to buy things that other people cast away, so he encouraged his neighbors to fill his yard with their throwaways. He didn't own the house, or the land it sat on, and management didn't seem to care about the way it looked so he figured he had a right.

Ernest Tubbs's twanging hillbilly voice singing "Have You Ever Been Lonely?" brayed from Marm's radio and out the open door. Lilibet smiled to herself. Ernest Tubbs wasn't a favorite of hers. Marm loved her hillbilly music, and Lilibet had been raised on it, but one day, while flipping the dial to find a baseball game, she'd discovered a radio station that played classical music. Curious, she'd listened awhile and decided she liked the old world melodies and symphonies. *Another subject I want to study in college,* she thought.

There was a time when she made fun of Marm's tunes, but Uncle East was teaching her to appreciate the history and tradition of Blue Ridge folk music and how it led to present-day hillbilly and country music. Her friend Donetta was teaching her to dance to rhythm and blues and the new rock and roll coming out of Nashville.

"Marm, I'm home," she called as she crossed the front porch.

"That's good, Lilibet, because I've been needing you. Margot needs her tutoring, and the garden needs hoeing." Regina Springer looked up from her ironing, reached to turn the sound down on her radio, and smiled at her oldest daughter. "Don't know what I'd do without you."

"I've got to hurry, Marm, I've got lots of homework."

"You study too long and too hard, Lilibet. You got all A's as it is. You know you're goin' to get one of them scholarships so just relax a bit."

"I don't want just any scholarship, Marm. I want to be valedictorian, and I want Judge Turner's scholarship."

Regina Springer set her iron down with a thump and turned to face her daughter. "Looka here, young lady, I think winning has become much too important to you. You are getting almost a full scholarship from the university as it is. Why do you need all of this, Lilibet? I think your sister could use a little of the attention you give to those books."

"You know why I want Judge Turner's scholarship, Marm. The person who wins it gets to live with Judge Turner's sister, Miss Mabel, in her beautiful house in Morgantown, and I want it." Then she lowered her voice and whispered to herself, "And I want to be valedictorian because I want to prove who's the best."

"What did you say?" asked her mother.

"Nothing. Where's Margot?"

"She's in the bedroom waiting for you like she always is."

Lilibet watched her mother smooth back her faded blond, gray-streaked hair, wearily wipe her arm across her brow, and lift the iron to get back to her work. Living in the camps had defeated her mother; the dirt, the dreary work that never let up, living from paycheck to paycheck.

The hell of it was there was nothing to look forward to but more of the same. If you ran out of money, you charged at the company store against your next paycheck. Some families were so deep in debt to the Hutton Company Store that they never saw the green of a dollar bill. The amount of their paycheck was deducted from the bill at the store month after month.

Depressing living conditions, frequent pregnancies, and the noncaring attitude of her husband had broken her once beautiful, laughing mother. Forty-year-old Regina Springer looked a wrung-out sixty. Lilibet promised herself that she would never let life defeat her as it had her mother. My life will shine brightly, she vowed. *I'll be safe. I'll have the security Marm has never had. I'll be damned if I'll live my life wondering if my husband can keep his job, and worrying if that same job will kill him.*

She crossed the cracked linoleum floor to stand behind Marm and, putting her arms around the thin back, hugged her. Her mother turned around to return the hug and they stood that way for a brief moment. Displays of affection were rare in this family. When they occurred they were precipitated by Lilibet.

As they drew away from each other, Lilibet caressed her mother's hand. "How's the arthritis today?"

Two fingers were missing from the work-worn hand, accidentally severed while Regina chopped wood one winter morning. Lilibet expertly massaged the misshapen hand and silently cursed her father, and her no-good brother.

"You got soothing hands, child," Marm said, but drew her hand away self-consciously. "But it's fine, just fine. Don't worry about me. Go to your sister. You're behind in her lessons and she won't be caught up with her class if you don't get your tutoring done." She glanced at a picture, an old *Life* magazine cover, tacked to the wall nearby. "I'll bet the Princess Lilibet takes good care of her little sister, Margot," she said as she turned back to her ironing.

Lilibet suppressed a sigh but entered the small bedroom she and her sister shared with a smile on her face. Fourteen-year-old Margot had what Marm called "weak lungs." Lilibet suspected it was tuberculosis and had suggested this to the company doctor. He ridiculed her and said that Margot had been born fragile and was susceptible to infections. Margot had missed so much school when she was younger that Marm got permission from the school board to keep her home. For the last four years Lilibet had tutored her younger sister.

Margot was a faded replica of Lilibet. She had the same pale-gold hair and skin, but the glow that made Lilibet special was missing. Margot's eyes were faded blue instead of violet, and the soft, delicate mouth that was so alluring on Lilibet was a bit petulant on Margot.

With a pair of scissors in her hand, and surrounded by magazines and clippings, Margot laughed when she saw Lilibet. "You'll never guess what Marm's got me doing, Sis. She found more pictures of the princesses and told me to cut them all out and paste them in her scrapbook. I thought after Princess Elizabeth married and became a mother that Marm would stop all this. Lord, isn't it enough that we're named after the insipid things? Do you think she will ever have enough of these dumb pictures?"

Lilibet laughed and gave her sister a hug. "No, I don't think she will, but if it makes her happy, what do we care? She has little enough to make her happy."

Lilibet and Margot had explained to their mother that she was an Anglophile. It amazed Regina that her fascination with all things English, in particular the royal family, had a name. Her daughters had shown the word to her in the dictionary and she had memorized its spelling and definition. They asked her once why she'd used the princesses' nicknames on their birth certificates instead of Elizabeth and Margaret. She told them that it would have been disrespectful to use the real names of the princesses.

They worked on Margot's lessons for the next hour and then Lilibet went out back to hoe the garden before it got dark. She attacked the pitiful patch with the same decisiveness she applied to everything. She resented the time it took from her studies, but she wanted to relieve Marm as much as possible, and she loved the smell of the fresh earth as she turned it over.

She heaved the hoe up and down and talked out loud to herself about the matters foremost in her mind. Her only close friend, Donetta Estep, lived in another camp closer to town and Lilibet saw her only at school. Early in her life, Lilibet realized that she'd have to confide in herself because there had never been anyone close to her who felt the way she did about things. At least talking out loud made it seem like she was talking to someone.

"God, I hope the MacDonalds and Eugene get what's coming to them someday. Deserve to rot in hell. Daddy'll say it's my fault and beat me." She paused, leaning on the hoe handle to rest for a moment, then attacked the undernourished earth again. "Can't believe that someone found my path. Dammit! Have to visit Uncle East soon. But I know that Indian can't possibly be his grandson. Of course I've never met the guy so maybe ... no ... couldn't be."

She grunted as the hoe hit a big rock. She knelt to work at it with her hands, finally dislodging it and tossing it to the side, adding to the large pile of rocks that was already there.

"I'll try to go to Uncle East's on Saturday. Sure am glad there's only a month of school left. Haven't told Marm yet that Sam Adkins asked me to go to the prom because I haven't decided whether to go or not. Should have known he was going to ask me. Ever since I helped him with his math he's been following me around, sitting beside me in all of our classes."

She hacked ferociously at a hard clod of dirt.

In a high falsetto voice, she asked herself, "Why didn't you discourage him, Lilibet?"

She answered mockingly in a lower voice, "Because he's Cledith's best friend."

"Lilibet," called her mother, "are you talking to yourself again? Can't you at least whisper so I can't hear you muttering? I swanee, people are going to think you're crazy. Your daddy's home so come in for supper soon."

"Okay," she called back, but continued her conversation with herself.

"I love you, Cledith Hutton. Maybe you'll notice me when I'm valedictorian. Sally Kay thinks she's going to win. But she won't ... please, God, I hope not." Her voice was faint and desperate now. "I have to win that scholarship. God, please help me."

Roy Springer yelled to Lilibet from the kitchen door. "Daughter, supper's on the table. Come and eat."

Lilibet gave the earth around the struggling carrots one last swipe, washed her hands at an outside pump, then joined her family for supper.

They ate in silence. Regina Springer, who so desired an education and read all that she was capable of in the few spare moments she could find, had long ago given up her attempts at intelligent suppertime conversation.

Roy Springer came from generations of dour, uncommunicative southern West Virginia coal miners. He favored his one surviving son in everything and had no patience for the women in his family. His wife was only a convenient and legal vessel for relieving his lust every night. God would strike him dead if he ever fucked a hussy, so Roy made sure Regina Spring was fed and clothed and made it to church every Sunday.

As he liked to tell Eugene, "What's a woman fer if it ain't to screw and raise children?"

He'd kept Regina pregnant since they were married when she was sixteen years old and he was eighteen. Three babies died during childbirth and two more in infancy. Two toddlers had succumbed to tuberculosis. Roy was ashamed that out of ten pregnancies only three children remained, and two of those were girls only good for doing chores. Roy expected his wife and daughters to cook, clean, garden, mend, do all the chores inside and out, including the wood chopping and heavy lifting.

Roy's small brown eyes, circled with the black mascara of coal dust that gave them a raccoon appearance which no amount of scrubbing seemed to erase, finally looked up from his plate and glanced around the table.

"Where's Eugene?" His impassive voice broke the strained silence.

Lilibet knew that Eugene had made himself scarce because he was afraid Lilibet would tell her father what had happened this afternoon, but she said nothing. She knew her father wouldn't believe her, and if he did, he'd only blame it on her, saying that she provoked the MacDonald brothers, had lured them and flirted with them.

"I don't know," she replied, hoping fiercely that Eugene was hiding out in the woods getting tortured by mosquitoes and bit by snakes.

"Probably out sparkin' that Bevins gal. He's somethin' with the women now, ain't he? Only thing makes me unhappy about Eugene is his not workin' in the mines. But he's making good money drivin' that coal truck so I shouldn't complain. Graduate this year don't you, Lilibet?"

Startled, Lilibet looked at her father in dismay. He seldom addressed her so she knew he must have something on his mind.

"Yes, sir."

"Good. We can use the extra money and your mother needs more help around here. Pappy Hutton will be glad to have you workin' in the main office."

"Daddy, I'm not going to work for Pappy Hutton. I'm going to college."

"Don't argue with me, girl. You do what I say. You don't need more schoolin'."

Shocked, her stomach churned sickly and she fought the tears that threatened to spill from her eyes. Lilibet cursed herself for not having thought of this turn of events, and then cursed herself for revealing her plans to her father.

Under the table, her mother reached for her hand and squeezed it, cautioning Lilibet to stay silent. Lilibet bit her lip and glanced at Margot. She caught a strange expression of satisfaction in Margot's eyes, but it passed quickly as Margot winked at her. Roy saw none of this because he had returned to his food, expecting his word to be taken as gospel anyway.

They sat mute, their hands folded in their laps, while Roy finished his meal. He lit a cigarette, bringing up a deep, wet, malicious cough. It was their signal to clear the table.

Lilibet ground her teeth until her jaws ached, her stomach still churning. Dear God, she couldn't wait to get to school tomorrow. At least she'd see Cledith there and just the sight of him made everything seem all right.

Chapter 2

The old yellow school bus lumbered its way cautiously down the narrow, looping mountain road. It was a humid spring morning and the windows were lowered. The younger children grabbed at tree branches that brushed the windows and then tossed the shorn, shredded green leaves at their seat mates. Older children shot spit wads back and forth at one another through paper straws.

Lilibet sat oblivious to everything, her head bent over a book as always.

A shout went through the bus as they neared the bottom of the mountain.

"Hey, look, there's Cledith and Clarice in their new Cadillac convertibles."

Everyone, including Lilibet, ran to the rear windows.

Tearing down the mountain behind the bus and attempting to pass it, were Cledith and Clarice Hutton, the fraternal twins of mine owner Pappy Hutton.

"Wow, will you look at those Caddies," someone declared. "How'd you like to get one of those for a graduation present?"

"I like Clarice's best. The bright red suits her, and the blue one matches Cle's dreamy blue eyes," said a girl close to Lilibet.

Lilibet shot her a dirty look but quickly turned back to watch the two cars racing down the road behind them. She held her breath as Cledith pulled around Clarice's red convertible, passed his sister, and then roared past the school bus.

"Hey, Bud," called a boy to the bus driver. "Watch out 'cause here comes Clarice. Look at her tool that baby around!"

Bud cursed, looking frantically from his rearview mirror to his side view mirrors, and all the time edging as close to the side of the road as possible without going over the edge. It would take only one tire off the road to flip the awkward, ancient bus down the ravine.

"Goddamn Hutton twins!" cursed Bud. "Pappy ought to be horsewhipped, spoiling them the way he does." Perspiration ran down his face as he saw Deadman's Curve coming up and saw Clarice edge closer and closer to the bus.

"Go, Clarice, go!" the kids yelled out the bus window. "You've never let Cle win yet!"

Clarice Hutton, her bright blond hair streaming behind her, laughed excitedly as she whipped around the bus, and the kids cheered her on. A tractor trailer, laboring its way up the constricted mountain road, came chugging slowly around the curve. Clarice expertly tucked her bright red car in front of the bus, missing the truck by inches. As the bus turned into the curve, they saw Clarice catch up with Cledith in his blue car and pass him on the straightaway into Yancey, West Virginia.

"Hooray!" everyone screamed.

Once again, the Hutton twins had brought some drama and excitement into their drab lives.

Lilibet sat down limply. How stupid of the twins, she thought to herself, but smiled proudly when she remembered how boldly Cledith had handled his car.

When the bus arrived at Yancey County High School, the two Cadillacs were parked sedately side by side in the lot reserved for students with cars. The stigma attached to riding the bus to school had never bothered Lilibet. Her superior academic abilities had kept her in classes with the "townies," which was important to her.

Students from the mining camps outside of town rode the school bus and were only accepted by the "townies" if they were good students or excellent athletes. In fact, most of the football team, except for Cledith Hutton, who was the quarterback, and Sam Atkins, who played center, were from the camps. It was Lilibet's shyness that kept her from being an integral part of the popular crowd, that and her dedication to surpass everyone in scholarship.

Inside the grimy, tan brick building Lilibet skirted her classmates surrounding Cledith Hutton, daring to steal a glance at the golden young god she'd adored since first entering the county high school four years ago. Cledith Hutton, blessed with his father's good looks and his mother's charm, was loved by everyone. He'd recently had his blond hair pared into a flat-top military crew cut and every boy in school had adopted the short style. President of the student body, captain of the football team, and all-around good athlete, Cledith seemed not to have been adversely affected by the lavish gifts showered on him by his father, or the lack of proper discipline.

His sister, Clarice, was a different story, as everyone in Yancey knew. Down the hall, Clarice leaned against the wall with one foot propped up behind her. Shoulders thrown back and large breasts teasingly thrust upward through her tight yellow knit top, she tilted her head alluringly at Jimmy Haynes, center of the basketball team. Jimmy stood facing Clarice, his arms bracing the wall on either side of her, enclosing them in a heated moment of their own. Lilibet saw Clarice lick her lips and pout at Jimmy, then so swiftly, run her hand over the hard knob forming in Jimmy's jeans.

"Dammit, stop it, Clarice," Jimmy said.

"Then stay away from me, Jimmy sweet thing," Clarice purred softly.

"You know I can't stay away from you," he muttered. Desperate, he looked around quickly to see if any teachers were near and then bent to kiss her lipstick-wet mouth.

"Ummm, that was good. Give me some more, Jimmy sweet thing."

"I'll see you at lunchtime." With obvious reluctance he pulled away from her to go to class.

Lilibet deposited her books under the lab counter she and Sam Adkins had been assigned. Sam had already arrived and was hard at work in his chemistry workbook. What Sam lacked in intelligence he made up for in diligence.

"Need help, Sam?" Lilibet asked quietly.

He looked up gratefully, his soft brown eyes adoring

her. "You bet! I don't think I could have gotten through chemistry without you, Lilibet. Where have you been all my life?"

"Right here." She smiled. "You just haven't been looking."

"That's for sure. I was so hung up on Clarice I couldn't see straight. Sure am glad to be over that."

A boy came by and gave Sam's shoulder a friendly shove.

"Congratulations, Sam. Hear you won the Yancey High Athletic Scholarship. I can't think of anyone who deserves it more. Now you won't have to study so hard," said Tom Tee Frye.

"Yes, I do." Sam said, frowning.

"What in hell for?" Tom Tee asked. "All your expenses will be paid at the university, and what ain't paid for, Pappy Hutton will take care of. Hell, I wish my mom was his private secretary."

Sam's fingers tightened on his pencil.

"It would be nice if my mom didn't have to work, Tom Tee, but she does and so do I," Sam said pleasantly. "I guess you don't remember that Pappy offered her the job when my daddy was killed at Number Three ten years ago."

Someone threw a pencil at Tom Tee and he turned away to see who it was.

"Let's get busy on your workbook, Sam," Lilibet said. "We'll get most of this finished before class starts."

She sat close to him so she could see his workbook and her arm rested next to his. The directions were difficult to follow and she went over them twice, explaining as she went, then asked him if he understood.

"What did you say?" Sam asked.

Lilibet looked up at him. His round face was redder than Marm's strawberry jam and he was looking at her real funny. She wondered if there was something wrong with the way she looked. Self-consciously, she touched her braided hair, which she'd twisted in a severe knot on top of her head.

"Is my braid coming apart?"

"Oh, no, your hair is beautiful . . . but why do you pull it up so . . . ?" He blushed again and stopped.

"Why do I braid and knot it?" she asked crisply. "Because it's so wild it gets in my way, that's why. Is there anything else wrong, Sam?"

She fingered the Peter Pan collar on her white blouse and looked down at the navy blue cotton jumper that hung loosely from her shoulders.

"Oh, no, Lilibet, nothing wrong at all."

"Then let's get on with thermodynamics," she said. "Here, you dropped your pencil."

His hand shook as he took the pencil from her. Big Sam was nervous this morning. Was it something she'd said or done? She hoped not. He'd have to concentrate if he wanted to pass chemistry.

The room was filling up now and conversation eddied around them as they hurried to finish Sam's homework before Mr. Stover arrived.

"Hey, Lilibet," Joe Carpozzoli yelled from across the room, "heard your brother, Eugene, is running moonshine for the MacDonald brothers. Can you get me some?"

"Yeh, me, too," shouted several others. The girls in the class started laughing.

The print on the page in front of Lilibet blurred and then swam crazily. She stiffened and tried to ignore the laughter but felt the color leave her face. She chanced a sideways glance at Sam and saw his face tightening with anger. He stood up and turned around to glare at his classmates.

"Shut up. Leave her alone. If I ever hear anyone say anything like that to Lilibet again, I'll bash your head in. Understand?"

Silence fell in the room. Lilibet's heart beat fast and furious. If there was anyone in the school as well-liked and respected as Cledith, it was Sam Adkins. Sam was everyone's "big, brown, cuddly bear." At six feet four inches and two hundred fifty pounds, he towered over everyone but never took advantage of his size. He was unable to train his curly brown hair into a crew cut like Cle's, so it sat atop his round-cheeked face like a monk's cap. He had friendly, brown eyes and an innate sweetness that captivated all who met him. Classmates with problems went to Sam for a shoulder to cry on.

After chemistry class, Lilibet gathered up her books but waited for Sam as Mr. Stover explained tomorrow's assignment to him. His face lit up with happiness when he realized she'd waited for him. As they walked out the classroom door, Lilibet said, "Sam, if the invitation is still open, I'd like to go to the prom with you."

Sam Adkins put his books in his locker, ignoring Cle Hutton's good-natured teasing.

"Hey, Sambo, come on, stop mooning around about your new girlfriend. We're skipping Latin and going to Tony's for a hot dog."

"Can't Cle—you know I can't afford to skip class. Go without me."

He grabbed his Latin book and walked away from Cle with relief. All he wanted to do was think about Lilibet. She'd blossomed later than the other girls and he knew the avid interest in the eyes of the boys embarrassed her, so she tried to hide the natural glow that came with her new maturity. It was impossible to hide, though she'd done her best this morning with her severe hairdo and drab outfit. His fingers had itched to take down her hair, unbraid it, and run his fingers through it. He blushed again. Gotta stop this, Sam, he told himself. This is worse than the crush you had on Clarice. This is different. With Clarice he had a permanent hard-on, and vivid dreams of screwing her. But, Lilibet, well . . . Lilibet. Mom said he was too young to be in love, but he thought he was.

He couldn't believe his luck. Lilibet was going to the prom with him.

Chapter 3

"Lilibet, try to be back early enough to go to the store," Marm called. "We was goin' to pick out the material for your prom dress today, remember?"

"Okay, Marm, I'll try," she called back. She maneuvered around a rusted refrigerator and out of the junkyard. Hurrying down the rutted lane that ran through the row of company houses, she soon came to the main road.

It was a beautiful spring morning. The soot-filled air couldn't dispel the feeling of cheer brought by the few insistent rays of sunshine that found their way to the deep hollow, warming and nurturing the lucky earth.

"Goin' to visit the mysterious mountain man, beautiful?" a raucous voice yelled across the mine yard.

A frown crossed Lilibet's face, but she gave the man a friendly wave, pushed her baseball cap further down on her head, and hurried on.

If the miner only knew how close he was to the truth.

Lilibet respected Uncle East's privacy, and she also didn't want anyone invading her own private place on the mountain. Only her mother knew who she visited on her trips up the mountain, and Marm had promised not to tell anyone. According to which legend you heard, Uncle East was either a dangerous recluse to be feared, or a wise man to be revered. To some, he was mere myth; the miners didn't believe such a person existed. The MacDonald clan made fun of the rumors, but were superstitious and cut a wide swath around the area the old hermit was supposed to inhabit.

"Better be careful, girl. Crazy 'old man' might keep you on the mountain—I would if I was him," called another crude, jesting voice.

She knew they meant no harm. She'd known most of them all her life, and though she disliked their rough teasing, she was accustomed to it.

Lilibet averted her eyes from the gaping mine entrance as it continued to disgorge miners from the early-morning shift. Shivering despite the warmth of the sun, she picked up her pace, anxious to get away from the chilling reminder of her most fearful memory. Her fear of the deep caverns beneath her feet was as potent today as it had been ten years ago when Eugene had deserted her there after a cruel game of hide-and-seek. He'd coaxed her into the mine with the promise of an ice cream cone and then left her alone, telling her to try and find him. Lilibet had searched through the gloom diligently, dying a little from fright each time Eugene jumped at her from behind a support beam or shuttle car.

Eugene had played cat and mouse with her for hours. Finally, reduced to a shaking mass of tears, she'd fainted, and he was forced to bring her out. Her nightmares consisted of black, cold, narrow spaces that led to never-ending nowhere. She hated the mines.

Modern mechanization had supplanted many of the mining jobs, and a frightening number of miners and their families were now on welfare, so Lilibet appreciated the work the mines provided for her father, but she hated the industry. She hated the paternal attitude of the management and wealthy mine owners. The company literally owned a miner from his birth to his grave. They gave you a place to live, a store to buy groceries, clothes, supplies, and everything you could possibly need. The health care offered, meager and pitiful as it was, was received gratefully by the families. To these uneducated and culture-starved people, any doctor's word was gospel, no matter how ill-trained or unsanitary his office.

Father company, thought Lilibet with disgust, also made sure there were beer joints close by, and a baseball field sat next to every elementary school. Father company had even been known to encourage the establishment of a Free Will Baptist Church in the vicinity. Never let it be said that the soul of a miner should be neglected. It was difficult to fight your way out of all this supposed caretaking, so the majority of the miners and their families accepted their lot gratefully.

The Hutton Company was different, Lilibet knew, only because it was privately owned and the owner lived locally, instead of in Charleston, New York, or Washington. To an outsider, Pappy Hutton's mines and camps didn't seem too bad compared to other places in southern West Virginia. He knew how to window dress and to give a good impression. Camp Huttonville even boasted a swimming pool and a recreational center for its teens. With its freshly painted houses and neatly tended lawns, Huttonville was the camp visitors were shown. Lilibet had never seen a visitor or health inspector in Big Ugly Creek, where she lived.

Even more distressing to Lilibet was the industry's effect on her beloved mountains. The lush natural beauty and wildlife that had attracted the early pioneer settlers was being slowly destroyed. Great mining scars cut into the once green land. Years ago a younger Lilibet had climbed high and hard and found the virgin wilderness that remained.

"It was nice of Marm to let me put off Margot's tutoring till after supper. Would have been even nicer if that good-for-nothing Eugene had got up to work the garden. But I don't mind getting up before light. I like it. Uncle East says it's God's quiet time."

She climbed out of the shadows in the hollow, lifting her face to the light, and took a deep breath, inhaling the high mountain air hungrily. She caught an animal scent, probably deer, but it reminded her to pay attention on this trip up the mountain.

"I won't get caught unawares again, and I refuse to be afraid. Those dumb cretins don't know I can track them by smell and sound," she whispered to herself as she climbed. "Jud smells like whiskey and Virgil smells like piss. Disgusting!"

Virgil loved the smell of his own urine and had a predilection for urinating whenever and wherever he pleased, which made him unpopular with the general population of Yancey County. The MacDonald brothers lived with their father deep in a hard-to-find gully high above Big Ugly

Creek. Part of a large clan of inbred mountain people who rarely mixed with anyone in the valley, the boys had never gone to school and had run wild since birth.

She caught the sharp, sweet aroma of catnip and searched for it as she climbed. Around a curve in the path, she spotted a patch with pale lavender flowers and knelt to break off several stalks to take to Uncle East. He used catnip to make tea for coughs and colds.

The sunny path soon turned into a barely discernible trail that entered dense, dark woods. For a while she walked beside a tinkling, laughing creek, but resisted the temptation to remove her boots and wade in its sparkling waters.

Finally, she reached a sheer, seemingly insurmountable rock face with no way around it or through it. Drawing a sigh of relief, she looked around, making sure no one had followed. She tucked the catnip down the front of her shirt and then climbed a sycamore tree that hugged the face of the huge boulder.

Halfway up the tree, Lilibet disappeared in the greenness of its leaves. Invisible to the ground beneath, she nimbly stepped off a sturdy limb and onto a narrow ledge that led to a natural stone bridge hidden by mountain laurel. She knelt, then crawled across the bridge and quickly exited on the other side into bright sunshine and her other world. Behind her the back of the cliff rose high and sheer. In front of her lay a green meadow filled with wildflowers, hepatica, lavender spring beauty, and white and pink May apple.

With a whoop of delight, she rolled over and over down the grassy incline that led to the flower-filled meadow. On her feet again, she gathered her fallen catnip, tucked the baseball cap in her back pocket, gave her hair an exuberant toss, and started off again. She still had a way to go before she reached Uncle East's cabin.

This roll down the hill was a ritual, a signaling that for a time she was free of the black, dreary life in "the bottom." It was also a fond reminder of how she'd met Uncle East.

Four years ago, while exploring she'd discovered by chance the path through Ironface Rock. At first glimpse of the enchanting meadow before her, the fourteen-year-old girl had spontaneously lain down and rolled, giggling self-consciously, but loving every turn and tumble down the hill. As she'd stood to right herself at the bottom, Lilibet heard a deep chuckling. Frightened, she'd looked up to see a tall, elderly man with a cloud of white hair and a thick beard standing beneath a massive red sweet gum tree.

"Don't be afraid, child. I'm laughing because I rolled down the hill the first time I saw it, and I was much older than you."

Lilibet had rubbed her eyes in disbelief.

He chuckled again. "I'm not an apparition. I'm real."

"What are you doing here?"

"I live not far from here, and you are the first visitor I've ever had. Call me Uncle East," he'd said. "Welcome."

Instinctively, Lilibet trusted him, and there began a friendship that transcended any relationship she had ever known. Uncle East never talked down to her. For the first time, someone accepted—and respected—her just as she was. With Uncle East she discussed books and music and art. He'd taught her to look at nature with new eyes—to see not just its beauty but also its underlying spirituality. He encouraged her intellectual curiosity as her parents had never been able or inclined, to do. A visit with Uncle East sustained Lilibet through many tension-filled moments in the barren, lifeless house at Big Ugly Creek. Uncle East, and the mountain, represented for Lilibet beauty, freedom, and the courage to imagine a better world.

Like most people, she'd heard the tales about the mysterious mountain man—that Uncle East had arrived in the southern mountains many years ago from an unknown northern city, and that most of his time was spent in the black hills with the ancients, the few Indians who were left, and the remaining elderly people who were direct descendants of pioneer stock. She'd heard that the old man had disappeared, never to be seen again. It was rumored that he had a schoolteacher daughter, Laura Brady, who lived in a town across the mountain, Matterhorn, West

Virginia. It had been a joyous surprise to know the tales of his existence were true.

A smile lit her face when she heard the soft, clear strains of a dulcimer and a baritone voice singing "Barbara Allen." She rounded a thicket of purple rhododendron and there was Uncle East's weathered cabin, tucked in the lee of a forest of pine trees. It sat with its back to the trees, protected from the never-ceasing breeze that blew this high. The wide front porch faced a vista of blue sky and distant mountaintops.

Uncle East said at night you could sometimes see, like tiny twinkling fireflies, the lights of the Charleston airport ninety miles away; Lilibet was sure you could see forever and ever.

Two rustic twig rocking chairs were on the tidy porch and Uncle East sat in one of them, his dulcimer in his lap. He finished singing the last verse of "Barbara Allen" and waved to her as she approached. Two coon dogs lay on either side of him. They lifted their heads to give a short bark of greeting, then went back to sleep.

"I made some sassafras tea for you. It's keeping hot on the stove," he said.

"You knew I was coming."

"Always do, but I had a little help this time."

Lilibet wondered what he meant but said nothing.

Lilibet went into the cabin, laid the catnip on a small pine chest by the door, and looked around her with pleasure. It was a simple, airy, two-room structure with many large windows, furnished with spartan handcrafted log furniture. Durable, but comfortable, the chair seats were filled with colorful patchwork pillows. Cream-colored cotton throws for cool nights hung on the backs.

She smoothed her hand admiringly across the surface of a mellow-hued, wormy-chestnut table. A large window next to it framed another breathtaking mountain vista. For a moment she sat in one of the four cane-back chairs placed around the table and imagined herself eating a meal here with Uncle East. In the center of the table sat an old tin watering can filled with a loose arrangement of pussy willow, mountain laurel, and trillium. Her eyes lingered on the watercolors of wild animals; a bay lynx, a red fox, a cougar, squirrels, and others hung pleasingly on the walls. A beautifully crafted stack-stone fireplace divided the living area from Uncle East's sleeping quarters. Shelves overflowing with books lined the walls on both sides of the fireplace.

Lilibet knew instinctively that this was not the home of your run-of-the-mill hermit. Though she had never been in a fine home, she recognized the taste and creativity that made this crude cabin a place of beauty. As she crossed the hand-milled, hand-rubbed pine floor, she knelt to caress the wood, feeling the soft golden glow flow right up through her fingers.

She lifted her tea from the wood-burning stove near the chestnut table and turned to join Uncle East on the porch.

A photograph on the stone mantel caught her eye.

It had always been there but she'd ignored it, respecting the unspoken pact that existed between her and Uncle East. They never asked each other personal questions. Their privacy was inviolate. She crossed to the fireplace and took the photo down to examine it closely.

A pretty young woman and a young boy sat with their arms about each other's shoulders on the steps of Uncle East's cabin. She studied the boy. Was this the Indian she'd seen on the mountain? It didn't look much like him. The woman wasn't an Indian either. She knew this was a photograph of Uncle East's daughter and grandson because he had told her that much. But that was all he'd told her.

"Samuel Johnson said 'Curiosity is one of the permanent and certain characteristics of a vigorous mind.' You have a vigorous mind, Elizabeth, so I'm not surprised at your curiosity." Uncle East's voice startled her and she nearly dropped the photograph.

Guiltily, she turned to face Uncle East, who stood in the doorway.

"I'm sorry. I didn't mean to be nosy."

"That's all right. I should have told you about them before now, but there was never a good enough reason. Now there is. Bring your tea and join me, Elizabeth."

He had called her Elizabeth from the beginning because he said she was an Elizabeth, not a Lilibet.

She followed him to the porch and settled into the rocking chair next to him. They sat in silence for a while. Lilibet drank in the cleanness of the blue sky and watched a red-tailed hawk spiral toward its nest high in a cliff across the gorge. Its shrill cry, the stirring of the pines behind them, and the whisper of the wind were the only sounds to be heard. The air was scented with pine and new grass.

"Black told me he thought he'd met my young friend so I figured you'd be hightailing it up here as soon as possible," Uncle East said, breaking the comfortable silence.

The tea in Lilibet's cup slopped around crazily.

"B-Black?"

"Black Brady is my grandson—he rescued you from the MacDonald garbage the other day."

"B-B-But that was an Indian, and Black Brady . . . from what I've heard of him . . . well, they say he's a savage. . . ." She stopped, embarrassed.

Uncle East chuckled and pulled his beautiful briarwood pipe from his shirt pocket.

"Black is one-quarter Shawnee, and he plays it up a bit. They talking about Black now, too?"

"Yes," she answered noncommittally. She didn't say that Black Brady had become a legend himself. In fact, the tales they told of him were so bizarre that she'd never really believed he existed. They said he wrestled with bears and could kill a squirrel at sixty paces with one swift fling of his knife.

He drew on his pipe and looked at her with a smile, his green eyes twinkling, and Lilibet recognized now the eyes of the young savage, their color dulled with age, but still bright with wisdom.

"That picture was taken twelve years ago, when Black was ten. The woman beside him is my daughter, Laura. I guess it's time I explained a few things."

He drew on his pipe again and stared out across the mountaintops. Lilibet knew better than to hurry him, so she waited.

Her tea had grown cold and was near the bottom of the mug before Uncle East's gruff voice spoke again.

"My wife Felice, Laura's mother, died when Laura was born. Her death was one of the reasons . . ." A flash of unforgotten pain flared in his eyes, and drew his mouth tight. With a deep breath, he continued. "When I came to Catawba Mountain, Laura was still a baby, and I put her in the care of good friends up north. She spent every summer here with me, even her college years. A Shawnee, Black Eagle, was my closest friend my first years on the mountain. Black Eagle kept the old ways of the Shawnee Indians and taught me much. He's one of the reasons I've survived so well up here by myself. Black Eagle fell in love with an Irish woman, Kathleen Brady, a Protestant missionary working in the Appalachian region. They had a son and they named him James Brady, after Kathleen's father. They knew the boy would have an easier time of it with an anglicized name."

He stopped to clean his pipe and then put it in his pocket.

"Jim Brady and my Laura grew up here together in the summertime. Eventually they married, and Jim went to work in the mines to earn money to go to college. Laura taught school in Matterhorn. After Black was born, Jim worked all the harder—wouldn't take help from anyone."

Uncle East set his rocking chair in motion.

"When Black was five, Jim had enough money saved to take all of them to live in Huntington, so he could go to school at Marshall. They never made it. Jimmy was killed in the Matter Mine collapse."

Lilibet reached over to caress his arm. "Oh, I'm so sorry, Uncle East."

He took her hand and patted it affectionately. "Never mind, my dear. It was a long time ago, though sometimes I think Black feels like it was yesterday. His grandmother, Kathleen, never got over it. She died of pneumonia the next winter. But it was grief that was the real killer."

He shook his head and then continued.

"Black lived with his mother during school seasons, but came up here to be with Black Eagle and myself in the summers. So, we are the reason he is as he is," he finished with a mysterious smile.

Which is what way? Lilibet asked herself. Black Brady

had created a terrifying legend in the mountains. That's why Eugene had been so frightened of him. A million questions raced through her mind. She gathered her courage to ask one of them.

"Why have I never met Black Eagle, or Black Brady?"

"Black Eagle was very old. He passed away four years ago, the spring Black graduated from Matterhorn High. I miss him more than I can say. You found your way here later that same summer."

"And your grandson?"

Uncle East sighed, and retrieved the pipe from his pocket. With meticulous care, he filled the bowl with tobacco, tamped it down, then lit it. Finally, he spoke.

"Black disappeared that summer. His grandfather's death affected him greatly. The three of us were very close. Black Eagle and I nurtured and tutored Black in ways that, in most respects, made him surpass other boys his age. It was a noble experiment, but there were side effects Black Eagle and I weren't prepared for."

He leaned over to scratch behind the ear of one of the coon dogs. Lilibet waited anxiously for him to continue.

"Because of his physical abilities, his extended reasoning capabilities, and the great freedom he'd been allowed, Black became intolerant of others, impatient. He believed that what was possible for him was possible for everyone else if they only reached for the best of themselves." Uncle East sighed again. The creases of age on his face deepened and he leaned his arms on his knees, gazing out over the panorama before him.

"Worse than that is his impatience with his lack of control over his life or the life of his loved ones. Black loves or hates intensely. There is no in-between for him. To him, death is lack of control. He hates death. Death is unacceptable to him. Separation from a loved one is unacceptable to him. When Black Eagle died, Black took to the woods where he is most comfortable. I didn't see him for a year. Since then, he checks on me periodically. He's matured some—thinks he can handle associating with inferior humans again," Uncle East said, saying this last with wry humor. "He's decided to spent this summer on Catawba so you'll be seeing more of him."

"He sounds like a selfish, unpleasant person to me," ventured Lilibet carefully, not wanting to hurt Uncle East's feelings.

Uncle East laughed. "Yes, I suppose he does. But that's the furthest thing from the truth. Actually, he's the most powerfully loving, gentle man I've ever known. He's just having trouble learning how to handle his capacity for love and caring."

He looked at her then as if he'd said too much, and she knew that was all he was going to tell her. She searched his seamed, weathered face to find a clue to his feelings. Except for a faint gleam of nostalgia in the wise old eyes, his face was expressionless. His head was nearly bald now except for a white gossamer fringe that fell on his neck in the back and came around to meet his glorious beard in front. All the snow-spun hair floating about his neck and jaws looked like a lowered halo made of cotton candy.

Lilibet caught a swift movement out of the corner of her eye and turned to see a white-tailed deer leap across the small meadow in front of the cabin. It disappeared into the rhododendron thicket.

"Freeze," Uncle East commanded in a low voice.

Caught in the act of scratching her nose, Lilibet froze as he'd taught her. Immobile, barely breathing, her hand still at her face, her eyes frantically searched the clearing. Nothing. There was a faint scent of something, but she didn't recognize it. Realizing something had spooked the deer, they sat waiting for the creature to appear. Lilibet was sure Uncle East knew what it was.

Minutes that seemed like hours crawled by. Lilibet's arm ached from its awkward position and her nose needed a good scratching. Her heart began to pound in anticipation. Would the creature show itself?

Suddenly, a black bear ambled from the pines behind the cabin. It stopped and stood not twenty feet from them. Slowly it turned around and around in the clearing, surveying the thicket, the cabin, and Uncle East and Lilibet sitting on the porch. The well-trained dogs, their muzzles quivering anxiously, moved not an inch.

They were a frozen tableau, the old man, the young girl, the dogs, and the black bear.

Lilibet tried to remain calm. She was safe because she was here with Uncle East. But it all depended on the dogs. Would they hold? If they angered the bear, then all was lost. Her heart tripped faster and faster, and her lungs ached with the need to breathe. The bear looked directly into Lilibet's eyes. She gazed back at him in horrid fascination. Was he as frightened as she was? Her arm quivered with the effort to keep it still. Neither she nor Uncle East nor the dogs had moved or made a sound in the last five minutes.

The bear raised up on its hind legs and stepped toward them. The dogs' legs were now trembling with the effort to hold back, but they would never move without the consent of their master. A great roar came from the huge animal, lifting the hair on Lilibet's nape, and then the bear fell on all fours and turned to charge in the direction the deer had fled.

Lilibet's arm shook as she lowered it and sank weakly back into her rocking chair.

"Stay," Uncle East commanded, as he placed a firm hand on each dog's head. "You may come out now, Raffles."

From underneath the porch emerged a raccoon. Raffles scampered up the steps and jumped into Lilibet's lap.

"I wondered where you were, you rascal," she said as she rubbed her nose affectionately against the raccoon's nose. "Where are Judy and the kits?"

"About the time that Raffles went under the porch, Judy disappeared with her babies. I have no idea where she went. She'll return when she knows it's safe."

"Did you know the bear was coming, Uncle East?" Lilibet asked in awe.

"I wasn't sure, missy. When the animals disappeared I knew something was in the area. A cougar, or maybe a bay lynx. Black told me he'd spotted a bear over on Christmas Ridge, so I figured it might also be the bear." He gave her an affectionate smile. "You did well, missy."

"Why didn't he attack, Uncle East?"

"Probably because he wasn't that hungry. He's been

out of hibernation a while now, so he's probably had his fill of berries and little woodland creatures."

Lilibet made a face, shivered, and hugged herself. She lifted Raffles to her breast and caressed him lovingly, smoothing the warm fur back and forth.

Uncle East tamped his pipe with fresh tobacco and gave her a stern look. "Told you that was the way of the wild, Elizabeth. The strongest survive with either their brains or their brawn, and they give no mercy."

"Life for us humans is much like that, isn't it, Uncle East?"

"Yes," he replied tersely. "Except for one major difference. We've been given a spirit-filled soul with which to communicate with all living creatures."

He lit his pipe as Lilibet thought about what he'd said.

"Don't you think that animals have souls?"

"You know that I do, Elizabeth. Their souls just aren't as highly developed as ours."

"Is that why you have the ability to communicate with them?"

"Now what do you think? Aren't you learning to do the same thing?"

"Yes," she said, realizing it was true. "It is a communion of sorts, isn't it?"

"Yes."

"Were you communing with the bear?" she asked tentatively, almost afraid of his answer.

"He knew we meant him no harm."

"Uncle East, why can't people commune with one another?"

The smoke from his pipe wreathed his shiny bald head.

"Because people have forgotten they are more spirit than body," he replied sadly.

A red fox, its bushy tail held high and proud, crossed the clearing toward them. Behind her followed two baby kits.

"There's Judy," Lilibet exclaimed. She put Raffles on the floor and stood to go and greet the fox, but her legs shook and, unexpectedly, she sank to her knees. She looked at Uncle East in dismay.

"You're all right, Elizabeth." He chuckled. "That's

called 'delayed reaction.' It's not every day you meet a black bear."

He stood to extend a hand and help her up.

She refused his offer.

"I'll do it myself," she said fiercely. "I don't like being on my knees for any reason."

His wise old eyes looked down into the young, beautiful violet eyes that were desperately trying to hide their anxiety, and he withdrew his hand. Swiftly, through his soul, ran feelings of sorrow for the pain and grief he sensed she faced in life, and at the same time twinges of envy for the living of it all. He stood back and watched her struggle to her feet.

Knees still shaky, Lilibet stood straight and defiant, her hands on her hips. Judy and her babies sat at the bottom of the steps and watched curiously.

"Stop staring, Judy," Lilibet said. "It's just me, and I'm just fine!"

Then, with a sheepish smile, she said, "I'm sorry, Uncle East. I didn't mean to be rude.'

"You weren't, Elizabeth. Determined is more like it." He smiled. "I'm going to the work shed to finish a new pair of moccasins for Black. Would you like to join me or do you have other plans?"

"I'd like to go to the glen. Do you suppose that bear is still around?" She had tamed small animals like Judy and Raffles and had coaxed a fawn from a bramble thicket, but a bear was way beyond her expertise.

"He headed toward the gap. He's long gone. I haven't heard anything or smelled a trace of him in a while. However, it never hurts to be cautious.'

"See you later then." She walked away from him toward the forest in the back of the cabin. Halfway between the cabin and the trees she stopped and called out to Uncle East.

"Uncle East, how did your grandson know about my glen?"

She couldn't see the mischief dancing in his eyes as he answered.

"You'll have to ask him, Elizabeth."

If she ever saw the savage again, she thought to herself, she'd not ask him a darn thing.

Lilibet never talked aloud to herself within Uncle East's hearing. Most people didn't listen to what they heard, but Uncle East heard, listened, and dissected every nuance of sound around him. She knew she should trust his opinion about the bear but the memory of the animal's roar was still too fresh in her mind.

Her eyes anxiously searched the gloom of the forest ahead of her. Seeing nothing, she stepped into the tall evergreens. Judy and the kits trailed behind her.

Chapter 4

Lilibet hurried along the back of the ridge. The forest became more dense, the trunks of the evergreens darker, and the air even cooler. Half an hour later she came to a rushing creek and nimbly crossed it, using flat, slippery, moss-covered rocks as stepping-stones. On another day Judy would have followed her, but the kits were too young to swim so the mother fox stayed on the near side of the creek. Judy watched while Lilibet traversed a fern-filled clearing and then entered a palisade of primeval forest and vanished. Her protective duties taken care of, Judy turned around and took her babies home.

Lilibet stepped into a glen of hallowed beauty and crossed herself. Her Catholic friend, Donetta, had said she must do that on crossing the threshold of a sacred place. To Lilibet, there were few places more sacred than this.

In the center was a quiet pond, which was the head of the rushing creek Lilibet had crossed minutes before. A green carpet of moss and fern embraced the tranquil pond. The white trunks of the silver sycamores surrounding the glen glowed eerily in the dimness. Dogwoods prayerfully lifted their fairy blossoms beneath the canopy of larger trees.

The yawning mountain gorge that plunged below this peaceful spot was just beyond a windbreak of saplings. Like spotlights shining on a dark stage, the sun filtered through the saplings and lit here and there upon the dogwoods, white solomon seals, and pink trilliums.

Lilibet pushed through the saplings and emerged onto a large, flat boulder. She sat cross-legged upon the boulder, closed her eyes, and lifted her face to the sun.

Feeling a little silly, she nonetheless repeated the ritual greeting Uncle East had taught her. "Thank you, Heavenly Power, for bringing me here again." Opening her eyes, she gazed with rapture on mile after mile, wave after wave of color-strewn mountaintops stretching before her against the sapphire sky.

The deep hunger that haunted Lilibet was always somewhat satisfied here on the boulder, or behind her in the hidden glen. She knew not what she craved or what caused the painful, lonely yearning that lived with her always. Once, she'd tried to explain the hunger to Donetta, but Donetta hadn't understood. She wondered if anyone ever would.

But here, on the mountaintop and in her secret place behind her, Lilibet was nourished and temporarily satisfied.

She uncrossed her legs, stretching them in front of her. She ran her fingers through her pale golden hair and tossed her head so that the wavy tresses hung down her back. Bracing her arms behind her, she shook her head back and forth and felt the shiny heat of her hair swing across her back. The image of herself sitting here naked flashed across her mind. Wouldn't it be wonderful to feel the sun on her body and her hair against her bare skin?

Lilibet rejected the pagan thought immediately, but experienced an odd pang of loss.

A lispy, dreamy *zoo zee zoo zoo zee* sound came from the glen behind her and she smiled with anticipation.

"Ah, there you are," she said softly. "Let's see if we can make any progress today."

Quietly she rose from the boulder and slipped through the sapling entrance into the glen.

She tiptoed silently across the pine-needled, fern-covered floor of the shaded glen and sat near the tranquil blue pond. A woodsy, clean scent of pine, fresh air and wildflowers filled the air.

Surreptitiously, she looked around to see if she could locate the black-throated green warbler whose song she had just heard. She couldn't find the bright yellow face or olive-green crown, but knew that the male bird was here and would show itself eventually.

She also felt the presence of something else. Something or someone had been here, or was here now. Marm said she had the 'knowing', a gift from her Scottish forefathers. Uncle East called it psychic ability that she could develop or ignore as she wished. Mostly, she tried to ignore it, but this impression was too strong to dismiss. Common sense told her that it couldn't be a person because no one knew of the glen but her and Uncle East.

Must have been a small animal, she thought with great relief. The noise of the clumsy bear would have alerted her to its presence. She lifted her nose to sniff and find a familiar scent, but could smell nothing but the glen. A deer probably passed through right before I came, she assured herself. Feeling better, she turned her attention back to the black-throated green warbler.

For a year Lilibet had tried to complete an assignment given to her by Uncle East. She was to charm the warbler out of the trees. At first she'd not believed it could be done, but he'd assured her she had the ability to achieve the task and he taught her how. The bird came close on several occasions, but had never come to rest on her hand or shoulder as Uncle East had said it should.

Lilibet sat in the lotus position, closed her eyes, and concentrated on her breathing. With each inhalation and exhalation her body grew more relaxed. She focused her attention on an imaginary spot in the center of her forehead and conjured up a flickering flame. She looked at the flame as if it were inside her head, and then lost herself in its orange mystery. Her eyelids tensed and then relaxed. Slowly the rest of her body followed suit. She imagined that she was inhaling directly through her skin, the oxygen in the air, the coolness of the glen, the song of the warbler.

And soon she could feel it all. Everything that encompassed her was within her. Peace filled her and she sent out waves of love to the warbler.

Immobile now, her breathing light and shallow, Lilibet could sit this way for hours. Her ears heard the soft lispy *zoo zee zee* of the warbler and the muscles of her throat vibrated with the same tremble of throat muscles exerted by the warbler as he sang. Her heart took on the intricate beat of the warbler's heart. Unaware of the passage of time—it could have been five minutes or an hour—Lilibet sensed the presence of the bird. Afraid to open her eyes, she smelled the warm feathers and knew it was closer still.

Soon now.

A slight weight settled on her knee and the bird was with her. Schooled to remain calm, she moved not a fraction, but swift elation swept through her. She'd succeeded! Love for the bird and for Uncle East welled within her.

"Don't move one inch. Don't even open your eyes," said a cool, calm voice.

Her heart bumped and tripped so fast that she thought she'd faint. For the second time this afternoon, she'd been warned of danger. This time was infinitely more fearful for she could not see the danger or the person who spoke to her so quietly. All her lessons with Uncle East came into play. She willed herself to keep her muscles relaxed, not to move, even though the peace within her had fled and been replaced with fear. Sadly, the bird sensed the fear within her and flew away.

"Sorry," said the voice. "He was a beauty."

A slight rustle in the ferns caught her ear.

"Six inches from your right thigh lies a copperhead," continued the relentlessly calm voice.

The thudding of her heart thundered in her ears.

"Listen to me and do exactly as I say," commanded the voice. "When I count three roll to your left and keep rolling. One, two, three."

A whistling sound sliced the air close to Lilibet's ear as she rolled swiftly to her left.

"It's okay now." The voice had turned angry.

Lilibet jumped to her feet and spun around to see who had invaded her privacy.

"You!" she spat out.

Black Brady wiped his bloody knife on his tattered jeans and bent to pick up the six-foot-long, headless copperhead snake and sling it over his bare shoulder.

"You're a little idiot! I know Grandfather taught you to

make sure an area was safe before you relaxed your vigilance."

"Who's an idiot? Anyone who runs around the mountains half-naked is the idiot!"

"I'm sorry I offend your delicate sensibilities," he said with heavy sarcasm. "Evidently you haven't yet experienced the joys of our forefathers."

"If you're implying that I need to revert to the primitive habit of nudity to fully enjoy the natural wonders around us, you're wrong." She blushed, remembering what he had witnessed earlier in the week. If he noticed the blush, he ignored it.

"Maybe," he replied in a more subdued tone. "Like the song says . . . 'to each his own'."

His voice was gravelly and smoky, when he wasn't angry, and it sent an unfamiliar sensation through her.

He walked toward the pond and Lilibet watched him warily. He was less Indian warrior today, more a handsome, virile, young man. His tight, tattered jeans pulled tautly against his long, well-formed legs, and the sleek, tanned muscles of his naked arms and shoulders moved in a beautiful harmony of motion. She acknowledged with grudging admiration the strength and catlike symmetry of his form as he moved across the clearing and knelt by the pond.

"Why do you wear that Indian garb anyway?" she asked, curiosity getting the better of her.

"Not that it's any of your business, but I wear it two or three times a year to remind me of my Shawnee forefathers and their reverence of the earth."

"How long have you been here?"

"Since you arrived." He skinned the snake swiftly, like the skin off a banana.

"How rude of you not to reveal your presence," Lilibet said primly.

"Didn't think it was necessary. You were the one who was intruding."

Angry again, Lilibet rushed to his side.

"No. This is my place. You are the intruder."

He looked up at her, his gray eyes filled with amusement.

"I don't think so, Lilibet Springer. I've been coming here since I was a child."

Crushed beyond belief that her secret place was not really hers, she desperately fought the tears that threatened. Gathering courage, she watched as he stripped bark from a sycamore tree and, rubbing hard, cleaned the inside of the snake skin. Ignoring her as he worked, he finished and rolled up the skin to place it in a shady place to be retrieved later. He muttered to himself, "Grandfather will find something creative to do with this . . . maybe use it in moccasins."

"Have you watched me here before this? Is that how you knew about this place?" she asked in a shaky voice.

"No. Grandfather told me all about you. He told me you had a retreat that you treasured, and when he described it, I knew it was the glen."

Black dug a deep hole in the soft earth around the pond and buried the entrails of the snake, apologizing to it for having to take its life. He washed his knife in the water then stood up and wiped the wet knife on his jeans. He sheathed it and then turned to face Lilibet.

"Look, I'm sorry I yelled at you. Actually, you should be proud of yourself. You did a great job with the warbler."

"Thank you . . . and thank you for probably saving my life. I'm sorry, too. I didn't mean to act ungrateful. I was so scared."

"So was I," he admitted and gave her a beautiful big grin.

She smiled back, her violet eyes dancing with delight.

"You know, beautiful things should be shared to be fully appreciated. Do you suppose we could share the glen?" he asked. "When you realize we are the only people in the world who know it exists, then sharing it with the other person doesn't seem so bad, does it?"

Lilibet had experienced a crushing sense of personal loss at the revelation that Black Brady had previous knowledge of her precious secret. But common sense told her any attempt to keep him away from the place that he obviously loved as much as she was ridiculous.

"I suppose not," she said. "I'll be going away to college in the fall anyway."

"So am I."

"Hah! That's a likely story. You, going to college?" Uncle East had not only created a misfit, he'd created a liar.

"Why is that so hard to believe?" he asked angrily.

She struggled to keep a straight face, not wanting to hurt his feelings.

"Well, in the first place, I think you're about twenty-two years old. In the second place, you've been out of touch with civilization for four years."

"So Grandfather told you about me. What difference does any of that make?"

"No college is going to take you."

"Wrong, Miss Lilibet Springer! I'll be entering the freshman class at Yale."

Lilibet whooped with laughter. "Yale? I don't believe it."

"Believe it. It disappointed Grandfather when I didn't go after high school. To please him, I'm going now. Besides, I've learned all I can learn from these mountains, and Grandfather's convinced me it's time to gather some knowledge about people and how they live with one another. I'm not real crazy about 'people' in general. They've killed off all the wildlife, polluted our streams, and shortened the life of this planet. But I . . ." he hesitated, as if afraid to reveal too much of himself. "I want to know more about everything. There's so much to learn out there. Oceans to cross and other mountains to climb.

She still didn't believe he was entering college, especially Yale, but decided to play along with him.

"That's all you want to do? Cross oceans and climb mountains?"

"It's just an expression, Lilibet," he said, in an obvious effort to be patient with her. "I want to experience many things."

"Don't you have any goals or plans?"

"Sure. Right now I plan on going swimming. Want to join me?"

"The pond isn't deep enough."

"Yes, it is. Eight feet deep in the center. A wonderful warm spring right in the middle. See what you don't know about when you're only willing to dip your feet in the shallows?" he said mockingly, and began to unbutton his jeans.

She watched in disbelief as he stripped his jeans off and stood stark naked in front of her. A gasp escaped her and heat flushed her face. She'd never seen a naked man before, and despite her vivid embarrassment, her first inclination was to study his body. Unbidden, her eyes dropped from his hard shoulders to his lean waist, to the thick thatch of dark hair that cushioned his vivid manhood.

Her hands flew to her mouth to stifle her gasp of shock. He laughed and her eyes flew to his face. The arrogance in his eyes infuriated her and she whipped around with her back to him, hiding from his body, his eyes, and her terrible curiosity.

"You are awful! I'm leaving," she declared, but was rooted to the spot.

"Don't leave. Swim with me."

She heard him wade into the pond and then the sound of splashing as he swam to the center.

"You can turn around now," he yelled.

Cautiously, she turned to see him treading water in the center of the pond.

"Sorry I embarrassed you. I really am. It's such a natural thing for me to do and sometimes I don't think before I play out my impulses."

She could tell he was genuinely apologetic so she sat down to watch him. Fascinated with this fiercely free creature, she told herself she would leave in just a moment. He dove down deep and surfaced a moment later, shaking the water from his long hair.

"Sure you wouldn't like to join me?"

She shook her head bashfully. The image of his forbidden thatch of hair and the scary, but wondrous, appendage it encircled still burned in her mind. A pleasant, mysterious tremor traveled warmly from her inner thighs into her tummy. Afraid to speak, she continued to watch silently as he swam for the next ten minutes.

"I've had enough. I'm coming out. If you're afraid to look at me, you better turn your back."

That made her angry. She wasn't afraid of anything. She jumped to her feet to shout at him. "I'm not afraid, but you're sure no gentleman. Gentlemen don't undress in front of ladies, especially ladies they don't know or aren't married to. I'm turning around because Marm taught me better!"

A silence ensued as she stood with her back to him and she heard him wade out of the water, then slide on his jeans.

"It's okay. I've got my clothes on," he said quietly.

When she turned back around, the first thing she saw was the look of chagrin on his face.

"You're absolutely correct," he said. "Grandfather would tan my hide if he knew I'd embarrassed you. I apologize again."

She laughed at the thought of Uncle East manhandling this tall, well-muscled young man, and said, "Apology accepted."

He reached for her hand. "Come with me while I dry off on the boulder."

She let him lead her through the saplings and they sat on the boulder together. The warm sun felt good after the coolness of the glen.

Black noticed she sat as far from him as possible without endangering her position on the precarious boulder. He cursed his thoughtlessness in the glen.

"How did you find the glen?" she asked.

He knew Lilibet was deliberately changing their avenues of thought, trying to forget what had just happened. For a moment, he stared out over the mountains, wondering how much he should tell her of his decidedly unorthodox upbringing here in the mountains with his two eccentric grandfathers? He knew Grandfather had taught her much, but he doubted that Grandfather would feel that Lilibet needed all that Black had learned. Besides, Black had been under the tutelage of his grandfathers since he was five years old. Lilibet had only been with Grandfather for four years, and she was leaving in a couple of months.

Black glanced at her profile as she gazed out over the mountain peaks. Her hair waved softly down her back and soft tendrils of the spun white-gold tresses curled tenderly around her face. There was a vulnerability about the delicate mouth, but a determined tilt to her small nose. There was strength there, great strength. Not that he had anything that horrible to tell her, just unusual for this day and age, and for the first time in his life he was concerned about someone's opinion of him.

That he should be concerned about what Lilibet thought surprised him. He'd been taught to be his own man, to lead his own life, to give of himself when he could help and then to pass on, asking for nothing.

He had to admit he liked this feeling of wanting Lilibet to like him, to not be afraid of him. He decided to take a chance and trust her.

"I found the glen when I was twelve years old. My grandfathers brought me to the middle of the forest and left me to live by myself for three months."

"They didn't!"

Black laughed at the expression of horror on her face. "Sure they did, but that was just the first time. The second time they put me on Christmas Ridge in the middle of winter for three months."

"B-but, your mother . . . didn't she object?"

"Sometimes my mother wouldn't give her permission, but generally she approved of what they were doing. Remember, my mother spent summers here with my grandfather, and she was married to a man who felt much the same way my grandfathers did about life. For several years she rejected the Christmas Ridge plan, but consented when I was fifteen. She told the county school officials that I was in boarding school for a special course. Grandfather had a friend who was headmaster of a school up north and he verified the information. My mother did a lot of tutoring later to get me caught up."

"Was your father raised the way you were?"

"Not as stringently. It took some years for Grandfather and Black Eagle to exchange and explore their philosophies."

There followed a tale of a young boy taught an odd,

but beautiful blend of Eastern religious philosophy, old Shawnee folklore, and Early American morality and goal setting. For three months every year, from five years of age, Black learned all there was to learn of nature, its beauty and its cruelty. He lived in caves with animals that most people would run from. He learned to heal injured animals and to heal himself. Survival in the wild became second nature to him, as did the making of tools, moccasins, clothing, and shelter from animal skins and other natural resources. Sitting at the feet of his grandfathers, he listened to the philosophy of Plato, Socrates, Buddha, Jung, Ralph Waldo Emerson, and Christ. He learned to delve within the deepest part of himself and use the ancient wisdom of the ages that resided within him.

"There was a time, in my teens, when I felt they were using me as an experiment, and I resented it. I rebelled and didn't come back the next summer. But during that year I realized several things. I realized I missed my grandfathers something awful and that they truly loved me ... and I realized I was better prepared for life than anyone else I knew. Or at least I thought I was—I've since discovered I'm only good for the mountain. They were experimenting with me, of course, but in a loving way; they wanted only the best for me. Also, they'd shown a great deal of faith in expecting that I could achieve all they had asked of me. So the next summer I came back to the mountain eagerly."

Lilibet and Black were facing each other now. Absorbed in this unusual story, she sat with her arms folded across her raised knees, her chin resting on her arms.

"What about your friends in Matterhorn? Didn't they think you were odd?"

"Not for a while. They knew I spent the summers with my grandfathers, but they didn't know what I did or where I was. During the school year I went to the Episcopal church with my mother, took piano lessons—which I hated—joined the Boy Scouts, played football in high school." He smiled then, remembering. "It was the scouts and the football that got me in trouble."

"What do you mean?"

"It was difficult to hide some of my skills, especially

in scouting. It didn't take long for my scoutmasters to acknowledge that my skills were far greater than theirs. I
was fourteen when our troop went for a week of camping
near the Peaks of Otter. My best friend disturbed a cougar
nursing her young and she attacked him. I killed the cougar with a stone from my slingshot . . . and then I . . ."
Embarrassed to be talking about himself, he stopped.

"Please, go on," Lilibet implored.

"Billy was bleeding real bad and I stopped the bleeding
by using pressure points I'd been taught. I'd done it before with animals. Everyone was grateful, but from then
on they looked at me differently. They thought I was
weird. It didn't bother me because my grandfathers had
told me not to be concerned about the opinions of man.
Not to measure myself against the excellence of the
masses, but against the excellence in myself."

"What happened in football?"

"You don't want to hear all of this," he said.

"Sure, I do. Please!"

He laughed. "I just ran a hell of a lot faster than anyone else. When you grow up racing with deer—and being
told you won't get anything for dinner unless you win—
you damn well learn to fly. Anyway, enough! Tell me
about yourself."

"Nothing to tell." She looked around her with dismay.
The sun was low in the sky. She'd been so entranced with
Black's story that she'd forgotten the time.

"What's the matter?"

"It's late! I'll never make it back down the mountain
before dark." She jumped to her feet. "Marm will be so
worried."

"I know how you come up. There's a more direct route
down, but it's rough. Are you up to it?" he asked, challenge in his voice.

"Of course."

"Then, let's go." He took her hand to pull her through
the saplings and into the glen. He stopped to look at her
face gazing up at him, her eyes trusting. "Realize that we
will be going straight down. Stay as close to me as possible."

She nodded her head in assent and he turned to leave the glen. She followed close behind.

Lilibet would never forget the next forty-five minutes. They ran through the thigh-grassed meadows and scrambled around rhododendron and mountain laurel thickets. They waded in icy streams up to their waists. Cold sweat beaded her brow as they scaled a small cliff and crawled across a canyon on a felled tree. She struggled to keep up with him, panting, her eyes tearing, her sides aching with pain. Once she lost sight of him and panicked. She opened her mouth to call for his help but shut it quickly. Never would she let him know that she couldn't keep up with him. He came back for her, though, which made her angry.

By the time they reached the bottom of the mountain her chest was bursting with the need for a lung full of air, and the calves of her legs burned. He stopped in a grove of pink dogwood and turned to beckon to her. Silently he pointed out Big Ugly Creek, which lay directly below them. It was the rear of the camp and she could see her house, light shining from the kitchen window.

"Thank you," she said softly.

Black looked at her in dismay.

"My God, what have I done to you? Have I been so long by myself that I've forgotten how to treat others?" he asked himself under his breath. Lilibet's hair was hanging around her face in a ratty mass of leaves and twigs. Her face was scratched and bleeding in places and her shirt was torn.

He reached to touch her face, then ran his thumb tenderly over a scratch on her cheek. "I'm sorry. I never meant to hurt you."

"It's okay. My daddy will never notice and Marm won't mind the truth. I kept up with you didn't I?" she asked proudly.

"Yes," he replied. He didn't want to let her go. A radiant warmth softened the sternness of his face.

One large, gentle hand held her precious face by the chin. The forefinger of the other hand came up to caress a scratch on her forehead.

She grew very still.

He lowered his head to kiss the scratch and a funny, pleasant tingle stirred her tummy.

"Goodbye, Elizabeth," he whispered huskily, then swiftly disappeared into the dusk.

Chapter 5

The Hutton house sat on three acres of lavishly landscaped grounds across the Tow River from Yancey. Other
prestigious homes were in the exclusive neighborhood
called Hutton Crossing, but only the three-story, red brick
home of Cle and Clarice Hutton commanded the valley.

A valet drove off with Sam's mother's Chevrolet as
Sam took Lilibet's arm and walked her up the path to the
house. Lights shone from every window, and music
blared from every brick corner and crevice. It took
Lilibet's breath away. She had read about valets, and cor-
sages, and parties such as this, but never expected to be
attending one this evening. When Sam arrived in Big
Ugly Creek to pick her up, he told her they were going to
a party at the Huttons' before the prom. He presented her
with a corsage of white gardenias and Marm had pinned
it to the shoulder of her pink organdy dress.

Sam told her she looked beautiful, and Marm whispered in her ear, "Hold yourself proud tonight, Lilibet,
and shine, shine for me."

She was scared but excited. On the Hutton twins' entrance into high school, this party had become a prom tradition and the "in" crowd considered it more important
than the prom. She was happy she was with Sam because
the Hutton house was a second home to him. Donetta
would be there, too. Sam had gotten her a date with a
friend of his.

They entered the front door without knocking and were
immediately swept into noisy bedlam. Adults and teenag-
ers alike roamed the house with drink in one hand and
barbecued rib, or cigarette in the other.

Lilabet's eyes took in as much as possible, but there

was so much to see that she found it difficult to focus on one thing. This was her first big party and she wanted to watch the people, see who was there, what they wore, and what they talked about. But she was torn between observing the people and looking at the house. She had never seen wall-to-wall carpeting before, or wallpaper, or Tiffany lamps. Her feet seemed to sink way, way down into the plush carpet and she had an urge to take off her shoes and wiggle her toes. She noticed many of the girls walking around barefoot.

It was then, as she watched the girls, that she knew her dress was all wrong.

Her homemade, waltz-length, pink organdy dress screamed of Big Ugly Creek and Marm's and Lilibet's naïveté. Marm insisted it was the latest thing because she had seen a picture of Princess Elizabeth in *Life* magazine wearing such a dress. Marm couldn't find a pattern for the dress at the company store and spent a whole Saturday in Yancey searching until she found one. It may have been just right for a young princess in England but not for Lilibet in southern West Virginia. The other girls' dresses were either chiffon with layers of crinolines under the big skirts, or tight taffeta sheaths. And most of them were strapless. Involuntarily, Lilibet's hand flew to the elbow-length sleeve of her dress, and she wanted to rip it off. She shrank behind Sam's big form and wished she were invisible.

Several voices called out to Sam.

"Hey, Sambo! About time you got here!"

"Sam, my man. The beer and dancing are downstairs. Old man Hutton hired a combo out of Charleston."

"Long ride to Big Ugly Creek, Sam, but you brought a pretty girl back with you. Hi, Lilibet."

Recognizing the voice, her heart jumped and she turned gratefully to the only person who had acknowledged her presence. Cledith Hutton's mellow blue eyes stared into her's and she swallowed the knot of nervousness that rose in her throat.

"Hello, Cle."

"You've never been here before have you? Come and meet my father and aunt."

Cle took her hand and she left the protection of Sam. She was exposed now as she had never been before. The young golden god of Yancey, West Virginia, had her by the hand and was pulling her through the crowd, Sam following along behind.

She saw the girls look at her dress and put their hands up to their mouths to laugh and talk about her to their friends. Their whispers followed her.

"Janie, will you look at that? I wonder what poop pile she pulled that from?"

"Honest to God! I can't understand why Sam brought her."

As they passed through a huge dining room with red satin walls and massive mahogany furniture, Lilibet's new high heels caught on the thick beige carpet and she stumbled. Someone giggled and she felt her cheeks pinken. Behind her, Sam reached for her elbow but she shook him off.

Never, ever, in her whole life had she been so miserable. Fervently wishing she hadn't come, she hung her head in humiliation. Suddenly, Marm's words echoed in her ears. "Hold yourself proud, Lilibet, and shine, shine for me."

She straightened her shoulders and stuck her chin up in the air. These people weren't acting any better than the MacDonald vermin. She wouldn't let them get her down. She'd much rather be on the mountain with Uncle East but she'd never let these jackals know that. Uncle East's face flashed before her and she heard him say to her as he had before. "You have a beautiful soul, Elizabeth. It will take care of you."

Cle seemed oblivious to the adverse attention she was receiving. He turned to smile at her and her heart melted.

"Pappy and Fat Sis are in the library. They like to meet all of our friends."

The book-lined den was filled with adults. Most of them were gathered in fascination around the first and only television set in Yancey. Lilibet glanced at the round, illuminated screen with curiosity. People were roller-skating around and around a rink, viciously jabbing their elbows, sticking out their feet, and knocking one another down as they went. How strange, she thought. It must be the roller derby she'd heard Eugene talk about.

Cle gave her hand a gentle tug and she turned to follow him again. An enormous portrait hanging over the fireplace caught her eye. The beautiful blond woman in the strapless light-blue evening dress lent a haunting presence to the room. Lilibet knew it was a portrait of Clada Hutton, young wife of Pappy Hutton and mother of Cledith and Clarice, who had committed suicide ten years ago when the twins were eight. Everyone said she killed herself because Pappy flaunted one too many of his other women in front of her.

Pappy Hutton, tall, reed thin, and immaculately dressed, stood with his sister, Fat Sis, in front of the brick fireplace.

Pappy's twin sisters, Mary and Margaret Hutton, had been unintentionally labeled for life when they were small. Identical twins, except one was heavier than the other, their nurse distinguished between them by calling them Fat Sis and Lean Sis. The names stuck and people in the valley were so accustomed to the nicknames they thought them not at all strange. Lean Sis lived in New York, but Fat Sis had taken care of Pappy and the young twins since Clada Hutton's death.

"Pappy, this is Sam's date, Lilibet Springer."

Pappy Hutton's cold blue eyes, recessed behind small, round, stainless–steel-rimmed glasses swept over Lilibet in her homemade dress and her discomfort, and he dismissed her as unimportant. He took the hand that she offered, however, and shook it, saying politely, "I'm glad you could be here, Lilibet. Any friend of Sam's is welcome in this house."

"Thank you, sir."

Fat Sis was a different matter. She took Lilibet's hand in both of her plump ones and in a warm, welcoming voice said, "We are very happy to have you here, Lilibet. I'll bet you haven't been fed yet. You boys take her and get her something to eat. Have a good time now, and come to me if you need anything."

Lilibet thanked Fat Sis, and then Cle and Sam led her downstairs to a big room with a low ceiling. It reeked of beer and cigarette smoke. A pool table, a Ping-Pong table, and a garish jukebox had been shoved against the wall. The walls shook as a rock and roll band beat out "Stagger Lee," and Yancey High School students gyrated back and forth to the music, their feet moving intricately on the tiled floor of their favorite room in the Hutton house. The light was dim but Lilibet could see Donetta in a corner with her date and moved toward her.

"Wait, Lilibet. Let's dance," Sam said.

"Do you mind if I say 'hi' to Donetta first?"

"No, but I think she might be a little busy," Sam replied.

"She always has time to talk to me," Lilibet said, and walked over to where Donetta stood in the arms of her date, Tom Tee Frye.

"Hi, Donetta. We finally got here. I've been looking for you."

Donetta turned around and smiled sloppily at Lilibet. Her fuchsia lipstick was smeared all over her face and Tom Tee's. "Hi, darlin'. How you doin'? Did'ja have a beer yet?"

Lilibet's heart sank. She had never seen Donetta like this. Her pretty dark brown hair was a mess, and the sophisticated red dress she'd borrowed from her older sister hung off one shoulder, exposing a bra strap. She and Donetta had talked about drinking and having their first beer, and how they would handle it. Donetta's father was an abusive drunk and she had decided that she would never drink at all. Tom Tee must have talked her into a beer, but it was obvious she'd now had more than one.

Donetta turned around and snuggled back into Tom Tee's arms, Lilibet stared angrily at Tom Tee and said, "She's drunk and you got her that way."

"She likes it," he said, staring defiantly back at her.

Lilibet took Donetta's arm to pull her out of Tom Tee's grasp but Tom Tee refused to let her go. Donetta, bewildered at this tug-of-war, finally jerked her arm from Lilibet's hand.

"Leave me alone, Lilibet. I'm havin' a swell time."

"Get out of here, you little shit," Tom Tee snarled at Lilibet.

"I won't—"

Sam put gentle hands on her shoulders and said quietly in her ear, "Come on, Lilibet. I think Donetta has already decided what she wants to do tonight, and there is nothing you can do but make trouble."

Reluctantly, and casting a furious look at Tom Tee, Lilibet let Sam draw her away.

The band from Charleston was now attempting Lavern Baker's "Jim Dandy." Sam directed her into the middle of the dancing crowd and patiently showed her a few basic steps.

Marm had taught her to clog when she was ten years old. They were secret lessons and there weren't many of them because Preacher Dunbar said dancing was a sin. If Daddy had known he'd have taken the strap to both of them. She remembered how pretty and flushed Marm's face was as she taught Lilibet the intricate steps. Laughing and breathless, she would urge her on, but with her ears perked for the sound of Daddy's truck.

The American Legion Hall, two miles down the road from Big Ugly Creek, held fiddling and dancing contests once a month. Many a night Lilibet sneaked out of the house after dark to go and watch. Finally, unable to control the itch of her feet, she'd begun to join in. When she began to win the contests in her age group she stopped going. She couldn't tempt fate by bringing attention to herself. Daddy would have found out real quick, and Marm would have gotten in trouble.

Clogging was a happy marriage of the old "buck and wing," the Irish jig, and the toe-to-heel movement of Indian dancing. You moved up and down, your arms hanging loose, and, except for a good kick now and then, kept your flying feet close to the floor.

Lilibet converted the up-and-down movement to side to side, and used a rolling gait in her hips and feet. Her body reacted instinctively to the rock and roll beat. She loved it. Before long, Lilibet was keeping up with the rest of the them, and perhaps going them one better.

She forgot the embarrassment of her dress, and the fear that somehow Donetta had gone beyond her into a world Lilibet had no wish to enter. Sam was a good dancer and they kept dancing and dancing, never stopping to rest or get a drink. Finally, flushed and out of breath, she fell against him, laughing.

"Sorry, Sam. Time for a break. I'm thirsty and I can't move another foot."

They worked their way out of the crowd and Sam told her to stay put while he got them something to drink. Sinking gratefully into a chair against the wall, she glanced casually at the sofa next to her and saw Clarice Hutton and Jimmy Haynes.

Clarice sat with her green satin dress hiked well above her knees. Jimmy's arm pumped in and out as his hand, hidden in the warm warren between her thighs, serviced her expertly. Clarice's blond head rested against the back of the black leather sofa, her eyes glazed and heavy-lidded. She rubbed the back of Jimmy's neck as his lank form hovered over her. His tongue licked hurriedly over the breasts that swelled partly exposed from her strapless dress. She moaned, "Ah, atta way, baby. Keep your finger right there. Oh, that feels so good, Jimmy sweet thing. Don't hurry. Make me come again."

Jimmy groaned and Clarice's body moved convulsively.

Hot and cold flames rushed through Lilibet. She stood up quickly to look frantically for Sam. He was walking toward her with two Cokes. When he saw the confused expression on her face and then observed Clarice and Jimmy, he moved swiftly to her side. "Sorry about that. Let's go to the other side of the room."

As they headed in the direction Sam had indicated, the singer crooned "Slow Boat To China" and she saw Cle and Sally Kay dancing dreamily to the slow tune. She'd had so much fun dancing with Sam that she hadn't had time to notice Cle and his girlfriend. Misery enveloped her and her eyes ached with threatening tears.

"Sam, could we just go to the prom?"

"Sure. Everyone is leaving soon anyway."

Lilibet felt she never really attended her senior prom. She and Sam danced a few times in the gaily decorated gymnasium and had punch from the refreshment table, but then the rest of the crowd arrived from the Hutton party. It didn't take long before Cle and Clarice and their friends decided the prom was too tame for them and it was time to adjourn to the lake and a blanket party. The rowdy bunch departed, much to the relief of the chaperones, taking Sam and Lilibet with them.

Driving to the lake along the dark, winding mountain road, Sam tried to relieve Lilibet's apprehensions.

"But—I don't have a bathing suit, Sam."

"That's okay. You don't have to swim," he assured her, thinking she probably couldn't swim anyway.

She wasn't really worried about swimming. She was worried about kissing. She'd heard there was a lot of kissing at blanket parties, and from what she'd witnessed tonight at the Huttons', there would be more than kissing going on. She'd never been kissed by a male before, not even her father.

With a jolt she remembered the tender kiss Black Brady had placed on her forehead but impatiently dismissed the tingling feeling it had sent along her spine. *Okay, I've been kissed, but never on the lips. I like Sam, but I don't want to kiss him.*

"What will we do if we don't swim?" she asked nervously.

"Fat Sis has probably packed up a basket with hot dogs, marshmallows, and potato chips. We'll roast hot dogs and marshmallows."

"Sam, maybe you should take me home."

"We're almost there, Lilibet." He reached over and smoothed the crown of her head with his big hand. "Relax. I know what you're worried about, and we're not going to do any necking. Trust me."

She heard the sincerity in his voice and believed him. Sam was a good friend and she was grateful he was her date.

The lights of several parked cars shone out on the black lake. A bonfire illuminated a clearing in the trees and music from Cle's portable radio floated across the water. Sweet honeysuckle and the mouthwatering aroma of roasting hot dogs met them as they walked to the clearing.

Clarice made her way up the rocky shore toward them. She had been swimming. Her skimpy red swimsuit displayed her tall, voluptuous body, sleek-wet in the beams of the headlights.

"Hi, Lilibet. Hey, Sam, do you still have the towels I left in the trunk of your car last spring?"

"Sure do. Ma washed them. I just forgot to return them. Wait a sec." He turned back into the darkness toward his car.

Lilibet stood there uncertainly.

Clarice, hands on hips, looked at her and Lilibet returned the steady gaze.

"Going swimming, Lilibet?" Clarice asked.

"No, I don't have a bathing suit.'

"I keep extras in my car. You can borrow one."

"I don't think it would fit."

Clarice smiled, a kind but humorous look in her blue eyes. "You are a bit smaller than me, aren't you?"

Lilibet smiled back and said, "Yes."

Clarice continued to study this new friend of Sam's and decided she liked what she saw.

In all ways, Clarice had matured much faster than the other girls in Yancey. She had little patience with their simpering, giggling, and posturing, and avoided their company whenever possible. To her disgust, they toadied and minced around her like she was the queen of Egypt or something. If she snapped her fingers they all came running. She'd always faced herself head-on and knew she was cynical beyond her years, knew that she was spoiled and demanding and expected instant gratification always, but she didn't care. There was a certain security in knowing yourself so well, no matter how rotten you were.

The only things that Clarice truly loved were her German Shepherd, Stud, and her brother, Cle. For Sam she held a deep affection and regretted the sexual runaround she'd given him since they were fifteen. Knowing that "going all the way" with Sam would eventually destroy their friendship, Clarice had never permitted the sexual consummation Sam had so desired. She was happy he was over his obsession with her.

"Do I have a smudge on my face or something?" Lilibet asked.

"No. You're just fine," Clarice replied.

When she hadn't been otherwise occupied with Jimmy at the party earlier in the evening, Clarice had unobtrusively scrutinized Lilibet. She'd begun to watch her when she realized the other girls were making fun of her. To spite the girls, Clarice had thought that she might offer Lilibet one of her dresses, but had held back as she noticed the pride in Lilibet's stance. She knew instinctively that Lilibet would have refused the offer. She liked the way the girl had gone onto the dance floor with Sam and enjoyed herself instead of hiding in a corner. Besides her love for Cle and Stud, and her fondness for Sam, there were two things Clarice found important and respected: innocence and honesty. Innocence because she'd lost her own willingly and defiantly when she was twelve years old, and honesty because all the unhappiness Clarice had ever known had been caused by deception. Innocence and honesty stood before her in this wisp of a beautiful, violet-eyed girl.

Clarice's steady scrutiny was making Lilibet uncomfortable and she started to move away, but Clarice caught her arm. "I'm sorry. I'm shitty rude sometimes. Next time, just tell me to stuff it. Can you swim?"

"Yes."

"I have a pair of my young cousin's cut-off jeans in my car, and an old T-shirt. Why don't you see if they fit and then you can swim."

Lilibet saw the dare in Clarice's eyes and impulsively decided to take it.

The slim crescent of the new moon in the indigo sky reflected no light on the convivial scene by the lake. Grateful for the darkness, but slapping at the bugs whining around her ears, Lilibet cautiously changed clothes behind a bush. She removed the gardenia corsage and wrapped it protectively with her shoes and hose in the folds of her dress, then put them in Sam's car. She knew she would not wear the dress again, but Marm need never

know that. *I'll take it with me to college and Marm will
never know the difference.*

She looked down at herself critically. The cut-offs fit
perfectly but the T-shirt was too large. That's fine with
me, she thought, as she picked her way through the couples lying on blankets in the woods. She stumbled over
an empty pair of blue satin high heels and recognized
them as Donetta's.

Eagerly, she knelt to say hello to the couple on the
blanket, but leapt to her feet when she saw that Tom Tee
had his mouth fastened on Donetta's breast. The two were
oblivious to everything. They smelled of beer, gin, and
something else . . . something Uncle East had taught her
to identify. With an embarrassing thump of her heart, she
realized it was the muskiness of animals mating.

Heart heavy, she continued toward the clearing, knowing Tom Tee had already placed himself between
Donetta's thighs tonight and that Donetta had lost her
much-prized virginity. Briefly, she wondered if Donetta
would tell her about it. They had always shared everything, but Lilibet didn't want to hear about this new experience of Donetta's. It was an ugly way to become a
full woman; drunk and vulnerable at the hands of a boy
who only wanted your body. *I want my time to be special,
really special. I want it to be loving, and beautiful; a time
I will carry with me in a precious part of my heart all the
rest of my life.* Wiping a quick tear from her eyes, she
stepped into the clearing.

Not everyone was in the woods rutting. With surprise,
she noted Clarice and Jimmy were roasting hot dogs
along with several other couples. Everyone knew that
Clarice tired of her conquests quickly. Maybe she'd had
enough of Jimmy. A crowd had gathered around Cle and
Sam as they organized a race at the lake's edge.

Sally Kay, sitting by the bonfire, called down to Cle.

"Cle, honey, don't you think it's dangerous to be swimming so far out in that awful old lake on a dark night like
this?"

"No, I don't," he called back. "I think it's going to be
fun. The winner gets my new Bo Diddly album."

"C'mon up here and sit beside me. I'm lonely."

"You come down here and get in the race."

"Cle, honey, come. . . ."

"Shut up, Sally Kay," said Clarice. "Leave him alone. He's having fun . . . are you?"

"Well, I . . ." Sally Kay ventured meekly.

"Just shut up," demanded Clarice, then noticed Lilibet standing on the edge of the clearing. "Hey, Sam. Lilibet is ready to swim. Maybe she would like to race with you all."

Sam hurried up the rocky incline toward Lilibet. His big, bearlike form stood in front of her, shutting out the light from the fire.

Quietly, so no one could hear, he asked, "Can you swim, Lilibet?"

"Yes, Sam, I can."

She moved around him, toward the lake, casting a quick glance at Sally Kay as she passed her.

Sam followed her anxiously. "You don't have to race if you don't want to. Sally Kay is right. It isn't the smartest thing to do on a night like this. But once Cle gets something in his head, there's no stopping him."

"I want to, Sam."

They reached the group by the shore. Cle had organized them into relay teams.

His face beamed with welcome when he saw Lilibet. "Hi, beautiful. We need one more person on Joe's team."

Her heart swelled, and she thought Sally Kay was stupid.

"Aw, come on, Cle," complained Joe Carpozzoli. "That's not fair. Hell, anyone who lives in Big Ugly Creek can't be a good swimmer."

Cle didn't know if Lilibet could keep up with the rest of them, but he was willing to give her a try. "She's going with us, Joe. Apologize to her."

Joe apologized. Cle took her by the arm and turned her toward the lake to show her where they were swimming. Her shoulder burned where his hand touched her and she shivered. "Are you cold?" he asked with concern.

"No, no. Just excited." His head crooked close to hers, he pointed out a platform in the center of the lake. She wanted to move an inch closer and touch her cheek to his.

Her golden god had just defended her. He had just included her in his life. Elation filled her.

"See?" he asked. His warm breath tickled her cheek. "Sam rowed out there earlier and left a kerosene lantern. Can you see it?"

Afraid to speak, she nodded her head in the affirmative.

"Good. Head for the light and you'll be fine."

Annoyed at first by their assumption that she was a poor swimmer, if she could swim at all, Lilibet was now amused. Uncle East had taught her to swim in the rapids of a rushing river high in a secluded valley on Catawba mountain. She had never raced with anyone but she figured she could keep up with the best of them.

There were four teams, and much yelling, jostling, and teasing as they all set out to swim madly back and forth between the float platform and the shore. One by one the players were eliminated until only Cle's team and Joe Carpozzoli's team remained in the race. By this time, Joe was grateful Lilibet was on his team. She proved to be the strongest of his swimmers. His team was now punching her on the shoulder and giving her words of encouragement. Cle eliminated himself on the last round. It wouldn't have been fair to win the race he had organized. The remaining member of Cle's team lost out to Joe, so Joe and Lilibet were to race against each other to determine the winner.

A noisy crowd had gathered on the shore now, interested in the showdown. Clarice swigged beer from a long-necked bottle. Jimmy Haynes stood behind her, his arms encircling her tightly. She yelled in drunken delight at Joe Carpozzoli, swinging her bottle crazily in the air.

"Hey, Joe. You're gonna get beat by a girl."

Joe glowered at Clarice. His happiness at having Lilibet on his team had dissipated.

Sam stood close to Lilibet. He put a towel around her shoulders and stood with his arm draped protectively about her. "Are you all right, Lilibet?"

"I'm fine, Sam, really I am. I'm a little tired and I'm cold, but as soon as I get back in the water that will all go away."

Sam looked at her with undying admiration. If he'd had any doubts about loving this gusty, vibrant girl, they were all gone. The T-shirt was plastered to her chest, clearly outlining her pert, full breasts, but she was so engrossed in the race she hadn't noticed. He realized the boys had noticed, though. They were staring at Lilibet, and Sam drew the towel closer about her. Clarice was yelling at him.

"Hey, Sam," she called anxiously. "Where the hell is Cle?"

"He stayed on the float because the kerosene lamp was burning low. He wanted to make sure it didn't go out."

He turned back to Lilibet.

"Do you want me to swim with you, Lilibet? Just in case you get tired, or get a cramp or something?" Sam had been eliminated early. He was a strong swimmer, but his bulk prevented him from being a swift one.

She glared at him. "No, Sam. I can do this by myself!" She turned to Jimmy who was going to start the race. "I'm ready."

"One, two, three . . . Go!" Jimmy yelled.

Lilibet and Joe dove cleanly into the lake. Joe outdistanced her quickly.

She swam by herself, acutely aware of the ominous depth of the black water beneath her. Her graceful arms cut efficiently in and out of the ice-cold wetness. The cheering of the crowd on the shore receded until it seemed an echo behind her. Close by, the only sound she heard was a soft splash as her legs knifed the water. Her long hair was a dragging weight and she wished she'd taken time to pin it on top of her head. She had wanted an upswept hairdo for the prom, but Marm had said no. She remembered her embarrassment, and then her anger at the way they had made fun of Marm's dress. The anger made her swim faster. Her arms flashed nimbly through the black water and she began to gain on Joe. She'd show these "townies" what a girl from Big Ugly Creek could do. Her tired legs found fresh energy as she resolutely propelled herself through the icy water. The coldness didn't affect her—she'd swum in much colder—but she hoped it was getting to Joe.

A splash ahead of her told her she'd caught up with Joe. She drew abreast of him and he glanced over in surprise. Lilibet, not wasting her energy to look at him, swam doggedly on.

Grimly, she swam neck and neck for a while, Joe grunting with his effort. Lilibet gritted her teeth and demanded more of her tiring body. Inch by struggling inch, she drew ahead of Joe, and then was by herself. Finally, she'd gone so far ahead of him she couldn't even hear his grunts.

It was scary being in the fathomless black water all by herself with only the inky night to keep her company. *You can do it, Lilibet. Keep kicking, pulling, breathing. Swim!" I'm a better swimmer than Joe. I'm a better swimmer than Joe. I'm a better swimmer than Joe. Swim. You're going to win. You're going to win. You're going to win.* She chanted in her mind until it was part of her stroke, part of her breathing, part of her.

Praying the race was almost over, she paused for a moment to get a fix on the float. Treading water with a tired dog paddle, she shook the wet hair off her face and peered anxiously into the distance.

A light flickered up ahead. She was closer than she'd thought. Cle was there. Waiting for her. Her spirits lifted, her eager heart pounded crazily, and she pressed on vigorously. Her legs and arms flew now as she raced to the finish.

Cledith Hutton sat in the dark, his arms resting across his knees, listening to the splashing sounds coming toward him. He'd be glad when this was over. He wanted to get back to Sally Kay and some serious necking. The fun had gone out of the race awhile ago, but he was the leader and the kids would have been disappointed if they hadn't seen it through to the end. He didn't know how he'd ended up head honcho of the crowd. They liked him and always had. They'd anointed him with their fun and adoration when they were in junior high school. Their blind willingness to follow him was now an intrinsic part of his identity and he would have been uncomfortable without it. Sometimes he grew tired of the responsibility but bluffed his way through, or let Sam cover for him.

The splashing noise was closer now. He knew it was Joe. He was the best swimmer in school. Lilibet was a good swimmer but she didn't have the strength Joe had. She'd probably given up and headed back to shore.

He was proud of himself, though, for picking her out and having faith in her. He was intrigued with Lilibet's beautiful face, but he and Sally Kay had been dating for a year and she had just let him break her "cherry" two months ago. She whined when they had sex, afraid she was going to get pregnant, but Cle Hutton wasn't going to get any girl pregnant. Pappy had taken him to a whorehouse when he was thirteen and he'd learned all about sex and contraceptives. Sally Kay sulked, but she liked sex. He wasn't going to give all that up just because he liked Lilibet's face.

The winner was here. A hand reached up toward him and he took it and pulled. Expecting Joe's heavy weight, he pulled hard, and a featherlike figure landed on top of him.

It was Lilibet, laughing excitedly. "Oh, Cle. I did it. I won!"

Exuberantly, she wrapped her arms around him and kissed him.

Aghast at what she had done, she swiftly rolled off him and sat with her head hanging. "Oh, Cle. I'm sorry. I was so excited . . ."

Impressed with the courage that made her a winner, and charmed with her unfeigned happiness and enthusiasm, Cle took her chin and turned her head toward him. Her silver hair, the color of moonlight, was plastered to her face and shone even in the darkness. The flicker of the kerosene lamp caught the depths of her intriguing violet eyes and the trembling of her delicate but full lower lip. Rivulets of water and tears ran down her face, dripping off her chin and on to her breasts.

"Congratulations, Lilibet. Don't cry," he whispered, and kissed her softly.

Lilibet thought she was dreaming. This couldn't be her,

alone with Cledith Hutton, in the middle of the lake, kissing.

His gentle lips moved carefully over hers, experimenting and tasting. A warm weakness spread throughout her and she caught her breath. He drew back to look at her again and she thought she would drown in the blueness of his eyes. Oh, God, is this really happening? He brushed the wet hair off her face and cupped both his hands around her face. There was a questioning look in his eyes and she nodded tentatively.

He kissed her again.

She loved the softness of his mouth on hers and the warmth of his hands on her cheeks. She felt the slight tug of his body toward the floor of the platform and never taking her mouth from his, she lay down with him. They lay on their sides, face to face, while he continued to kiss her, his tongue now making gentle forays between her lips to touch her teeth.

Lilibet wondered if she was supposed to do something, but lay there enjoying the sensation Cle was creating in her body. His hand moved from her face to her breast and she stiffened reflexively, but tried to relax as he continued to explore. Cle pulled her closer to him and she felt the distinct hardness of him through the thin nylon of his bathing trunks. Startled, she schooled herself to lie still. She knew what the hardness was. She had seen enough animals mating to know that Cle was aroused. As much as she enjoyed the tingly arrows of warmth and excitement caused by his stroking, she was worried. Nervously but affectionately, she ran her hand up and down the smooth skin on his back and then pulled away.

He stopped kissing her and said, "It's okay, Lilibet. I wouldn't hurt you for the world."

Cle was filled with wonder at the water nymph who lay here beside him letting him touch her beautiful breasts. And they were beautiful. Full, perfectly shaped, not too large and not too small. He wanted to pull up the wet T-shirt and kiss them but he dared not right now. Later.

Lilibet brushed her fingers across the top of his crew cut, enjoying the bristly feel of it against the palm of her hand, and sighed. "Thanks for the kiss, Cle. It was better than a Bo Diddly record."

He laughed, amazed at her guilessness, and bent his head to kiss her again, but Joe's head popped up over the edge of the platform.

"Shit, Cle, if that's what you're giving out for a prize, I'm glad I didn't win." He grumbled as he climbed clumsily aboard the platform. "You're lucky Sally Kay can't see out here."

Cle and Lilibet sat up. Lilibet felt guilty, but Cledith Hutton knew that Sally Kay was history.

On the way home to Big Ugly Creek, Sam and Lilibet were silent.

It hadn't taken long for Sam to figure out what happened between Cle and Lilibet. He knew Cle too well, and he recognized the look of triumphant excitement on Cle's face. The dazed expression on Lilibet's face confirmed his suspicion. Nobody could resist Cle's charm. He simply had been endowed with all the things that impressed people and made them feel happy: good looks, genuine charm and interest in others, wealth, and an uncertain vulnerability that made women want to take care of him.

There was a light coming from Lilibet's house and Sam could see her mother and her sister waiting behind the screen door. Mrs. Springer and Margot disappeared as he steered Lilibet between an old car and a broken-down sofa, to her porch. She smiled up at him and then stood on her tiptoes to put her arms around his chest and give him a warm hug.

"Thank you, Sam. Thank you so much."

As he drove away, Sam decided he wasn't going to give up without a fight. He had the rest of the summer to win her. Deep in his heart, however, he was afraid he'd already lost, and an enduring sadness began to fester.

Chapter 6

The brightly lit Yancey County High School auditorium was packed with family and friends of the graduates. Lilibet wished the lights were dim so she couldn't see anyone; maybe then she wouldn't be so nervous.

In the front row sat Pappy Hutton and Fat Sis. Fat Sis, her mass of gray hair piled high on her head and fastened with combs, was perspiring and fanning herself with the program. Pappy was cool and collected as always. Men came to shake his hand, trying to get his attention because of problems at a mine, or a political situation that needed tending to. He waved them away with impatience. Tonight was not the night for business or politics. He only had eyes for his two handsome children who sat on the stage with the rest of the class.

Lilibet saw Sam's mom sitting behind the Huttons. Anna Adkins was a short, buxom woman with pretty brown hair and eyes.

Marm, Daddy, and Margot were sitting toward the middle. Marm had a big pink hat on. Lilibet had told her not to wear it because people behind her wouldn't be able to see, but Marm had insisted this was the occasion for a proper hat.

For the sixteenth time, Lilibet shuffled the prompting cards she held in her wet, shaking hands. They were damp and smudged now, hardly readable. It was time for the principal, Mr. Satterfield, to introduce her valedictory address.

Cledith and Sam sat on each side of her in the first row of graduates. Cle, because he was president of the student body, and Sam, because he was class president. She'd become accustomed to their dual presence and at times felt like the filling of a sandwich. Neither one of them had let her out of their sight since prom night a month ago. It was the hot topic of conversation at school. Uncomfortable at first with the sudden attention, she was beginning to enjoy it and the subsequent whirl of social activities.

She felt Sam's hand on her arm and looked down to see that he was offering her his handkerchief. He had noticed her wet hands. How like Sam. She used it to dry her hands, then gave it back to him with a smile. Cle patted her other arm, and when she looked at him, he winked at her and gave her a thumbs-up sign. Her heart flipped as it always did when he touched her.

"Parents, friends, and students, I now present to you the Valedictorian of the Class of 1950, Miss Lilibet Springer."

Somehow she made it to the lectern without fainting, cleared her throat, and began to speak in a quaking voice.

"Parents, friends, and families, thank you for coming tonight. I would like to address my remarks to my classmates . . . "W.E. Henly said, 'I am the master of my fate, I am the captain of my soul.' We must remember these words as we embark on the rest of our life's journey. You have a divine appointment with yourself." With each word, her voice grew stronger, she stood straighter, her shoulders set more confidently.

Uncle East had helped her write the speech. Much to the chagrin of Cle and Sam, she'd spent one whole Saturday with Uncle East, rehearsing and polishing her delivery. Her mysterious refusal to tell them where she'd disappeared to only created more frustration on their part.

"It matters not if you become a doctor, shoe salesman, or coal miner. Be true to the best that is within you. Do not be diminished by those who would control your wages, control your health, control where you live and how you live. Demand your right to live as a whole human being. . . ."

In the middle of her speech, she didn't need her notes anymore. She found she was having a wonderful time. A flash of silver danced off Pappy Hutton's glasses and she dared a glance at him. Uncle East had warned her that the mine owner wouldn't like this speech about human rights, and charting your own course. At the time, she hadn't cared. Now, as she noted the grim, tight look about his narrow face, she began to have second thoughts. She didn't want Cle's father angry with her, and she didn't want her daddy to lose his job. But she had made her decisions about what she wanted to say, so, by God, she would say it. She might never have another such opportunity.

Caught up in the rightness of her words, and the excitement of this big moment in her life, Lilibet spoke eloquently. Forgotten were her fear and shyness. Before the amazed eyes of the people of Yancey, the shy, beautiful girl from Big Ugly Creek metamorphosed into a dynamic young woman. Her voice, clear and firm, clipped each consonant, and rounded each vowel like an embrace. Every phrase carried the correct emotional nuance as she took her audience up with her, and then down. She had them in the palm of her hand and she loved the magic of it.

As she neared the end, for a brief moment, she focused on Marm and Daddy. Marm was sitting tall and proud with a big smile on her face. Daddy was slumped in his seat, his face red and glowering. Lilibet's eyes swept to the front and she wasn't surprised to see a look of consternation on Pappy Hutton's face. But he wasn't looking at her. He was looking behind her at Cle. Was something the matter with Cle?

What Pappy Hutton saw, and Lilibet couldn't see, was the look of absolute adoration on Cledith Hutton's face as he watched Lilibet. Speculation sharpened Pappy's wintry blue eyes as he returned his gaze to the fair-haired young woman who spoke so entrancingly and dangerously. He knew Cle had seen a lot of her this past month, but so had Sam. Pappy knew his son well. Never before had his son been so affected by a female. She was, of course, exquisite, and he'd bet his hairy balls she was an innocent little charmer. The Hutton men had a connoisseur's eye for beautiful women. What concerned Pappy was her obvious intellect and . . . Holy Jesus, she had guts, making a speech like that in front of him. It was almost union talk.

He'd been ready to magnanimously forget about her speech. It was graduation night and kids said a lot of things. Now, however, he recognized she was a force to be reckoned with. She didn't know that, though. That was his ace in the hole. Lilibet Springer didn't know she could make his son, Cle, dance like a puppet on the end of a string.

Another set of male eyes in the audience absorbed every sound and movement Lilibet made. The slip of a girl in her simple, sleeveless white cotton dress captivated him. Her brave, shining spirit lit up the whole auditorium. Everything else, and everyone, was dimmed and unimportant in comparison. A knot of dread twisted in his chest, as he, too, noted the look on Cledith Hutton's face.

"Keep your divine appointment with fate. Don't be late. You need to be the best you can be for your country ..." Lilibet paused dramatically, "and maybe even more importantly, for yourself."

As her eyes scanned the crowd, Lilibet saw two very tall figures, way in the back, in the last row, stand up. One, a bit shorter than the other and with aged shoulders, raised both his arms over his head and clasped his hands in a big victory shake. He shook his arms so vigorously that his white panama hat fell off his head, and with a start she realized it was Uncle East. Next to him stood Black Brady.

Pure happiness shot through her.

Nothing could have made this evening more complete than having Uncle East here ... Black, too, she supposed. She hadn't seen him since that day in the "secret place." She saw him pick up Uncle East's hat and put it on his grandfather's head, and then the two of them slipped quickly out the rear door.

She became aware of the utter silence that filled the auditorium. Had they not liked her speech? A smattering of clapping began, then it gathered, and grew until a thunderous sound echoed in the room. They were standing on their feet now, applauding and applauding. She was stunned. She turned around to walk back to her seat, but Mr. Satterfield brought her back to the lectern. He whispered in her ear that she should stand there until they finished acknowledging her. She looked out over the audience and smiled, then waved at Marm, who waved proudly and energetically back.

Then through her haze of joy she heard Mr. Satterfield announce that the winner of the Turner Scholarship was Miss Lilibet Springer. Portly, gray-haired Judge Turner crossed the stage to shake her hand and give her an envelope. Tears streamed down her face. She wiped them away impatiently. *Thank you, God.*

The Home Ec Club and The Future Teachers of America served refreshments in the cafeteria. Yellow and blue crepe paper crisscrossed the ceiling and looped around the tan walls. Lilibet was surrounded by well-wishers. Embarrassed but glowing, she could only smile warmly and say thank you.

Marm, Daddy, and Margot stood on the outskirts of the crowd until Sam noticed them and drew them close to Lilibet. Marm hugged Lilibet so tight she hurt her ribs. Then she put both hands on Lilibet's shoulders and said in a shaky voice, "You have done us so proud, Lilibet."

"Thank you, Marm. I couldn't have done it without your encouragement."

"Congratulations, Lilibet," Margot said, giving her a quick hug. Donetta was there and hugged her, too.

"You've done fine with your grades, daughter, but I didn't like that speech of yours. You're bitin' the hand that feeds you," said a glum and angry Roy Springer.

Marm put her hand on his arm to quiet him down, but he shook it off. "And you needn't think you're goin' to college jest because you won that fancy scholarship. You're stayin' home and workin' cause we need the money."

"Well now, Roy, let's not be so hasty about that," a smooth, cool voice intruded.

As Pappy Hutton walked through the crowd, the people who remained around Lilibet fell away. As always, he wore a neat, black, pinstriped three-piece suit, the trousers slim and tailored to perfection, the vest festooned with a gold watch fob.

Cle and Sam stood at attention, and Roy Springer's

face grew beet red. Lilibet's heart was pounding. Oh, God, what had she done? Pappy Hutton was going to fire her father because of her speech.

"Let's not be so hasty," Pappy said again and patted Roy on the shoulder.

"Mr. Hutton!" Roy gulped. "Nice to see you, sir. This girl of mine didn't mean nothin' by that speech...."

"I thought the speech was wonderful," Pappy interrupted. "It's time our young people began thinking for themselves. Of course, we know they'll feel differently about things when they've grown up a bit, don't we, Roy?"

"Yes, sir."

"I thought you were making good money up there at Big Ugly, Roy, but maybe you could do with a raise. I've been watching you and I think you'd make a good section foreman."

"Y-yes, sir! Thank you, sir!"

"You see, Roy," Pappy Hutton said, putting his thin, elegant arm around Roy's worn, blue-serge shoulder, "I believe this young daughter of yours should go to college. With the scholarship and your promotion that should be more than possible. What do you think, Roy?"

"Yes, sir. Absolutely, sir," said an astounded Roy Springer, and began to cough his wheezy, wet cough.

A huge gratefulness filled Lilibet. All her resentment toward Pappy Hutton fell away. She couldn't believe her ears. He had just ensured her entering college in the fall.

Pappy's eyes narrowed imperceptibly as he turned to Lilibet. Swiftly, he took in Cledith's hand at Lilibet's waist, and Sam's hovering presence. So that's how it was. Cledith would win her, of course. There was a difference in the way she looked at Cle and the way she looked at Sam.

"Now, young lady, it's time I congratulated you," he said as he shook her hand.

"Thank you, Mr. Hutton, and thank you for helping my daddy," she said with quiet dignity.

He brushed her gratitude aside, but noted how much poise she'd gained since the night of the prom. Learns quickly ... and has an inbred confidence she's not even aware of yet. Yes, it was best to have her where he could keep an eye on her—and on Cle.

"You are attending the university of Morgantown with Cle and his friends, I assume." He interrogated her casually.

"Yes, sir. I'll be living with Miss Mabel Turner."

"You couldn't be in better hands." He turned to Regina Springer. "Mrs. Springer, you won't have to worry about your daughter. Mabel Turner is an old friend of mine and I can assure you she will take good care of Lilibet."

"Thank you, Mr. Hutton. Thank you so much." Marm blushed, overwhelmed and embarrassed by the sudden attention from Pappy Hutton himself.

Several fellow classmates were whistling and making arm motions to gain Cle's attention. He waved to them and said to his father, "Pappy, if it's all right with you, we're leaving now."

"Sure, Cle. Coming to the house for a party?"

"No, sir, not tonight. We're going to Ruby's."

"Kind of a rough place, Cle. Are the girls going, too?"

An arm entwined in Pappy's and a velvety voice said, "What a dumb question, Pappy. Do fat babies fart? You know I wouldn't miss a party."

Clarice kissed her father on the cheek and squeezed his arm. He kissed her back. She looked like her mother tonight.

"The sky would fall if my little girl ever missed a party," he said, laughing. "But you all be careful."

Pappy already knew they frequented Ruby's Beer House, but he didn't want them to discover just how much he *did* know about their lives.

Sally Kay Nolan acknowledged the week after the prom that she'd lost Cle to Lilibet. She'd spent the last month without a boyfriend and wasn't happy about it. Accustomed as she was to being Cle's girl and receiving the afterglow of the attention showered upon him, she had grown more miserable every day.

On the night of graduation, outside Yancey County High School, Sally Kay Nolan pitched a fit. She screamed and yelled and cried and said there was no way she was

going to Ruby's unless she had a date, and if she didn't
have a date then Cle must take her. Cle prevailed upon
Sam's chivalrous nature and convinced him he should
take Sally Kay to Ruby's, then he swiftly tucked Lilibet
into the Cadillac.

It was a hot, thick summer night. The breeze created by
the rushing of the car was restorative. Lilibet rested her
head on the back of the seat of Cle's baby-blue convertible, and gazed happily up at the starlit sky. West Virginia
valleys are narrow and deep so her view was limited, like
lying in the bottom of a rectangular box and looking up
to see the restricted view directly above you. In fact, the
miners and old mountain people called the floor of the
valley "the bottom." The stars she could see were bright
and sharp. The air was sweet with honeysuckle. She was
alone with Cle. What a wonderful night.

Cle silently gave thanks to Sally Kay and her theatrics,
and congratulated himself. Finally, he'd gotten rid of
Sam. It was great being alone with Lilibet. He treated
himself to a quick glance at her. The wind whipped her
hair back and the lights from the dashboard reflected on
her face, giving him a clear view of her profile. He loved
the way her perfect nose tilted up just slightly, and her
delicate but generous lips turned down a bit at the corners. God, she was gorgeous. How could he not have
spotted her before now? He knew Sam was in love with
her and it was hard for him to deny Sam anything, but,
this was different. It was more than her beauty.

Cle was inexplicably drawn to Lilibet Springer. He
couldn't figure out why, nor did he care. Being with her
made him happy.

The neon sign at Ruby's garishly proclaimed GOOD
BEER AND GOOD EATS. It flashed on and off, blinking orange then blue. Long before they screeched into the
crowded parking lot, they could hear the outside loud-
speakers blaring out "Little Bitty Pretty One."

"Didn't I hear you tell your father that Ruby had hired
a combo for tonight?" Lilibet asked as they entered the
dark, smoky bar and dance hall.

"Yep, but just for part of the evening," Cle replied. He waved to their crowd taking up a large corner section of the room.

A few of Ruby's faithful were there, leaning on the bar or slouched against the wall. Mostly young miners, and several mountain men of the MacDonald ilk, with tattooed arms, tight jeans, and hobnailed boots, they drank their beer and watched the younger set with tolerant amusement. Knowing the high school crowd would be there and not wanting trouble, Ruby had discouraged most of her regulars tonight. With relief, Lilibet noted that Eugene was not there.

The Platters's "Harbor Lights" swooned out from the jukebox and before Lilibet could say hello to anyone, Cle put his arm about her waist and danced her onto the scarred dance floor. She saw Sally Kay staring daggers at her, and Sam looking crestfallen, but Cle's arms were around her and nothing else mattered. Donetta and Tom Tee joined them, and soon the dance floor was crowded.

Coins clinked continuously into the jukebox for the next couple of hours, while they danced and consumed an abundant beer supply.

"Ain't you afraid the sheriff will drop by and check out the age limit, Ruby?" asked a miner leaning against the bar.

"Hell, no," Ruby replied in her whiskey voice. "Pappy paid him to stay away."

"Don't he worry about their gettin' drunk, or smashin' them fancy cars?"

"Sure he does, but he wants 'em to be happy so he indulges them. Way too much if you ask me. But he pays me and everyone else to look the other way, so I keep my mouth shut."

Ruby stood behind the bar watching the action, her eyes missing nothing.

"Besides," she said, "if they get too pissed I call Pappy, but mostly Sam Adkins makes sure they all get home safe."

"Ain't that Sam dancin' with that dark-haired girl?"

"Yeh. Gawd, I don't know how poor Sam got hooked

up with prissy Sally Kay. She's been datin' Cle for almost a year now. Looks like Cle's got himself a new date tonight."

Ruby noticed that Sam and Sally Kay were sticking close to Cledith Hutton and the Springer girl. The Springer girl was a new one to the crowd. A nice addition, but a lamb among wolves. Wonder how Pappy feels about Cle datin' a miner's daughter?

"Who's the hot blond number sittin' in the booth arguin' with Jimmy Haynes?" another man asked.

Ruby eyed the man with disbelief.

"Honey, you mean you've never noticed Clarice Hutton before? Hell, since she was twelve years old she's been shakin' that ass of her's at every male in the valley who wears long pants. She's been fuckin' Jimmy for two or three months, but she's gettin' tired of him. When she finds someone else to get her hot enough, she'll dump him like shit."

Her sin-weary eyes carefully viewed Clarice and Jimmy. Hope there's no trouble with those two tonight. That slut, Clarice, was shovin' Jimmy's nose with her finger and laughin' like crazy. She was already drunk, and so was Jimmy. Time to bring on the live music. She didn't know how good these guys were, and she didn't know if the kids would like their music, but the young man had been convincing. Said he was goin' to college in September. He and the other four guys was workin' their way through the college and needed the money.

Lilibet paid no attention to the band setting up their equipment. She and Cle were sitting in a corner booth holding hands and talking.

"I'm excited about going to the university, Cle."

"I always knew I'd be going to school in Morgantown so it's not all that exciting to me."

She wished she could relay to Cle a small portion of the wonderment she felt at just the thought of attending classes in a university, of learning, advancing, pulling herself out of Big Ugly Creek. But she couldn't tell him how much it meant to her, and to Marm.

She could never tell anyone how when she was seven

years old, she'd lain awake nights listening to Marm and
Daddy arguing. Eugene had hated first grade and Daddy
never made him go back to school after Christmas. In
southern West Virginia a father had all the rights to his
son, a mother none. Daddy said Eugene wouldn't need
schoolin' anyway because he was going into the mines,
and the girls didn't need to go past third grade. That was
enough for learnin' to read, write, and figure numbers.
Marm told him she wouldn't sleep in the bed with him
anymore. Said she'd sleep on the floor, or even worse, on
the porch where all the neighbors would know his wife
wasn't sleeping with him and taking care of his "needs."
Lilibet didn't know what "needs" Marm was talking
about at the time, but she did know that Marm slept on
the porch for three nights in the dead of winter until finally Daddy relented and said the girls could go to
school. Now she knew, of course, what "need" Marm was
referring to. It was the only time she'd ever known Marm
to stand up to Daddy about anything.

No. She could never tell Cle things like that.

"You're smart, Cle. Didn't you ever want to go to one
of those prestigious schools like Harvard or Columbia?"

"Nope. Pappy says I'm going to the university because
it's insurance that I'll become part of West Virginia's
'good ol' boy' system. I'll be running the mines one day
and I'll need to know people all over the state who
count."

"What's the 'good ol' boy' system?"

"Well, you have to join the right fraternity and make
friends with the right people so that you'll have powerful
connections later when you need them."

Privately, Lilibet thought it sounded cold and calculat-
ing, but it also made sense. After all, who was she to argue with the son of a successful man?

"I suppose you'll think I'm kind of naive, but I just
want to go to college to get a good education. I want to
learn about everything!"

"I don't think it's naive at all," Cle said, and gave her
a soft kiss on the cheek. "I think every woman needs to
be well-educated so she can be a benefit to her husband
and children."

Lilibet blushed and hesitated but said, "I don't want to get married right out of college, Cle. I want to go to law school. I want to be a lawyer."

Cle's eyebrows rose in surprise and he drained the last of his beer.

"A lawyer! Well, I'll be damned. I don't know any female lawyers. Pappy says there are a few in Charleston and Washington. Why do you want to do that?"

"I suppose I want to be powerful, too, just like you do . . . but for different reasons. I'd like to help improve the living conditions of our people in the mountains here, and to get laws passed to protect the nature around us. You need power and money to do those things."

Wonder and puzzlement gathered in Cle's eyes.

"Our miners are living pretty good. They've had tough times lately because times are tough. Production is down."

Lilibet tamped down her sudden anger. Of course, Cle wouldn't understand. He had never lived in a mining camp. He picked up her hand and kissed her little finger, which made her smile with tenderness.

"And protecting nature? God does that," he said. "You are strange sometimes, Lilibet. I've never heard anyone say they were worried about our natural wonders. I mean, God made them so they will always be there, right?"

Sam and Sally Kay sank breathlessly into the seat across from them, Sally Kay's crinolines filling up the space. They leaned across the table, hanging on every word Cle said, so Cle shut up and glared at them. Tom Tee Frye slammed a fresh pitcher of beer on the table and he and Donetta squeezed into the booth, too. Lilibet wasn't happy to see more beer, but she knew it was a big night in their lives and they deserved to celebrate. She'd even had one herself, though she didn't like the taste. Cle drank beer like it was water and he seemed just fine, but some of the kids were getting drunk. Tom Tee said not to worry, this was nothing compared to other parties they'd had.

"Lilibet, honey, wherever did you get that precious little dress?" Sally Kay asked. "I suppose your Ma didn't know that crinolines and big skirts are in now."

"My mother bought this at the company store for my birthday and I like it," Lilibet replied. Several nasty retorts came to mind but she held them back.

Actually, she liked the simple white dress she wore. There was an elegance to its line that she knew enhanced her slim figure. For once, Marm had gotten lucky. Even had she hated the dress though, she would have loyally defended Marm.

"Well, honey, if you're going to be dating Cle you need to be wearing some better . . ."

"Shut up, Sally Kay," Clarice interrupted. She leaned drunkenly against the booth. "Cle, sweetheart, I need money. Got any?"

Cle chugged his beer. "What do you need money for, twin? Jimmy got his paycheck from Kroger's today."

Tom Tee poured more beer into Cle's mug and watched as Cle downed it quickly again. He shook his head in awe.

"Jimmy's in the john throwing up and I could care less. Just give me some money, Cle, darn it!"

Cle reached into his pocket and pulled out a huge wad of bills. "Swear to God, Clarice, you have got to start carrying money with you."

The sweet sound of a clarinet sang through the murky room. The small ensemble onstage, comprised of just a piano, clarinet, trumpet, bass fiddle and drums, began playing "Red Sails in the Sunset." They were pretty good, but some of the crowd complained that it sounded like their parents' music. Cle told them to be quiet and listen. One by one, they drifted onto the dance floor and found they liked the smoothness of the sound coming from the small band. The band segued into a rollicking version of "Music, Music, Music," and the dancers stood around clapping their hands in time to the beat. Then came "Kansas City," and the graduates were back to dancing again. Then it was time for a slow dance, and the piano player began "Smoke Gets In Your Eyes."

His hands fingered the beautiful song with love, sending the melody out to curl around them like a caress. Even the drunkest of them, even the rowdiest, even the most cynical, recognized the magic in his music. For the first time that evening they stood quietly and listened, their arms around one another, swaying in time to the music.

Cle downed another beer and peered across the table at Sam. "Anything about the guy playing the piano seem familiar to you?"

Sam squinted through the murky light. "Hell, Cle, his back is to us. I can't see his face."

Cle kept staring at the piano player's broad shoulders and muscular back. He wore a white dinner jacket with blue jeans, as did the whole band. Nice touch, thought Cle. His beer-hazed blue eyes gleamed with startled recognition.

"Sam, take a real good look. I'll never forget that back as long as I live, and you shouldn't either."

Lilibet wished that Cle and Sam would stop talking so she could hear better. The musician was spellbinding. It seemed as if the piano and the music were speaking to her alone, trying to tell her something. If she closed her eyes, she could hear the soft wind blowing over the tinkling creek on the way to Uncle East's and the sycamore leaves whispering high in the glen. But soon, the melody grew seductive and the velvet notes courted her heart and hummed in her veins. How strange yet wonderful it made her feel. Lilibet, come to me, it said. He was a sorcerer spinning a mood of enchantment.

The enchantment turned to restlessness and the familiar discontentment and hunger pulsed at her, leaving her unsettled . . . and something else. The back of her neck tingled and her knees grew weak. The "knowing." What was it trying to tell her? Her eyes popped open and she shook herself.

"I don't know what the hell you're talking about, ol' buddy," Sam said.

"Holy Jesus, Sam! Remember in the eighth grade when Coach Jackson invited us to sit on the bench during the last game of the season because we were going to be on the high school team next year? The score was Yancey seven, Matterhorn sixty. They wore white shirts with blue numbers. That's Black Brady, Sam! All we saw of him that night was his back because he was always running down the field away from us."

"By God, Cle, I think you're right."

"What did you say?" asked a startled Lilibet.

"The piano player is Black Brady, Lilibet. Do you keep up with football?"

"No, I've never been to a football game. Lots of baseball games though."

"I've never seen anyone run so fast, and neither had any of the college football coaches. Brady won every athletic and scholastic scholarship available in the state that year."

"Yeah," said Sam with a note of reverence in his voice. "He runs like the wind."

You would, too, if you'd raced with deer, thought Lilibet wryly.

"He got appointments to West Point and the Naval Academy," continued Cle, "and the dumb son of a bitch turned them down."

"You're joking," gasped Lilibet. Throwing away golden opportunities was tantamount to a criminal act to her.

"Cle's not joking, Lilibet," Tom Tee said. "Brady's a bum. He's weird, too. Lives in the mountains by himself. They say he can heal wounded animals and all sorts of bizarre stuff."

Clarice had long ago forgotten about getting money from Cle. With arms folded, she had plastered herself to the side of the booth and listened raptly to the music. "Runs like the wind, heals wounded animals . . . plays piano like an angel," she muttered to herself. "And has the sexiest damn shoulders I ever saw."

She pushed herself away from the booth and, walking carefully erect, as drunks try to do, made her way through the crowd that surrounded the band. As Black finished and the crowd applauded their approval, Clarice selected a chair near the piano where she could watch his face.

Lilibet was shaken by the knowledge that the talented pianist was the savage she'd encountered on the mountain. She remembered his strong fingers disemboweling the snake and shivered. The same fingers had just courted the keys of the piano as if they were a woman. Was there no end to the contradictions of Black Brady? She saw Clarice smile at him and he returned a friendly nod.

Ruby's regulars had had enough of the rock and roll on the jukebox, and what they considered the corny sound coming from Black's band. They'd been grumbling among themselves. One of them said, "Shit, Ruby, get them horn-tootin' dudes out of here. Plug the jukebox back in so we can play some hillbilly."

The man was an overgrown bully who always caused trouble. Ruby signaled hastily to Black that it was time for them to stop playing.

Lilibet watched with interest as Black stood to help his fellow band members gather their equipment. He turned and looked directly at her. He had known she was there all along. His luminous green eyes bore into hers and he smiled, an odd, sad sort of smile, and then left.

The high school crowd began to disperse as the jukebox, fed by Ruby's regulars, gave forth a steady stream of country music. It was time to find a new scene where they could dance to rock and roll, or rhythm and blues. They turned to Cle for guidance and he told them to meet at his house.

Jimmy Haynes, chastened and half sober by now, argued with Clarice about who was going to drive her red Caddie. He said she was in no condition to drive but she insisted she was. They fought over the car keys until Sam intervened. He took the keys from Clarice and gave them to Jimmy.

"Clarice, get in your car. Jimmy will drive you home," Sam ordered.

She gave Sam the crude finger but walked out with Jimmy, and Ruby drew a sigh of relief.

"Do you think they'll be okay, Sam?" Lilibet asked anxiously.

"Sure, for a while, but she's not fooling me one bit. Jimmy will take her home and then later she'll sneak out by herself." He looked at Cle. "Come on, Cle. Let's go to the john."

He put his arm around Cle, and as they walked away

Lilibet could have sworn Sam was holding Cle erect, yet Cle hadn't seemed drunk.

Tom Tee Frye, spoiling for a fight, was confronting a miner at the jukebox, insisting he play "Since I Met You, Baby." Donetta went to try to entice him away or calm him down.

"What sluts they are," Sally Kay said.

"Who?" Lilibet demanded.

"Well, Donetta and Clarice, you dummy."

"Donetta is not a slut!" Lilibet declared, and then remembering Clarice's kindness to her at the lake, she defended her also. "And neither is Clarice."

"Are you blind, girl? Just because Donetta is your best friend doesn't mean you have to stick up for her. She and Tom Tee are screwing every chance they get."

"They are not! And even if they are, it's none of your business!" Lilibet said hotly.

"You are really stupid, or just blind loyal. And I suppose you're defending Clarice because she's Cle's sister. Everyone knows she's the town whore."

Lilibet knew she was, but her inbred loyalty prevented her from admitting such a thing to Sally Kay.

"You ... you ..." She wanted to tell Sally Kay she was a bitch, but she had never even said the word before unless she was referring to a dog.

"You, what, Lilibet?" taunted Sally Kay.

"You are mean," declared Lilibet.

She was tired of waiting for Cle and Sam, and she sure didn't want to sit here with Sally Kay any longer. The bar was getting smokier and noisier, and the beer had given her a headache. She needed fresh air Without a word, she got up and left Sally Kay.

She stepped out into the half-empty parking lot and found the sky had clouded up. A fine mist fell, cleaning and cooling the summer night air. Some thoughtful person had put the top up on Cle's car. She walked to the center of the parking lot and spread her arms wide. Tilting her head up toward the falling rain, she closed her eyes and opened her mouth to catch the sweet coolness.

"It doesn't taste as good down here as it does on the mountain," said a smoky voice she now recognized.

She opened her eyes to find him. With graceful nonchalance, his arms folded and one foot propped behind him on the bumper, Black leaned against the rear of a car parked in the shadows. She couldn't see his face.

"Thought you had gone," she said.

"No, I've been waiting for you."

"What do you mean . . . waiting for me? I'm with Cle."

"Grandfather wanted me to tell you he was proud of you. That's high praise from Grandfather."

"How did you know I would come out here?"

"Because you're like me, Lilibet. You need the wind, the rain, the sun, the moon, clean air."

I'm not at all like you, she thought fiercely to herself. *I have plans for my life, places to go, things to learn, security to gain for my mother and sister.* But she remembered the way his music had called to her, an invitation in the wind, a summoning to be free, and she was suddenly nervous.

"What are you doing at Ruby's anyway? I thought you hated the piano," she said quickly.

"Used to," he murmured, his voice sounding disembodied in the dark. "I lost some scholarships I was awarded when I turned them down, so now I'm earning money for school, and the more I play, the more I find I enjoy it."

"You play beautifully."

"Thank you, but there's another reason I've come off the mountain and rejoined civilization." He stepped into the light and smiled, a slow, lazy smile. "I wanted to dance with you on the night of your graduation."

Ivory Joe Hunter's "Since I Met You, Baby" came from the speakers hanging in the eaves of Ruby's roof. Black came toward her, into the wavering neon light. She couldn't take her eyes off his long legs in their tight jeans.

"Here?" she questioned, her heart beating wildly. "Here in the parking lot?"

"Yes," he said quietly as he reached her.

He'd changed into a white, short-sleeve cotton knit

shirt. Tucked without a wrinkle into his jeans, the short
sleeves showed off the sleekness of his tanned, muscular
arms. Her eyes traveled up the bronze column of his
throat, over his strong jaw, sensual lips, and stopped at
the glint of purpose in his eyes.

He put his arms around her. Heart in her throat now,
and with the brief sensation that this was the beginning of
something that couldn't be finished, she drifted naturally
into his body, and they began to dance around the misty
parking lot.

Ivory Joe's mellow, whiskey-smooth voice poured over
them like a benediction.

Smoothly, he guided her, his strong arm about her
small waist, their shoes scuffling faintly on the pavement.
The orange and blue neon sign reflected on and off their
slow-moving forms. The raindrops sparkling in Lilibet's
silver-gold hair looked like a crystal tiara. Reverently,
Black lowered his head to bury his face in the fresh fragrance of her damp hair.

A wild, hard wanting rushed through him, jerking him
erect with its violence. She looked up at him and the confusion in her violet eyes tore at Black's heart. He knew
what she was feeling but he couldn't explain it to her. She
would have to learn for herself.

Lilibet saw Black's eyes grow mysteriously smoky.
The slow, sensual, earthy beat of the music enveloped
them and, giving in to it, she laid her head on his chest,
letting the spell take them around and around the center
of the parking lot. An unfamiliar heat pulsed in her stomach and then melted languidly down into her hips and
thighs. She felt dreamy and restless at the same time. Un-
consciously she moved closer to Black, wanting to feel
the whole, long, wonderful length of his warmth. His
shirt was damp now, except for where her head rested,
and she could feel his heart beating. An inexplicable feeling of poignancy filled her and, unbidden, hot tears
coursed down her cheeks.

The music stopped. The song had come to the end, but
still he held her.

"Elizabeth?"

She looked up at him again.

He smiled the same sad smile she'd seen before, then wiped a tear away with his thumb. Gently, his thumb moved to caress the tiny mole near the corner of her mouth.

"Yes?" She wanted to reach up and feel the place he'd touched; it was still warm and tingly from his thumb.

"What are your dreams on this important night?"

His penetrating green gaze made it difficult to think. She hesitated for a moment. "I wish for other nights like this."

"I'm sure there will be. Anything else?"

"You'll think I'm silly," she said softly.

"No, I won't."

"I've always dreamed of waltzing in Vienna or Paris or Washington in one of those beautiful white dresses," she whispered.

A rustle in the dark behind Black alerted him seconds before Virgil MacDonald pounced on his back, yelling, "Gotcha, you Indian bastard."

With the grace of a ballet dancer, Black spun on the ball of his foot, but Virgil clung to his back like a leech. Jud MacDonald and Eugene Springer had climbed onto the hood of a battered pickup truck and cheered Virgil on.

Lilibet, shocked into immobility, stood with her hand over her mouth, forcing back a scream. How could they not have smelled Virgil, or heard something? She couldn't believe their complete absorption in each other. Only Cle had ever before claimed such attention from her.

"We'll teach you not to come on our side of the mountain and mess with our girls," Virgil growled in Black's ear.

Furious with himself for letting his guard down, Black reached behind him and, catching Virgil's ears, yanked him fiercely over his head. Virgil landed at Black's feet with a howl of outrage. Black picked him up by his collar, landed an uppercut on his chin, and then dropped him.

Virgil jumped to his feet, a knife gleaming in his hand. He crouched into a fighter's stance and circled Black menacingly. The odor of his filthy clothes contaminated the space around them.

Jud and Eugene had shut up now. The cheering was over. The fight had turned deadly serious.

"Go back inside, Lilibet," Black commanded in a steely undertone.

"No," she refused with a frightened whisper.

Like quicksilver, Black kicked the knife out of Virgil's hand and then caught the arm and twisted it cruelly behind Virgil's back. Virgil went to his knees, groaning with pain.

Suddenly, Jud and Eugene charged at Black, one landing a blow to his head, the other kicking him in the kidneys.

Lilibet, scared but furious, flew into action. Hurtling through the air, she landed on Jud's back and began to beat on his shoulders. He shook her off like a flea. She jumped back on and pummeled his shoulders with all her strength, grunting with the effort. Again he batted her off and continued to punch Black in the kidneys.

Undaunted, Lilibet leaped back on, but this time she fastened her teeth on Jud's dirt-crusted ear and bit down hard. He squealed like a pig and letting go of Black, slapped backward at Lilibet, trying to remove her from his back.

Lilibet felt her eye swelling up where Jud had slapped her. It hurt like nothing had ever hurt before.

I've just received my first black eye, she thought irrelevantly.

Her legs were fastened determinedly around Jud's waist. She dug her fingernails into his neck and wouldn't let go of his ear. It tasted like sour cooking oil and she held her breath so she wouldn't gag.

Jud twisted around and around like a whirling dervish, trying to remove the clinging irritant on his back.

Black, keeping a firm twist on Virgil's arm and battling Eugene at the same time, was exasperated with the whole debacle. He didn't want to hurt anyone, but when he saw Jud whirling around with Lilibet on his back, his exasperation turned to fury. He wanted this over with quickly so he could get to Lilibet. He released Virgil's arm and swiftly grabbed his neck. Finding the soft spot just above the hard bone on the nape, his thumb dug deeply and unerringly to contact a sensitive nerve. Virgil screamed in agony and passed out. As Black gave Eugene a karate kick to the chin, Cle's concerned voice cut through the night.

"Lilibet? . . . son of a bitch!" Cle declared, as he and Sam took in the fight in the parking lot.

Sam roared like a lion and cannonballed himself toward Jud and Lilibet, ramming his head full-force into Jud's stomach.

"Oooof . . ." All Jud's air left him.

"Get off now, Lilibet," Sam ordered.

Lilibet dropped gratefully to the pavement, landing hard on her butt. In a daze, she watched Jud land on the ground beside her like a deflated inner tube. She spat, trying to rid herself of the sour taste of his ear. The spittle landed on Jud's cheek. A secret, satisfied smile cornered her mouth.

Cle had run to help Black, but Black had already taken care of Eugene. In a matter of seconds, Black had ripped the shirt off Eugene, stunned him with a clip to the right ear, and then tied his hands together with his shirt. Eugene sat in a heap beside Virgil.

Seeing that everything was taken care of, Cle went to help Lilibet to her feet. Shakily, she stood and he ran his hands up and down her arms and shoulders checking for broken bones.

"Stop it, Cle," she demanded. "I'm not a horse!"

"Are you all right, Lilibet?" all three of them asked simultaneously.

"I'm fine . . . a bit dizzy, but fine."

They all reached for her, but she took a step backward. "I'm just fine, I said. Don't touch me. I don't need any help!"

"My God, what happened here?" Cle asked. "What are you doing out here, Lilibet? And what are you doing with Brady? I've been looking everywhere for you."

"I'm sorry, Cle. Tom Tee looked like he was going to start a fight, and it was stuffy in there anyway, so I came out for some fresh air . . . Black was out here and . . . we were talking."

"You've met before?" inquired an intrigued but jealous Cle.

"Lilibet is a friend of my family," Black said swiftly, brooking no more discussion of the subject.

"Didn't know you had a family, Brady," Cle said, and didn't notice Black's quick intake of breath. With the Hutton loftiness, Cle looked Black over casually and then turned back to Lilibet.

"Cle, that was rude," Lilibet gasped.

Black masked the disgust he felt at the odor of beer emanating from Cle and Sam, and the bleariness of their red-rimmed eyes. What idiots they were to waste their bodies and endanger their lives. Couldn't Lilibet see that Cle was drunk? Only a fool would have left Lilibet alone in a place like Ruby's.

Black had little tolerance for fools. The weaknesses of others were a mystery to him. He supposed his lack of understanding was partly due to his stern, unusual upbringing. All he knew was that what he could achieve, others could achieve. His grandfathers, aghast at this attitude they hadn't foreseen, had told him it would take some living in the outside world to undo his intolerance. Not bloody likely, he thought, if tonight was any example of what he was supposed to accept.

Right now, the scene in front of him only filled him with nauseating repugnance. Cle and Sam were stupid. Maybe this idea of going to college was wrong. Maybe it would be better to stay on the mountain. If the cost of learning more about people, life, and love, meant dealing with dunces like Cle and Sam, he didn't know if he wanted to pay the price.

"Cle, that was rude," Lilibet said again. "Apologize."

"Don't concern yourself, Lilibet. I always consider the source," Black said calmly.

Never would he forget her standing there in the misty neon-lit night, her hair clinging to her angelic face in damp, wispy tendrils; her dress torn and dirty, Jud's blood staining it; one lovely violet eye swollen shut. He wanted to kiss the hurt away. How courageously and fiercely she had defended him.

"You got a real shiner there, kid."

She laughed and gingerly felt her eye.

"Thought maybe I did. How am I going to explain this to Marm? But we got 'em good, didn't we, Black?" She hated violence but it gave her a feeling of pride to have shared the crazy experience with him. What a victorious night it had been, from beginning to end.

"We sure did . . . with help from Sam . . . and Cle," he added belatedly.

"You should have stayed inside, Lilibet. It's safer in there," Cle said, casting an accusing look at Black and placing a possessive hand on Lilibet's arm. "Besides, I will never let anything happen to you, Lilibet. I'll always take care of you. You're my girl."

A muscle tightened on the proud, sculpted jawline of Black's otherwise impassive face. Sam's heart boiled and bubbled like a brewing pot of corn whiskey. Cledith Hutton had just staked his claim on Lilibet Springer.

Chapter 7

Black ran with the wind. His long legs stretching to their limit, always reaching for the ultimate stride, he vaulted over boulders and bounded gracefully over creeks and crevices that would have daunted another man. His feet barely skimmed the surface and he felt the vital earth humming and living beneath him.

Darting a glance from the corner of his eye, he saw the cat gaining. She was almost parallel with him now. Silently, her powerful, perfect body covered the ground with arrow swiftness. Heaving for air, his heart drummed madly in his ears as he asked more of his body.

The cougar was a beauty and one of the few remaining in the mountains. She could attack and kill in a matter of seconds. Black had eluded her for an hour and didn't know how much longer he could keep up the pace. Perspiration beaded on his normally cool brow and he felt a tremor in his thighs. He could hear her easy measured breathing.

She pounced on his back and they fell to the ground, Black's face hitting the dirt. He jerked his elbows backward to jab them into the ribs of her sleek body, but she batted them away with one powerful paw. She used the same paw to effortlessly turn him over. He grabbed her neck with both arms and wrestled with her, but she licked his face with her big, rough tongue and he lay back laughing.

"You win. You let me think I'm going to win, but you always do. I don't know why I bother to race with you, Cat."

Cat purred in response. He could feel her chest vibrate with the sound and he laughed again.

"Get off me. You're too heavy."

Black gave her a shove and the orange, thick-furred cougar gave his face another quick lick and then rose to all fours. With regal grace she lay down beside him, and placing her head flat on the ground between her two front paws, stared at him with yellow feline eyes.

Black stared back.

He would miss her. Half grown when they'd first met, he'd watched her develop into the powerful creature she was today. *I guess I was half grown, too,* he thought.

It was the winter he'd spent on Christmas Ridge when he was fifteen. Rifle shots had awakened him early in the morning. Amazed that hunters had ventured this high in the middle of February, his first thought was to seek them out. He had been on the ridge since the first of January and was eager for the sight of a human face. On second thought, he realized his grandfathers would disapprove. He was to have no human contact for three months.

Later in the morning, while tracking the flight of a rare Golden Eagle, he'd come across blood in the snow. Forgetting the eagle, he followed the bloody prints for two hours. He could tell it was a small cougar and, from the way she eluded him, she knew he was tracking her. Her energy gave out on a rocky, concave ledge that hung out over Catawba Gorge.

He lay on his stomach to peer down at her and she growled. From his vantage point it looked as if she'd been wounded twice. Once in the chest and again in the hindquarter. She was bleeding to death. When he climbed down onto the ledge, she hissed and clawed at him and wouldn't let him near her. Several attempts at soothing her failed.

From his cave he retrieved the best of the deer meat he'd preserved for the winter, and returned to the ledge to tempt the cougar. For the rest of the day, he threw her bits of meat. She rejected them. He slept through the night on the ground above the ledge. At dawn he could see that she was considerably weaker. He climbed down to sit closer to her and she raised her head to hiss weakly at him. Every hour he moved a bit closer. Finally, sitting not two feet from her, he shoved meat in front of her nose.

She pawed at it listlessly and closed her eyes. His heart fell. Tentatively, he placed his hand on her side and could feel a faint heartbeat. Elated, he moved closer. He sat for a while caressing her and murmuring reassuring sounds, all the while planning how he would move her to his cave.

Cougars were called "the spirit of the mountains." Solitary and mysterious, at one time they roamed the United States from the Atlantic to the Pacific. The lord of its domain, it retreated with the arrival of modern civilization. Of the great predators, the grizzly, the wolf, and the jaguar, only the cougar had survived in the mountains of the South. Magnificent animals, they kept their home range for life unless it was altered in some way. His grandfathers had told him fifty thousand cougars had been killed in the last forty years for sport or bounty.

Black couldn't imagine killing anything so beautiful unless it threatened his life.

To get her off the ledge he'd rigged a pulley made of deer hide. He wrapped her in a large square of hide, and fastening rawhide lines around his neck, pulled her to his cave like a horse pulls a wagon.

For the next week he used every healing skill he'd been taught, and a few more he'd devised himself. The bullet in her hindquarter had passed through, but the one in her chest had to be dug out with his knife. Using pressure points and pine resin, he stopped the bleeding. Then he applied hourly poultices made from ginseng powder and soot from the fire. Close to death when they'd reached his winter cave, Cat, as he called her, responded slowly.

Toward the end of the week she developed penumonia. He devised a vaporizer system using a gourd of heated water laced with turpentine, and a tent made of his clothes. He spoon-fed her sassafras tea. He prayed.

His periods of meditation, required by the grandfathers, grew longer and deeper. He knew meditation was concentration in its highest form focusing on God. He had, on previous occasions, touched the oneness with the universe that he desired, but now he needed an extra-special strength. He needed healing power.

Late one evening, he sat in the mouth of his cave as the

winter sky darkened to a burnished amber and then a
deep purple. He had reached the state of "peace beyond
understanding" when he heard a voice.

"Hello, Black."

He opened his eyes to find a lovely raven-haired lady
standing in front of him.

"Do you remember me? I'm your grandmother,
Kathleen."

"Yes, Grandmother, I do remember you. Thank you for
coming."

"We are always close by, Black. You were right to ask
for help. Do you love the cat, Black?"

"Yes, I do."

"Physically you have done all that's possible, but the
cat will die unless you convey your love to her."

"How do I do that, Grandmother?"

"Lie down with her, Grandson. Transfer to her all the
peace, love, and strength you are feeling now. You have
within you all the powers of the Universe. Use the healing powers of love to heal her."

She began to fade away.

"Stay with me, Grandmother, please!"

"You know I can't do that, Black. You'll do just fine."

She was gone, but the great sense of love and peace remained.

Black walked into the cave and sat down beside the
cougar. Fighting for air, she breathed fitfully; otherwise
she was motionless. He stroked her orange coat. The
week of illness had paled its colors and thinned it. He
stroked and stroked, and underneath the thin layer of fur
he began to feel a new warmth. He knew what he must
do. Black lay side by side with the cat. He managed to
get both arms around her and hugging her to him, willed
her his love and strength. He imagined the sun with all its
energy and he poured the same energy into the cougar.
All night long he moved over her, laying on top of her or
with his arms around her, heating her body with his love
and energy.

He whispered to her, over and over again, "I love you,
Cat. You are so beautiful. Feel me, Cat. Know that I love
you."

At dawn, he could feel a slight vibration in her chest as she tried to purr. The healing had begun. By the time Black left Christmas Ridge that winter, Cat was as good as new and a bond had formed between the two forever.

Now with one hand resting on Cat and the other under his head, he gazed up into the brilliant blue sky. Directly above him, the leaves of an old oak tree glowed russet, gold, and orange. It was late in the afternoon and there was a definite chill in the air. It would be cold tonight, but he was sleeping next to Cat in her lair so he would be warm. He had come to say goodbye to her. In two days he was leaving for Connecticut and Yale.

He knew it would be difficult at first, being four years older than the other freshmen, but World War II veterans had done it—were still doing it—and Korean veterans were beginning to enter college, too. It was time to leave the mountain, expand his horizons. He'd never admit it to Grandfather, but he'd been itching to leave even before Grandfather began to urge him to go back to school. His thirst for knowledge and exploration had only been whetted in his years of isolation and learning in the forest.

High in the sky, his eye caught the faint silver trail of a jet. His heart caught at the sight. With every fiber of his being, he wanted to be up there, too. Someday he would be. He had promised himself that he would fly someday, fly higher and faster. His hand caressed Cat as he watched the jet climb into the clouds and then disappear.

"I'm going to miss you, Cat. I'm going to miss you, and Grandfather. I'd ask you to keep an eye on him, but I know you won't go near there. Fortunately, I know both of you can take care of yourselves."

All summer long, he had helped Grandfather lay in supplies for the coming winter. Tomorrow Black would bring up the last of those supplies from town. Grandfather was getting older and some of his survival skills were more difficult to accomplish. Black had chopped a huge pile of wood, but had also bought a supply of kerosene in case of emergency.

His mother had told him not to worry, that she would keep an eye on her father. Black didn't like the idea of his mother traipsing up the mountain in the winter. Great, he thought! Now he'd worry about both of them. *Enough of that, Black. Worry is a wasted emotion.* He switched it off and searched the sky for the jet.

"There is someone else I'll miss too, Cat. But she thinks she loves another, and she needs a chance to grow up. She'll do that while I'm gone. I wish she were ready now, but we both want to go to college and she deserves time to do whatever she dreams of."

Deep within him, he acknowledged his own selfish need for freedom, then shook his head in irritation at the notion that such a thing was wrong. A fascinating world beckoned, one that Black yearned to discover. Like Lilibet, he needed time to realize his destiny. He also knew that Lilibet truly was not yet ready for him or a mature love.

"Somewhere within her she must know we belong together. We'll be ready for each other when I come back."

Cat purred a response. She rose to her full height, and standing over Black, nuzzled him gently. She walked away from him for a few paces, and then back. She nuzzled him again.

"Ready to go, aren't you?" The cougar had been restive all day. She sensed he was leaving.

He got up and, with an easy lope, ran into the forest, Cat by his side. Cat growled as they passed a rocky incline. They were near the area where Black had first seen Cat's blood that long-ago winter. Black's mouth tightened with anger. Later that same winter, after Cat had healed, Black had found the rotting carcasses of two sister cubs. Unable to carry all of their bounty, the hunters had taken only the mother's body, and perhaps another litter mate of Cat's. Cat would never forget and neither would he. He pitied the hunters if they ever ventured this far again. Black would have little mercy on them. Cat would have none.

Cat stopped. Black braced himself for what was coming.

Low in Cat's throat and from her soul, came a guttural sound. Slowly it gathered volume and rose from a growl to a poignant wail, then gave way to a full-throated howl. The high-pitched, tormented keening of a cougar in pain reverberated through the mountains. The harrowing anguished scream was enough to raise the hair on the back of a person's neck. Black had heard it the first time he and Cat had come upon the carcasses of her family. Since then, he had also heard it during her mating seasons. It still struck the fear of God into him and his heart tripped quickly. He knew she was telling him that she remembered this place, and also that she knew he was leaving.

With disciplined practice, Black had perfected the cry for himself. But it was such a soul-wrenching experience that he found he couldn't give way to it unless he was truly tormented, and then it came with urgency. When Grandfather Black Eagle died, Black had gone to the secluded glen and roared his grief using the cougar's cry. Emptied then, he'd gone to weep in the arms of Grandfather East.

The sound continued to ululate around him and he knelt to bring Cat to him. With his arms around her neck, she lessened the scream and then stopped.

He held her big, whiskered face in both of his hands and looked directly into her eyes. "I know," he said. "It hurts."

Black sighed and rose to his feet. He wished he could convey to her that there were other worlds he needed to see, other paths he needed to travel, more knowledge he needed to gather, but that he *would* return. He would always return to the mountains.

He reached to scratch her ears and he could have sworn she smiled. Maybe she did understand his thirst for adventure. After all, there was within her the same ancient knowledge that lay within him.

"I'll be back, Cat. The roots of my being are here. I'll always come back."

Chapter 8

The red satin walls and massive dark furniture in the Hutton dining room seemed oppressive to Lilibet, but who was she to make a judgment? She'd never been out of Yancey County. She was just grateful to be here having a farewell dinner before they all went off to college.

Summer had sped by quickly. The picnics, swimming parties, and forbidden rendezvous at Ruby's had kept Lilibet in a social whirl. For the first time in her life, she felt a part of the young crowd in Yancey—not only a part of it, but at the helm with Cle. She and Cle were now considered a steady couple, and Sam was her dear friend. The brief moments she'd stolen to spend time on the mountain with Uncle East had been far too few.

Tomorrow she was going to say goodbye to Uncle East. She had promised herself she'd spend the whole day on the mountain with her elderly friend. Cle and Sam still had no idea where she disappeared to now and again.

"Goddamn unions are going to be the ruination of this country," Pappy Hutton declared, his fist slamming the table for emphasis.

"Ah now, Pappy, they aren't that bad," Clarice teased, putting her hand affectionately on his arm.

She sat next to him, her yellow hair tamed into a proper chignon, but her voluptuous breasts spilling out of an off-the-shoulder, blue cotton dress.

"What do you think, Lilibet?" he asked.

Startled, she almost withered under his cold stare. His blue eyes pinned her in place like a dead butterfly in a display case. Conditioned to silent meals in her own home, Lilibet was always undone by the lively dinner conversations at the Huttons'. Although completely dominated by Pappy and his opinions, they were at least a window into a new world of ideas and events. Up to this point, she had kept silent and just listened.

She swallowed and opened her mouth, but only an odd squeak came out.

"Well, girl, what do you think?"

"Pappy," Cle intervened. "Lilibet is our guest. She doesn't have to give an opinion."

"Maybe she doesn't have any opinions."

Lilibet knew he was testing her, but she didn't know why. But she did know that she was angry and she quickly shed her reserve.

"When Eugene Debs and Samuel Gompers organized the unions early in this century, they were very much needed. American workers were poorly paid and ill-treated. There was—and still is in some cases, sir—an absolute demand for leadership. Organizing the workers so they could improve their conditions through collective bargaining was essential."

"Eugene Debs was a Socialist!"

"Yes, sir, he was. I didn't say I liked his politics. I said I liked the initiative he showed. Samuel Gompers was an honorable man. He kept the American Federation of Labor free of radical and socialistic elements, and he won higher wages, shorter hours, and freedom for workers."

"You've been speaking in the past tense, Lilibet. What do you think of the unions today? What do you think of John L. Lewis?"

Pride had begun to glow in Cle's eyes, but Sam and Clarice were still holding their breath.

Fat Sis said, "Let Lilibet eat her dinner, Pappy."

Lilibet turned to Fat Sis, sitting next to her at the hostess end of the table, and said, "That's all right, Miss Hutton, I'd like to answer." She turned back to Pappy. "I think the miners in West Virginia would be starving today if it weren't for John L. Lewis and the United Mine Workers. Their work is dirty and dangerous, and the general public doesn't appreciate them one bit. They had to strike to get what belonged to them!"

Pappy's face was getting red. Cle was getting worried.

"Do you think Hutton Mines should be unionized?" Pappy said in a quiet voice laced with steel.

Anna Adkins, sitting next to Sam across the table from Lilibet, said quickly, "Pappy, I think Lilibet feels as if she's being grilled. Could we change the subject?"

Sam gave his mother a grateful glance.

Lilibet smiled at Mrs. Adkins but answered Pappy.

"Yes, sir, I think the Hutton Mines should be unionized," she said bravely. "However, I also feel that the United Mine Workers, the AFL, and the CIO, have garnered too much power. John L. Lewis has become a tyrant and strikes have become a way of life. Also, I don't believe in the closed shop. Everyone has a right to work whether he belongs to a union or not."

"Aren't you equivocating, Lilibet? First you say I should let the unions in here, then you say they have too much power." His cold blue eyes never left her during their entire discourse.

"I'm saying, sir, that if the union was operating the way it was in the twenties, thirties, and forties, it would be welcomed in Yancey. However, to paraphrase William Pitt, 'power corrupts, absolute power corrupts absolutely.' The unions are now corrupt with power."

"Well, I'm certainly relieved to hear you say that, Lilibet."

"I'm not finished, sir."

Beneath the table, Cle have her arm a warning squeeze. He knew what Lilibet was about to say. You couldn't have spent the last three months with Lilibet and not know how she felt about the conditions in his father's mines.

She ignored Cle's cautioning hand and continued.

"If the unions are no longer a viable answer to the plight of the miner, then private ownership has a *moral* responsibility *not* to take advantage of its employees."

Pappy Hutton's eyebrows lifted sharply into an inverted *V*, and his fixed stare became glacial.

Clarice leaned over quickly, her bosom resting on Pappy's arm. She hoped Lilibet was smart enough not to venture further, but just to be safe, she intervened. She kissed her father's cheek and, pouting her lower lip, said,

"Pappy, sweetie, I've had enough serious talk for one night. We're supposed to be celebrating, and you're supposed to be crying buckets of tears because your beautiful, charming children are leaving."

Everyone laughed, breaking the thick tension around the table.

"What are you going to major in when you get to college, Clarice?" Anna Adkins asked.

"Boys, Mrs. Adkins, boys!"

They all laughed again.

"I don't care what Clarice takes in college, or what kind of degree she gets. She'll come home and get married anyway. But Cle is going to get a degree in business," Pappy Hutton stated emphatically.

Cle shrugged his shoulders noncommittally.

"What about you, Sam?" Fat Sis asked.

"Gee, I'm not sure yet. Maybe law. I think I'd like to go to law school."

Lilibet kept her plans to herself. She'd said enough tonight. Besides, Cle, Clarice, and Sam knew she wanted to be a lawyer. This was the first time she'd heard Sam mention a similar interest.

"That would be great, Sam. You might end up the Hutton Company lawyer," Pappy said with delight.

Lilibet saw a peculiar expression cross Sam's face, then vanish.

Anna Adkins proudly patted her son's shoulder.

"Sam's going to do well in whatever he does. Thank heavens for the athletic scholarship." She didn't mention the hefty account Pappy had deposited for Sam in a Morgantown bank. He'd said he didn't need it, that he would get part-time work. His mother and Pappy had insisted the money should be there just in case.

The Huttons' cook and housekeeper, Belle Richards, served apple pie and ice cream for dessert.

The few black families in Yancey County kept to themselves. They had their own schools and most were in service-oriented businesses. Years ago, Belle's husband, Henry, had created a catering company from scratch. It was now a sign of success, an announcement that you'd arrived, if you used Henry Richards to cater a party.

As often as she'd been in the Hutton house during the summer, Lilibet was still unaccustomed to being waited on. She glanced up at Belle and smiled tentatively. Belle gave her a big smile and winked. She had been with the Huttons since the twins were babies, and she was the only person in town who spoke up to her employer.

"Mr. Hutton, you keepin' these nice young people here in this gloomy old room talkin' big talk! I have a feelin' they'd rather be out doin' some partyin'. What's the matter with you, sir?"

Pappy laughed. "You're right, Belle. But before I excuse you, children, let's have a toast to your future."

Lilibet raised her delicate crystal goblet with the others.

"Here's to four of the nicest young people in Yancey. Here's to your journey into adulthood. May you know nothing but wealth and health."

They drank and Lilibet's head felt a bit woozy.

She was anxious to get out into the fresh air.

Cle took her hand and they walked through the heavily landscaped front yard. Fat Sis's garden still held a few faded pink roses. Bronzed hydrangea drooped heavily from branches ready to give up the ghost for the winter. They passed through the garden gate and crossed the road to the river. It was chilly. Lilibet pulled Clarice's borrowed sweater closer about her shoulders. They sat on a stone bench Pappy had installed next to the river. At night, if the conditions were right, this was a romantic spot.

In the daytime you could see the Tow River's filth. Black residue washed off the coal by mine machinery, sewage, and garbage from the mining camps upstream had turned the once beautiful blue water into a runny, brown sore.

But it seemed a nice place to sit this evening. A half-moon shone weakly on the surface of the river, reflecting a faint silver gleam, and a light breeze, carrying nuances of Fat Sis's last roses, helped dispel the stench from the dying river.

They leaned back against the bench and Cle put his arm around Lilibet's shoulders.

Lilibet's mother had given her permission to ride up to Morgantown with him. He would have her all to himself for a whole day. Clarice and Sam were taking their own cars. Sam's mom had given him a second-hand Chevy for graduation. Cle was happy about that. Sam would have his own car instead of borrowing Cle's.

Cle wondered again if Lilibet was telling the truth about sewing with her mother tomorrow. She was mysterious sometimes, which only made her more interesting. He pulled her close to him.

He kissed her ear, licking the outside of it with his tongue. She responded by blowing softly on his neck. Soon they were kissing each other deeply. Cle ran his hands over her full, perfectly shaped breasts. He was so hot. He wanted her desperately but never went any further than touching her breasts. She meant too much to him. She wasn't an easy lay like most of the other girls, and she wasn't playing games with him like Sally Kay. He knew he would have competition when they got to the university, but he would get rid of it quickly.

Her breathing came faster now and perspiration beaded her upper lip. He knew she was as hot as he was. God, how he'd like to take her right now. But he wouldn't even try because Lilibet had told him that giving her virginity to a man was going to be a special occasion. Besides, he wanted it to be special, too. They would save it until the time was right.

There had been a few times when he'd lost control and decided to throw caution to the wind and go all the way. Cle didn't know whether Lilibet would have allowed him but it didn't make any difference, because, somehow, Sam always mysteriously appeared to interrupt them. Where Lilibet was concerned, Sam was like a homing pigeon, thought Cle wryly. Just as well. He was going off to college, and he sure didn't need to be getting anyone pregnant, especially Lilibet. So far, he'd been able to hide his physical misery from her. On the evenings after he drove her home to Big Ugly Creek, he relieved himself by visiting Baby Blue at the whorehouse in Mud Flats, or coming home and masturbating like crazy.

Someday, though, he would have her.

* * *

Up in the Hutton house, dim light flickered from the library windows. Pappy Hutton sat in the dark. A silver candelabra on the mantelpiece, holding eight lit candles, chased shadows across Clada Hutton's portrait. He stared at Clada as he sipped his brandy, moving the smooth liquid around slowly on his tongue, savoring the richness of its smoky flavor. He rolled his fat brown Cuban cigar appreciatively between his thin fingers, then lifted it to his nose to inhale its sweet, pungent smell. Never taking his eyes off the portrait, he drew on the cigar and let the smoke drift from his mouth.

"Cle's like you, you know, Clada. He doesn't suspect yet. They've made an idol of him because he's handsome, and because he's sweet and generous, and because he has money. He's good at playing their games."

He drew on his cigar again, letting the smoke mingle with the taste of the brandy.

"I was right about the Springer girl. I've watched her all summer. Very immature in some respects, especially in the ways of men and women. Also rather naive and innocent, but then those kind are always more fun to twiddle about with. She did well tonight. She's bright. Very bright. More importantly, she's got spunk. She's tough, not as tough as she thinks she is, but tough enough. Lilibet will never turn tail and run the way you did, Clada. Only cowards commit suicide. That was a treacherous thing you did, Clada, leaving me. A breach of faith. Those other women don't mean anything to me. They're just pieces of flesh. You knew I needed extra cunt now and then. You should have understood, and you should never have taken a lover of your own. A mistake, Clada. No one fools around with what belongs to me."

He smiled, a thin smile without warmth.

"Now, I'll tell you who is like both of us. Your darling daughter, Clarice. Hell, her pussy's as hot as my cock. If she weren't my own daughter, I'd take a tumble myself. Fat Sis thinks I don't know about the trip she and Clarice took to Huntington this summer. It was her second abortion. Hell, she had her first at age fourteen. I don't care as long as she marries the right man and keeps the right baby. She's beautiful like you. No one in the valley, or the state of West Virginia can hold a candle to her. She has one major fault, and I'll have to admit, she gets it from me. When she falls in love, it will be forever. She'll never let go. It may be her undoing. I'll have to keep an eye on that."

In a mocking toast, he raised his glass to the portrait.

"Here's to our children, Clada. You needn't worry about them. I'll find a man who can handle Clarice. I've found someone to take care of Cle."

He made a mental note to telephone Mabel Turner in Morgantown. Lilibet needed cleaning up around the edges. God knows where it came from genetically, but there was a look of the thoroughbred about her. He'd noticed it right away. Grudgingly, at first. Then with great relief as he realized Cle was in love with her.

Mabel would rid Lilibet of that awful hillbilly twang. Teach her how to dress. Teach her about fine art and antiques. How to be a gracious hostess. She'd be an asset to Cle instead of a liability. It would have been easier if Cle had fallen in love with one of the Morgans in Charleston. The money and connections were there. But he didn't need the money, and shaping this girl was better than breaking in a spoiled, rich brat.

There was no one better than Mabel Turner for the job. A grand lady in the tradition of the Old South, she'd been the belle of Virginia and West Virginia in their younger years. He smiled to himself. He and Mabel had taken a tumble or two. He'd wanted to marry her but she wouldn't have him. Independent Mabel had opted not to marry anyone. She'd gone back to school, gotten a doctorate in philosophy, and taught at the university. Just as well. He'd soon fallen madly in love with Clada, and still was to this day.

He raised his glass again.

"Good night, my dear."

Chapter 9

With a satisfying thump, Black closed the door to his grandfather's smokehouse. It was filled with cured venison, squirrel, and smoked trout. Only the middle of September, there was already a bite in the air on top of the mountain. High in the sky a flock of geese headed south.

Raffles the raccoon followed as Black walked through the remains of the garden, checking to make sure the last of the summer squash had been gathered, then headed toward the shady glade behind Grandfather's cabin. Before leaving the sunny meadow, he looked to the sky again, searching for planes, and found nothing but pure azure space. Space so sharply blue and honest it made your soul ache.

The thought of being enclosed in a classroom for the next four years was almost unbearable, but he wanted all Yale had to offer. His lessons in control and discipline would be challenged to their fullest as he accustomed himself to four walls.

The sheltered, shadowy glade held the springhouse. Black opened the door and stepped inside, indicating to Raffles that he should remain outside. It was cool and quiet, only the sound of water rippling beneath the damp rock floor. He stooped under the low ceiling and surveyed the shelves of colorful preserved vegetables. Even in the windowless dimness their bright colors were cheering. Glass jars twinkled proudly with red tomatoes, orange carrots, yellow squash, and green beans. Other shelves were laden with jars of blackberries, blueberries, and raspberries. On the floor slumped burlap bags filled with potatoes he and Grandfather had dug up just yesterday.

Black never ceased to marvel at nature's lush generosity. She gave and gave. Sadly, he thought, we've learned too little about returning to her what is hers, and we must. We've been selfish, taking and giving nothing back. How long can she support us?

"Black? Yo, Black! Lunchtime."

"Coming, Grandfather."

As they ate their lunch on the spacious porch of the cabin, sharing bits with Raffles and Judy, they looked out over mountain ranges stretching forever before them. Daubed now with fall's ruddy golds and bright reds, one could sit there for an eternity and never tire of the wonder of it all.

Their sandwiches were thick slabs of cheese, and thicker slabs of sweet juicy beefsteak tomatoes, between hefty slices of homemade brown bread slathered with mustard. They chased them with cool, clear spring water.

Black wiped his chin with a napkin and gave a big sigh.

"I wish I could take it all with me, Grandfather. You, and the mountains."

"The sandwich, too?" His grandfather chuckled. "You've had three, son. Would you care for another?"

Black laughed. "No, thanks. I've had enough. I'll dream about that sandwich."

Grandfather drew on his pipe, one of the few luxuries he'd brought with him from his earlier life. He caressed the polished wood stem with appreciation.

"You'll take it with you, Black. It's all there within you. Every leaf, every ray of light every race you ever ran with Cat. And you'll draw on it time and again."

"I'm anxious to go, Grandfather."

"I know you are. Been feeling your itchiness all summer. I'm not surprised. When Black Eagle and I saw how you soaked up knowledge, we knew you wouldn't confine yourself to the mountains. What you've learned here is just the tip of the iceberg, Black. Sometimes I'm sorry the university refused to take you this time. Morgantown is a lot closer than New Haven and you could have come home more often. You're lucky Yale still wanted you."

"I'm sure your being a distinguished alum had nothing to do with it," teased Black. "Especially a mysteriously deceased alum. Do you ever regret those decisions you made years ago?"

"Yes, I made mistakes that I regretted later."

"Come with me, Grandfather."

"No, I'll stick with what I have. I'm happy here now."

"I've never known anyone happier, Grandfather."

They sat in companionable silence while Grandfather smoked his pipe.

"Thank you, Black, for taking the corn to be ground. Black Eagle and I always did it ourselves, you know. But you don't need to concern yourself about me this winter."

Black knew there were winters his grandfather had subsisted on nothing but smoked venison and berries. Soggy or dry summers had ruined his gardens, leaving little to put away for the winter. Those summers were usually followed by violent winters. Confined to the cabin with rare opportunity to hunt for game, Grandfather used every survival skill taught to him by the old people and Black Eagle. He enjoyed the challenge and the inherent danger. Steadfastly, he refused to come and live with his daughter and grandson. Neither would he step foot in a town for provisions. He insisted on being self-sufficient. As Black grew older and watched his grandfather age, he'd invented subtle ways of making sure the elderly man had supplies.

"I know you can take care of yourself, but I took the opportunity to spend every last second here with you and the mountain, and Cat."

"Was that you or Cat I heard yesterday? I can hardly tell the two of you apart anymore. Although I didn't think you were that torn up about leaving."

Black laughed. "No, I'm sad but not in pain. It was Cat. We were passing the cavity where we found her murdered family that winter seven years ago. She's also hurting because she senses I'm leaving."

"I wish she would at least prowl through the clearing here so I could see her, but I know she won't. Maybe I'll catch a glimpse of her while I'm hunting in November."

"Only if she wants you to see her, Grandfather."

"Black Eagle told me stories of cougars bonding with humans. He said they helped lost wagon trains find their way through the desert, and rescued convicts sentenced to death in the wild. Has she ever accidentally scratched you or injured you?"

"Never. Sometimes, when we're wrestling, I can feel her holding back all that leashed power within her and I have to remind myself that she could kill me with one swat of her paw. Her restraint is awesome."

They rocked back and forth, the runners on the lovingly crafted chairs silent, as they feasted on the colorful landscape before them.

"Thought about what you're going to do after college, Black?"

"Some, but not enough to talk about it. You know I want to fly, Grandfather. The war in Korea is gearing up and things don't look good in Vietnam. Seems kind of foolish to make plans for the future because I don't know where I'll be or how long I'll be away."

"Have you seen Elizabeth this summer?"

"Yes, we've talked several times. I see her when my band is playing in Yancey County."

Memories of his jealousy-plagued moments watching Lilibet dancing in Cle's arms jarred him. Jealousy should be beneath him, but all his stoic training fled at the sight of their two blond heads together. When the urge to hold her became more than he could bear, he would let someone else take over at the piano and he would tap Cle on the shoulder to cut in. Cle would grunt a reluctant assent and go to sulk in a corner, glaring at them the whole time they danced.

He would soon forget about Cle as he whispered in Lilibet's ear. Small conversations that were intimate and revealing in their urgency, on his part anyway, to learn more of her. She laughed at some of his questions, but answered seriously. When he'd ask her if she liked to walk in the rain, she'd answered, "Sure, doesn't everyone?"

But everyone *didn't* like to walk in the rain, and he'd bet no one had ever asked her questions like that before.

"She still dating that Hutton boy?"

"Yes."

"What do you think of him?"

"He's a parasite. Lives off his father," Black ground

out between clenched teeth. "I hate parasites. Sam Adkins is the only one in that crowd who works. He's digging coal at Number Four."

"Maybe Cledith Hutton hasn't had the opportunity to prove himself."

Black flashed his grandfather a glance of fury.

"You, of all people, how can you say that?" he demanded.

His grandfather didn't answer right away. He rocked awhile and puffed his pipe.

"You're going to encounter fools along the way, Black. Probably meet a few at Yale. But I hope you'll form some friendships there."

"The friendships I make will be with people who believe in giving their ultimate in whatever they do. Do you think friendship is necessary, Grandfather?"

"Probably not, but empathy for others is. Elizabeth has that. . . ."

"Yes, too much," interrupted an irritated Black. "Why do you insist on talking about Lilibet, Grandfather? I know she visited you this summer."

The older man looked at his grandson with interest. Black was never rude, never interrupted, and rarely became angry with him.

"Yes, but not as much as I'd like, and when she comes we don't often talk about her life in Yancey. She's coming today."

Black's heart lurched. He held himself very still. He, too, knew Lilibet would be visiting today. He'd sensed it since early morning when he'd awakened with Cat's fur warm by his side. He'd taken the kernel of happy knowledge and tucked it away inside of him to draw on and savor at intervals during the day. He admitted to himself that he was jealous. Grandfather knew also. Of course, Grandfather knew. Grandfather and Lilibet were very close.

Uncle East gave a sidelong glance at his silent grandson. Black's strong, carved profile was stern and unmoving, betraying not a single emotion. The green eyes stared straight ahead at the vista before them. Intrigued by the lack of response, East's heart gave a joyful leap of surprise. Only he could read his grandson and he knew he was hiding something. Should he hope . . . no, don't be an old fool, East. Elizabeth and Black are worlds apart in culture and ambitions. Besides, this young man has mountains to climb and rivers to cross. His love of freedom was tantamount to a holy quest. He knew Black would never be happy until he conquered other frontiers—and a few demons within himself. Still, he sighed, an old man could hope.

Abruptly, Black stood up.

"I'm sorry, Grandfather. I have something I have to do. Will you excuse me?"

"Certainly, son. I have two pairs of moccasins that have to be finished. One I lined with fur to warm Elizabeth's feet on cold mornings in Morgantown. The second pair she can wear here on the mountain."

He watched with concern as Black strode away.

He and Black Eagle had made a mistake with their grandson. But he was sure they hadn't bred the humanness out of him . . . only submerged it for a while. Black was too intrinsically passionate and sensitive to be uncaring about anything. The first summer he'd spent with them, Black's small five-year-old body and soul had continually quivered with anger. Anger at the cavernous mine and the cavalier attitude of the men he felt had taken his father's life. East, Laura, Black Eagle, and Cathline had loved and coaxed the anger away, but it wasn't Black's nature to let a hurt or injustice go unchallenged. There still simmered within him a spark of anger that needed quenching.

Black's physical and spiritual communion with nature, his understanding and rapport with animals and every aspect of the natural world was an attainment worthy of the most studious, transcendental mystic. He was afraid of absolutely nothing: man, beast, or storm. Uncle East knew Black had had experiences and adventures he'd never spoken of. From the lessons he'd had in philosophy, Black understood that human beings were all part of the same family, were as kin to him as the cougar or the marigold. But his frustration for people and their foibles began to grow when he realized few of them understood or respected the power within themselves. The frustration had now become intolerance and anger.

They'd brought Black to the mountain to teach him the best of the ways of men, and then turned him loose in a society that knew nothing of the mountain. His lessons on the mountain would eventually stand him in good stead, but until he learned the illnesses of mankind, accepted them, and learned to deal with them, Black was ill-suited for polite society. Black, unfortunately, needed grounding.

Uncle East sighed.

You should have broken your vow, East, and spent time with him down there. If anyone understands anger at fools and parasites, it's you. He got it from you. You should have remembered what a potent force anger is.

He and Black Eagle did well in all respects but one. They had created a man who used all his faculties to the best of his abilities—physically, mentally, and spiritually—but they forgot to teach him how to handle the disappointment of others not living up to their potential. And they assumed, mistakenly, that he could handle the great, awesome power of deep emotion, the depth of emotion that men such as Black are capable of.

The death of his beloved grandfather, Black Eagle, had sent Black into isolation for four years. He'd come out unscathed and more mature, but he'd never lost that loneliness—or regained his trust in others. Because of the pain of caring, Black had been cautious, connecting only with his parents and grandparents. Except for Elizabeth.

Elizabeth had broken through. Her honesty, her faith in love, and her enthusiasm for life itself could make Black complete. Her love would help fill some of the emptiness East and Black Eagle had not foreseen. Had Black already sensed what Uncle East knew about Elizabeth?

A huge smile broke Uncle East's sober countenance.

Down the mountain, in the social room of Big Ugly Creek Freewill Baptist Church, Lilibet swiftly laid flatware on tables covered with red-checkered oilcloth. There was a revival meeting tonight and the women of the church were preparing to feed the big crowd. She, Marm, and Margot were helping set tables.

Female chatter rose and fell throughout the room.

"Laria Sue's diabetes is botherin' her a whole big lot."

"She eats too much sugar."

"Preacher says eatin' too much is jest as sinful as drinkin' too much."

"I heer'd tell of young'uns who ate so much candy at Halloween they dropped dead the next mornin'."

"I cain't believe that. I jest thank Jesus for sparin' my young'uns from polio this summer. They was sixteen cases of it in Yancey County. Only five of them children lived an' they is in iron lungs."

Lilibet thought if they talked less they'd get more work done. She had almost finished her six tables. Marm was about done, too. Margot hadn't completed her first table. She'd complained of being tired when they were leaving the house.

"Mary Beth, how's your pa doin'? Heer'd you took him to the hospital last week."

"Got him back home. He jest sits thar on the porch coughin'. Got the black lung. He'll be sittin' thar till he dies, an' I'll be takin' keer of him the rest of my born days."

"Lord God, I hope my Chester don't get black lung. We cain't afford no doctor bill's, even the Hutton Company doctors."

Lilibet was sure that Daddy had black lung disease. His cough was getting worse. The sputum was discolored, almost black. She had tried to get him to go to the doctor but he wouldn't. He said it "wouldn't do no good." He was right. Coal dust was filling up his lungs and nothing could be done to repair them. He would die slowly, fighting for every breath. She gritted her teeth, clenching her jaw till it ached. Someday, she would get a law passed that ensured protection of a miner's lungs, or ensured complete medical treatment. She closed her eyes and shook off her anger. That was tomorrow. This was today. *See to the needs of the here and now, Lilibet.*

She hurried, knowing she would have to finish Margot's tables before she left for Catawba Mountain. She let the incessant chattering of the women go through one ear and out the other, hearing but not listening. She knew they were being sociable; they needed one another's company. They chattered because they were scared. They don't recognize it as fear, but she knew it was. The constant gossip and friendly news served a deep underlying need to chase away their fear of accidents, illness, death, and debt. If they stopped talking, their fears would catch up with them. She reiterated her silent, ferocious vow that her life would be safe and secure and free of fear.

She didn't know what the future held for her, but it was not Big Ugly Creek and her mother's miserable life.

After she'd arranged purple asters and joe-pye weed in a glass jelly jar and placed them in the center of her last table, she turned to help Margot. Marm and Margot were whispering as they worked.

"What are you two whispering about?" Lilibet asked with a smile. She picked up a handful of flatware and moved swiftly about the table.

"Mrs. Blackburn says the preacher was talking about you," Margot said in sotto voice.

"Well, what did he say?" Lilibet asked.

"Now, Margot, Lilibet doesn't need to hear this the day before she goes off to college."

"Preacher Dunbar says you have backslid," Margot said, ignoring her mother. "Says you're a wicked sinner because you went to the movies, and you've been dancing at Ruby's."

"Did Mrs. Blackburn think Satan was coming to get me?"

"I know you think it's funny, Lilibet, but we have to stay here and listen to him preach at us in church every Sunday," Margot said with a sour look on her face. "He'll make Marm's life miserable for the next few weeks."

Immediately contrite, Lilibet hugged her mother and said, "I'm sorry, Marm. I didn't think of my fun causing you any harm."

"You never think of anyone but yourself, Miss High and Mighty. Cledith Hutton is being nice to you because you won all those scholarships. In the meantime, you're going off to college and I have to start the tenth grade in

Yancey County High School because there's no one to tutor me. Then, on Sundays, I have to come here and listen to Preacher Dunbar talk about the sinner in my family."

"Margot Springer, you apologize to your sister this instant," Marm demanded. She looked around, hoping no one was hearing this family argument.

"It's okay, Marm," Lilibet cautioned, laying a comforting hand on her mother's arm.

"Or maybe Cle's screwing you, is that it?" asked a sneering Margot.

Marm gasped and her hand flew up to slap Margot but stopped just short of Margot's cheek. Ever conscious of the eternal gossip that circled through the camps, she restrained herself, glancing around again to see if anyone had noticed. Even Lilibet was shocked. She knew Margot was jealous of her—jealous of Lilibet's going off to college, and jealous of the attention Cledith showered upon her. But the depth of the jealousy surprised her.

"I'll take care of this, Marm," Lilibet said. She took Margot firmly by the arm and nudged her toward the outside door.

Outside, they walked over to a wooden bench under a buckeye tree. Putting her hands on Margot's shoulders, Lilibet forced her sister to sit down and then she stood in front of her, hands on hips, eyes blazing.

"You listen to me, you little snip. The doctor says your lungs are stronger and there's no reason you can't attend school. After you've been in school a few weeks you'll love it. You'll make friends and go to parties just like I did this summer. In fact, I'll make sure because I'll ask Tom Tee's little sister to watch out for you. Okay?"

Margot nodded her head sullenly.

"As far as church is concerned, you don't have to go. I wouldn't sit and listen to that blathering hypocrite even if they paid me. I stopped going when I started thinking for myself. I realized God doesn't belong to any particular church and He loves us always no matter who we are, and no matter what the preacher says. If you think Preacher Dunbar has a franchise on God then you'll believe Virgil MacDonald pisses Pepsi."

"Daddy will switch me if I don't go to meetings," Margot whined.

"Daddy tried beating me for a few Sundays, but he couldn't make me go. Preacher puts fear into you. Makes you want to just give up and let life defeat you. I think *that* is evil. Nothing can make me come to church. Coming here to help Marm on days like this is different. Do you understand?"

"Yes," Margot muttered. She looked up at Lilibet with shame in her eyes, and tears rolled down her wan face. "I'm sorry, Lilibet."

Lilibet's heart contracted and she wished she hadn't been so adamant with Margot. She reached to caress her blond head.

Margot stood and gave Lilibet a stiff hug. Marm came out of the dingy clapboard building and hovered anxiously around the two of them. "Everything all right now, girls?"

"Yes, Marm," they said in unison, and giggled.

"Lilibet, I know you have some place to go, so Margot and I will finish her tables. If you stop by the house on your way up the mountain, please don't wake your brother. Eugene is still in bed with the flu. I gave him catnip tea, but he don't seem no better this morning."

"Thanks, Marm. I really do have to get going."

She turned to wave as she walked off and Margot gave her a listless wave. Even Margot didn't know much about where Lilibet went on her trips up the mountain. She told Margot that she went to find unusual specimens for her botany collection. She also told her she had a friend she saw once in a while, but because he was an old man, Margot wasn't interested.

Lilibet ran past her house. She was late and she hadn't planned on going home first anyway. Eugene wasn't sick. He was drunk. He'd been drunk for three days.

"If he's sick it's because he got hold of some bad corn liquor," she said with disgust as she hurried across the creek. "He's getting so he smells as bad as the MacDonald brothers. If he continues running around with them, he's going to end up in jail. I just know it."

She didn't talk to herself as much as she used to. She

had Cle and Sam, and sometimes even Clarice to talk with. But personal problems like family, and the hunger and discontent that plagued her, still were aired only to herself. Sometimes she thought that Cle might understand but so far she'd been afraid to venture into unknown territory with him.

Guilt hit her as she thought of leaving Marm and Margot here alone with Daddy and Eugene. But she couldn't stay with them. Staying here would defeat her purpose. She would never be able to help Marm and Margot unless she took advantage of the education she'd been offered. Someday, when she'd made something of herself, she'd take them out of this cheerless gray splotch on the face of the earth.

"Someday, I'll get you out of here, Marm. I swear I will!"

In the glen, Black sat with his back to the gorge. Sunlight filtered through the saplings. It cast dancing, leafy shadows on the paper propped on the easel before him. That was fine with him. The shadows helped him transfer the mystical mood of the glen to paper. His strong fingers moved the watercolor brush with sure but delicate strokes. He preferred working in oil or chalk, but this hallowed place called for the soft hues only watercolor could produce.

He was almost finished. He wanted it to dry before Lilibet left so she could take it with her. He knew she had arrived at Grandfather's. He could feel her presence on the mountain. She would be here soon. They hadn't shared the glen since the first time they had both been here early in the summer. He knew she'd visited several times, but he had respected her privacy and stayed away.

He'd held her in his arms as they'd danced for a few minutes every week through the summer, causing a growing animosity between him and Cle, and even good-natured Sam. Black could have cared less.

But he hadn't been alone with her since they danced in the parking lot at Ruby's. He remembered the crystal tiara the mist had formed in her hair and his tongue tasting the honey of it. His heart tripped a double beat but he willed it to return to its steady rhythm. *Yes, she's special, but you cannot let your emotions control you,* he told himself. There is a whole fascinating world out there to learn from, to enjoy, to conquer, to be free and unfettered. *Don't get sidetracked, Black.*

He knew Lilibet was close by. He'd tracked her for the last half mile. He smiled. She was trying to surprise him and doing a darn good job of it. He would let her.

Suddenly, she stood there before him, hands on hips, laughing. Brush suspended in air, he stared at her, pretending shock.

"How did you . . .?" he started, but stopped when she knelt down and removed the moccasins on her feet. She dangled them happily in front of her.

"My moccasins. I have my own pair. Aren't they beautiful? Uncle East said they will last forever. He told me you were probably here."

He said nothing. He was drinking in the sight of her. He should have put her in the painting. She belonged in it. She wore a discarded white shirt of her father's tucked loosely into her tattered jeans. A white grosgrain ribbon held her pale golden hair up in a ponytail. Her huge violet eyes shone even in the gossamer light of the glen.

"What's the matter, Black? Angry because I surprised you, or jealous that I'm almost as good as you are at being silent in the forest? The moccasins make it easier. . . . I'm sorry, I'm disturbing you, aren't I? I'll leave."

A look of disappointment on her face, she returned the moccasins to her feet and turned to go.

"Wait. Please stay. It's my turn to apologize. You really did surprise me."

"Are you sure you want me to stay?"

"This place is yours as much as it is mine. I knew you'd want to visit before you left, so I was expecting you. You realize the moccasins mean that Grandfather trusts you will use your knowledge of snakes. Otherwise he would insist you continue to wear your heavy boots for protection."

He cursed himself for taking a formal, almost parental tone with her. It certainly wasn't how he felt.

"I'm very good at spotting snakes," she said indignantly.

"You weren't three months ago," he reminded her.

She blushed. "I was so entranced with the bird . . . anyway, I promise to be careful if you promise not to be so . . . so superior!"

He had to laugh at that. A rich, throaty chuckle came from his bronze throat, and she smiled.

"You don't laugh often, I like the sound of it. May I see what you're painting?" she asked shyly.

"Sure. I'm about finished. Come and look."

He held his breath as she appraised his work.

She said nothing for a moment, and then sighed.

"Oh, Black, it's beautiful. It reminds me a little of a picture I saw in an art book once. I think it was by a man named Claude Monet. The colors make me think of Monet's painting. But the work is definitely yours. Oh, it's wonderful. All pastel lavenders, and pearly pink with touches of cornflower blue. I love the jade green you've used for the pond and the shadows under the trees. You've been painting this since summer, haven't you? Because here I see the white trillium and . . . and here the purple violets .. and how did you get that hazy phosphorescence throughout?"

She paused for breath and then looked at him with embarrassment.

"I'm sorry. I sure talk a lot sometimes, don't I? It's just that I've never seen anything like this before. I mean, I've never known anyone who could paint a beautiful picture like this."

He laughed again.

"Are you kidding? I love all the praise. Thank you."

Her hand moved toward the watercolor as if to touch it, but she jerked it back.

"I wish I could do that," she said.

"You can," he assured her.

"I've never tried, or had any lessons. But even so, I'd never be able to make anything so lovely," she said with reverence.

"Well, I haven't had any lessons myself and my first

paintings were god-awful, but maybe I could get you started."

"Oh, yes."

"I'll put some finishing touches on this and then you'll have a painting lesson."

Leaning over his shoulder, she watched as he completed the image he'd created of the glen. He removed the paper carefully from the easel and, slipping through the saplings, laid it out to dry on the flat boulder overlooking the gorge, fastening the four corners with rocks.

When he returned, he found her sitting on his stump, the easel before her, her fingers hovering over various colors in the paint box.

"They won't bite. You can touch them."

"They're so beautiful. I can't wait to put them on paper. What do I do first?" she asked eagerly.

They spent the next hour experimenting with colors, mixing and shading them. Then he showed her various strokes and painting techniques. He told her that everyone eventually developed a style of their own, as she would if she painted enough. She had great fun splashing huge reds and yellows on the paper, then tearing off the sheet to splash the next one with oranges, browns and purples.

"Feeling comfortable with the brush now?" he asked.

"Yes."

"Would you like to try painting something?"

"Yes. You've done the glen as it was in summer. I'd like to try it now, with its fall colors."

"Okay, let's start with the sycamore trees near the gorge. What color would you paint them?"

"A lemony yellow with rusty spots here and there."

He held her small hand in his as he directed it back and forth from paint to paper. The angle he was working from was awkward so he settled himself behind her on the wide stump, his legs straddling hers, his body snug against her back as they worked. The peace of the glen settled on them as they became entranced with the scene they were creating. A bright orange and black butterfly lit on the corner of the easel and rested while it watched them. High above, a pine grosbeak whistled a musical *tee-tew-tew*. A dragonfly skimmed across the tranquil green pond. A breeze, blowing cooler all the time, sifted softly around them, ruffling the edges of the paper.

Black knew it was time to get up from the stump. She'd learned enough to work by herself. He should take his hand from hers. But the sight of his tan hand holding her fair one bewitched him. Earlier trying to see the paper from her perspective, he'd crocked his head in close to hers. Acutely aware now of his cheek resting against her ear and wisps of her hair tickling his nose, he held himself motionless, suspended and still on the outside, smoldering on the inside. He opened his mouth a fraction and caught one of the tendrils between his lips, praying she wouldn't notice. The fresh, light lilac scent of her drifted through his nostrils and into every cell of his body. The hush in the glen accentuated her easy, even breathing. It echoed in his ears.

He tried to concentrate on the paint and paper before them but the fragrance of her, the breath of her, the warmth of her sent his mind reeling. His thighs encircled her legs and his crotch hugged her bottom. Through his jeans, he could feel the crevice that divided her rounded buttocks. He hadn't meant to get so dangerously close. *Yes, you did,* he told himself. *Admit it. You've been wanting to feel her, be with her, since the first time you saw her. Since she put her hands on her hips, glared at you with those enormous violet eyes, and belligerently told she was "just dandy."*

He gently moistened his lips to keep the wispy tendril of hair inside his mouth, and then closed his eyes in silent agony.

Lilibet, first vaguely annoyed but now embarrassed at the distractions intruding sharply upon her studied concentration, was losing the battle to ignore them. The heat of Black's inner thighs pressing against her legs, and the imprint of his sizable maleness against the small of her buttocks caused a flush of warmth in her cheeks. Fighting the strange and wonderful sensations, she clenched her brush and concentrated fiercely on the paper before her, but a pulse beat tugged incessantly in an unfamiliar place ... the softness of her own inner thighs. Her heart was beating between her legs! The throbbing beat traveled up to her private parts and climbed to her stomach. Oh, my God, it was the wanting, only a physical wanting so powerfully strong and demanding this time that it hurt. Against her ear and cheek, Black's breath was warm and tingling on her tender skin. Her nipples tightened, the buds rubbing painfully against her cool shirt. Was a piece of her hair caught in his mouth? It was her imagination. Her hand shook and an orange line wavered uncertainly down the palette.

Concentrate, Lilibet.

Don't let him know how he affects you. It's the intimacy of the glen, his physical closeness, the knowledge you will be saying goodbye soon. It's just that you've never known anyone like Black. She caught her breath as she heard the rhythm of his breathing change, felt it quicken and grow hotter on her cheek.

Black grew more uncomfortable, an erection beginning to harden as she squirmed to dip her brush in a new color. God, how he wanted to put his arms around her, cuddle her to him.

No, it wasn't cuddling he wanted.

He'd explored sex before with his girlfriend in high school. It had been a hot, groping, searching effort but had eventually led to a satisfying relationship for both of them. This was different—an overpowering force he'd never dealt with before. As angelic and ethereal as Lilibet looked, and as innocent and naive as she was, what he was feeling at the moment frightened him. He wanted to plunge himself into her again and again, bury himself deep, deep, deep and stay there until she told him he'd made her happy. The scorching, volcanic feeling consumed him.

Hastily, he moved backward off the stump and jumped to his feet, startling her.

"Did I do something wrong, Black?"

"No! You're doing great. You should be on your own now. I'll sit on the log next to the pond and watch."

"Okay." Both relieved and disappointed, Lilibet watched him settle himself beside the pond.

Black knew it was wiser to watch from a distance. The turbulent emotions in him subsided somewhat. He drew several deep breaths and bid the gods of the forest and the spirits of his Shawnee forefathers to come forth and draw a cloak of protection around them both. When he was satisfied they were safe, he pillowed his head on the log and dozed as she worked.

An hour later, a chill wind woke him. The sun was low in the sky and the glen was cold. Lilibet was still painting, a look of determination on her face. From where he lay, he could see her quivering with cold. Quietly, he removed his flannel shirt and walked over to wrap it around her, his hands resting on her shoulders.

Her concentration was so great that she merely nodded her thank you and continued painting. He marveled at the painting he saw before him. She had worked swiftly, as if she knew there was little time and she wanted to get everything on paper before it was too late. It was primitive in form but breathtaking in the choice of colors and shading. The splashes of red, rust, and yellow were bold and brave. She lifted her brush to add more rust to a tree trunk but, gently, he squeezed her shoulder. She was about to make the mistake most beginners made.

"That's enough," he said. "You've finished."

She turned to look up at him. "I have?"

"Yes. Step back to look at it and you'll see."

He let go of her shoulders and she stood up. He said nothing while she surveyed her work. Then she smiled and joy filled him.

"It's not bad, is it?"

"It's very good for a beginner. You should take lessons when you get to school."

Lilibet looked at him now, startled. "Black, you gave me your shirt and it's very cold."

With concern, she reached to touch his naked chest but he stepped back quickly before she could reach him. He took her hand in his. "It's all right I don't mind. Cold doesn't bother me."

"Thank you for the shirt." She pulled it closer around her and they stared awkwardly at each other for a moment.

"You're going to have to leave soon. Let's see how my

picture is doing," he said. "Stay here. It will be too cold on the boulder."

He disappeared through the saplings and a moment later returned with the parchment rolled up neatly. From his hip pocket he pulled a strip of deer hide, and tied it around the cylinder. He handed it to her.

"This is for you ... if you'd like it. It's your going-away present," he said.

"Oh, Black, of course I want it. Thank you so much. It will hang in a place of honor in my room at Miss Mabel's." She looked perplexed for a moment.

"What's the matter?" he asked.

"Well, I was wondering how I could pack it without ruining it. Maybe I shouldn't try to put it in a box or suitcase. Cle can find a safe hidey-hole somewhere in the car."

"Cle?"

"Yes. He's driving me up to Morgantown tomorrow. Isn't it wonderful?"

"I suppose so." He shouldn't be surprised, Black thought. If he'd read Cle correctly, he won't let Lilibet out of his sight. He'll keep her to himself as long as he can.

"I earned a lot of money this summer doing clerical work in Pappy Hutton's office, but half of it would have gone for bus fare if Cle hadn't offered to take me. In fact, if it weren't for the Hutton family, I probably wouldn't be going to college. Pappy Hutton talked Daddy into letting me go, and he gave Daddy a better-paying job. I know a lot of people don't like Cle's father. I hate the way he manages his mines, and I'm scared to death of him, but he's got some good in him, Black."

He clamped his teeth together, willing himself not to say anything.

"And guess what? she continued with excitement. "Clarice taught me how to drive a car. Sam says I'm a menace on the road, but he lets me drive his car sometimes. Cle says I can drive partway to Morgantown tomorrow."

Early on, he'd recognized Lilibet's strong sense of loyalty to her friends and family. It was as strong as her will and determination to succeed. But gratitude was a dangerous thing. It could be good or bad. It could blind you to reality. Lilibet's excitement at stepping into the Hutton's world, at learning new skills, her gratitude for the friendships she'd formed, and her inherent protective nature had colored her vision of Cle Hutton and his family.

She stopped talking and stared at him. Her next words caught him off guard.

"Black, sometimes you look at me so sadly. It's puzzled me before. Have I done something wrong or disappointed you?"

How could he tell her he knew it was a gamble to leave her? They belonged together. He'd known it since they'd danced at Ruby's. When he'd seen the tears roll down her cheeks then, he knew she'd sensed it, too, but hadn't recognized what she felt. He wanted desperately to take her with him. He didn't think it would have taken much to convince her, but neither one of them could afford to do that monetarily. All summer he'd fought the desire to spend more time with her. In time she would have recognized what he already knew.

He couldn't deprive her of the fulfillment of the plans she'd so carefully made, the dreams she'd worked for. He couldn't take away the dream of a university education, and then law school. If he denied her that experience she would eventually resent him. He wanted to join the air force and fly jets. She wanted to go to law school. She had just begun to discover herself, and his own thirst for adventure was overwhelming.

Was he being noble or selfish? He didn't know. He only knew it hurt like hell.

The danger was Cle.

He could only pray that sometime in the next four years she would see through Cle.

It slipped out before he could stop it.

"Cledith Hutton is a damn fool."

Her violet eyes darkened with fury. "He's not! How can you say that? You don't even know him."

"I know his type well enough," Black said tightly.

"He's not a type! He's sweet and good, and he's generous. He may not know as much as you do about life and nature but he . . . you're older . . ." she sputtered as words failed her.

"Cle Hutton has pulled the wool over your eyes, Lilibet. He's not the kind, generous leader of the crowd you're so willing to believe he is."

"He's a lot more than you are," she said, her eyes flashing gold. "He's practical and has goals. He would never have thrown away those scholarships like you did . . . or . . . or run around the mountains in Indian garb!"

"Who says I don't have plans, things I want to do, dreams just like everyone else?" demanded Black. "Cle just talks a bigger game than I do."

"Not true!"

"It is true, and what Cle can't possess by charming everyone, Pappy Hutton buys for him. What's Cle really done for anyone lately?" asked Black with heavy sarcasm, angry with himself for ruining their time together but unable to stop himself.

"Why, I think you're jealous," she said, her eyes widening in sudden understanding. "I thought the great noble savage was above such base emotions!"

She tore his shirt from her and thrust it at him, tears in her eyes. "Here! I don't want your dumb old shirt."

Like two children, they shoved the blue flannel back and forth between the two of them. Finally, he grabbed it, wrapped it around her like a cocoon, and pulled her tightly to him.

Her arms were caught in the shirt but she didn't struggle to get loose. Her heartbeat slammed against his ribs. He gloried in the feel of her small body adhered to his. She felt perfect.

She stared up at him, her eyes filling with wonder and suspense.

He bent his head and placed a soft kiss on her lips, but he was still angry and his lips became hard and demanding. Breathless, she gasped when he released her mouth and kissed her ear, then placed swift kisses all over her heart-shaped face. He returned to her delicate mouth, wanting all he could have of her. Automatically, she responded, her little tongue searching for his, and their kiss grew deeper. Jealously, it flashed through his mind that Lilibet had done some serious kissing this summer. Cle, dammit!

Black wanted more. An urgent erection grew tight in his jeans but he gained control of himself. Almost in benediction, he kissed her forehead and reverently smoothed back a strand of her hair. He gave her back a light caress. With regret he would remember the rest of his life, he drew a deep breath and stepped away from her.

"Why did you do that? You shouldn't have done that," she said, her body shaking, obviously dismayed at herself and him.

Lilibet's angry words hid her dismay at the effect of his kiss. Shaken beyond belief, she'd wanted Black to prolong the wondrous feelings he'd stirred within her. But she couldn't tell him. Nice girls didn't admit to such feelings. Besides, she'd already figured out that it was the glen, and the poignancy of saying goodbye that had caused all this inner turmoil.

"Why? Why?" she demanded.

Black wanted to answer, *because you're mine, you belong to me*. But he knew it wasn't true. She would never belong to anyone and neither would he.

"I want you to remember me," he said quietly.

"You didn't have to kiss me . . . like that."

"I think maybe I did."

He retrieved the cylinder of parchment from where it had fallen and handed it to her.

"You'd better go, Elizabeth," he said. "It's getting dark. Go the way I taught you. You'll make it in time."

He saw the confusion on her face, but he could do nothing to help her. They both had rivers to cross before they came together again.

Trembling, she briefly ran her hand down his bare arm. Then, swiftly, she turned to go and never looked back. He watched her disappear into the tree line.

He glanced down and saw in her haste she'd forgotten her painting. Carefully, he removed it from the easel. It was his now.

The die was cast. He'd taken the gamble.

PART TWO

SUMMER 1954

Chapter 10

"Keep an eye on Lilibet this summer," Pappy Hutton said into the telephone. "Report to me every week. Do a good job and that manager's position you want is yours."

He replaced the receiver and motioned to the waitress, Eulonie Bevins, to come and take the phone away. The long cord, installed for Pappy's use, trailed its way back to a desk in the kitchen.

"What creep you got watchin' the Springer girl, Pappy?"

"None of your business, Sheriff."

They sat in Pappy's accustomed lunchtime corner in the Rainbow Diner, Yancey's only excuse for fine dining. This is where he dispensed his godfather favors: fixing a traffic ticket, giving money to a miner with a terminally ill child, paying car insurance for a miner's widow. Insignificant serfs found him here every day. More prestigious patronage, having to do with governors, and banks, and presidents was bestowed in the evening at the Yancey Country Club.

"That was a mighty fine college graduation gift you gave the twins. Hear you offered it to Lilibet, too. Shame she didn't go to Europe with them."

Irritated, Pappy ignored the comment. The girl was much too independent. He'd taken care of that by making her Anna Adkins's assistant for the summer. Doing a damn good job, too.

"Did you tell me Eugene Springer was still in the county stockade?" he asked.

"Yes, sir."

"What for?"

"One of my deputy's caught him carrying hooch across

the county line. I didn't tell the Feds because I don't want them nosin' around Yancey. Eugene's been there for three months. The Springers haven't got the money to get him out, and Lilibet won't give them any of her savings. Says he deserves to rot in jail."

Good for her, thought Pappy, a scant smile breaking his cool facade. "Let him go. Tell Eugene if he embarrasses his sister again, if he as much as picks his nose or scratches his balls, I'll have him picked up again."

"Yes, sir."

Pappy's glacial gaze darted about the long, narrow room with its worn, once colorful plastic tablecloths, but always came back to focus on the four women who sat near the front. The dim wall next to their table held large, yellowing black-and-white photographs of early century miners. Lilibet Springer's blond head lit the room in contrast.

Mabel had done an excellent job with Lilibet, not only in her mode of dress but in her whole demeanor. Her wild mane of blond hair had been tamed into a shorter cut that swept back over her ears and lay gracefully just above her shoulders, complementing her heart-shaped face. Her narrow-lapeled cotton blazer, silk blouse, and cream linen slacks had the soft nuances of class that Pappy required in a daughter-in-law. She'd always been self-assured but she now had an air of ease and a sense of self and style.

"Your future daughter-in-law's a beaut, ain't she?"

"Keep your opinions about Lilibet to yourself, Hager," said Pappy coldly, and waved his hand negligently to indicate that it was time for the sheriff to leave. The dickhead was getting too big for his britches.

He watched as the sheriff tipped his cap when he passed the table where Lilibet sat with her mother and sister, Regina and Margot Springer, and her old high school friend, Donetta Frye.

Pappy's glance caressed Lilibet for a moment, flickered over the Springer women, and landed on pasty-faced, very pregnant Donetta Frye. Donetta had gained a permanent thirty pounds in the four years since Cle and Lilibet's class had graduated from high school. Her cheap, green maternity smock clung to every unattractive, fat-laden droop on her body, hiding nothing. Tom Tee has rutted her till she's about good for nothing, he thought.

He watched as Donetta whispered something in Lilibet's ear, and the indignant expression growing on Lilibet's face. Keenly, he observed the reactions of the other two women to Donetta's rudeness. Regina Springer wore an expression of benevolent tolerance. Margot Springer's pale prettiness twisted into ugly jealousy. She masked it quickly, but Pappy Hutton made a mental note of it. Margot was jealous of her sister.

"Have you eaten of the tree of knowledge yet, Lilibet?"

Donetta whispered her question into Lilibet's ear so Marm and Margot couldn't hear.

Lilibet had been feeling sorry for worn-down Donetta, but now she bristled indignantly, and glanced swiftly around the Rainbow Diner, hoping no one had heard, in particular, Pappy Hutton, who sat in the rear at his favorite corner table with his cronies.

"Are you asking if I'm still a virgin, Donetta?" she returned fiercely in a low voice.

"Well, surely you couldn't be." Donetta looked at her slyly. "I mean, lordy, you've been dating Cle all this time, all through college. A girl can only hold out so long."

"It's none of your business!"

Incensed, Lilibet tried to calm herself. This lunch date was a treat for Marm, and Lilibet didn't want it ruined.

"Please, Lilibet! A soft answer turneth away wrath," sniffed Donetta.

Lilibet sighed. Donetta was no longer a Catholic. "Saved" shortly after her shotgun wedding to Tom Tee Frye the same fall the rest of them had gone off to college, Donetta was now a Freewill Baptist. Her conversation was liberally sprinkled with biblical terms.

"What are you two whispering about?" Margot asked.

"Oh, we're just talkin' about womenly things, you know, babies and pregnancies and stuff like that," said Donetta, with a tone of matronly superiority.

"Well, if anyone knows about having babies it's you, Donetta," said Margot snidely. "Jane Etta's only three,

Tom Tee, Jr.'s two, and another due next month. Must be a lot of shi ... dirty diapers at your house."

"Yeh, but I don't mind. Tom Tee's proud, says I breed like a rabbit. The Lord told me to multiply, so that's what I'm doin'."

She leaned to whisper in Lilibet's ear again. "Honey, come over tonight while Tom Tee's out with the boys, and you can tell me everything."

Donetta would worm nothing out of her, thought Lilibet. She was still a virgin and proud of it. She understood how difficult it was for Cle, but he seemed to be as intent as she on waiting for their wedding night. Lilibet wasn't naive enough to think that Cle was a virgin. She detested what was called the "double standard," but Marm had explained that men were allowed to do things nice girls didn't do. There were periods of time when Cle disappeared and she wondered if he was out "catting," as the boys liked to say. That would have to stop if they got married.

"I'm sorry, Donetta, but after I take Marm and Margot home this afternoon, I have to come back and catch up on some work at the office."

"What do you need to work overtime for? Come and have a beer with me?"

"I need money for law school."

"You're crazy to work so hard," Margot said. "You should have gone to Europe with the twins when Pappy offered it as a graduation present. I'd have jumped at the chance."

"I wish you could have gone."

Every time she saw the metallic brace on Margot's right leg, she felt guilty. Guilty because she, Lilibet, was healthy, had a college degree, and a bright future in front of her.

Polio had swept the valley two years ago. The Hutton Company doctor decided Margot had tuberculosis about the same time she came down with polio. Lilibet had stormed home from Morgantown and demanded the doctor find a sanitarium for her sister but he had refused— said she'd have to recover at home like all the rest of the miners' children who had managed to survive. Cle informed Pappy and soon Margot was ensconced in a lovely clinic high in the mountains in Pocahontas County near Bald Knob. She'd recovered from the tuberculosis but the mild case of polio had crippled her for life. She got around well enough, with her brace and a sturdy cane. She'd graduated from high school last year and attended a small business college in Charleston. This summer she had taken over Lilibet's old job as filing clerk at the Hutton main office.

Lilibet was uneasy with her promotion to assistant office manager. There were many others in the company who had worked for years for such an opportunity. Uncertainty at Pappy's motive gnawed at her.

"We're beholden enough to Pappy Hutton," she said. "Besides, I'm not a member of his family. I had no business going to Europe with Cle and Clarice."

"Well, you're practically engaged to Cle, for heaven's sakes!" Margot cried.

"Wearing someone's fraternity pin doesn't mean you're engaged."

"People in Yancey think it does," said Margot.

Lilibet knew this was true.

"I don't care what they think," Lilibet said irritably. "There are a lot of things Cle and I need to resolve first. He hasn't accepted the idea that I'm going to law school. He wants to settle down right now. If he can't wait three years for me, then it wasn't meant to be."

"You girls leave Lilibet alone. She knows what she's doing," said Marm gently.

"Why didn't Sam come home after graduation?" Margot asked.

Lilibet smiled. Margot had a huge crush on Sam.

"He made a high score on his law school entrance exam so they offered him a good-paying job in the law school library for the summer. He couldn't pass it up."

What she didn't say was that she'd made a higher score and been offered the same job but turned it down when Pappy Hutton said he'd pay her more. It was a golden opportunity to be home with Marm and Margot this summer before the rigors of law school in the fall.

"'Twas awful nice of Mr. Hutton to let you use Cle's

car to get back and forth to work," Marm said. "When will the twins be back?"

"In about a month. Around Fourth of July week."

"And then the partying will begin. Hooray! Cle can't go a week without a party, and things have been dog-down dull without Clarice here," said Donetta. "I heard about her traipsin' up to Yale, chasin' after that Black Brady hunk. Heard he sent her packin' more than once. Now she's hot and heavy over that trucker, Mike Crisp. During spring break this year, someone saw them fu . . . excuse me, Mrs. Springer, screwing in his truck in Kroger's parking lot."

"Did you see it yourself, Donetta?" asked Lilibet.

"No, but you know it's . . ."

"It's gossip."

"Sure, if that's what you want to believe, Lilibet," Donetta said sarcastically. "Excuse me, but I have to go potty again . . . one of the burdens the Lord gives us when we bear the blessed fruit."

Donetta got up to waddle through the tables to the la-dies' room and Margot said, "Humph, doesn't look to me as if the 'blessed fruit' has done her any good. She looks like a slow-melting lump of lard, and look at the varicose veins in those stumps she calls legs! I bet she hasn't washed her hair in a month, and that cheesy smock must have come from Murphy's Five and Ten where Tom Tee works."

"Margot, be nice," said Marm.

Behind the look of settled domesticity in Donetta's eyes they had all detected a hint of desperation, but no one could sympathize more than Marm. She was just happy her daughters had escaped the trap Donetta, and most miners' daughters in Yancey County, found them-selves in.

"Got some hot cherry pie a waitin' in the kitchen fer you, Mr. Hutton," said the waitress. Her mouth worked diligently to camouflage the obvious lisp that overlaid her mountain twang.

"No, thank you, Eulonie, but give me Lilibet Spring-er's check."

She laid the bill on the table in front of him.

"Yes, sir. More coffee?"

"No, thank you, Eulonie." He waved her away, as he had the sheriff, and got up to leave.

She wondered sometimes if Pappy Hutton ever really thought of her as a person, someone other than the waitress who brought his lunch every day, and never gave him a bill because the owner had instructed her not to.

You're a piece of furniture to Pappy Hutton, Eulonie Bevins, but that's okay. She adjusted one of the stiff-permed gray curls that rimmed her disfigured face, and ran wrinkled fingers over the scar, an old, comforting gesture. She was five when an unlicensed doctor in the back hills had botched an attempt to remove a birthmark. The result was an ugly, rutted, red welt that twisted one corner of her mouth up to meet her earlobe. She remembered the day, thirty years ago, when she'd been hired at the Rainbow, and how grateful she was for the job. She never said much because she was self-conscious of her lisp, and she knew people thought she was stupid. She sure wasn't stupid, and she'd discovered early that you learn more listening than you do talking, and that suited her just fine.

Pappy Hutton stopped to greet the nice ladies having lunch, and Eulonie shivered as she saw him caress the top of Lilibet Springer's sweet blond head.

Lilibet switched off the desk lamp, sending her office into darkness. She needed the darkness for a moment. It was shielding, soothing. The only light in the big, empty, silent Hutton office building came from beneath Pappy's door at the far end of the hall. She knew Pappy and Anna were in there, and she knew what they were doing. It hadn't taken her long this summer to figure out that Pappy Hutton and Anna Adkins enjoyed more than a business relationship. She wondered how long the affair had been going on and if Sam knew. She was amazed that Anna, a woman of seemingly strong moral convictions and kindness, would indulge in a sordid relationship. She hoped Sam didn't know. He would never hear it from her.

Marm said she took too much on her shoulders, said

she worried too much about others. Maybe. If she did, it was just her nature. Absorbing herself in work helped her put aside her concerns for Marm and Margot, her anger at Eugene, her suspicions that her father's lungs were deteriorating faster than she'd thought. There was also the fear of not having enough money for law school. She was saving every cent, but would it be enough? On top of everything, she missed Cle everyday. His happy personality always made things brighter.

Suddenly, the old familiar hunger and yearning hit her hard, and she wished she were on the mountain, in the glen, or on a trout stream with Uncle East. *Stop it, Lilibet, you don't have time to wander about the mountains like . . . like an Indian.* Like Black.

The telephone clanged loudly in the silence, making her jump. Who would be calling at this hour? She turned her desk lamp back on and answered the phone.

"Hello," she said tentatively.

"Lilibet? Is that you? Your mother said you were working late. I knew my old man was an S.O.B. but he's going to have to lay off my girl and I'm going to tell him so. He's working you too hard."

"No, no, Cle. He doesn't know I'm here." *At least, I hope he doesn't.* "What are you doing calling me so late? It must be three o'clock in the morning over there."

"Right you are, my bright and beautiful girl. In Paris it's the best time to party. I'm just getting started." She heard loud music and someone giggling in the background.

"Cle, are you okay?"

"Sure, honey. Say hello to Babette."

"Cle, is Clarice there? Let me speak to her."

Muffled voices and some arguing ensued.

Clarice's voice finally came on. "Don't worry, Lilibet. We're partying and there must be fifty extra women here. They all love my twin, of course."

"He sounds drunk, Clarice."

"He's a bit looped, but you know Cle, he can handle it. I'll take care of him."

Cle came back on the line. "I miss you, honey."

"I miss you too, Cle."

"When I get back we'll announce our engagement." His voice lowered and he sounded almost sober. "You're my only . . ."

Transatlantic crackling broke up his last words. She thought he'd said 'hope'.

"What did you say, Cle?"

"Nothing. I love you."

She hesitated. Cle said the word "love" frequently. She was more cautious and often hesitated before replying. Did she love Cle? Yes, she was sure she did.

"Lilibet?"

"Yes. Love you, too. Cle. See you in a few weeks."

She hung up and wearily dropped her head to the desk, wanting to sink into forgetful sleep for just one delicious moment. The pile of back orders for Hutton coal, which Margot had neglected to fill, fell to the floor. She bent to pick them up and bumped her head on an open drawer.

"Dammit"

She rubbed the rapidly swelling bump and viewed the restacked pile with distaste. They were the only things she hadn't gotten to this evening. Maybe if she had a bite to eat her energy would return. She twisted her chair to raise the window behind her desk. Sultry summer night air wafted into the dark room, and with it the mouth-watering aroma of Tony Carpozzoli's garlic-laden chili sauce.

Carpozzoli's Chili House, directly opposite the Rainbow Diner on the square and across the street from the courthouse, was owned by Joe's father, Tony. Lilibet hated the Rainbow because it was Pappy's domain, and a bowl of chili from Tony's seemed the perfect solution. Her spirits lifted.

At Carpozzoli's, Black Brady tried to listen to the conversation of the man opposite him. But he'd seen Lilibet enter the Hutton offices earlier, and the thought of her being so near and yet so far was intruding on his ability to concentrate.

In the last four years, his focus had never shifted. He had dated and developed a social life of sorts at Yale, but Lilibet had always been the beacon. the light he'd held in his heart and mind. Other girls were beautiful, other girls were intelligent, other girls had shining souls, but he knew with every fiber of his being that Lilibet was the partner fate meant for him to have.

He was sure she'd seen through Cle Hutton by now.

Keeping in mind that Lilibet wanted stability and security, Black had forced himself to partake of some business courses and also investigated the possibilities of teaching. To his great surprise, he discovered he'd inherited his grandfather's natural affinity for business. He would prove to Lilibet that he could be as steady and practical as anyone.

The strength and wildness of the mountains would always be within him and the mountains would always be there for him when he needed them. He had only to step outside and look across the courthouse roof to see Blair Mountain. During summer breaks he had pursued a few of the challenges that would forever draw him: kayaking in Alaska, climbing the Himalayas, and crossing the Atlantic from Florida to England in a single sloop, alone. But for the rest of his life, he dreamed of doing his adventuring with Lilibet.

His years in college and the rigorous summers had taught him not to judge others so harshly, and that everyone seemed to have different lessons to learn. He knew life wasn't finished with him yet; he knew he was still stubborn, and hotheaded, and egotistical, but he was grateful for these new insights.

He'd come back to the valley to help Lilibet understand they belonged together.

Mike Crisp slapped his hand on the table and roared with laughter at the raw joke he'd just told. Black laughed automatically and jerked his attention back to his dinner partner.

Lilibet headed eagerly toward Main Street. Accustomed to the company of Cle, Clarice, or Sam for the last few years, she'd found the freedom of the last few weeks surprising and exhilarating. So it wasn't such a big deal to go to Tony's by herself late on a Friday night, she thought, but she loved her newfound independence.

Friday and Saturday nights in Yancey were busy. A drunk miner bumped into her, excused himself, and stumbled on. She wasn't afraid of him. The miners drank to relieve the tension they endured all week, and to dull their unending fear of poverty and illness. Generally, they were nonviolent men intent only on finding a state of oblivion. She was safe as long as she stayed on Main Street. It was the beer halls on the side streets and back alleys that spewed out brawling men.

The "loafers bench" around the tan brick, begrimed courthouse was filled with night-sitters hawking, spitting, and gossiping. Brown splotches of tobacco spittle permanently stained the cracked sidewalk in front of them, visible even in the spill of sallow illumination from the street lights. She saw Virgil MacDonald whizzing into bushes behind the bench, and two old men shaking their fists at him, while Jud threw dice in a crap game on the sidewalk.

She hurried past on the opposite side of the street and opened the door to Carpozzoli's. Tony, a surprised look on his face, waved from his open cooking counter at the rear. He adored Cle, his son Joe's friend, and always remembered Lilibet. He flashed her a happy smile, his big black mustache quivering in the process. She crossed to the nearest red Naugahyde booth and sat down.

The place wasn't busy. The dinner crowd had emptied out, and late-nighters hadn't come in yet. Candles, in squat wine bottles coated with thick aprons of dribbled wax, flickered at the center of red-checkered tables and booths. The only other light came from the jukebox, and Tony's cooking area. It splashed out on the waitress attending two men in a back booth.

Tony had created a cozy atmosphere, and it was the only place in town to boast two jukeboxes. One was stocked with rock and roll, country, and rhythm and blues records for the high school students who came for a hot dog in the afternoons; the other played classical and pop at night. Gershwin's "Someone to Watch Over Me" purled tenderly throughout the intimate interior. The song was one of Lilibet's favorites.

The gum-cracking waitress interrupted her reverie.

"What fer ya, Lilibet?"

"A bowl of chili, Gloria . . . and," should she have a glass of red wine, another of the niceties of life in which Miss Mabel had initiated her? No, she had to drive to Big Ugly tonight, " . . . and, a glass of iced tea."

As Gloria left, Lilibet heard the laughter of the two men in the back booth. She glanced over and was startled to see Black. Even in the dimness he was instantly recognizable. The other man looked like Mike Crisp. Both were big men, but Mike was burly and broad and rough-hewn, whereas Black was sculpted, lean and measured. She hadn't seen Black since the summer four years ago. For a split second her mind played back the picture of Black stripping off his jeans beside the pond. *Stop it, Lilibet. Think of the pile of unfilled Hutton orders instead.* But her hand shook as she picked up the glass of water Gloria had left with her.

Mike was an independent trucker who lived with his common-law wife in a house trailer on the edge of town, his semi parked in the front yard. A lusty, earthy man, he loved beer, women, and baseball, in that order. Lilibet had met him at Ruby's

Strange, the two of them together, thought Lilibet.

She knew the moment Black spotted her. He sat straighter, and his eyes gleamed through the dimness. Can he see through the dark? Probably . . . he can do everything else an animal can, she thought angrily. Why am I angry? She squirmed on her seat, confused at this disruption of her normally well-organized thought processes.

They paid their bill and got up to leave. They shook hands and walked toward her, Black leading the way. He was wearing his favorite worn jeans and white cotton knit shirt. They stopped as they reached her booth.

"What a nice surprise, Lilibet. It's been a long time."

"Hello, Black. Hi, Mike."

"Well, hey there Lilibet!" Mike roared. Mike never spoke, he roared. "Where the hell's Cle? Hell, I never seen you without him."

"He's in Paris. I just talked with him."

"Clarice with him?"

"Yes."

"Next time you talk to them, tell Clarice Mike said 'hello.' "

"Sure."

Gloria brought Lilibet's chili and, giving Mike an arch look, rubbed her thigh casually against his. As she turned to walk away, he gave her jiggling rear end a quick squeeze with his huge hand and she giggled.

"See you later, Mr. Brady," said Mike.

"Right, Mike . . . I'm Black, not Mr. Brady."

Mike gave him a friendly punch on the shoulder and left.

Black looked down at Lilibet.

"Your chili is getting cold," he said. "May I join you? I could use another cup of coffee."

"Yes, of course." How could she say no?

For a second they stared at each other, remembering the last time they had been together, and the devastating kiss they had shared. Embarrassed, her throat went dry and the rhythm of her heartbeat thudded loudly in her ears.

Lilibet was relieved when Gloria brought Black's coffee. He sat quietly and drank the steaming liquid, studying her as she self-consciously ate the chili.

"Good?" he asked, finally.

"Yes, but I'm beginning to wish I'd had ice cream instead. Ice cream in the summer, chili in the winter. For some reason, I had an urge for chili in the middle of June." She gave a little laugh. "But it does taste delicious."

"Maybe something else brought you here," he said, looking at her strangely.

"What would that be? Spirits?" she asked jokingly.

"Yes. Probably your guardian angel."

"Do you believe in guardian angels?" she asked nervously, not wanting to indulge in a personal conversation with Black but unable to help herself.

"Yes," he said. His green eyes reflected the flickering candlelight, and a tiny, delicious shiver ran down her spine.

She moved her bowl away and leaned over to whisper, "Don't tell anyone, but so do I."

She smiled and he laughed, taking her hand in his.

"Thought maybe you did," he whispered back.

It seemed natural for her hand to be in his. He raised it to his lips and kissed it.

A jolt of pure pleasure hit her. Frightened at the ferociousness of the feeling, she tried to pull her hand away, but he held it firmly. His eyes locked with hers and she couldn't look away. She wanted to swim right into the greenness of Black's eyes. Get caught up, swallowed, immersed in their mystery and their strength. The sensation was overpowering. He held her eyes with his as he turned her hand over and softly kissed the palm. The jolt of lightning hit her again, but this time when she jerked her hand he let it go.

"That's why your guardian angel brought you here tonight, Elizabeth," he murmured quietly.

Gloria's voice broke the spell he'd woven. "How about another cup of java?"

"Lilibet?" Black questioned with a raise of his eyebrows.

"Well, I . . ."

"Two coffees, Gloria," he said, ordering for her.

Stunned by the feelings she'd experienced in the last few moments, Lilibet sat very still.

"You've grown up, Lilibet. Even more beautiful than you were before."

"Thank you, Black, but I expect you're just seeing the effect of my wonderful Miss Mabel's tutelage, new clothes, and such."

"No, you'd be beautiful in rags, but tell me about Miss Mabel."

Happy his attention was diverted for a moment, she said, "I miss Miss Mabel every day. Aside from Uncle East, she is my favorite person in the whole world. She's great to talk to . . . teaches philosophy at the university, and it seems she knows everyone. Her house is always filled with interesting people from all over the world. I met the King of Denmark, a prince from Egypt, and our very own President of the United States came and spent an entire afternoon with her."

He smiled at her enthusiasm, but said nothing.

She rushed on, wanting to fill the pregnant silence as he continued to watch her intently. "The last two summers, she hired me as her assistant, taking notes and doing research, and took me with her when she traveled to New York, San Francisco, and even to London for a week. I loved it. We visited museums, and art galleries, and fine restaurants, and . . ." She stopped, suddenly angry with Black's scrutiny.

"Why are you staring at me, Black?"

"Why didn't you answer my letters, or return my phone calls?"

"Because I was busy, because I'm practically engaged to Cle, because . . . because there is no room in my life for you, Black! I'm going to law school! You may have graduated from Yale but I see little improvement in your . . . in your . . . I mean, what are you doing hanging out with Mike Crisp, for heaven's sakes? It's typical of you—like running around the mountains wild."

A brief, wry smile turned up the corners of his sensual mouth, and her heart jumped again.

"Yes, that's a part of me—always will be. Is that the only way you think of me, Lilibet. running around the mountains dressed like a Shawnee? You love the mountains as much as I do."

It was her turn to be silent. She was embarrassed at her attack on him.

"If you must know, I graduated cum laude," continued Black, with no hint of self-importance, simply stating a fact. "I've come back to the valley for . . . two reasons. Mike Crisp is my first employee in an electronics company I'm starting in Matterhorn."

"You're going to be a businessman? Here in the valley? I had no idea you were even interested in such things, Black."

He laughed. "Neither did I. I took a class in Investments in my junior year and, much to my amazement, found I had a knack for the stock market, buying at the right time, and all that. I also became interested in the budding electronics industry, and began to toy with the notion of bringing a manufacturing company here. The people here need to be able to make a living at something other than the mines."

"That's wonderful, Black." Briefly, she wondered what had happened to his dream of the air force and flying. "What will you be manufacturing?"

"Television components. Anything to do with making television sets. It's a natural, Lilibet. Especially for this area. I can't believe no one has done it yet. In twenty years there will be a television set in every house in the nation. The people here need work. Steady work. This will give them and their children plenty of opportunity to make a good living."

"But what about transportation of supplies and product in and out of the valley?"

Black let out the breath he'd been holding. He'd made a mistake when he'd kissed her hand earlier. He knew she'd been ready to bolt from the booth, but now her innate curiosity had her captivated with his plans. For a moment, she'd forgotten her nervousness. She'd caught his excitement and her quick mind was already searching for problems and solutions.

"The biggest problem I've had is in getting organized. Ample rail lines are already in place, of course. The hang-up is air and truck service. In Korea they learned the value of helicopters in mountainous areas. Until I can afford anything so extravagant, I will use trucks, which is where Mike Crisp comes in. He's a crude, rough sort of guy but he gives all of himself to a job, and everyone I talk to says he's always on time, works late if necessary."

Black talked on, knowing she needed time to sort out her thoughts, to adjust her old impressions of the young savage she thought she knew. Bubbling red and blue lights from the jukebox skipped on and off the brightness of her hair, but he couldn't see her eyes. When he'd let go of her hand, she'd drawn away from him into the shadows.

"I don't care where a man comes from, or how he looks or talks. If he works hard and likes his work, I like him. There's one more important thing about Mike." He paused. "He's the only trucker in the valley who's not in Pappy Hutton's pocket."

"Is Pappy giving you trouble?"

"He's thrown every roadblock he can. No one will rent

a building to me, so I have to build my own factory. When I try to hire carpenters, brickmasons, or electricians, they're always tied up for some mysterious reason. Some are honest enough to come right out and tell me that Pappy's threatened to shut them down if they do any work for me."

She moved forward into the light, her voice concerned. "I'm sorry, Black. Maybe I can help."

"You will not," he said, trying to keep the hardness out of his voice. "I don't want your help or anyone else's. I'll do it on my own. Stay away from it, Lilibet!"

She brushed a lock of hair from her forehead and he saw a nasty purple swelling. His hand reached automatically across the table to caress it, and she tried to draw away, but he caught her by the chin and held her face so he could see the violet of her eyes.

"Let go of me, Black," she whispered faintly, and his heart caught at the softness of her tone, the vulnerability she tried to hide.

"Why?" he whispered back. "Does my touch bother you?"

"Yes . . . no, of course not."

"Well, well, well," a snide voice intruded, and Lilibet jumped, startled out of the magic Black was creating with his fingers. Tom Tee stood behind Black, casually resting his arms on the back of the booth.

"Tom Tee!"

"Yes, it's me, Lilibet. The one and only Tom Tee. One of Cle's best friends," he smirked. "Isn't he going to be interested in this little assignation with Black Brady? Late on a Friday night no less. You can believe I'm going to be the first one to tell him. In fact, I might just shoot off a lil' ol' postcard to the south of France today."

"Why don't you go home, Tom Tee?" Lilibet asked.

"And miss all this fun? Hell no. I haven't had a chance to speak to you since you got home. I've seen you cruising around in Cle's Cadillac. Must be nice."

Wanting to forestall the storm she saw brewing on Black's face, she forced herself to be polite.

"Yes, well, I needed a way to get Margot and me to work."

Black sat silent during this exchange. He couldn't see Tom Tee, but his insinuating voice came directly across the top of Black's head. His inclination was to shut him up, to turn around and crumple Tom Tee's moon face with one crushing squeeze of his hand. But he'd learned long ago that violence served little purpose, so he kept his feelings and his inclination to himself.

"Yeh, gotta get to work, don't you? Especially since you got an important promotion. Shit, I should have married Clarice. It pays to fuck a Hutton."

With that, Black turned, his arm flashing upward. He grasped Tom Tee by the jaws, and rising swiftly from the booth, jerked Tom Tee toward him. His fingers closed in a ferocious grip and Lilibet, with a sick turn of her stomach, heard a bone crack in Tom Tee's jaw.

Tom Tee couldn't utter a sound, but the pain in his eyes hurt Lilibet, too.

"No, Black, don't!"

He ignored her and increased his pressure on Tom Tee's jaw. Another snap of bone could be heard clearly in the silence, as the jukebox quietly changed records. Tony and Gloria stood in frozen horror, Gloria with her hand to her mouth as if to stifle a scream.

His face implacable, Black said in a cool, emotionless voice, "I've broken two small bones in your jaw near your ear, Mr. Frye. I can't recall their names right now, but your dentist will know. You will probably have your jaws wired together for a while, which couldn't please me more. Send the bill to me. Should you ever be so foolish as to say anything like that to Lilibet again, I'll make sure you speak with a lisp for the rest of your life."

Through the pain, Tom Tee knew with incredulous certainty that Black meant every word he said.

Black released Tom Tee, who backed away from the booth, gingerly holding his jaw. Tears running down his face, he stumbled backward in disbelief, finally bumping into Carpozzoli's plate glass window. He slid slowly down its smudged perpendicular surface until he sat, dumbfounded, on the floor.

Black turned to speak to Tony, who walked cautiously toward them. "I'm sorry, Mr. Carpozzoli, if I've caused a disturbance here. Mr. Frye needs a dentist, but he will be just fine. I've already paid Lilibet's check, so we'll be leaving."

He grabbed a stunned Lilibet's wrist, pulling her from the booth and out the door.

"Why, you, you . . ." she sputtered. "How could you do something like that? You're still an uncivilized savage—and dammit, I could have paid my own check! That's the second time today someone has paid my bill."

He ignored her comments and took her by the elbow to nudge her down the street. "I'll walk you to your car. It's almost midnight and the street is getting rough."

They walked in strained silence toward the Hutton office parking lot.

Black tried desperately to keep his hold on Lilibet's elbow loose but reassuring. The residual violence he felt kept his free hand gripped into a painful fist. His primal urge to protect Lilibet, and to make Tom Tee suffer for insulting her, shocked him. He'd thought his years at Yale and his summer travels had leeched some of the wildness from him. Evidently, he had more to learn.

"I'm sorry, Lilibet. The evening has ended badly. Certainly not the way I intended."

An odd sound came from her. He looked down to see her body shaking. Was she crying? He took her other arm and turned her to him so he could get a good look at her. She was laughing.

"Oh, God, Black, what you did was absolutely atrocious, but I've been wanting to hit Tom Tee for as long as I can remember. I loved the look of disbelief on his face."

"I don't like what I did, Lilibet, but he deserved it."

They both felt the almost undeniable urge to put their arms about each other right there on Main Street.

This is crazy, thought Lilibet. *First he breaks Tom Tee's jaw, and now I want him to kiss me?* She broke away from him and hurried down the street.

He caught up with her.

"Have you been to see Grandfather yet?"

"I'd hoped to go next weekend."

:"Great. I'm going rafting, and leaving from Grandfather's. Go with me."

"I can't, Black."

"Have you ever been whitewater rafting?"

"No."

"Then come with me. You'll love it. I won't take no for an answer. I want to make up for this evening."

"Well, I . . ."

They had reached her car. They stood under a street light, and he watched her struggle with uncertainty as he opened the car door for her.

"Good! I'll see you next weekend at Grandfather's. Don't forget to bring a sleeping bag. I'll bring everything else."

"Sleeping bag? I don't have one, and I can't go on an overnight trip. What would everyone think?"

"No one has to know, and you can use my mother's sleeping bag. Not afraid, are you?"

"No! Absolutely not!"

He shut the door and reached through the open window to take her chin in his hand and tilt her face up so he could see her eyes.

"The river and I are waiting. Next Friday afternoon, Lilibet."

Before she had a chance to protest again, he walked swiftly away into the dark.

In spite of the warm air coming through the window, she shivered. What was she getting herself into?

From a gleaming expanse of window on the top floor of the Hutton Building a slim, elegant figure watched with keen interest as Black walked away from the circle of light and Lilibet drove off toward Big Ugly Creek. He removed his gold watch from its pocket on his vest and wound it slowly and methodically, his eyes narrowing shrewdly.

Chapter 11

Leery of Eugene and the MacDonald brothers searching for her if they knew she was camping on Catawba Mountain somewhere, Lilibet swore Marm to secrecy. Unable to bring herself to lie to Marm, she'd told her of the overnight rafting trip with Black. Marm, who thought Lilibet worked too hard anyway, was happy with the news and more concerned with the safety of the trip than the morality of an overnight stay. Marm's trust in her didn't make Lilibet feel better about lying to everyone else. The family thought Lilibet was visiting a friend in Charleston for the weekend, as did Anna Adkins, because Lilibet had to ask for the afternoon off.

She knew she shouldn't have come, but the mountain had drawn her. Honesty made her admit that the temptation of Black's company was even more potent. She was afraid of him and all he represented, but she needed to confront those fears and was curious about what would happen when she did face them.

Unaccustomed to the guilt she felt at asking Marm to lie for her, Lilibet had been unhappy the entire afternoon. Her time with Uncle East was marred because she was a bit worried about what lay ahead.

Uncle East, aware of her discomfort, had drawn her out, wanting to know of the courses she'd most enjoyed in college, and about the trips she'd taken with Miss Mabel. She'd gradually relaxed and animatedly told him of the trip she and Miss Mabel had taken this past year to San Francisco. But as the time for Black's arrival drew closer, her worries returned. Should she be going with him? What if Cle found out? What difference did that make? Black was just a friend . . . but an exciting one. If

Cle really knew Black, he would like him. Then, forgetting about Cle, she worried about being a hindrance to Black. She didn't know much about rafting, but she knew one must be quick and alert. Rafting demanded implicit trust of one's partners.

When Black arrived, eager and ready to leave immediately, she forced her unspoken worries to the back of her mind.

Uncle East accompanied them to their point of departure: a rugged, rockstrewn beach on a flat section of No Name River in the highest reaches of the mountain. Black poled the sturdy rubber raft out onto the silent river, and Uncle East waved goodbye to them. As she waved in return, the guilt and worry left her. The clean, cool, pine-scented air; the sparkling, clear water beneath them, and the strong, sure presence of Black as he stood in the prow of the boat looking remarkably like one of his noble Shawnee forefathers, all seemed awfully right to her.

He turned to give her a reassuring smile, and the sparkle in his eyes reminded her he also had a lot of Irish mischief in him. Openly elated at being away from the valley, his usually stern face was an expression of contentment.

"Well, Mountain Sprite, are you ready for your first lesson in rafting?"

"Yes, Captain." She gave him a mock salute.

He handed her a short paddle and sat down beside her.

"When I'm by myself on the river, I use a single-man kayak that belonged to Grandfather Black Eagle. This raft is for two people but on occasion, just for fun, I have handled it alone. We need only one paddle at the moment, and while we're on calm water you should learn how to use it."

For a second she knew an unfamiliar twinge of jealousy at the thought of Black sharing the raft and river with someone else, but she had no time for speculation. His firm hand on hers, he gave her instructions in how to hold the paddle, how deep to immerse it, and how to affect the direction of the boat. She caught on quickly and he decided to let her take them down the first stretch of river by herself.

Black lay back, his arms folded behind his head, his wide-brimmed hat tilted over his eyes, hiding the rapt interest they held as he watched her.

As they traveled along, the narrow canyon walls became higher and more sheer. The mountains of the West were breathtaking in their grandeur, but these mountains, in the southeastern United States, were awesome in their eternal strength and determined wildness. They dared you to conquer them. Men took minerals from their bowels and scarred their surfaces with tracks and machines, but when man was gone, the mountain would endure.

Tiny puffs of lazy white clouds floated aimlessly above them while the river moved swifter and louder. The silent river began to make ripping sounds and then to rumble.

It was talking to Lilibet; she knew it was daring her, telling her she couldn't tame it.

"Oh yes, I can," she muttered. "Give me a chance."

So absorbed was she in her task of subduing the now restless river, she'd reverted to her old habit of talking to herself. Forgotten were Black and Cle and the valley. Only she and the rumbling river existed. She could feel the sun beating on her face, and the gentle wind whispering in her ears. The smooth wooden paddle she used to control the river and its challenge. was warm to the touch, and as she dug it into the churning waves, she sensed the river laughing. *Cease and desist, Lilibet. I am too much for you.*

"No. No, you aren't," she hissed. "I can do this."

Black watched and heard. He knew she was talking to the river. A knowing smile curved his mouth. He had done the same thing many times. He also knew exactly where they were and when he should take control of the boat himself. They were in no danger at the moment. He loved the way she threw her lower lip out as she grew more determined. Splashing water plastered her chambray shirt to her breasts. She'd lost her canvas hat and her silvery-gold hair flew wildly about her intense face, her cheeks pink from the last hour in the sun. She was unaware of her wet shirt or the loss of her hat.

As he feasted his eyes with the delight of her, he recalled his conversation with Grandfather early this morning.

Breaking Tom Tee's jaw had been cruel, and he'd needed Grandfather's counsel. Grandfather's words still rang in his ears.

"Accomplishment comes easy to you, Black, because you learned early to expect the utmost of your mind and body. It's second nature to you now. That's why you chase after new challenges. You need the edge of daring new elements, of conquering."

"But I don't want to conquer Lilibet, Grandfather."

"I know you don't—she's unconquerable anyway. But you've never wanted anything as much as you want Elizabeth. Problem is, you can't wade in and take her as your Shawnee forefathers took their women. In the meantime, you're like a tiger protecting his tigress. Any threat to her calls up your protective instincts."

"Yes, I'd already recognized that ... but I can't go around breaking jaws when someone insults her."

"Humph. Sounds like Mr. Frye deserved to have his jaw broken, but, no, you can't continue such behavior. You are encountering the strongest emotion you will ever have to deal with—love. Do you love her, Black?"

"Yes. More every time I'm with her, and I think she loves me, too. I don't understand her refusal to recognize it."

"Elizabeth has set a course for herself, a course she thinks will solve her problems, give her the safety and security she craves for herself and her family. You don't factor in. Be patient, Black. Remember the power and strength that lie in control and patience. You'll have to sublimate your desires, Black. Bring peace to your heart and soul."

He'd spent the rest of the morning on Christmas Ridge meditating and had regained his perspective. Now, seeing her struggle with the rigors of the river, his love for her gained even broader dimensions, and he knew the control of his heart and emotions would require eternal vigilance ... until the time was right.

He sighed with regret. He could spend forever watching her but it was time for him to take charge. The boat was beginning to buck and jump. He lifted the brim of his

hat, replaced it squarely on his head, then moved forward
to retrieve the paddle from her.

"Lilibet, time for you to rest a while," he said as he
reached for the paddle.

She turned to him, startled, and kept a tight grip on the
paddle.

"No. Not yet. I'm not tired."

"I know, but I'll need your help later, so let me take
over while you rest."

Reluctantly, she relinquished the paddle. Following his
instructions, she crept cautiously to her seat.

Black glanced at the sky. The sun was still high but
dusk came quickly in the mountains and they'd started
late. He figured they had another hour before they
stopped for the night.

Lilibet watched as he reached down into the water, and
then tossed a handful on the back of his neck.

"What are you doing, Black?"

"The river takes care of those who respect it. It's a way
of acclimating yourself to the water temperature. Puts you
in harmony with the river gods."

Shivering with cold, Lilibet now realized her shirt was
soaked. She wasn't surprised at the coldness, for she
knew it came from icy springs and snow beds that lay all
year long in shaded crevices high in the mountain peaks.
In summer it rushed pell mell down to the river, never
stopping to warm up. She ignored the shirt and the cold
as her fascination with Black and the river gorge grew.
They'd hit the first of the white water and the river's din
hissed loudly. The vertical walls of the gorge continued to
rise in a solid copper-colored mass, buttressing them on
both sides.

As entranced as she was by the wild beauty of the
gorge, her eyes were drawn again and again to Black. He
still stood, though the raft was rolling like a roller coaster.
His long legs braced firmly against the rubber sides, he
rowed instinctively and gracefully with the raft. He'd
removed his shirt. As he paddled, muscles worked
smoothly on the insides of his arms. His tanned chest and
broad shoulders etched a chiseled contour against the
rugged horizon. She remembered the time in the glen just

before they'd gone off to college. How warm and smooth his skin had been to her touch, and how she'd wanted to run her fingers through the light matting of black hair that formed a diamond from his rib cage to his collarbone. Feeling her cold cheeks warm at the thought, she shook her head to clear it of dangerous images.

She thought he'd forgotten her, but he turned to give her a quick smile. The look of happy anticipation in his eyes told her of his love of the challenge to come. She'd never met anyone with such vast self-confidence. He was in his element, testing himself against Nature's might. It was, she realized suddenly, a contest of equals.

The blue water had turned to silver and was getting rougher. She tightened her hold on the rope handle at her side and turned her attention to the white-churning channel in front of them. She loved the rush of the water and the uncertainty of what was to come next.

The rapids were increasing in size. Large boulders and rocks were turning their uneventful journey into a bumping, twisting adventure. Two large boulders loomed ahead of them. Black deftly maneuvered the raft between them but a whirlpool at the end of the eddy caught them and whirled the raft around and around. Her head dizzy, she heard Black laugh. Finally, it tossed them out onto calmer water and she sighed with relief.

Over the roar of the water she heard Black's voice.

"We'll stop soon," he yelled.

"Okay," she yelled back.

An hour later, dusk had fallen and they were settled in a deep, tree-filled cove near the river.

Lilibet gathered firewood while Black secured their raft and supplies. Too proud to ask for help, she struggled with building the fire as he fished for trout for dinner. Years ago, when Uncle East had taken her to the river for swimming lessons, he'd taught her how to build a fire. But there had only been three or four of those trips, and her memory had dimmed. Eventually, though, she got the knack of it and had a roaring fire going by the time Black arrived with two large red-speckled trout.

Amazed at the bonfire blazing before him, Black started laughing.

"What are you laughing at?"

"Do you think your fire is big enough?"

"What's the matter with my fire?" she asked belligerently, her fists on her hips.

Four years of college and Miss Mabel's polish gone, she looked like the enchanted waif he'd first encountered on the path fighting off the MacDonald brothers.

"It's so . . . big." he got out, convulsed with laughter.

"So, isn't it supposed to be? How are we going to keep warm without a big fire?"

"Well, it's fine for a pep rally . . . or if we were cooking an ox." He struggled to control his laughter. "But we're cooking trout and . . ."

Seeing the stricken look of embarrassment on her face, he took a big stride to where she stood and hugged her to him. "Sorry, you did a great job."

She shoved him away from her.

"Darn right, I did. "Then, pausing she looked around her. "Uh . . . how do we make it smaller so we can cook? I'm starved."

Black tamed the fire with dirt and wet leaves, and soon had the trout cooking on a hot bed of coals. They ate the delicious feast with their fingers, pulling the tender, moist meat apart easily. Their dessert was plump, juicy huckleberries from the woods just behind them. Licking all the purple juice off their fingers was the best part.

Black watched as she sucked her fingers free of huckleberries. A smear of charcoal from her fire-building smudged her forehead and purple berry stain circled her lips. Her wet hair had dried in a crazy circular shape, half plastered to her face, half swept behind her ear. He smothered his desire to laugh again. He wanted desperately to take her into his arms and kiss away the smudge and the stain. He ached to feel her hair in his hands as he mussed it even more.

Unaware of his eyes on her, Lilibet gazed into the fire.

In a very small voice, she said, "Black, do you know that, except for one other person, we are the only people who have ever been in this cove?"

"Grandfather has been here with me."

"Yes, and he's the only other person besides ourselves who has ever, in all the eons of time, been here."

"I've sensed that before, but how do you know, Lilibet?"

"I just know, Black. I have what Marm calls the 'knowing'. Mostly I try to ignore it and not listen to it, but sometimes it calls to me so strongly that I can't ignore it anymore. I knew the minute I stepped ashore here. How glorious the whole mountain must have been a hundred years ago," she said, happy that she'd confided in Black, and he'd accepted her "knowing" without question.

A wistful note crept into her voice as she contemplated the flickering flames. "I'd love to go back for just a day to know how it was hundreds of years ago."

So, in the ebony night with only the small fire for light, with the wood smoke drifting above their heads, the scent of evergreen filling the air, and the gurgle of the silver river rippling close by, Black told her what Grandfather Black Eagle had told him.

He told her of wild headwaters, of great clear, clean rivers leaping down precipices and scurrying through the dark gulches of Allegheny wilderness. He told her of great oaks, white pine, and the majestic chestnut, and forests so densely timbered they were dark at midday. He told her of sparkling mineral springs from which all could drink without fear of poisoning, and the abundance of game caught fairly and squarely only for food. The southern Indian had understood the ecosystem's delicate balance, changing the environment when necessary to suit their needs, but living within its bounds more fully than most civilizations in history. But others had come after them. The black bear, wolf, cougar, and wild turkey were now almost nonexistent. The white-tailed deer, once the prey of the bear and cougar, was now the only animal surviving in abundance.

She could hear the regret in his voice as he told her how the white settler had conquered the pristine wildness. Innocently, he had forced the land to serve him, but had destroyed it for future generations of man and nature. His powerful locomotives came screaming up the valleys. Soon the narrow gauge railroad crept up the hills, its branches reaching into gorges to bring out the hardwood until there was none left. Great trees were left rotting on ridges and the hills began to erode. And there was a treasure yet undiscovered. Coal. With industrial might demanding more fuel, the coal mines were soon in full operation, and the mountains were gutted of another mother lode. With coal dust and sawdust in their streams, the trout began to die. Food was now easily accessible from grocery stores, but the hunting of game continued for sport instead of survival. Unable to quench his caveman instincts, a hunter's trophy on the wall seemed more important than living in harmony with all living things.

"Ravaged," Black concluded angrily. "They ravaged these hills and the money-men left without a care, their leavings a poor substitute for what they took."

"Don't be bitter, Black. There was a need for most of what they took. Civilization was growing and most of them didn't realize the damage they were inflicting."

"They should have taken the time to care, to look, to think before they raped the very land that succors them," he said, still angry.

Not wanting the magic of the night to be broken, and hating the fierce look on his face, she reached to comfort him. She touched his arm and patted it. "It's okay, Black. Man and nature have to learn to live together. We've just been slow learning."

He covered the small hand on his arm with his hand and looked into her face. The anger had been replaced by amusement and he grinned, his white teeth gleaming in the darkness.

"What's so funny now? I seem to be a continual source of amusement for you," she said, annoyed.

"Wait right here, urchin. I'll be right back."

He returned shortly, bare-chested with his shirt rolled up wet in his hands, and knelt beside her.

"Hold still while I clean up the damage you've done to your face."

"What are you talking about?"

He grasped her chin in one hand and rubbed at the smear on her forehead.

"Let's just be thankful that ten years from now, when you're trying a case before the Supreme Court, the eminent justices will have no idea about the dirty mug you once sported on top of a mountain in West Virginia."

Silenced by his words, she let him minister to the rest of her face. Then, tentatively, she said, "Do you really think so, Black? Most of my friends at the university were studying to be teachers, nurses, or secretaries. Even the dean at the law school tried to talk me out of entering. But he couldn't say much because I made the highest scores on my entrance exam. I wonder if a woman has ever . . . Do you really think I'll be arguing a case before the Supreme Court one day?"

"If that's what you want, 'Miss Lawyer to-be.' "

He'd reached the huckleberry stain around her mouth and she talked as he cleaned. "I don't know if I'll ever be such a good lawyer, but it's nice to dream. There's so much to do and see and be, isn't there, Black?"

"Will you shut up so I can get the last of this purple off your mouth?"

She laughed and puckered up her lips to make it even more difficult for him. Black caught his breath. As he'd progressed from her forehead to her mouth, he'd realized this was a dangerous undertaking. He should never have gotten this close to her. Every movement of her eyelids, the flush of her cheeks, the softness of her lips were a burning temptation. He dropped a swift kiss on her puckered mouth and she gasped.

"Kiss me again, Black," she whispered.

"No."

He placed his hands on either side of her head and combed his fingers through her damp, matted hair. He rubbed at it until it stood out dry with electricity. Just the way he was feeling, he thought. She hadn't taken her eyes off his face.

He stopped rubbing and they stared at each other.

"Sorry, I shouldn't have asked you to kiss me again, but I've never forgotten the kiss in the glen, Black," she said softly. "Uncle East says I'm curious. I suppose I wanted to see if it was what I remembered."

"You were supposed to remember it."

"I didn't need another kiss to remind me—one was enough. I was afraid to come on this trip because ..." She was too embarrassed to finish.

"Because of this," he said, and leaned down to kiss the tiny mole near the corner of her mouth.

From the thick forest surrounding them came a deep, booming *whoo-hoo-hoo*. Unhappily distracted, Lilibet shuddered and looked around her apprehensively.

"What was that?"

He smiled and sat down on the ground. Legs crossed, he lifted her easily onto his lap.

"That was the great horned owl. He's harmless, and he'll watch over us tonight. Black Eagle said owls are wise because they are awake at night to monitor our dreams, the dreams that come from the soul center of us. During the day they sleep while we run about in a frenzy of unreality, trying to achieve unimportant things."

Whoo-hoo-hoo.

"You're sure about that?" she asked.

He answered her with a kiss. His tongue worked wondrous magic between the parted fold of her lips and she opened them even more. He ached to absorb all of her, to lick every delicious inch of her, to awaken every nerve in her exquisite body, to take the parted lips and make them hot and full with desire. Desire for him. But he held back, knowing the beauty of control and the exquisite torture of foreplay. He wanted only to give her pleasure.

He brushed the hair away from her neck and kissed the sensitive skin beneath her ear. A small moan escaped her and he stiffened. He wanted desperately to please her, but he knew it wasn't safe to continue. Willing away his hardness, he stopped kissing her, took a deep breath, and drew her to him in a big bear hug.

"Is that why you were afraid to come with me, Elizabeth?" he whispered hoarsely in her ear.

"Yes," she whispered back.

"Are you still afraid?"

"No ... I don't know ... yes."

He laughed softly. "You should be. Don't test your curiosity on me again. Remember what curiosity killed." He sighed deeply and stood up with her in his arms. "It's time for sleep. We'll be up early in the morning. There's a lot of river to cover."

He set her on her feet but she stumbled weakly against him. He held her by the shoulders and looked into her eyes, all business again. "You okay?"

"Yes," she muttered.

But she wasn't. She knew Black had been the wiser one. It would have been folly to continue with the kissing. Just exactly what she'd been afraid of . . . the ignition of those feelings she had every time he looked at her. She had felt so right in his arms. She wanted to be held again, feeling the knitting of the muscles beneath his bare skin, the moist, sleek, damask-fine feel of his warm chest against her cheek.

He was showing her how to arrange her bedroll.

"What did you say?"

"I said, we'll put it here on the soft moss beneath this big oak."

"Why can't we sleep near the fire?"

"We have to tamp the fire to small embers. It's too dangerous, Lilibet, even in wet summers. You'll be warm enough. Trust me."

"Where will you be?"

"I won't be far away."

"Sleep next to me, please."

He hesitated a fraction, then agreed.

Feeling safe now, Lilibet snuggled deep into the down-filled sleeping bag. The dark night held no fears for her. She could feel the welcome of the mountain and the comforting presence of Black. She was just Lilibet here—no one's daughter, no one's sister, no one's employee, no one's girlfriend. She drew a deep breath of satisfaction and scrunched even deeper into the sleeping bag. It smelled like Miss Mabel. Then she identified the expensive fragrance. Chanel No. Five. Black's mother must wear it too. She smiled happily to herself and went to sleep.

* * *

She woke up to the smell of boiled coffee and fried trout. Ravenous with hunger, Lilibet inched her way up to the opening of the sleeping bag and stuck her nose out to sniff. Delicious. As she worked her way up further, cold air hit her face and she retreated back in her shell a notch. The growling of her stomach made her brave so she quickly poked her head through the opening and opened her eyes.

A downy white fog filled the clearing. It muted everything, making their camp quiet and mysterious. She searched for Black and made out his form near the fire, watching fondly as he prepared breakfast. Even through the haze of fog, the smooth efficiency of his movement fascinated her. He was so sure of himself. No time or energy was wasted. He wore a heavy cable-knit navy sweater over his jeans.

"I know you're awake, lazy-bones," he called without turning around. "Time to get a move on."

"Do I have to? It looks cold out there, and it's so warm in here."

He turned to stride toward her with something slung over one shoulder. He stood over her, hands stuck in his pockets, and looked grumpily down at her.

"If you want breakfast, you'd better climb out of there and put this on."

He gave her the extra sweater on his shoulder. It was identical to the one he wore, except hers was dark green.

For a second she was tempted to make him pull her out of the bag, but thought better of it when she saw the look on his face. The green eyes held no amusement this morning, no teasing, no sense of play as they had last night. He was serious.

"All right," she returned testily, unhappy that he'd spoiled the mystery of the fog-shrouded dawn.

Later, as they ate, he told her what to expect for the rest of the day.

"There's been a turn in the weather, Lilibet. The front that wasn't supposed to arrive until tomorrow has moved in sooner. Nothing serious. It will be colder than I'd expected and the river will be rougher in places. Nothing to worry about as long as you obey me implicitly. I know

you learned a lot from Grandfather about nature and survival, but nothing has prepared you for mean water. This
won't be the ordinary rafting trip I'd planned."

"Is that why you're so serious this morning, Black?"

"Among other things, yes," he said, not mentioning the
restless night he'd spent sleeping close to her.

"I can do anything you can do, Black. You don't have
to worry about me."

He raised a sardonic eyebrow but said nothing. He
reached into his supply pack and brought forth an ugly
rubber thing with legs.

"Good grannie! What is that?"

"A wet suit. Ordinarily, you wouldn't need it, but the
water will be cold today and you never know when we'll
take a dunking."

She whooped with laughter, but when she saw the
frown on his face, she put her hand over her mouth to
muffle the sound.

"If you think I'm going to wear that, you're crazy. It
looks like my Grandfather Springer's long underwear,
only it's black instead of red."

"I don't care what it looks like—you're wearing it."

"I am not!"

"You are so."

"Are you wearing one?"

"No."

"Why?"

"Because I'm used to the water. Go behind the big oak
tree and put this on."

"No! If you aren't wearing one, neither will I."

He stood up to tower over her.

"On your feet, Lilibet," he ordered.

She stood and stared defiantly up at him.

"If you don't put this on, I'll take off your clothes and
put it on you myself." he said in a steely voice.

She glared into his green eyes, hard with purpose, and
she knew he meant every word. Defeated, she tore the
suit from his hands and stomped to the oak tree.

"And put the sweater on over it," he called after her.
"You'll need it for a while."

While Lilibet struggled into the offending rubber object, Black struck camp.

Shortly after, they moved out and were back on the river.

The first hour of the trip was relatively calm, but Lilibet began to understand Black's concern. He'd explained that although he knew the river well, it would be his first time over it this summer. It was impossible to tell the size of the rapids until you were upon them, and they changed from day to day or week to week. The size of the rapids depended on the amount of water released this past spring from the dark crevices high in the peaks. Had the cold front not come in, the water would have been calmer, warmer, and easier to predict. Instead, they wouldn't know what to expect. She moved about in the raft, paddling where he needed her.

Ice cold water sprayed incessantly over her and she was grateful for the sweater.

She hadn't much time to observe Black but she did notice as the water got rougher and the challenge greater, the smile on his face grew broader. She understood for she felt the same rush of adrenaline as the river roared in her ears and the swirling rapids tossed them about higher and higher. She wouldn't have missed this for the world. Her arms grew tired from the constant paddling, but her excitement was so great that soon she'd passed the threshold of tiredness.

By midmorning, she'd shed her sweater. It was heavy with water and more an encumbrance than a comfort. She began to appreciate the warmth of the repulsive wet suit.

As the river grew rowdier her strength grew to the challenge. They broke through the first big rock barrier and the raft dropped into a huge trench with boulders erupting all around them.

"Hold tight," yelled Black.

Her stomach fell to her toes as the raft was flung on its side and she faced a wall of water that looked like concrete—which is just what it felt like when they hit it. Her head jerked back against the bottom of the raft as it bucked, throwing them back into the rocks again. She wanted to close her eyes but knew she couldn't.

She fought to remember all he'd told her about the paddle and how it could help, and about "high-siding," moving to the left or to the right of the boat to prevent the boat from overturning. Moving to the correct place in the raft became automatic. There was no time to stop and think. Only time for action and razor-sharp reactions.

Over the boom of the water, she heard Black calling to her.

"We're coming into Crooked Elbow. Your paddle will do no good now. Come up here."

Stowing her paddle, she crept cautiously forward.

"I'm using you as ballast," he yelled to her over the increasing din. His face wild with excitement, he showed her how to lean in either direction, left or right. She was to throw her weight into the waves as they came. "But hold tight to the rope or you'll be thrown out."

She nodded. He gave her a blazing smile, deftly dropped a kiss on her lips, surprising her by sucking quickly at her tongue, and then moved to the rear of the raft. The water was rising faster and higher, but Lilibet soon caught the trick of throwing her weight where it was needed.

Black shouted with exuberant joy as they crested a shoot and landed once again in raging water.

They bumped and tore down raging No Name River, and the gorge walls grew higher and higher. Lilibet felt small and insignificant. With a growing sense of vulnerability, she realized they were riding a savage, spasmodic sluiceway with no way out except inexorably onward. They were at the mercy of the river and its caprices.

The roar was deafening. They shot through a sluice, whirled on the edge of a killer drop, and were immediately thrown up against the left wall of the gorge, plastered almost vertically against the smooth rock. Lilibet high-sided and then was thrown to the bottom of the boat.

Black shouted something about "balling" herself up.

The current was relentless in its fierce power. Lilibet no longer had time to think about anything but survival, as the rocks and water tossed the raft at will. Numb with fear, she clung desperately to the rope, her hands raw from the savage back and forth rubbing.

She heard Black yell something . . . something about "boils," and then they were in a maelstrom of water, rocks, and deafening clamor.

The raft was sucked into a deep void and then crashed down between two huge boulders. A wave of churning water flew over the raft and filled it. Then, like a bullet out of a gun, they were shot through a barreled channel of water.

Lilibet caught a blurred glimpse of Black's face. The exuberance was gone, replaced by a look of grim concentration. Through the spray and endless foaming water ahead of them, she thought she saw an abrupt drop and turned to warn him, but it was too late. They fell over the falls, overended, and Lilibet knew only angry, heavy water in her ears, mouth, filling her lungs as she tried desperately to hold onto the rope. It slipped through her fingers and she was free of the raft and on her own in the boils of No Name River.

The river threw her deep against its bottom, and her eyes and hair filled with grit as she scraped along a sandy flat. Oddly, it was calm down here and she tried to swim along the bottom, hoping she could emerge farther downstream in calmer water.

It was impossible.

Caught in a whirlpool, she was twirled and twisted violently back up to the choppy surface. She hadn't time to search for Black and the raft. Choking and coughing, she grasped at an overhanging branch but it broke off and the icy, raging current threw her back out into the middle of the maelstrom. It turned her over and over like a helpless ball. She rolled herself into a fetal position, hoping her body would receive less damage if there was less of it to hit. She'd lost her shoes long ago and every time the current beat her against a rock she could feel parts of the wet suit rip away. *Thank God for the wet suit.* So far it had kept her from freezing to death, and had absorbed most of the damage her skin would have suffered.

Tossed against a boulder, she held her rolled-up position.

Losing consciousness.

Too much water in my lungs. Blacking out. No oxygen.

Thrown against another boulder, an agonizing pain brought her mind back into focus. She fought to the surface. Walls of water tossed her back and forth like a rag doll.

I won't . . . be defeated . . . you can't take me, river. But the darkness was closing in again.

No, not me. It isn't time.

An overwhelming peace filled her, and she slowly ceased her struggles.

Black, fighting against all odds, had known their only chance of survival lay in his staying with the raft. It upended him time and again but he clung to it like a barnacle. Beaten, bruised, and choking, he rode it out, fear pushing up into his throat like it never had before. Fear for Lilibet. Through all the twisting, turning, and battering that he took, he reminded himself of her courage, of her stubbornness, of her will to win. Each time he managed to surface, he searched frantically for her. Once he saw the black of her suit rolling like a ball through a channel of rocks. Good girl! Then he lost sight of her again.

It seemed an eternity before the river showed mercy and began to flatten out. Swimming, he pulled the raft toward a rock outcropping near the shore.

Then he saw her. A heap of limp black rubber and golden hair caught between two rocks in the middle of the river. He would have to release the raft to reach her. Letting go of the rope and swimming against the raging current, he headed toward her, praying all the time. All the years of mental, physical, and spiritual training concentrated within him, focused on reaching Lilibet. His strong limbs seemed as light as feathers, and the air in his lungs as plentiful as the air around him. He didn't feel the freezing water, or the rocks and branches tearing at him. He only saw the golden-haired rag doll ahead of him.

Chapter 12

Lilibet fought upward to the sound of Black's voice. If she swam hard enough she could reach him. Her arms churned wildly. Something caught both her wrists and held tight.

She opened her eyes to see Black staring down at her, vast relief spreading across his wet face.

"Thank God," he muttered.

He kissed the inside of her wrists reverently and placed them gently at her sides.

Dazed, she continued to gaze up at him. She felt grass beneath her and there were leafy tree branches overhead. Where was the water?

"Black?"

"Don't talk. Rest quietly. The river flattened out in time for both of us. We made it to the only accessible wilderness area between our campground last night and the landing we were heading for."

He didn't tell her of the despair he'd felt when he'd reached her limp body, or the brutal half hour he'd spent pulling her through the icy water with his teeth clamped securely to the collar of her wet suit.

When he finally got her ashore, he realized she was breathing, but barely. He carefully examined her cut and bruised body, checking for broken bones. Then he blew life-giving air into her lungs. She was breathing easier now but her usually vibrant face was drained of color. The freezing water had caused hypothermia, which was both good and bad. The reduction of her body temperature had caused her metabolism to slow and that was good. In response, all her bodily functions required less blood and oxygen, at least for the moment. Her pulse was slow and she was shivering. The confusion on her face told him she wasn't alert. To keep her from going into shock or developing pneumonia, he would warm her gradually.

"Black, we're in the glen."

"Yes, darling, we are," he said, humoring her. "Listen to me carefully. I want you to move your fingers and toes for me. No matter how difficult it is, I want you to move them and when you can move them well, I want you to move your hands and feet. I want you to move as much as you can. I have to leave you for a moment to build a fire."

"Yes, of course, I'll do anything you say, but . . . how silly. We don't need a fire in the glen."

With urgent haste, Black searched for dry firewood. He talked to her as he gathered the wood and built the fire.

"Are you wiggling those fingers and toes? Are you moving your hands yet? Talk to me, Elizabeth."

"Trying, Black. Why am I so weak?"

Using a splinter of wood and flint stone, he sparked the fire, coaching it high and hot. Tearing off his wet chamois shirt and denim jeans, he draped them to dry over two large stones he'd rolled near the blaze. He made a bed of supple pine needles and covered them with moss.

He stood over her naked, and she looked up and smiled, the dazed look still in her eyes.

"Black, this really isn't the time to play Indian."

He picked her up, carried her over to the fire, and laid her on the bed of moss.

"Lilibet, I'm going to remove your wet suit."

"But, Black—"

"It's okay. We have to get you warm."

"But, I only have on my undies, and . . ."

"Don't worry about it. I won't look if you won't look," he said with amused irony. She passed out and the forced smile left his face.

He worked her arms out of the rubber suit she hated, and pulled it down to her waist, trying not to stare at her full, creamy breasts. They poked teasingly up through her soaked, white cotton bra. He swallowed hard as he took in the delicate fragility of the rest of her. His hands could easily span her waist. He couldn't help but wonder if her slim form was capable of absorbing the shaft of a large man. When he exposed her panties he saw her curly, pale-golden triangle plastered wetly through the thin cotton material and he forced himself to remember the task at hand. Using his knife, he quickly finished stripping the wet suit from her slim, vulnerable form and laid it aside, then removed her bra and panties and placed them to dry on the hot rock with his clothes. With a deep breath he laid down beside her.

He'd wanted her for so long. At the feel of her body in his arms, the years of mounting desire almost overwhelmed him. She was as he'd imagined—beautiful, fragile, sensual. He took a moment to enjoy the silky impression of her skin against him. Fiercely, he fought his need. Her vulnerability helped him win the struggle. He relaxed.

Hoping she could hear him, he said, "You have to be warmed slowly and this is the best way. Rest while I warm you."

They were in a heavily wooded gap. The primeval timber hadn't allowed the sun entrance for many a year. Black remembered the time he'd warmed Cat's body in the cave that winter on Christmas Ridge. It had been colder then, but Cat had fur on her body and Cat was a wild animal with centuries of built-in reserves. The precious body in his arms had only him and her stubborn will to win. He didn't think she would die from freezing now—she hadn't been in the water that long—but the danger of developing pneumonia was high. He couldn't let that happen.

He rubbed her arms and legs briskly until they were pink from friction. He blew on her face and into her ears, patted her cheeks, and massaged her shoulders, her hips, and her thighs. The potent sexual fascination he'd initially felt while undressing her disappeared, transposing itself into a spiritual fission as he focused on healing her. His long, hard body covered hers and he warmed her, not with a sensual love, but a universal love. As the warmth of his body seeped into hers, he talked to her.

"God loves you, Elizabeth. The sun, the moon, and the

stars love you. Uncle East loves you. Marm loves you.
Feel the warmth of Raffle's pelt as you soothe him in
your lap. Remember Marm's hot chocolate and steaming
vegetable soup. Think of the hot pavement under your
feet at noon. Feel, Elizabeth. Remember. Please, think."

For two hours, they lay together while he healed her
with his body and with prayers. He never let up, never
stopped talking to her, never stopped concentrating on
Lilibet.

His warmth transferred to her. It soothed her fragile,
chilled body. He could feel her warming slowly, slowly.
He willed his strength, his health, his healing power into
her perfect form, sensing she was receiving and recovering.

Then, through the intenseness of his trance, he was
aware of her hand patting his shoulder. He raised himself
to lie on his side, leaning on one elbow, and looked at her.
Her cheeks were pink, her eyes were glowing, and she'd
stopped shivering.

"Elizabeth?"

"I'm fine, Black. Really, I am."

Black was speechless with relief. He broke into a cold
sweat, a fine quaking shook his body, and he closed his
eyes. Until this moment he'd refused to think about the
possibility that he might lose her. Now that he could
breathe freely again, he was unable to breathe at all. Now
that he knew she would be all right, he was sick with
gratitude. He controlled the pain in his chest, forced himself to breath evenly, and slowly opened his eyes. Gratitude to God and the Spirits of the Woods filled him. He
could only gaze at her in happy wonder.

The hand that soothed his shoulder stilled as she took
in the implications of her nudity. She blushed and looked
away from him.

"There's nothing to be ashamed of," he muttered. "It
was the only way I could warm you properly."

"Well, at least I got rid of that wretched wet suit," she
said, laughing. "I don't know how you retrieved me from
the river or how you got me so warm, but I'm grateful.
Thank you."

"That wretched wet suit may have saved your life,"

Black growled. He reached for her dry underwear and his chamois shirt. "Here, put these on."

He grabbed his jeans and jumped to his feet. Turning his back to her, he put them on.

"Your shirt is soft and warm. Thank you."

He turned around to see that she sat with her legs crossed Indian-fashion, his big brown shirt covering most of her. In the gloom of the grotto, her violet eyes shone at him trustingly. Inwardly, he groaned. As he watched her, he saw her eyes change, growing wide with fear and then wonder. She was looking beyond him into the woods.

He sensed what she saw and smiled to himself.

"What's the matter?"

"Uh, Black . . ." Her voice shook. "Do you have your knife? I mean . . . oh, my God."

He couldn't resist the opportunity to tease her.

"Sure you're feeling okay, Lilibet?"

"Y-yes. Behind you . . . oh, God . . . look behind you." She covered her mouth with her hand, determined not to embarrass herself by screaming.

Black made an imperceptible motion with his hand. Mischief leaped in his eyes as he watched Lilibet's mouth gape open.

He didn't have to turn around to know that Cat was heading toward them.

Lilibet wondered if her traumatic experience on the river had affected her mind. *I'm hallucinating.* Gliding gracefully toward them was a golden cougar. Two dead squirrels dangled from its white saw-edged fangs. Speechless with fear, she raised her arm and pointed with her finger as Black stood there, refusing to turn around. She started to get to her feet, but remembered Uncle East's lessons. She froze, moving not an inch.

"Good girl," Black said. He didn't turn around. He stood there, hands on hips, legs spread apart, his tanned chest gleaming in the leaping firelight. "Stay still for a while. Cat will become accustomed to you."

Astonished, Lilibet realized Black had known about the cougar all along. Mesmerized, she watched as the beautiful animal sat sedately on her haunches beside Black. He looked down at the huge cat and smiled.

"You brought our lunch, Cat. Thank you." He knelt, gave the cougar a hug and took the squirrels from her mouth. She licked his face with her big tongue and then lay down, swishing her tail.

Across the dancing flames of the fire, Lilibet couldn't take her eyes off the exotic scene before her. The cougar returned her stare, its unblinking eyes glassy orange in the firelight. Its steady scrutiny was unnerving. Black sat beside the cougar, smoothing her coat, and ruffling the fur between her erect, pointed ears.

"Everything is fine, Cat. This is my friend, Lilibet." He glanced over at Lilibet. "Lilibet, this is my friend, Cat. Sorry, I teased you. She won't hurt you. Don't know whether she will let you come close or not. I'm the only human she knows . . . or wants to know. We'll see. She's shown a great deal of trust in coming to the fire. She could have dropped the squirrels at the tree line and disappeared."

They're true . . . all those tales they told about Black are true. She felt as if she'd stumbled into a forest primeval. She dared a questioning glance up at the towering oaks and dark evergreens that hid the sky, then returned her gaze to the wild cougar, and Black, who seemed dangerously primitive. She'd been dropped into a world before time, and there before her sat a God of the Forest with his hunting mate. She remained motionless but the pulse in the hollow of her throat trembled. Black began to speak and his calm, steady stream of words soothed her. Lilibet knew he was giving her and Cat time to become accustomed to each other.

"Cat knew I was in trouble—has probably known since the river sucked you from the raft and my heart turned over. She's been following us ever since, and knew we would need food. Would you like to hear about me and Cat?"

She nodded her head.

Black told her of his fifteenth winter spent on Christmas Ridge, of the slaughter of Cat's family and his rescue of the half-grown cub. While he talked, he skinned and gutted the squirrels, speared them with a stick, and placed them across a Y-shaped branch to cook above the fire. By the time he'd finished his story, the meat was sizzling with a delicious roasting aroma. Cat's eyes had blinked shut with sleep, and Lilibet was relaxed and comfortable.

"Ready for some food?" Black asked.

"Am I ever!" She stood. Cat's eyes blinked open and she stood, too.

Lilibet froze.

"Come here, Lilibet."

Her bare feet felt like cement blocks.

"Come here," he ordered.

She closed her eyes. *Hunker down, Lilibet. Center yourself. Uncle East says beasts love, too.*

She opened her eyes and walked to stand beside Black and Cat. Black put one hand on Cat and took Lilibet's hand in his other to place it on Cat's rough golden coat. A tremor ran through the cougar and Lilibet realized the big cat was as frightened as she was.

The fear left her as she hastened to reassure the cougar. "It's alright, Cat. Any friend of Black's is a friend of mine. You feel so warm and strong. Maybe we'll be good friends someday."

With feline grace, Cat moved away. She disappeared into the forest as silently as she had come.

"Did I do something wrong, Black?"

"No, you did everything right. Cat was ready to leave. Sit down and we'll have our lunch."

Lilibet decided the tender white squirrel meat tasted like chicken. She tore it hungrily off the bone. When they finished, they went to the bank of the river and cupped their hands to drink the clean, clear water. Lilibet washed her face and hands and returned to sit on her bed of moss while Black went to scout the area.

For the first time since she'd recovered from her waterlogged stupor, she began to worry about their precarious situation. Black had told her they'd lost the raft, and she thought they must be miles from civilization. She was sure Black knew exactly where they were but no one else did. Suddenly exhausted, she decided the problem could better be dealt with from a prone position so she lay down on the soft moss. Despite the niggling worry, her eyelids drooped heavily and her weary body, replenished with warmth and food but desperate for rest, settled thoroughly into welcoming hollows in the pliant moss. As she drifted off to sleep, she realized that Black had called her Elizabeth when he was off guard. . . . The way he said it made her seem desirable. Had she been dreaming earlier when she heard him call her "darling"? He'd said his heart had stopped when she'd been thrown from the raft. Mmm, she thought drowsily, it felt wonderful to be cared for. She'd think about the implications of all this tomorrow. . . .

Black returned and sat beside her while she slept, remembering the fullness of her breasts, the slimness of her hips, the delicate look of her exquisite body. Now he memorized the curve of her lips, the flutter of her eyelashes on her porcelain cheek, the graceful arms flung carelessly over her head. He would let her sleep. She needed her strength for the next part of their adventure.

An hour later the gap grew chillier as the sun dropped lower in the sky. He saw her shiver and it was natural to lie down and take her in his arms. As he gathered her to him, he cursed himself for convincing her to come on the trip, but he had to admit he would have it no other way. And she was safe . . . here in his arms.

He murmured into her ear. "As long as I'm around, you will never be cold again, will never be hungry, or sad, or in pain. No one will ever hurt you again, my precious darling. I promise."

"Umm. What did you say?" She spoke into his chest, stirring the coarse black hair.

"I didn't know you were awake."

"What did you say?"

"Someday I'll tell you. Not now."

Fully awake now, she drew back to look at him, curiosity burning in her eyes.

"Why not?" She felt cozy and protected in Black's arms.

Black didn't answer, just gazed at her, studying her face with infinite care.

High above them, the primeval pines soughed softly in

the small clearing, their dark green branches moving gracefully in the gentle breeze. Close by, the river, having lost its anger, lapped quietly at the shore. The fire next to them crackled with reassurance, the smell of its wood smoke melding smoothly with the freshness of the pine. The moss beneath Lilibet felt velvety warm.

She swallowed hard, as his study of her face grew more intent, and he curved his fingers around her jaw, his thumb trailing lazily across to her mouth. Gently, he brushed his thumb back and forth across her lips. The beauty mark near the corner of her mouth drew special attention. A tremor ran from the back of her neck down her spine. She drew away, remembering her doubts about coming on this trip. Her near-death experience on the river had swept away many pretenses. She knew now that because of her plans for her life and her obligations to others, she'd been running away from her attraction to Black. She wondered if it wasn't time to grow up, to face the music, to explore what lay behind the promise in his eyes.

He held her chin between his thumb and forefinger and drew her back to him. His thumb returned to her lips and the brushing became a sensual rubbing. He tugged her bottom lip down and bent over to graze it with a kiss.

She stared into his eyes and the look there summoned the same feeling she'd had in the cafe. She wanted to swim into their green depths and get caught up in their mystery and strength. How could she deny what seemed the most natural thing in the world? She couldn't tear her eyes away from his steady gaze, and any thoughts of fear, or guilt, or denial were swept away.

He leaned closer to cover her mouth with his. Tentatively, Lilibet returned his soft kiss. His lips moved over hers in supple pulls and tugs. It felt like nothing she'd ever felt before. She responded, giving him her mouth. His demanding lips sought entry and she opened hers eagerly and felt his tongue touch hers. Their kiss grew deep and all-absorbing until she was lost in the wonder of it.

Wanting this new, exquisite pleasure to continue, she put a hand around his neck to hold him to her. Her fingers explored his nape, his ears, and the shining black hair that swept back from his temple.

He dragged his mouth away from hers and murmured her name. He kissed her temple, her cheek, then returned to the honey of her mouth. "Elizabeth," he repeated hoarsely, the ache in his voice shaking her to her toes.

Her insides knotted, convulsed with sweet wanting. She ached to have him even closer, to feel even more, to absorb him into every part of her. Her body responded willingly, moving with an age-old, natural back and forth rhythm against his long length.

The complete artlessness of the sensual movement of Lilibet's hips against his heightened Black's already raging desire. He struggled to regain control of the torrential passion rushing through him. Tearing his mouth away from hers, he tried to lift his head. A small moan escaped her and she pressured his mouth back to hers, rubbing her other hand softly across his back. Black realized she was offering him more than lust. She was offering her faith in him. The knowledge shook him and he tried again to pull away from her, but she tugged on his shoulder and he couldn't resist. He groaned into her mouth and his hand moved up beneath the chamois shirt and caressed her breast with exquisite gentleness.

Lilibet's breath left her and the sweet knots low in her belly changed to a spiraling heat. Suffused with a fierce wanting, she put both arms around him and pulled his broad shoulders to her until they shut out the twilight in the cove. His skin felt hot and alive. Even had she willed it so, her hips couldn't stop their rhythmic movement. Her yearning body touched and teased his taut male organ again and again. His searching hands and the movement of her body had pushed the chamois shirt up to expose her panties and her bare waist. She ached to be fulfilled. His body was hard and unyielding. He wasn't giving over to her. His hands were tender and searching, but his body remained guarded and defensive.

Oh, please, Black. She'd never felt like this before. *Please let this never stop. Please make me feel more.*

As if in answer to her silent plea, she felt a quiver of response, a release of the control in his form. He tore his mouth from hers and in desperation quickly pushed the shirt up to expose her breasts. He gave a small cry when he saw the twin pink peaks, and grasped her bottom with his hand to press her tightly to him. She wasn't prepared for the rock-hardness of his large organ. It strained for release beneath the zipper of his jeans. The rough material pushed hotly against her panties and against the bare skin at her waist.

They lay tight together, her tender breasts buried in the crisp black hair on his chest; his steel-hard, jean-imprisoned erection nested heavily in her feathery gold curliness.

Black lowered his mouth to play a slow, seductive game as he rimmed her lips with soft, satin licks. Lilibet found herself responding with quick, tiny nips to his full bottom lip. Her breath came in ragged gasps, his gossamer kisses grew hard and demanding. His hand massaged her bottom with gentle, squeezes, and Lilibet felt an unfamiliar wetness soak her panties and dampen her inner thighs.

Mindless now, his mouth left her lips and searched for her breasts.

Lilibet released his shoulders and, in a flash, pulled her shirt up and over her head. He caught her chin roughly in his hand and for the first time she saw the raw, primitive passion that burned in his luminous eyes. She closed her eyes to shut out the fierceness, and raised her head to kiss his eyelids shut. He released her chin and, nudging her bra aside with his chin, found what he'd been looking for: the sweetness of her breast. With reverence he circled each one with light kisses, drawing closer and closer to the tender, aroused nipples. As his hungry mouth closed over a taut peak, they both moaned, and Lilibet was swept into an ecstasy she'd never thought possible. He moved to the other breast. The gentle nuzzling gradually became a hard suckling, his teeth nipping, his tongue hard. She grabbed the pain and drew it into her.

As he moved his mouth lower, covering her waist with kisses, he tugged at her panties and she helped him pull them off. With his hand, he parted her thighs. Gently, he fingered the sensitive folds hidden in the golden, curly hair there and found the nub he was looking for. He suckled her breast while slowly, he inserted his forefinger inside her. Lilibet gasped with delight. Her body writhed and she ached with such tormented longing that she thought she would faint. Black raised his head and looked directly into her eyes, his pupils dilated with lust, while his finger moved sensuously in and out of her swollen, wet warmth.

Black's mind had left him. All he knew was that Elizabeth was with him, and that she wanted him as much as he wanted her. At first, he'd just wanted to taste, to tease, to satisfy himself with a kiss or two. Never in his wildest dreams had he imagined Lilibet would react as she had. Her swift, hot response had shocked, then pleased him enormously. It also inflamed him. He sensed that her passion was boundless and the call to explore it was overpowering. Every nerve, every muscle, every atom of his body seared with the agony of wanting her. He watched her violet eyes darken to purple as his finger pleasured the warm, velvety tightness of her. Surprise flared in her eyes and crossed her face as she reached a zenith and cried out. Hot liquid rushed over his loving hand. A fierce, possessive joy filled him. He'd given her her first climax.

Limp, she whimpered with wanting.

He could stand it no longer. He wanted all of her. He wanted to feel himself inside of her. He wanted to supply her with the ecstasy she deserved.

"Please, Black," she implored.

He tore his jeans off and pulled her roughly to him. His naked erection, inflamed and rigid, nested hot in her golden curls and stretched the length of her belly to reach her waist. Unable to help himself, he whispered hoarsely in her ear, "You are beautiful, Elizabeth. I want you . . . all of you." She shivered and a deep sigh escaped her.

He laid her onto her back. Using his knee, he spread her legs and slipped between them. His full weight upon her, he took her face in his hands and covered it with kisses.

Lilibet felt the hot tip of his erection nudging her vagina. She wanted this but, oh, she was scared.

Black, attuned to every nuance of her, felt the tensing of her body and knew it signaled more than wanting. On the edge of plunging into the maelstrom of desire that overwhelmed them both, her sudden fear jolted him back to awareness. He lifted himself, braced on both arms, and looked at her again. The trust in her passion-filled eyes haunted him. He'd taken advantage of her innocence and honesty, and of her trust in him. He groaned with the enormity of what he'd been about to do. Chest heaving and gasping for breath, he shook his head to clear it of the whirlpool of lust into which he'd been sinking. With a groan of self-disgust, he jumped to his feet. He would have despised himself had he given into his desires.

"Black?"

"Everything is fine, darling." He covered her with his shirt and then stalked off a few paces, his back to her.

"Please come back, Black."

"No, I can't take you like this."

"I want you to." Her voice shook with passion.

"It's not right, Elizabeth."

"Turn around and look at me," she demanded.

He turned, breathing easier now and she marveled at his mammoth self-control. His eyes, however, still burned with a savage need. His cock stood, large and erect, like a stallion's. The sight of his tall, taut, powerful body, tanned and brimming with primitive energy, bright against the background of dark evergreens, would live in her mind forever.

"Why isn't it right?" she asked, trying to get her own breathing in order.

"I want the moment to be perfect."

"What could be more perfect than this? This is you and me, Black, here on the mountain."

"You're young, Elizabeth. You aren't sure what you want yet."

He reached for his jeans and struggled into them.

"You're only four years older than me!"

Ah, but I've done a lot of living and learning in those four years, my darling. I've seen and experienced things I'd never want you to know exist.

"And I don't think there's any doubt about what I

wanted a few moments ago—maybe you just don't want
me," she continued, her voice soft. Tears of embarrassment rolled down her cheeks. Perhaps she'd made the
wrong decision when she'd given in to her desire to explore their attraction. She sat up and pulled the shirt over
her bare breasts.

Black knelt beside her, wiped the tears from her
cheeks, and kissed her chin. Her eyes still held the drugged delirium of passion. He got up quickly.

"Elizabeth, you'll never know how much . . ." He
stopped. He couldn't tell her how important she was to
him—not yet. He was a man and, as much as she'd matured in the past four years, there remained about her an
air of innocence. Her simple faith in him still shook him.

She stood up, hands on hips, stance wide, and glared at
him. "So, we chalk it up to the madness of the moment,
right, Black? All that adrenaline we pumped while we
were on the river, all the danger, caused an excitement we
wouldn't ordinarily feel, right, Black?"

"Maybe. Probably."

"I don't give a fig what you say. We both know what
just happened was more than animal lust," she said.

He grasped her firmly by the shoulders. "Have you forgotten Cle so easily, Elizabeth? The young man you're
planning to marry?"

"No, of course . . ." She *had* forgotten Cle.

Completely.

How could she? Maybe her sarcastic remarks to Black
were correct. Maybe the passion they'd just shared had
been a brief madness.

He gave her a small shake. "Do you love him, Elizabeth?"

"Yes, I . . . I thought I did."

"You don't know, do you?"

She tried to conjure up Cle's face and couldn't. She
tried to remember the way she felt when Cle touched her
and couldn't.

"No, I don't know." She did know she would never be
the same again, nor could she pretend any longer that
Black was simply a friend.

He let go of her and walked over to a huge spruce tree.

Bracing both arms against the fat trunk, he dropped his head between them for a brief moment. Then he turned around, folded his arms, and leaned against the tree to face her.

"My body is an instrument that gives me superlative joy—the joy of uniting flesh and spirit. Elizabeth ... when *your* spirit knows what it wants, *then* ..." he stopped, unable to continue.

She started to walk toward him, but he held up his hand to ward her off.

"Even had I wanted to take advantage of the moment, Elizabeth, I wouldn't have because I don't have a rubber. We weren't prepared." His smoky voice came soft across the small clearing. "I only tempt fate with my own life, not someone else's."

He'd silenced her. They stared at each other for a moment.

"We have to leave here now. There's an hour of dusk left and we have two hours to travel."

"But we'll be trying to find our way in the dark. I thought we'd spend the night here."

"No," he said quickly, unwilling to further test the shaky control he'd fought so hard to regain. "My mother is waiting for us at the parking area at the foot of Catawba. She knows I can take care of myself but she's waiting because you are with me, and we have to get you home."

"I can take care of myself, too."

"Sometimes," he said. He ignored her bristling manner and moved to the fire. "Let's put out the fire and get going." A double entendre if ever he'd heard one, he thought cynically.

They covered the embers of the fire with damp earth and buried the bones of their lunch.

"Let's go," said Black. He picked her up in his arms and walked into the trees.

"Put me down."

"You have no shoes and I don't have time to make moccasins."

"You don't have any shoes either. I'll walk, too. Put me down!"

"Certainly, milady, but when it gets dark, I suggest you take hold of my jeans."

He walked unerringly through the thick growth of tall timber and fast darkening night. Luckily the struggle to keep up with him kept her from reflecting on the passion they'd shared in the cove. She stumbled painfully over exposed roots, logs, and boulders. Black never paused, never looked back. She wondered how he could be so sure about the direction they were taking. The towering canopy of trees hid the sky from them so he couldn't be using the stars. Finally, admitting she needed his guidance, she hooked her finger into the waist of his jeans.

The ebony forest closed around them but Black never stopped. Lilibet wondered if he had night vision, like his friend the cougar.

After an hour, Black whirled around, picked her up and turned back around to stride forward again.

She struggled to get loose but he held her firmly to his chest. Her stomach went soft and her limbs felt watery.

"It was taking too long," he muttered. "We'll go faster this way. I don't want my mother waiting in the dark any longer than necessary."

Lilibet gave up. It was useless to argue. Besides, she would never admit that her feet and knees were torn and bleeding where she had stubbed, bumped, and abused them on the treacherous ground. She was no dummy. Riding in Black's arms was much nicer. She gave into the feeling of protection and caring that emanated from him. But her mind was free now to worry about the intensity of her emotions.

All this time, she'd thought she loved Cle—had even told Cle she loved him. Yet what she was feeling for Black was stronger than anything she'd ever felt for anyone. Could she have been so wrong all these years? It had to be that "madness of the moment" sort of thing. She'd heard girls at school talk about that. But the wild, hot feelings she and Black had shared seemed more than "a moment." It was as if Black knew the right switch to flip—that was it! The explanation was simple. Because of his sensitivity to nature. Black was a sensual man. How good of him not to take advantage of their mutual loss of control, she told herself. Satisfied with this theory, she relaxed.

As they traveled through the blackness she found herself doing ridiculous things, like mentally counting the strong beat of his heart against her ribs, inhaling the husky maleness of him, and listening to his even breathing as if it were the New York Philharmonic.

Black's gait was steady and smooth. The gentle rocking motion lulled Lilibet and she slept.

Meeting Black's mother and traveling to Matterhorn in a jeep in Black's arms was all a weary blur to her. Laura Brady helped her bathe, medicated her bumps and scratches, lent her a nightie, and put her to bed in a big four-poster.

The next morning, Lilibet offered to help prepare breakfast but Mrs. Brady shooed her away, urging her to explore her charming cottage in the woods. Lilibet wore a faded red shirt and a pair of slacks that had been left behind by one of Black's old girlfriends. The too-large slacks dragged on the floor as she walked, and Lilibet looked down with a grimace. Hah! The wench must have been big and awkward. She was grateful for something to wear, but couldn't wait to take off the offensive garments.

The cottage exuded a unique, fairylike, tucked-away-in-the-woods sort of charm, yet had an elegant sophistication. The walls were windows bringing in the outside, a panorama of cleared but not cultivated woods.

She stood in the center of a large, beautiful room and looked about her with appreciation. The sparse furnishings were simple but elegant. She'd learned enough from Miss Mabel's tutelage to recognize rare antiques. A low, primitive, bent-willow table sat in front of a deep-cushioned navy and burgundy plaid sofa. Two Sheraton armchairs sat on either side of an empire table in the corner, and a burgundy, Georgian-style wing chair serviced a classic mahogany desk. The cream walls and mellow oak floor were bare and beautiful.

Dominating the room was a massive Steinway piano sitting near an even larger stone fireplace. This was where Black worked and practiced. She marveled at how it all came together, the antique and the modern. Someone with excellent taste had taken great care to create a workplace of simple beauty without distractions.

"This is where he comes to compose. He wants no distractions, so there are no paintings or books." Laura Brady's gentle voice came from behind her.

"It's beautiful," Lilibet said.

"I'm happy you like it." A smile touched the reserved but pretty face.

"You resemble Uncle East."

"Thank you. You have given my father much joy, Lilibet. I worry about him, up there on the mountain alone. Knowing he has someone besides Black and me who cares about him gives me a good feeling. It's also nice to be able to mention him to someone other than Black."

The willowy, still youthful, dark-haired woman standing in front of her bore echoes of Uncle East on her patrician face. She wore her white twill slacks, blue cotton shirt, and white Keds with an elegance few would have been able to achieve. Her manner of speech suggested a Northeastern boarding school education. Up until now, Lilibet had only enjoyed Uncle East's attention and company, accepting without question his self-imposed exile on top of the mountain. Since learning more about Black, and now acknowledging the obvious breeding in Laura Brady and the exquisiteness of this cottage in the woods, for the first time she wondered who Uncle East was and where he came from. Curiosity burned in her as she realized Uncle East wasn't the simple soul she'd assumed he was.

Biting her tongue to hold back the questions she was dying to ask, Lilibet followed Laura Brady into the cozy, yellow breakfast room of the cottage. Black joined them, freshly shaven, hair slicked wetly back, and dressed in his favorite ragged jeans and white shirt. He smelled delicious, like spices in mulled wine.

He looked up and winked at her as he ate with gusto the huge plate of pancakes his mother had placed in front of him. About to take a bite of pancake herself, Lilibet's stomach flipped. There was no way she could eat anything. She lowered her fork, dripping with syrup, to her plate.

"What's the matter? Don't you like my mother's pancakes?"

Embarrassed, she said, "Of course I like them. They're delicious."

She brought the fork to her mouth again and forced a bite down, her stomach objecting all the way. *Please don't wink at me again, Black. Or smile at me, or touch me, or look at me.* The thought of trying to eat her breakfast with Black directly across the table from her made her dizzy.

Lilibet, this is ridiculous! Get hold of yourself. The wild passion you shared in the woods last night means nothing. A madness of the moment, right? Right!

Not wanting to hurt Mrs. Brady's feelings, she choked down a few bites of pancake and crisp bacon. Laura Brady's discerning eye watched her with sympathy.

"Lilibet, you're probably tired from your adventure yesterday. Please don't eat more than you want. Black, she's not hungry. Stop teasing her."

Black knew exactly what was wrong with her and winked at her again, a wicked gleam in his eyes. "Not as good as the squirrel we had yesterday, or the dessert later, right, Lilibet?"

"I, ah . . ." she stuttered, remembering the way he'd tugged at her bottom lip and kissed it.

Her hand shook and a drop of syrup fell on the borrowed red shirt. "Oh, I'm sorry."

She wasn't really. She hated the red shirt. Red certainly wasn't her color and she had to admit she was jealous of the anonymous former girlfriend to whom it belonged.

"Don't worry about it," Black said. "It'll wash. Cynthia's forgotten about it anyway."

Taking mercy, he glanced at his watch and then looked at her. "When we called your mother last night, she said to have you home by nine o'clock this morning, before your father gets off the night shift So we better get going."

The ride over the mountain to Big Ugly Creek was a silent one.

As they crossed the narrow, rickety wood bridge to Big Ugly, Black reached over and covered her hand with his. "Would your father really be angry if he knew you spent the night at my house chaperoned by my mother?" he asked in a disbelieving tone.

How could she explain that her father didn't care much what she did as long as she maintained her relationship with Cle Hutton, therefore ensuring his job?

"I can handle my father. It's my mother who's afraid of him."

Black frowned but changed the subject.

"I'd like you to see the building I've finally got going up for my manufacturing company. It's not much but it's a beginning. Would you come and give it a tour?"

"Absolutely."

"Next Saturday okay?"

"Yes."

He stopped the car in front of Lilibet's house, leaned over to kiss her smack on the mouth, and then got out to open the door for her. Startled by his brazen behavior at eight o'clock in the morning, she looked around to see if anyone from the camp was watching. No one was in sight.

Hand at her waist, he shepherded her through the junkyard.

"I'll call you."

She nodded. She watched as he walked away, her heart in her mouth. Would he call? Don't be silly. . . . What if he doesn't? She would see him when they toured his plant. Sam was coming home this week, and Cle and Clarice the next week. Things would be back to normal then. She would get these disturbing new feelings for Black into perspective.

She stepped onto the porch and, with a loud, cracking sound, her foot sank through the broken plank Eugene had promised to repair two months ago. The rotting wood splinters scraped painfully at her wrenched ankle as she pulled it out of the offending cavity.

Moaning softly, she sat down on the top step to rub her ankle. She viewed the junkyard in front of her bleakly.

Suddenly her concerns about Cle, and her newly discovered feelings for Black seemed inconsequential. Her resolve to go to law school and learn to take care of herself and those she loved hardened.

Chapter 13

Sam, Lilibet, and Black stepped out of the sweltering corrugated Quonset hut that contained the embryo of Brady Electronics Company, and into a baking July afternoon. Sam was glad he'd invited himself along when Lilibet told him of Brady's invitation to visit the budding company. He'd learned a lot. More than he wanted to know, not about Brady and his budding business, but about Brady and Lilibet.

Black shook Sam's hand and said, "Thanks for coming with her, Sam. I worry about her driving over the mountain by herself."

Sam felt a flash of annoyance. Brady had no right to concern himself with Lilibet's safety. Sam put his arm possessively around Lilibet's waist, hiding his thoughts behind a congenial smile.

Brady took Lilibet's hand to say goodbye, and the lightning intensity of the look in Brady's eyes when he touched Lilibet, electrified Sam. He had a sudden burst of insight that frightened him to the core. At that moment, Black and Lilibet were in their own world. A palpable awareness simmered between them and everything else—including Sam—was forgotten. It was as if he didn't exist.

As swiftly as it happened, Sam saw Black mask his eyes and the strange, timeless interlude ended. Sam shivered with the knowledge he'd discovered. Long ago he'd given up hope for himself, but he knew he'd always have Lilibet in his life because she'd be with Cle. Knowing someone had the power to upset this apple cart was unnerving.

They waved goodbye, and Sam drove his car down the

bumpy, dusty back road toward the main highway to Yancey.

Sam's curly brown hair stuck wetly to his brow, and sweat rolled into his ears. He loosened his tie and unbuttoned his collar button. He pulled a big white cotton handkerchief from his rear pocket and swiped it across his brow, then returned it to his pocket.

"Why don't you take off your tie, Sam? It's too hot for a tie today."

"Thanks. Believe I will." He pulled the tie off, threw it on the back seat with his jacket, and unbuttoned another button on his shirt, wishing he'd never worn his new blue and white seersucker suit. He'd wanted to impress Brady with his law school status, but realized too late that Brady couldn't care less about such things. "Ma said Pappy is buying new Cadillacs with air-conditioning."

"Yes. I ordered three of them for him last week—for him, Cle, and Clarice. Fat Sis said air-conditioning was a waste of money and she'd keep her old car."

"Wow! Next thing, he'll be putting air-conditioning in the house and office."

"You're right. He told me to take care of a cooling system for the house. They're coming from Charleston to install it next week. No such luck for the office."

Sam mopped at his face again and left the handkerchief on the seat beside him, knowing he would need it again. He thought of Black Brady and how cool he'd looked despite the oppressive heat in the Quonset hut.

"Too bad that fancy cooling system Brady installed for his workers got sabotaged last week, right in the worst heat of the summer, too. You think someone is out to . . . discourage him?"

Lilibet gave him a withering look. "Really, Sam, don't play dumb with me. You know the mine owners in the valley, most particularly Pappy, don't like the idea of a new industry coming in and giving their 'slaves' an opportunity to make a decent living. But Black's well aware of it."

"What do you mean?"

"It didn't take him long to figure it out. His first building was burned to the ground."

"How do you know so much about what's been happening? You been seeing a lot of Brady, Lilibet?" He dared a quick glance at her and saw her stiffen briefly.

"Some."

"What's that mean?"

"Not that it's any of your business, Sam, but Black took us to the movies. Margot wanted to see *From Here to Eternity.*"

"Is that all?" Sam said. Relief filled him, but all the facts still didn't fit. He decided to pursue it further. "Seemed like to me you two were real chummy. I mean, how did he know you're always hungry?"

Memories of the unusual meals she and Black had shared in the wilderness came to Lilibet's mind, but she thought better of mentioning them.

"If you must know, Sam, I had dinner at Black's house last Wednesday evening. His mother invited me. Is there anything else you'd like to know? Is it a crime to make a new friend? There are other people in the world besides you, and Cle, and Clarice!"

Her anger deflated him. Wilted by the heat and worried about her anger, he drove on silently for a while.

Lilibet was the only person in the world who could make him angry, or sad, or happy. Sometimes her effect on him scared him, but he couldn't live without her. So far, he'd been able to manage his life, and Cle's, and keep an eye on Clarice without much effort. It had always been like that, and he didn't mind. People looked up to him and respected his ability to control a situation, to take over and clean up the mess someone else had made. He had discovered early that taking care of others and having them rely on him gave him a sense of power, and he truly did love to make people happy. He guessed because he was so big and looked so capable, people just assumed he could handle about anything. And he could—except his love for Lilibet.

She was always in his head, so much so that it was beginning to worry him. Lilibet had become an obsession. Common sense told him this wasn't healthy but the more he tried to exorcize her, the more the image of her, the sound of her, the smell of her, rooted in his mind.

He cleared his throat.

"I'm sorry. I just ... well, Brady used to be kind of wild. ..."

"They cleaned him up at Yale, Sam," she said with heavy sarcasm.

"Yeh, now he seems ... uh ... sort of sophisticated ... and he seems real interested in you. I. ..."

"Spit it out, Sam!"

"Do you think you can handle him?" he said hurriedly.

"There's nothing to handle, Sam," she retorted angrily. "Drop it!"

Dear God, she was lying through her teeth, thought Lilibet. Handling her feelings for Black was becoming a full time job. She had to constantly battle the giddiness, she experienced whenever she was in Black's presence. She took a deep breath and let it out slowly. No point in taking her confusion out on poor Sam.

"I'm sorry, Sam."

"I'm sorry, too, Lilibet. Let's not be angry." He reached over and covered her small hand with his large one.

"No, let's not," she replied softly, patting his hand with her free one.

Sam could feel the perspiration rolling down his face and into his collar, but the sweat could fill his ears for all he cared. Nothing could persuade him to take his hand away from Lilibet's, he treasured the feel of her hand in his. It seemed so small, and fragile and he held it carefully. He imagined it caressing his brow, rubbing his back.

"Oh, Sam, look!"

A deer bounded out of the woods and crossed the road in front of them, interrupting his fantasies.

"Beautiful, aren't they? Don't see many of them down here anymore."

"No, but up on the mountain, Black and I have ... seen a few. They're getting plentiful again." Angry with herself for bringing up Black again, she changed the subject. "I think we're going to have a great Fourth of July celebration. Pappy gave me some of the responsibility in organizing it, and I loved it. The mayor calls my office every day to make sure the fireworks people are coming, and the baseball field is ready."

"I know. Every year, Pappy pulls out all the stops to make a good, old-fashioned celebration. The parade starts at eleven. I'll pick you, and Margot, and Marm up at ten."

Lilibet slowly pulled her hand from his. "Thank you, Sam, but . . . I'll be driving us in the truck."

"But, we've always spent the Fourth together," he said, surprised. "Is it because Cle and Clarice aren't here? Cle expects me to take care of you."

Lilibet bit back an exclamation of frustration and gathered her courage.

"Sam, I promised Black I would spend most of the day with him. He won't be here for the parade because Brady Electronics is having their own celebration in the morning, but he will be here for part of the game, as well as the picnic and fireworks."

"Doesn't he have family to be with in Matterhorn?" Sam asked, disgruntled.

"His mother is celebrating with . . . someone else," she hesitated and then continued. "Sam, it's not really a date with Black. He doesn't know many people in Yancey, and you know how everyone gets together on the Fourth. Sally Kay is home from Atlanta. Why don't you ask her to buddy around with you?"

"Good idea. Think I will," he said pleasantly, although he was seething inside. This was getting out of hand. Thank God, Cle would be home soon.

Chapter 14

Eulonie Bevins came out of the Rainbow Diner and locked the door. Would wonders never cease? Eulonie's miserly boss had closed the diner for the parade and given the overworked waitress the morning off. Virgil and Jud MacDonald leaned against the Rainbow Diner's grimy glass window. There was a cleared space around them. Eulonie guessed there was an advantage to smelling bad. People gave you a wide berth.

Eugene Springer must be around somewhere. She saw Virgil sneak a drink out of a brown paper sack–wrapped bottle, then slip it underneath his shirt. A man dressed in conservative brown slacks, plaid shirt, and green aviator sunglasses leaned against a telephone pole nearby. Stupid Virgil. Most people could spot a "revenuer" right off. Maybe that's why Eugene wasn't in sight. The three of them had managed to keep their still hidden for years, but the government men must be close to finding it or they wouldn't be hanging around town.

Red, white, and blue bunting draped on the front of buildings and around telephone poles gave the coarse, gritty street a festive air.

"Hey! How are ya? How are ya, cuz?"

Mayor Seth Browning, dressed like Uncle Sam, interrupted Eulonie's survey of the decorations and the crowd. The retired real estate salesman made his way down the sidewalk, shaking hands, a perpetual smile on his face. He called everyone "cuz" for cousin because, unless they were important, he couldn't remember their names. She heard him call a booming greeting to Lilibet Springer. That old wind bag, Eulonie thought, he's buttering her up because he thinks it'll pay to spend time with Lilibet. After all, she's going to be Cle Hutton's wife.

Lilibet endured Mayor Browning's gushing words of praise for her work in planning the parade. She was embarrassed, but knew Marm was thrilled to receive a personal greeting from the Mayor. After patting a blushing Margot on the head, he left, and Lilibet settled back in her folding chair with a sigh of relief.

Lilibet was happy they'd arrived for the parade early. She'd found them a shady spot under Carpozzoli's striped aqua-and-white awning. Fat Sis had told her she was to do nothing today but enjoy herself, and that's exactly what she intended.

Across the street, in front of the courthouse, she saw Tom Tee and Donetta with Jane Etta and the baby. They spotted Lilibet across the street and waved. Lilibet waved back, hoping they wouldn't decide to join the Springers.

"Here comes the parade," Marm said with excitement. "Wish your daddy had felt like coming."

The bang of drums and clang of cymbals could be heard down the street.

Yancey, West Virginia's Fourth of July had begun with a flourish, and Lilibet found herself wishing Black were here to share the fun. She shook her head, annoyed with herself. Cle would be home tomorrow. She knew he'd be upset when she told him she'd been spending time with Black. But she couldn't deny how much she'd enjoyed herself the past few weeks with Black. Like a good book she couldn't put down, she didn't want it to end.

When Cle returned, she would sort it all out. In the meantime, there was the baseball game later and the rest of the day with Black.

Black found the baseball field easily. He'd played high school football against Yancey on an adjacent field. He searched the wooden bleachers for Lilibet and spotted her Cincinnati Reds baseball cap midway up in the stands. Climbing carefully up through the crowd, apologizing as he went, he saw Margot wave at him. Lilibet was so absorbed in the pitchers warming up, she didn't see him. He reached them as "The Star Spangled Banner" came over the loudspeaker, and he put a cautioning finger over his lips, indicating to Margot that he wanted to surprise Lilibet.

Lilibet, impatient for the game to begin, heard a decidedly off-key male voice singing the national anthem. It was so grating she longed to put her hands over her ears. The longer the song went on, the louder and more off-pitch the voice sang. Heavens, would it never end? Where *is* Black, anyway? Finally, it was over and everyone sat down.

She glanced behind her, to see if she knew the unfortunate singer, and caught her breath as she came nose to nose with Black. He was leaning forward with his arms on his knees, an easy-fitting white T-shirt tucked into white shorts, a blue New York Yankee cap on his dark head. He looked irresistibly handsome, and a sweet heaviness gathered in her lower belly. If she moved forward just a bit, she'd be able to kiss him—and the urge to do so was almost overwhelming.

How long had he been there?

Margot giggled.

"Hi. Made it in time for the opening pitch," he said, a big grin on his face.

"Good. I've miss . . ." She couldn't tell him she'd been missing him all day. Margot would hear. "Was that you singing just now?"

"Yes. Awful, isn't it? Grandfather says I should just mouth the words, but I can't resist. Now you've been forewarned and can put cotton in your ears the next time I get the urge to sing."

She laughed. "Somehow it's comforting to know there's something you can't do."

"I'm ashamed to tell you, Miss Smug Face, but there's a list of things a mile long that I can't do."

"For instance."

"Well, let's see . . . I can't skate, or whistle, or cook, except for wilderness cooking. I can't type, or write a good story, or . . ."

She held up a protesting hand stifling a giggle.

"Please, no more, you wretched failure. Don't disillusion me further."

"Margot, would you mind scooting over so I can sit between you and your sister?"

"Sure, go ahead."

"Where's your mom?"

"At the picnic grounds. She doesn't like baseball," answered Margot. "Unlike my sister, who is a fanatic."

Lilibet gave her a dirty look.

The umpire brayed, "PLAY BALL!," and Lilibet forgot about everything but the game.

The pitcher on the Hutton Company Hound-Dogs, a wad of tobacco bulging his cheek, let go with his first ball and it whapped into the glove of the catcher.

At the end of the first inning the score was Wildcats, three, Hound-Dogs, one.

Black liked baseball but found he far preferred watching the changeling who sat next to him. Lilibet, so ladylike since her college years, was suddenly a whirlwind of intense absorption. From her angelic face there sparked the devil's own fury. She was constantly moving up and down, challenging the umpire's every call, and directing scathing running commentary at the players and coach. He thought she must be exhausted at the end of a game.

Cupping her hands around her mouth, she shouted, "Come on, hustle out there, hustle! Put something on it! What's the matter with you Jimbo, got glue on your glove?"

The umpire called another ball. "Oh, for Christ's sake—you're not going to walk him, are you? Hey, Coach, take Jimbo out of there. Let him sit it out!"

"Strike him out, you idiot!" The bat connected with the ball with a solid sock and the ball whizzed out of the park. A home run.

Lilibet beat her fists on her knees, then lowered her head to cover her face in frustration. Lifting her head to get back into the fray, she shouted, "Come on, Hound-Dogs, shake the lead out."

Sam Adkins and Sally Kay Nolan, Southern Airlines's newest stewardess, arrived and scrunched themselves into the seats in front of Black and Lilibet. Lilibet didn't even notice. Sam turned around and gave Black a nod.

The Hutton Hound-Dogs were up to bat.

Lilibet yelled, "Atta way, Georgie. run for third, run for third . . . oh, for cryin' out loud, why didn't he slide?"

Sally Kay turned around and gave Lilibet a look of disgust, then smiled sweetly at Black. "She's a bit hard to take at a baseball game, isn't she?"

Sam gave her a warning look and Sally Kay returned her attention to the game.

The Hound-Dogs squeaked by with a nine to eight victory. Lilibet, flushed with happiness, threw her arms around Black. He held her to him, wanting to crush her little body tight against him, but nobly resisting the temptation. If she was this elated when they won, he wondered at the depth of her dejection when they lost.

Black knew he wouldn't have Lilibet to himself much of the day, but he couldn't help the irritation he felt when Sam took Lilibet's other arm as they left the ballpark. She talked animatedly to both of them about the game, swinging her head back and forth. He wanted to lick away the tiny crystals of moisture above her upper lip.

He consoled himself with the knowledge that he and Lilibet would have the evening to themselves. Marm and Margot had promised to watch the fireworks with visiting kin from upstate.

"Lordy, I can't wait for the picnic. I'm starved."

Black threw back his head and roared with laughter.

Regina Springer sat on the ground beside her clean, but frayed, red-checkered tablecloth and viewed its largesse with satisfaction. An old tin held her fried chicken, a round, covered glass bowl was filled with potato salad, and her battered bean pot was warm with baked brown beans. A cardboard shoe box contained her best raisin cookies. The picnic was ready for everyone to enjoy when they arrived from the game.

She leaned back against the trunk of the tree that sheltered her and looked up into its leafy canopy with gratefulness. She closed her eyes and said a prayer of thanks.

It was rare to have a moment alone, and to be in town with the children was heaven.

She opened her eyes to enjoy the scene unfolding in front of her.

In the distance Anna Adkins helped Fat Sis and Belle Richards set up the Hutton picnic enclave. Near the river, the man who owned Carpozzoli's was selling pizza from a booth. She must remember to have Lilibet buy her a pizza. She'd never had one.

Next to the pizza booth a woman with a disfigured face propped a Rainbow Diner Ice Cream sign on a table with an awning. It was that waitress the women whispered about. Had six different children by as many different men. Eulonie Bevins was her name. Seems like someone should be helping her with those heavy ice cream canisters.

Regina struggled to her feet and made her way over to the woman.

"Howdy, I'm Miz Springer. Looks like you need some help."

"Thank you, ma'am. But no need. I'm used to liftin'," Eulonie Bevins said.

"So am I," Regina said, "and I always wish I had someone to help." Trying not to stare at the poor woman's face, she lifted one of the cold, sweating metal cans and put it on the table.

"You're Lilibet's mom, ain't you?" asked Eulonie.

"Yes."

"Hope you're proud of her. She's a fine young'un."

"I am proud of Lilibet."

Eulonie stopped loading supplies on the table for a moment, resting her elbow on a box of candy cones. "You happy about Lilibet's bein' engaged to Cle Hutton?"

"Lordy, yes. Wouldn't any mother be?" What a strange question, Regina thought.

Eulonie grunted and went back to work. They worked silently until Eulonie had the ice cream counter set up to her satisfaction.

"Thank you, Miz Springer. 'Twasn't necessary, but I can see where Lilibet gets her kindness."

Regina made her way back to her sheltered place under

the tree wondering about Eulonie's curious question about Lilibet and Cle.

A harsh whisper startled her. She looked around but could see no one she knew. She rose to her knees and poured herself a cup of lemonade from the cool thermos. Lilibet had bought the expensive thermos especially for this picnic. Regina ran her hands proudly over the shiny aluminum surface.

"Hey, Marm . . . psst . . . Marm."

Eugene was whispering to her from behind the tree.

"Why are you hiding, son? Come and have some chicken."

"Jest hand me a leg and I'll eat it right here. Marm, has anyone been askin' for me?"

She handed him a chicken leg. "Come out from behind there, Eugene. What's the matter with you?"

"Anybody lookin' for me, Marm?"

"No one's been asking for you or looking for you."

"You ain't seen a man with green sunglasses snoopin' around?"

"No."

"If he comes and asks about me, tell him you ain't seen me. Save me some chicken. I'll be back after dark."

Anxiety about Eugene and the trouble he might be in lessened when Regina saw Lilibet and Margot approaching with other young people in tow. Margot was chattering like a magpie to Sally Kay, and Lilibet was smiling up at Black Brady.

Oh, dear. She'd never seen Lilibet glow like that. Mr. Brady was awful nice, and he worked so hard at his new business, despite all the mysterious setbacks he'd had, but he's so . . . so kind of worldly and mysterious, or something she didn't understand. And that way he moves, sort of like Laria Sue's cat, smooth and graceful. His body is powerful hard looking. She blushed . . . Lord God, Preacher would be angry with her, thinking about a man's body like that. She brushed her cheek with the back of her hand as if to do away with the blush and the thought. She didn't understand a lot about Cle or the Huttons either, but at least it was a familiar ignorance. Lilibet's much better off with Cle. Cle could give Lilibet everything she ever needed and keep her here in the valley.

She could see Sam wasn't happy with the situation either. His brow was wrinkled with concern as he watched Lilibet smile at something Black said.

"Hi, Marm," Lilibet shouted happily.

Dear gussie, Regina thought, Lilibet's shed four years today. Looks like she did on her eighteenth birthday . . . before she had law school and her daddy to worry about.

They settled on the ground around her red-checkered tablecloth, and Regina forgot her anxiety as they dug into the picnic she'd prepared. They'd eaten just about everything when a tanned, healthy-looking young man approached them.

"Hey, Sam, Lilibet. Done any swimming lately?"

Lilibet jumped to her feet to give Joe Carpozzoli a hug. Joe had joined the Marine Corps the same September the rest of them went to college. They'd seen him during Christmas vacations, but that was all. Cle and Joe corresponded sporadically, so Joe was caught up on the crowd and how they fared.

"Hey, Joe, how long you home for?" asked a jovial Sam.

"Just a week. Gotta report to Cherry Point next week. They're going to teach me how to fly, man. I'm staying in the corps. Love it. Cle be home tomorrow?"

"Sure will. Pappy's throwing a coming-home party for them tomorrow night," Sam said.

"Man, two whole days of partying. Today and tomorrow . . . what a great time to come home," Joe said. "Come on, you all, let's get some of my dad's pizza, and then invade the Hutton table for a dish of Henry's homemade ice cream. Pappy's got a beer keg set up over there, too."

Joe walked off, pulling Lilibet and Sally Kay with him. Margot was struggling awkwardly to her feet and Black helped her up. Sam saw the yearning in her eyes and said, "Come on, Margot. Let's go. Thank you very much, Mrs. Springer. I enjoyed everything." He hooked a blushing Margot's hand over his arm and they followed Joe's trio.

Black supposed he should feel left out, but he

didn't—he was angry. He wanted Lilibet. He watched with relief as she jerked from Joe's grip and turned to run back to him.

"Black, I haven't seen Joe for a while, do you mind . . . or would you like to come with us?"

He could see she wanted to spend time with her old friends. He tucked a flyaway strand of burnished gold hair back under her baseball cap, and trailed a finger around her ear. He felt her tremble at his touch and the memory of her fragile, yet sensual body laying beneath him on the moss in the cove flashed through his mind. Heat began to climb up through his groin. *No, Black, turn it off.*

"No, I don't mind. Go ahead. I'll help your mom clean up, and I see Mike Crisp down by the river. I need to speak with him. But you and I have an unbreakable date tonight. Dancing and then the fireworks. Meet you at nine at the Sons of Italy Hall."

She nodded her assent and gave him a grateful smile. "Marm, everything was delicious. Thank you. I'll come back before the fireworks to make sure you find Uncle Bub and Aunt Roo."

"Never you mind, darlin'. You jest go and have a good time." Marm waved her off.

Regina watched the sun slip behind the mountains with regret. What a lovely day.

One of the oldest buildings in town, the tan, stuccoed Sons of Italy Hall squatted near the Hutton office building. Most of Yancey's community dances were held here. The sound of "Harbor Lights" came from its opened windows.

Black had completed his business with Mike Crisp long ago, and had spent the intervening time talking to people who were curious about future employment at Brady Electronics. He hurried toward the dance hall to meet Lilibet. The doors of the building burst open, spilling yellow light into the darkness. Lilibet, Joe Carpozzoli, Sam, Sally Kay, and others came out running full tilt, Lilibet leading them and pulling Joe by the arm. She caught Black's hand as they ran by.

"Come on, Black, Joe and I have a bet. He doesn't believe I can clog."

"What's the wager?" he asked, running along beside her.

"Five dollars."

Ten minutes later, Black grinned in the dark as he watched Lilibet climb on the wooden platform set up in the town square next to the courthouse. He figured Joe had already lost his bet. Pigs would fly before Lilibet would wager her hard-earned money on a bet she wasn't sure she could win. Not wanting to miss a thing, Joe stood up close, the lights from the stage falling on him. Black stood in the back on the edge of the crowd. He knew Sam and Sally Kay stood near him. He could smell Sally Kay's Fabergé. Margot was next to him. He folded his arms across his chest and prepared to enjoy the next few minutes. He remembered Lilibet's complete participation in the ball game, and he'd sensed a wildness in her as she pulled him along to the square. She'd obviously decided to live this day to the hilt, almost as if it was her last day of freedom.

Did Cle's coming home have anything to do with her behavior? The thought discomfited him. He didn't like it. Besides, he loved what he was seeing in Lilibet today. More of her bright, honest, enthusiasm for life.

A cigarette glowed in the dark as the smoker drew on it. Pappy Hutton stood unnoticed in the recessed doorway of Murphy's Five and Ten, not liking what he was seeing. He'd chosen a daughter-in-law who was bright, beautiful, and courageous. But it wouldn't do for her to make a spectacle of herself in public, especially at these hillbilly doings. He should have taken all of the twins' crowd to the country club tonight . . . Lilibet would have had to go along. But all of his thoughts had been focused on the coming-home party tomorrow night. When she was finished dancing, he would find an excuse to take her home with Fat Sis.

Lester Jones and his West Virginia Pickers swung into a bluegrass favorite, "Watermelon Smilin' on the Vine."

People from the audience had joined the professional cloggers. A young man Lilibet had gone to grade school with took her as his partner, and off they went. Lilibet's feet moved as quick as the excited beat of her heart to the lively, intoxicating music. Lester Jones's fiddle had every toe tapping and every knee wiggling up and down.

Hearing only the music, absorbed in the movement of her body, her feet, the wildness of her heart, Lilibet felt unshackled. She forgot about the people watching and her bet with Joe. She forgot about everything: Cle, Black, Pappy Hutton. The vague, disquieting notion she'd harbored that this was her last unfettered day before Cle came home, left her. All her fears of the mines, and her grim existence on Big Ugly Creek, and her craving for security, flew away as her feet flew. Her true spirit soared. All the courage, energy, and love of freedom of her mountain forefathers expressed themselves in her uninhibited movement. She didn't realize she was laughing with delight. She wasn't aware when the rest of the dancers cleared a circle to stand back and watch as she threw in innovations of her own. They clapped their hands, and yelled, "Go, Lilibet, go!"

In the middle of the audience, Marm stood with her cousins.

"What ya cryin' fer, Regina? That girl of yourn's a dern good dancer."

How could she explain that the tears she wiped hastily off her face were from joy, not sorrow? She'd taught Lilibet to dance like that. She, Regina, had felt like that once.

Black could hardly breathe. Tears pressured the back of his eyes. His throat closed with the effort to keep them back. My God, she was unbelievable. Her head flung back, she'd lost her hat a long time ago and her flying hair shone in the spotlights. Lilibet was the embodiment of love, excitement, freedom. There poured from her an inexhaustible, spontaneous display of spirit—a wholehearted letting go of all she felt, of all she was, of all she wanted to be. For just a moment, he gave himself the luxury of imagining that unrestrained passion in bed with him.

"Oh, Jesus," Sam muttered. Black's acute hearing picked up the agonized groan, indistinguishable to anyone else. He glanced sideways. It hurt to see the misery and adoration on Sam's face. *Dear God, he loves her, too.*

The music stopped and Lilibet walked to the side of the stage. Her fellow dancers urged her to stay with them, but Black saw her throw Joe a look of triumph and then look out over the crowd. *She was looking for him.* She climbed down from the stage, out of his sight, and he moved to find her.

Lilibet descended the last step, and rested for a moment in the shadows of the scaffolding. Still breathless and flushed, and trying to regain her composure, she moved out into the light to find Black in front of her.

He stared at her for a second, taking in her tossed hair, her excited face, the wildness in her eyes, and extended his arm to her. The magnetic pull between them was not to be denied. She took his hand and, in one smooth motion, he brought her to him and stepped them both into the shadows. They kissed . . . a long, soft kiss. Unaware of anything or anyone, they each gave themselves wholeheartedly to the kiss and its loving promise. Finally, he lifted his head and kissed the wisps of hair away from her cheeks, then took her hand to walk away into the night.

Pappy Hutton emerged from beneath the scaffolding and lit a cigarette. *Humph. The miner's daughter and the Indian bastard. Water seeks its own level. What did you expect, Hutton? Well, you're not going to have Lilibet, Brady, I've invested too much time in her, and no one disrupts my plans, especially you. Cle's coming home just in time. Lucky Cle—from the looks of the two of them, Brady's got her all primed. She should be real ripe. Hope the girl is still a virgin.*

Black and Lilibet drifted aimlessly, hand in hand, content just to be together. They passed the crew setting up the fireworks display at the ballpark. Black noticed the wire mesh gate to the football field. Finding it unlocked, he directed Lilibet through and closed the gate behind them. They walked quietly onto the field, the dark, empty, stadium around them. They were in a cup of silence with the distant sounds of celebrating echoing over the edges. From the dance hall floated the strains of "Mona Lisa."

Black brought her firmly to him and they danced in the middle of the field, remembering the feel of each other's bodies in the cove, remembering their urgent wanting. Suspended in a floating world of their own, they danced, mesmerized with each other and the night. The tune changed to "Stranger in Paradise" and they danced on, feeling it was an apt song for this magical night. The slow sweeps they were making in the center of the field tightened, until they moved in place, their feet barely lifting, their bodies massaging each other.

"Look at me," he demanded.

She tilted her head to look up at him.

"Happy?"

Spellbound from the last few hours, and now hypnotized with his arms about her, she could only nod in the affirmative.

"You were meant to be."

Black lowered his head and their mouths met in another long, deep kiss. He flattened her to him. His knee pushed closer, slipping between her inner thighs. *Oh, yes, Black.* Silently, she urged him on. Harder and higher he pressed until she was riding his knee. The heavy, honeyed ache in her loins, the exquisite torture of wanting him, made her groan as the insistent pressure of his knee rubbed hard against the very center of her desire. Her wetness soaked her slacks and she knew he felt it on his bare thigh. Their physical need for each other beat stronger and wilder each time they were together. Their joy in being together brought wonder to Lilibet's heart, and expectant hope to Black.

A loud sizzle and then a bang broke their self-reverie. Beyond the blackness of the field, where the edge of the stadium met the sky, a rocket rose bright against the indigo night. It exploded into a million dazzling golden particles and seemed to shower over them.

"The fireworks," he muttered in her ear.

"Yes." She sighed with happiness, leaning back against his encircling arms to gaze at the extravaganza in the sky above them, her hips braced against his hard length. Fireworks were a passion with Lilibet and seemed a proper finish to this enchanted day and night.

The lights burst and broke above them, red, green, and gold, like the feelings Black evoked within her. Pappy Hutton had wasted no expense. Bright red, white, and blue stars sparkled in the sky, then rockets of orange and yellow. Silver shots and showery sprinkles of colors filled the sky, conjuring up an evening of wonder, romance, and patriotism. Pappy didn't know it, but he was providing Lilibet and Black with a private showing. So far, no one had discovered their retreat and she prayed no one would. This was a night of enchantment.

Black couldn't take his gaze from her glowing face. Reflection from the exploding lights above shimmered in her eyes. The lips he'd kissed were swollen with passion. He watched as they quivered and moved with unsaid words. She said something so quietly he couldn't hear her.

"Say again, please, Elizabeth."

"When I die, I want fireworks. Not a funeral, or a service filled with weeping people. I want fireworks bursting beautifully, happily, triumphantly in the sky, proclaiming Lilibet lived . . . Lilibet lived!"

He wove his fingers in her hair and, holding her head between both his hands, bent to reverently kiss her forehead. She threw both arms around his neck, yanking his head to meet hers in a desperate motion. He kissed her, murmuring softly against her lips, "It's all right, darling. Everything's all right."

He heard a faint sound and jerked his head up. Someone was in the stadium with them.

In a low voice, he said to her, "Don't move."

She nodded. Holding her upper arms tightly, he turned toward the sound and said in a menacing voice, "Identify yourself pronto, or you'll find a knife at your throat. I know you're thirty feet to the right of me. It won't take me but seconds to find you."

"I-I-it's me, Brady. Lilibet's brother, Eu-Eugene."

Black swung around, thrusting Lilibet behind his back.

His eyes took on an unearthly glow as they pierced through the night and found Eugene s quivering form.

"Stay where you are, Springer. What do you want?"

"I have to t-t-talk to Lilibet. I seen you come in here a while ago, and I waited for you to come out ... but I can't wait no longer."

"Talk to her from where you are.'

"Gotta talk in private."

"No. Start talking."

"It's all right, Eugene," Lilibet said over Black's shoulder. "Black won't rat on you ... he'll kill you first."

Black heard the humor in her voice and relaxed a fraction, but kept her behind him as she listened to her brother.

"I'm l-l-leavin' town, Lilibet. Them revenuers are gettin' too close to the ... the still." He cleared his throat, gathering courage to continue. "I want you to tell Marm and Daddy."

"Where you going, Eugene?"

"Don't know. Think I'll hitch a ride with Uncle Bub and Aunt Roo to Dixie Lick, and head out from there."

"The MacDonalds going with you?"

"I ain't tellin', and I ain't tellin' where I'm going," Eugene said, a belligerent note in his voice.

"Frankly, Eugene, I couldn't care less. Don't come back. Marm's better off without you.' Her words bit cruelly through the distance between them.

Eugene advanced a step, and Black said, "Told you not to move, Springer."

Eugene turned to run and soon disappeared through the far gate.

Black turned around and gave her a little shake. "I wouldn't have killed him, you imp."

"I know," she said, laughing, "but he thinks you would."

"Only if he'd harmed you," Black said, his face solemn.

"Oh, heavens, Black, I forgot Eugene was to drive Marm and Margot home." She pulled out of his arms. The spell was broken. "I have to find them. They'll be getting worried."

He put his arm around her shoulders and they walked slowly, reluctantly toward the gate.

"I'll pick you up sometime this week and we'll go to Matterhorn for one of my mother's famous barbecues."

"Black, you know Cle is coming home. I promised I'd go to the country club dance with him."

"Lilibet, sooner or later, you're going to have to tell Cle that you and I—"

She cut in before he could finish. "I know, I mean, I don't know. I need to be with him for a while . . . to be sure. Cle's so anxious to get home, and he's so looking forward to all the parties and the rest of the summer. I . . ."

He turned her to face him, both hands on her shoulders. "Are you afraid of him, or of Pappy?"

"Of course not. No."

Chapter 15

The late afternoon sun drew a languid halo around Cledith Hutton's golden head. His crew cut a thing of the past, he wore his hair continental style, swept back without a part. His navy blazer, white duck trousers, and white buck shoes were immaculate and held a hint of the playboy yachtsmen on the French Riviera. He stood in Fat Sis's rose garden saying goodbye to guests. Flicking a piece of dust from his blazer with one hand, he kept the other anchored about Lilibet's waist.

"Goodbye, Mayor," Cle said, shaking hands heartily.

"Been good to see you, good to see you. Glad you're home where you belong. I expect you'll be taking over mine operations soon, right?" said Mayor Browning.

"No, sir, it'll be a while yet. I have a lot to learn. I'm happy you could be here. Tell Mrs. Browning we're sorry she's not feeling well."

"Yes, yes, sure will, sure will. Bye now, Cle, Lilibet."

Cle leaned to whisper in Lilibet's ear. "Good. One more gone. Soon they'll all be gone and I'll have you to myself."

He picked a white rose from the bush next to him, stripped it of its thorns, and tucked it in Lilibet's hair above her ear.

"Perfect," he said, and surveyed his handiwork.

She was perfect, he thought. Her white piqué sundress, skimming her slim waist and flaring gracefully at her knees, showed off the light tan she'd acquired this summer. The tiny spaghetti straps exposed her delicate shoulders, the fragile collarbones framing the heart-shaped hollow at the base of her throat. Her only jewelry was a pair of pearl earrings, and a pearl bracelet on her bare arm. Someday, he thought, he would give her real pearls.

"Hey, Cle. Can't wait till the blast tonight. Things aren't the same when you're gone." Tom Tee gave Lilibet a meaningful look and she glared back at him. "We gotta take Jane Etta home first, but we'll be back in time for the party."

Cle patted Jane Etta on the head, and gave Donetta a brief hug.

"When are you going to tell me why those flapping jaws of yours are sewn together, Tom Tee?" Cle laughed. "It's about time some broad socked you a good one."

"Says he ran into a door at the store, Cle, but I think he saw a pretty girl and God ran him smack into a wall!" said a giggling Donetta. "Bye, see you later."

"God, she looks like a tub of lard. Disgusting! How does Tom Tee put up with it?" Cle muttered.

"Some women get that way after they've had a few babies, Cle."

"You won't, will you, sweetheart?" He gave her waist a squeeze.

"Well, I . . ."

"Goodbye, sir, happy you could be here. Yes, ma'am, we had a wonderful time over there . . . Clarice is in the house helping Fat Sis and Belle . . . yes, ma'am, I'll tell her . . ." And so it went.

From the kitchen window, Clarice surveyed the garden scene with speculation, wondering how soon she could escape. She was bored, bored, bored. Cle was doing his duty nicely, but then he always did. He had scarcely let Lilibet out of his reach. Lilibet was such a nurturer, she hadn't yet caught onto Cle's talented manipulating. Cle had found the perfect mate in Lilibet. Everything he'd wanted and hadn't gotten from our dear, sweet mother, Clada. Wonder what Freud would make of that?

Clarice dipped a shrimp in cocktail sauce and nibbled on it as she eyed the two of them.

She wondered if what Tom Tee said about Lilibet and Black Brady was true? She hoped not. Cle needs Lilibet. An angel with guts. *And you need Black Brady, Clarice Hutton.* But she was afraid of Black. He wasn't someone she could diddle with and then throw away. The minute she'd looked into his eyes that night four years ago at Ruby's, she knew he was the one savage she couldn't tame. She'd made a fool of herself chasing after him up to Yale those weekends. He doesn't know it, but someday he's going to have a hell of a ride with me. She sighed. In the meantime, she had Mike Crisp to look forward to.

She ate another shrimp.

She'd never fucked Mike but she'd gotten him hot when they'd danced the last time at Ruby's. She'd hated Europe and everything it entailed. She'd spent the whole trip wanting to come home and fuck Mike. Her pussy actually itched with the craving. She knew he was forbidden fruit, almost as dangerous to fool around with as Black, but the danger only made the game more enticing. She craved Mike almost as bad as she craved Black. Thinking about the humongous cock she'd rubbed and hardened two month's ago at Ruby's made her weak in the knees. Biggest cock she'd ever felt. Time to split this joint. Lollipop time, Clarice, baby.

She licked the cocktail sauce from her fingers, took the pins from her piled-up strawberry blond ringlets and, shaking her head with relief, let her hair fall to the middle of her bare back. Mike had said to reach him through Gloria at Carpozzoli's. Tugging impatiently at the top of her strapless red sundress, she reached for the phone.

Fat Sis had redecorated the rec room since high school days. Lilibet didn't like it. The overstuffed furniture was black patent leather, the tables were triangular-shaped yellow Formica with black metal legs, and the walls were a rusty orange. The lamps were funny-looking globes without shades and light glared without mercy on the homely room. She was ashamed of herself for being so picky.

Cle and Joe finished a game of pool, pounded each other on the back, and grabbed another mug of beer. "Well, buddy, you haven't lost your talent for beating the shit out of me. I owe you ten bucks," Joe said.

"Forget it, Joebo. Put it in the collection plate for me on Sunday."

The sound of Lloyd Price and "Stagger Lee" came from the jukebox. Cle gave his beer to Joe, fastened his arm around Lilibet and danced her onto the new black linoleum.

Cle brushed his lips over her forehead, and her heart jumped to her throat. No, don't do that, she protested silently. Black kissed me there. Oh, God, how was she going to tell Cle about Black, and about law school? Cle was so sweet. She had loved him for a long time. But things had changed. The awesome depth and power of the feelings Black generated in her were not to be denied. Then there was law school. She'd wanted to be an attorney for as long as she could remember, but if Cle had his way she would marry him and stay here in the valley. He couldn't hog-tie her, she thought defiantly. She sensed that Black would be more understanding of a woman practicing law. But Black hadn't even told her he loved her. Did he? Her brain swirled as dizzily as her skirt. One thing she knew for sure: Nothing would keep her from law school. Nothing.

Cle whirled her around expertly, her skirt flying above her knees. He laughed, kissed her again, and whirled around faster and faster. Cle had always been a good dancer, and he'd perfected his techniques to the point where he was a joy to dance with and a joy to watch.

"Hey, Cle, do it again," yelled a drunk Tom Tee. "I wanna see Lilibet's legs."

Cle ignored him but said to Lilibet, "Come on, honey, let's show them what we can do."

He twirled her around faster and faster, his steps getting more and more intricate. Lilibet had no trouble following him.

"Gawd! How can Lilibet follow him? I couldn't do that if you paid me a thousand bucks," Donetta said.

Sally Kay sniffed. "Oh, she can dance, that's for sure. Didn't you see her clogging the other night, up there in front of the whole world like she was . . ."

"Shut up, Sally Kay," Clarice growled.

She sat in a corner with Joe, nursing a beer. Mike couldn't meet her until midnight so she was killing time, but she was getting hornier and hornier. Joe Carpozzoli was even beginning to look good. She looked around the room. Jesus, even Jimmy Haynes was here. Cle still had the magic, still commanded the loyalty and the following he'd garnered in high school. All the old crowd was here. She hadn't seen Jimmy since high school. He worked in his father's bakery shop. Looking at Jimmy's lanky form, dressed in tacky plaid trousers and white nylon shirt, she wondered how she could have ever been hot for him.

"Cle, the keg's running dry," Jimmy yelled.

"Tell Sam. He'll take care of it."

Hadn't any of them noticed that Cle was an amalgamation of Sam, Lilibet, and herself? He was a vacuum without the other three. She supposed they never would see the real Cle. He was too beautiful, too generous, too charming, too much fun. She loved her twin to distraction, but she knew him well.

She'd learned to love Lilibet, too. She didn't want to, but she did. Lilibet accepted her as she was. Lilibet was the only true friend she'd ever had. Other people played up to her because of Pappy's money, or to be a part of Cle's magic circle, or, if they were men, because they wanted a good fuck. Her sorority sisters had either envied or hated Clarice. Clarice hadn't really cared what they thought but found herself spending more time with Lilibet at Miss Mabel's. Memories of the late nights they had shared, making fudge, exchanging confidences, tears and laughter brought a sharp pang of guilt. She thought of what Pappy had asked her to do and her stomach fluttered nervously.

The son of a bitch is up to something, and she wished he wouldn't involve her. She wanted nothing to do with his Machiavellian plots. However, he'd threatened to curtail her freedom, putting a tail on her, so she'd told him she would find out what he wanted to know.

She had to admit that she needed Lilibet almost as much as Cle did. Besides, Lilibet might be the only hope for this evil-seeded family. *I'm sorry, sweet Lilibet, forgive me just this once.*

She caressed the bodice of her strapless dress and casually squeezed an aching nipple. Joe looked at her hopefully. She took a big swig of her beer and laughed.

"Want some of Clarice, Joe? You didn't get any in high school, did you?"

"Shouldn't talk that way about yourself, Clarice."

"Why the fuck not?"

"You're Cle's sister."

Clarice licked her lips, then leaned over to lick Joe around his ear. "Come on, Clarice, stop it."

"Want some, don't you, Joe?"

"You're my best friend's sister," he said, his voice shaking. He crossed his legs and drank the rest of his beer in one swallow.

Sometimes, her guilt and shame shoved her hard, made her do things she didn't want to. For a second, she placed her hands over her ears to blot out the sounds she heard in her head, the sounds a ten-year-old girl heard as she hid beneath her mother's bed and listened to strange moans and sighs. She'd been jealous of her mother—jealous of Pappy's intense obsession with her, and jealous of the physical attention he lavished on her. Cruelly honest with herself, Clarice knew now that her jealousy had grown to incestuous desires for her own father, and the shame of it was the seed of her nymphomaniacal journey through life. Pappy had never touched her, but she knew he sensed her physical obscenities, and was amused. He had goaded her young jealousy by fondling other women in front of her and her mother, and by making a big to-do over any female friend she brought to the house.

No wonder her mother had done what she'd done.

She no longer desired Pappy, but the early forbidden and exciting sexual encounters she'd initiated with other men to hurt Pappy had created a craving for more of the same. She squeezed her aching nipple again, and thought about running her hand across Joe's crotch. No, waiting for Mike would make their sex even more erotic.

Sam came in lugging a new keg. Joe lurched up to pour himself another mug.

"Haven't you had enough, Joe?" Clarice asked when he sat down again.

"Never too much, when I'm here with you all. 'Sides, I don't know when I'll be home again."

"Cle, Pappy wants to see you," Sam called out over their heads. "Said to meet him in the library."

"Okay. Come on, honey. Let's see what he wants."

"No, Cle," Lilibet said, trying to pull her hand from his. "I'm sure he doesn't want me."

"Where I go, you go."

The library was empty when they arrived. The always-lit candles on the mantel cast flickering yellow light on the portrait of Clada Hutton. Except for the candles and a small lamp on a table near the fireplace, the room was dim.

Lilibet walked up close to the mantel, wanting a better view of the painting. "She was so beautiful, Cle."

"Yeh."

"Heavens, look at her necklace. Are those real sapphires?"

"I expect so."

The dull sound of his normally vibrant voice made her turn around. His back was to her. He was inspecting the cover of a book.

"Don't you know?"

"Never thought much about it." His tone was almost sullen.

He hadn't turned around. She walked over to him, tugged on his sleeve and forced him to face her. "Is something wrong?"

"No. What could be wrong? I'm home. I'm with you."

She let go of him and returned to the portrait. She stood on her tiptoes trying to read the signature of the artist. "Cle, who painted this?"

"Some artist from Virginia." He'd turned his back again and was searching for another book.

"Will you come and read this signature for me?"

"No!"

Surprised at his uncharacteristic rudeness, she went to him again, but he wouldn't turn around. She knew it had nothing to do with her. It must be the portrait. Cle never looked at the picture of his mother. She tried to remember times with him here in the library and realized he always stood with his back to the fireplace. He didn't want to see the portrait. Curious, since all reports said Cle had adored his mother. Come to think of it, he never talked about her. When Clarice or someone else mentioned Clada Hutton, Cle would change the subject.

Lilibet walked back and studied the image of the beautiful woman, wondering what secrets were hidden in the sapphire blue eyes.

"There will never be another woman to match her, Lilibet." Pappy Hutton's dry, cool voice startled her.

She turned to find him staring at her from across the room near the library door. "I'm sure you're correct, Mr. Hutton. I wish I could have known her."

"Lilibet, would you excuse Cle and me for a while? He's been busy with our guests and with you. I'd like some private time with him. It's been a while since we've had a father and son chat. I'm sure you understand."

"Yes, sir."

"Lilibet can stay, Pappy. She can read a book while we're talking."

"No, son. These are private business matters."

Lilibet walked to the door. Wanting no argument between Pappy and Cle, she exited quickly.

Pappy sat in a leather wing chair by the garden window and lit a cigarette.

"You're looking fine, son. I like the polish you picked up in Europe."

"Thank you, sir. I enjoyed the trip but I'm happy I'm home. This is where I belong."

"Yes, it is. Come and have a smoke with me."

Cle sat in the adjoining chair and lit a cigarette. "What's this all about, Pappy?"

"Have you and Lilibet been engaging in sexual activities?"

"Now, Pappy, I really don't think that's any of your business." Cle laughed. "But . . . yeh, we do some pretty heavy petting."

"You fucked her yet?"

Cle grew red in the face and fidgeted in his seat. "What's the problem, Pappy? Think I'm not man enough?"

"I know better than that, son. I have my reasons for asking."

Cle drew heavily on his cigarette, then tilted his head back to vigorously dispatch the smoke into the air above him.

"No, I haven't. We wanted to save that for our wedding night. You always said there were girls you marry, and girls you diddle. I've done a hell of a lot of diddlin', but not with Lilibet."

"Ask her to marry you."

"I have, but she keeps putting me off. Wants to go to law school. I'll talk her out of that before the summer's over."

"Knock her up, Cle! Get her pregnant now or you're going to lose her."

A brief silence ensued in the dim library. Cle stubbed his cigarette out, and cleared his throat.

His voice strained, he said, "I don't like being told what to do, even by you. But you always have a good reason, Pappy, so I'll listen."

"Quite simple, son. Black Brady has a hold on her. She's falling in love with him."

Cle stood up abruptly and raked his fingers through his neatly combed hair. "That's impossible. She loves me."

"I'm sure she does, but from what I've seen and from what's been reported to me, the attraction between her and Brady is something you would . . ." It was difficult to admit that your son was an "empty suit." He'd started to say Cle would never fathom the powerful emotion that was possible between people like Lilibet and Brady, but thought better of it. He didn't want to insult his son, especially at this point.

Cle walked about the room, running his fingers through his hair, and muttering to himself. "It's just impossible. How did she get so involved with Brady? I can't lose her, I can't."

He couldn't let anyone discover how much he needed Lilibet. Everyone knew he loved her, but he needed her more than he loved her. Her strength, her soft heart, her loyalty. He couldn't survive without it. When he'd discovered her, spotted her genuineness, he had known

women like her were few and far between. Well, actually
Sam had found her for him, but Sam hadn't minded when
Cle had taken over. She was his only hope. He knew this
like he knew his hair was blond and his eyes were blue.
Lilibet wouldn't fall in love with someone else, wouldn't
betray him, wouldn't leave him like . . . like his mother
had.

"It's not important how she got involved with the bastard. Sit down, Cledith."

"I can't. I've got to figure this out."

Pappy walked over to Cle and stood in front of him,
halting his frantic pacing.

"There's nothing to worry about. Clarice is going to
find out when Lilibet's fertile time is, and you can take it
from there."

"How's she going to do that?"

"At Clarice's invitation, Lilibet is spending the night
here tonight. Clarice plans one of those late-night female
gabfests, and she'll maneuver the conversation around to
monthly periods and so forth. Then we'll know when
she's ripe."

"But, Jesus Christ, Pappy, how is that going to help
me? I can't just wait until Clarice says the time is right
and then rape Lilibet." His face was pinched and white.

Pappy gave an inward sigh of relief. He'd given into
the idea faster than Pappy had imagined. Cle didn't like
unpleasant situations. He wanted his life to run smooth
and undisturbed. There had been the possibility Cle
would say, "Oh, the hell with it, let Brady have her." Evidently, somewhere along the way, Lilibet had truly become indispensable to his son. Exactly what he'd
surmised four years ago.

"You'll figure out a way, boy. You've been wanting to
fuck her, right?"

"Hell, yes! It's driving me crazy."

"You're my son, and no man can satisfy a woman better than a Hutton. You get her pregnant, boy, and we'll
have a wedding by the end of the summer. She'll forget
all about Brady, and law school. I know women like
Lilibet. They take their maternal and wifely duties seriously."

She's also intensely loyal and honest. Sickeningly endearing qualities that will keep her by your side through thick and thin, thought Pappy. *I have great plans for you, my boy, and Lilibet is going to make sure they happen. Neither of you will ever know it's me pulling the strings.*

Cle's cheeks were pink again, and a gleam had entered his blue eyes. *Ah, the idea was taking hold. He was thinking about fucking her. Good.*

"Well, what do you think, son?"

"I'm thinking you're going to be a grandfather next winter, Pappy." Cle shook his father's hand and thumped his back, smiling.

"You can join your friends now, Cle. Don't forget you're starting work at Hutton headquarters first thing Monday morning."

"Yes, sir."

Pappy watched the door close behind his son and then turned to face Clada's portrait. "A grandchild, Clada. Odd, I never thought of the added benefit of a grandchild. A nice addition to this house. The more I think of it, the more I like it. Denying Brady access to Lilibet is going to give me great pleasure. I don't like him or that new factory he's trying to get started. Getting too big for his Indian britches. Cle will have Lilibet, and I'll have a grandchild, and Brady will live with eternal disappointment."

He took his time lighting a fat cigar, rolling it wetly between his lips. He exhaled and let the smoke drift lazily up toward her portrait. "How sad, Clada. You won't be here to enjoy the progeny of your favorite child." He paused a moment, a thin smile on his face. "He doesn't like what you did, you know. Cle doesn't like it at all."

Chapter 16

Lilibet woke up late the next morning with a heavy sense of foreboding. In the stillness of the morning there was apprehension, a loaded impression of waiting for something to happen. It was the "knowing." She fought the feeling, blaming it on the nightmare she'd had. She'd had it before . . . rats crawling over her as she sat alone in a cold, black tunnel, her wrists and ankles bound. As awful as it was, she'd become accustomed to the eerie dream she'd been having in the past few months. No, this feeling wasn't generated by the dream. The "knowing" was telling her to prepare for something now.

She shook her head irritably. Everything is fine. You're just tired from the party. She stretched her arms above her head, yawned, and looked about Clarice's spacious bedroom.

The whole house at Big Ugly would fit into this room. She knew Clarice had spent a fortune refurbishing her bedroom the same time Fat Sis did the rec room. She smiled to herself. The new look was a big change from the frilly, pink and white organdy room of Clarice's high school days. It certainly reflected Clarice's personality and it wasn't very restful, but Clarice wasn't restful. The colors were bold: bright blues, and vivid purples, with splashes of white. This was the first time she'd ever slept on sheets decorated with flamboyant blue and purple flowers. The furniture was all chrome, angular, and modern. One whole wall was mirrored and so was the ceiling.

Why would one want a mirrored ceiling? She stared up at her reflection. Kind of interesting to see what you looked like in bed first thing in the morning. She glanced over at Clarice, still asleep on the other side of the immense bed. First time she'd ever seen or slept in a king-size bed. Fat Sis had wanted to put her in the guest room but Clarice insisted Lilibet sleep with her.

Lilibet, exhausted after two days of celebration, had begged off when the rest of them went to Ruby's at midnight. She'd been asleep when Clarice sneaked in at three o'clock in the morning, but Clarice had awakened her. They'd had a grand time gossiping and talking about female things, like they used to in college sometimes. It was fun.

Lilibet looked at the clock on the bedside table and was surprised to find it was ten o'clock. She'd never slept so late before. She started to get out of bed, but then lay back down with a smile. Pappy had given her the day off. What a great week this was turning out to be. She'd needed some fun time. The party last night, and getting the old crowd together had been wonderful. Maybe her sense of foreboding was simply a letdown after all the fun. Fourth of July was the magic day.

Oh God, Fourth of July.

Her heart skipped a beat when she thought of Black and the questions Clarice had asked her in the early-morning hours. She'd slipped them in just as they were drowsing off to sleep, but Lilibet knew Clarice well enough to know they were more than just casual questions.

She remembered them now, anxiety forming in her chest. Unaccustomed to deceit of any kind, guilt hit her hard. She hated it. She detested the confusion of her feelings toward Cle and Black. She loved Cle, but knew now she didn't love him the way she should. With an ache deep in her heart, she reviewed Clarice's questions.

"Lilibet, that time you danced with Black Brady at Ruby's, and the rest of that summer . . . what was it like?"

"What do you mean?"

"You know . . . how does he feel? Does he wear an after-shave? What's the brand?"

"I don't remember, Clarice, and besides, you pay more attention to things like that than I do. Good night."

Just as she was drifting off to sleep came another question. "Tom Tee says you've been seeing a lot of Black. Is that true?"

"Go to sleep, Clarice," she'd said, and turned over on her side away from Clarice.

"Tell me. I won't tell anyone."

Lilibet knew this was true. Clarice had her own code of ethics and would never betray a friend.

"Black and I are just friends."

"What's he like?"

"He's . . ." brave, exciting, exhilarating, kind . . . sometimes he's mysterious and dangerous . . . there's no one like him, she wanted to say. "He's . . . very talented—and fun to be with." She feigned a yawn. "Oh, I'm so sleepy. Good night, Clarice."

"But . . . has he ever kissed you? I won't tell Cle."

Lilibet pretended she was asleep.

She remembered the whispered conversation now and searched frantically in her mind for any revelations she may have made. Earlier they had talked about old high school friends, how fat Donetta was getting, how shallow Sally Kay was . . . and then they had talked about the painful, difficult monthly periods Clarice experienced, and how easy and regular Lilibet's were. No, nothing there to worry about . . . it was the conversation about Black that bothered her.

You've got to take hold, Lilibet. Decide what you should do. She'd promised Cle she would go to the country club dance with him on Saturday night. She told herself she would face up to her dilemma before then.

The telephone rang in the upstairs hallway. She heard Belle's soft voice answering. Moments later, she heard Fat Sis on the phone, and then a muddle of conversation between Belle, Fat Sis, . . . then Cle's voice was added. What was going on?

A knock came at the bedroom door. She got out of bed, hastily put on her bathrobe, and opened the door. Fat Sis stood there, her face white, Cle behind her, his pinched and drained.

"Lilibet, darling, we have some bad news. I think you'd better wake Clarice," Fat Sis said.

"What's the matter? What has happened? Is Marm all right, or is it Daddy?"

Cle pushed past Fat Sis and hugged Lilibet to him, his voice high and thin. "No, honey, it isn't your family. It's Joe. He never made it home last night. He's ... dead."

Shocked, Lilibet asked, "No! How?"

Cle clutched her to him. He was clammy, covered with a nervous sweat, and smelled of stale beer. She could hardly breathe. She could feel the stuttering of his heart.

"We tried to stop him, Lilibet, honestly we did."

"What do you mean?"

"He was drunk when he left Ruby's. He never made Deadman's Curve."

Her stomach churned sickly. Her knees almost gave way. Then her spine stiffened and she shriveled inside. She jerked away from him.

"You were drinking too much! All of you. How could you, Cle? You're their hero, their leader. You shouldn't have let him leave." She hurled the words at him. He drew back as if he'd been wounded, his face pained, an unfamiliar glistening in his eyes.

"Sam tried. Sam took his keys but somehow Joe got them back."

Oh, God, poor Sam. He'll be suffering worse than any of us, she thought. He always feels so responsible for all of us—takes such good care of us—and we take him for granted. She'd find both Sam and then Tony Carpozzoli later. First she had to repair the damage she'd done. Cle had come to her for comfort and she'd given him anger. Joe had practically grown up in this house—he'd been here almost as much as Sam—and she knew his loss would hit Cle hard.

Clarice was sitting up in bed, hugging the flowered sheet to her chest, her hair disheveled, her eyes round and shocked. A note of hysteria in her voice, she said, "Dead? Not Joe. You're kidding, aren't you, Cle?"

There was no answer from Cle. The twins stared at each other, their eyes bleak, their faces bleached of color. Lilibet remembered the last death they'd dealt with was their mother's. Were they recalling the tragedy? It seemed so. Fat Sis stood immobile in the hall, globular tears dropping from her plump cheeks. Belle stood behind her. Belle and Lilibet exchanged a significant glance. Someone had to take charge here.

Lilibet submerged her anger at Joe's useless, wasteful death, knowing she would have to deal with it later, and began giving orders. Within her something shifted. Cle had looked to her for strength and guidance. All of them had, and she had given it, was giving it. Why did she feel cheated, set apart, in charge when she didn't want to be?

She shrugged it off and said, "Belle, fix breakfast for the twins and me. I'm sure Fat Sis has already eaten." Fat Sis nodded weakly.

"I'm sorry I yelled at you, Cle," she continued and kissed him on the cheek. "Call Sam and get him over here. Your father needs to be told, so call the office. Then call the Carpozzolis and tell them we'll be over as soon as we get organized. Now you'll have to leave so Clarice and I can get dressed."

"Lilibet, do I have to call the Carpozzolis right now? I don't think I can face talking . . ."

"Of course not, Cle. Perhaps it's something Fat Sis better do. Fat Sis?"

Fat Sis wiped the tears from her cheeks and nodded to Lilibet, a look of relief on her face. "Yes, I'll do that."

She hurried off, happy to have something to do. Cle reached for Lilibet's hand and kissed it. "I love you," he whispered to her.

She smiled at him. "Everything will be fine, Cle. We'll get through this. Go on now. We've got people to call, and food to prepare and take to the Carpozzolis. They're going to need all the support we can give them."

He left. She turned around to find Clarice staring into space. "Get dressed, Clarice!" she ordered.

The day of Joe's funeral was hot and still. Nothing moved unless it had to. Everyone and everything was hidden away in whatever cool shelter could be found. Heat shimmered off the asphalt and dusty green leaves hung limply from the trees. Dogs lay listlessly in the shade of porches, awnings, drooping bushes—although even these provided little relief.

Despite the sadness of the occasion, walking from the hot, bright sunlight into the dim, cool interior of Saint Jude's Catholic Church was a relief. Joe's parents sat in the front pew with the remainder of their six children, and assorted grandchildren. Behind them sat the Hutton family, Lilibet, and Sam.

Cle's clammy hand clasped hers tightly. She could feel his arm trembling, and she gave him a smile of reassurance. On her other side, Sam sat solid as a rock, his brown eyes filled with sadness. His warm hand covered her free one, and she marveled for an irrelevant moment at the contrast of Cle's cold hand and Sam's warm one. Their presence on either side of her reminded her for a poignant moment of graduation night. She nudged each of them with an elbow and they smiled.

She looked around to see who had come. Most of Yancey's business community. That was good. She took a moment to enjoy the beauty of the stained glass windows and the colors they cast on the faces of the people and the polished wooden pews. People talked in hushed tones, some with grief on their faces, some not. This was a social occasion for a few people. In the smugness of their faces they carried their self-righteous pride in having come to dutifully honor the deceased. They gossiped back and forth over the backs of their pews, their whispering hissing over the quiet organ music. The Carpozzoli family sat silent, their shoulders bowed.

The organ music grew solemn and loud and the talking ceased. A marine honor guard marched in and the mass for Joe Carpozzoli began. Cle tightened his hold on her hand until it hurt. She looked at him but he avoided her eyes. Sam winked at her and Lilibet finally let her tears for Joe flow.

The Yancey Valley Country Club was nestled in a secluded meadowland ten miles outside of Yancey, the only wide open space of its size in the valley. It was an incongruous spot of manicured, money-green luxury in the midst of the poverty-ridden community. As much as she hated to admit it, Lilibet enjoyed coming here and now and then. Though she disliked many of the phony and stilted people who made this their enclave, the idea that man could create something this beautiful among the slag heaps encouraged her. She respected beauty and achievement in any form.

This middle-of-the-summer dance was a tradition. The first time she'd attended with Cle four years ago, she'd been shaky with nerves. Now, with the cachet of the Hutton family stamped on her long ago, she moved with assurance and poise among the upper crust of the community. They treated Lilibet and Cle as if they were the heir apparent and his fiancée.

Cle brought her another drink, and she accepted it gratefully. It was a hot night, and she was thirsty, but she was drinking much more than usual. Ashamed, she knew the gin was giving her false courage for the conversation that must take place between her and Cle sometime this evening.

Lilibet wore a dress Clarice had given her. She loved the way Marm had cut it down to fit her. Clarice had dared her not to wear a slip underneath, and Lilibet had taken her up on it. The long, cerulean-blue, silk gown rustled sensuously about her legs as she walked. A few years ago the sensation would have embarrassed her, but Black had made her proud of her body, had awakened . . . no, don't think of that. The off-the-shoulder neckline made her feel practically naked, but cool and daring, maybe even a bit decadent. She worried, though, about the hungry glances Cle cast at the suggestion of breasts curving above the edge of blue silk. They were the same looks he gave her when he was in the mood for heavy petting. There would be none of that this evening.

She had decided to tell Cle about Black. The last thing she wanted to do was hurt him, but she needed time to sort out her feelings. She didn't want to see either Cle or Black for a while. She planned to spend the next few weeks sorting out her future and should know what to do by then. There was law school in the fall. She would be away from both of them for long stretches of time. Deep down, she knew she wasn't facing the issue squarely . . . but she'd adored Cle since the first moment she saw him

eight years ago, had nurtured his wants and taken care of
his needs. She dreaded hurting him.

"Come on, honey, let's get another drink and walk
down by the pool," Cle said.

She agreed. This was the opportunity she'd been waiting for. "Just a lemonade for me this time, Cle. I'm a bit
woozy."

"Stay here. I'll go to the bar and be right back."

She watched him engage in charming banter with the
bartender for a few minutes, and then come back to her
carrying their drinks. With concern, she noted his sunken
eyes and the quivering of his hands. The liquid in the
glasses slopped dangerously back and forth. Only three
days since Joe's funeral. Cle had locked himself in his
room for two days. Tonight was the first time he'd been
out in public. On the surface he seemed fine, but she
knew he was battling sincere sorrow. He flashed her a
beautiful smile as he approached and her stomach
clenched.

Could she go through with what she'd planned this
evening?

They walked hand in hand over the pampered emerald
lawn. A bright full moon cast light on other couples wan-
dering about. Tall trees stood etched in shadow against
the night sky, and lilacs scented the darkness. They
skirted the eighteenth tee and entered the pool area. It
was empty. No swimming permitted tonight. Several of
the cabanas looked as if they'd been recently occupied:
an empty glass, a crumpled napkin, a discarded tie, a pair
of silver high heels.

Cle directed her toward the Huttons' enclosed private
cabana at the outer edge of the area. "Pappy gave me the
key," he said.

"Let's stay out here, Cle, in the moonlight. It's so
beautiful tonight."

"I know, hon, but I have some private things to say to
you . . . and I don't want anyone interrupting."

"Well, okay . . . I want to talk to you, too."

Pappy Hutton had built this small frame cabana years
ago when he wanted privacy while at the club. Several
wealthy families followed suit. The cabanas were dis-

creetly situated among the trees between the pool and the golf course.

Cle unlocked the door, switched on a small lamp standing near the door, and cranked open a whole wall of wooden louvers. Lounge chairs, meant to be pulled out to the pool when needed, sat flush against the three other walls. A well-stocked bar filled one corner. There were armchairs, and a telephone for Pappy's use. The newest model television sat in another corner. The place smelled of old bathing suits, chlorine and rich bourbon.

Fresh air filtered through the open louvered wall. Lilibet stood close to it, staring out at the stop-and-go flash of fireflies in the darkness. They reminded her of the fireworks on the Fourth of July. She shook herself irritably. Cle came to stand behind her.

The thought of what she had to say to him made her throat dry. How could she? He'd been so good to her. Pappy had given her daddy a better job. Daddy was sick a lot and she knew most miners would have been fired by now, or put on pension. Daddy had kept the job and she was sure it was because of Pappy. The whole Hutton family was kind to Margot and Marm. Cle was so happy, so fun to be with, so loving . . . oh, God. Her mouth dry with fear, she cleared her throat.

"Drink your lemonade, beautiful. Harbert put something special in there for you. Takes the tartness away."

The strains of a fast-paced "Kansas City" drifted down from the clubhouse.

She took a few nervous sips. Refreshing. She could barely swallow but forced half of it down. Afraid to look at Cle, she drank the rest of it quickly, then set her glass on a table at her side and returned her attention to the darkness outside. A wave of dizziness swept over her and she wondered idly if the bartender had put vodka in her lemonade. She'd told Cle she wanted no more liquor. They said you couldn't taste it. More likely, it was the strong emotions she had been dealing with all week.

Harsh, strained breathing caught her ears. It was Cle. She turned to face him, and the sight of him nearly broke her heart. He was sitting on a cabana lounge, his elbows propped on his knees, his head lowered, his face hidden in his hands. He moaned. Faint-headed, and a little sick in her stomach, she walked cautiously to sit beside him and put her arm around him.

"Ah, Lilibet, Jesus Christ! Why did Joe have to die?"

She rubbed his back soothingly. 'I don't know, Cle. No one knows those things. We just have to accept."

"But it's not fair. I can't stand it. I don't think I can live with this."

"Yes, you can."

He reached for her, and she let him wrap her close to him. He needed something to hold. "No, you don't understand. It's my fault. He died because of me."

"Cle, sweetheart, that's not so," she said, trying to comfort him.

His hot, harsh breath filled her ear and she could feel the staccato beat of his heart next to her ribs.

"Yes," he got out with difficulty. "We had a chug-a-lug contest. My idea ... and you know Joe, anything I wanted to do was great with him Oh, Jesus, Lilibet, I need you so."

"Cle, Cle, It's okay. I'm here and everything is fine." She smoothed his cheek, wanting desperately to ease his suffering. He caught her hand and kissed it, then placed it around his neck and cupped his hand around her face.

"Tell me it wasn't my fault, honey." A sob tore from him and tears rained down his face.

He was crying. Cle was crying. She'd never seen a man cry before, not even her daddy. Huge tears poured down his grief-ravaged face. Sunny, charming, happy, carefree Cle was sobbing uncontrollably. He fell back on the lounge pulling her with him. The movement on the slippery plastic surface gathered her silk skirt to her knees, but she paid little attention, more concerned about Cle.

"Joe's death wasn't your fault," she assured him. "Joe didn't have to chug-a-lug with you. That was his choice."

He hugged her closer to him and her dress slithered up her thighs. He kissed her, first her ear, then her cheek, her chin, and then her lips, his tears wetting her face. She knew he needed her and was comforted by the feel of her, so she said nothing. Sobs interlaced his kisses. She stroked the back of his neck. For a while, nothing could be heard in the dark cabana but Cle's sobs and Lilibet's soft, soothing shushes. Every time she shushed him, he would catch her lips in his to kiss her again.

"I'm scared. I need you, honey. Help me," he sobbed.

"I'm right here, Cle. I'll help you." Thank God, he was crying. He needed to cry.

His tongue entered her mouth and she started to protest but thought that wouldn't be fair. After all, they had kissed this way many times before. Cle wouldn't understand if she pulled away, especially now, when he needed her more than ever. The two of them were soaked with his never-ending tears. Their faces, her hair, his loosened shirt collar, even her neck and the top of her gown were wet. She wished she could stem his tears, relieve his suffering.

His tongue became insistent, his mouth pulling on her lips to deepen the kiss. Freeing her mouth for a moment, he uttered over and over again in her ear, "I need you, Lilibet, help me. I need you." Over and over again, interspersed with sobs.

He captured her mouth again, his tongue thrusting deep in her throat. Her head whirled crazily again, and she could hardly breathe ... why would Harbert lace her drink? Cle's hand moved down to her buttocks and brought her hard against him. She lay softly against him, letting him soothe himself with the feel of her warm body.

He was still crying. It was killing her.

His hand moved down and she felt his fingers on her exposed thighs. She hadn't realized her skirt was up so high. He jostled the silk skirt higher and found the bare skin at the top of her hose and then the straps of her garter belt. Swiftly, his hand slipped between her thighs and then up to finger the downy patch of triangular golden hair.

She stiffened.

Cle had never touched her there before. He'd touched her breast and his hands had roamed over her, but never in her most intimate place. She wanted to tell him that she didn't think this was a good idea, but his kisses held her mouth captive.

She tried to pull away but her head, filled with airy cotton, betrayed her. She was only able to murmur, "Please, Cle. Don't do that."

"Oh, honey, it feels so good down there. Let me, please. You've never let me before. All these years. Please."

"Well, I . . ."

He kissed her again, his fingers working for entrance to the velvety canal. He found it and inserted one finger gently, working to mellow and moisten her. Despite herself, she felt a tenderness for Cle and a corresponding response. Her head whirled dizzily. She was wet. He continued to fondle her, coaxing a response, and she found she enjoyed it. He inserted a second finger and it hurt but she tried to relax while he moved them up and down within her.

The sage, vigilant core of her was telling her this wasn't right. No matter how sweet, not matter how good Cle had always been to her, no matter how many years she'd thought they would someday be together like this, it wasn't right. She tried to pull her arm from beneath his shoulder but his body was too heavy.

He was panting in her ear and mumbled something about needing her. He extracted his fingers and fumbled with his zipper. It opened quickly, as if it was oiled, and just as quickly he rolled on top of her and she felt the hardness of his erection.

"Cle, I really don't think . . ."

"I love you, Lilibet. Please, honey. You're going to be my wife. Please, honey, please." His face was still wet with tears. A few of them dropped to land on her nose as he hovered close above her. "I need you, honey."

This was darling Cle. Sunny, kind Cle, who was unhappy and miserable now. He needed her.

No. This must not be. We will not do this. This is your fault, Lilibet. You've indulged him, and for all the wrong reasons. You should never have let him get this far.

She pulled on the back of his jacket with one hand, pushed at his chest with the other, and said, "Cle, this is a mistake. Let's—"

He pushed hard and hurriedly into her—oh, God, it hurt—and it was too late. For a moment she thought about fighting him off but knew she was partly to blame, so she lay still, her heart beating frantically, her own tears forming. Her nurturing nature had betrayed her.

She wasn't ready for him. It burned. She said nothing, just held him stiffly to her as he shoved in deeper and the burning became a hot hurt. A sharp pain ripped through the burning and she bit her lip. He pumped harder and harder, breathing harshly, his saliva dripping on her ear. Dear God, is this what all the excitement is about? Where's the music and the stars bursting above? It seemed to her that even animals she'd seen mating on the mountain enjoyed it more than she did. Was there something wrong with her?

Her hip jarred painfully against the wall while he pumped incessantly against her and she held to him. It didn't hurt so much anymore. She endured, waiting patiently for this to end. Clarice had said the first time was never good for anyone, not even Clarice. Cle seemed to expand and his climax filled her, the excess spilling down her legs.

With a groan of relief, he relaxed and rolled off her. He lay on his side panting, and pulled Lilibet around to face him. He wasn't crying anymore. "Oh, God. That was wonderful. Are you okay?"

"Yes." She wondered at her feelings. Relief that it was over with, disappointment that the loss of her virginity had come and gone without music or magic . . . but mostly she felt wretched sadness—and a sickening sense of having betrayed someone.

"Thank you, honey. That was exactly what I needed. I feel so much better." He nibbled on her ear. "Don't move an inch. Stay right here close to me for a while."

He kept her next to him, not bothering to straighten his trousers or her dress. His coarse, wet pubic hairs strayed awkwardly over the rim of her garter belt. The metal fasteners of the garters bit into her bare skin where he pressed against her, and her inner thighs, her hose and dress were sticky with his semen. Cle had emptied himself into her but she was not filled. Why should the strange hunger that claimed her time and again be so strong now?

Over Cle's shoulder, she stared out into the quiet, firefly-flecked darkness, and knew with deep, utter certainty that she loved Black. Like a balloon torn abruptly from its owner's hand, bereft of help or guidance, she blew alone and unanchored. Cle had fallen asleep. Weak with the knowledge of what she'd allowed him to do, she wept. Her bitter tears dropped unnoticed on the shoulder of his white dinner jacket.

Chapter 17

The unpainted wood walls of the tiny new bathroom still smelled of sawdust. Marm was so proud of this addition right off the kitchen. Hutton Mining had given Daddy another raise right after the Fourth of July, and Marm had finally gotten her long desired inside bathroom.

Lilibet sat in the old claw-footed bathtub, retrieved from the front yard junk pile, and ran hot water into the tub until it reached her shoulders. Everyday for the last four days she'd sat for an hour in water so hot it make her skin red. Marm, amused, thought it was because Lilibet loved the new bathroom and bathtub. She suspected Margot knew the real reason.

She had done all the things she'd heard her college friends discuss when their monthly periods were late: long hot baths, hard, jarring running and exercise, painful enemas, nasty doses of Epsom salts—all of which had done nothing but give her a sore and aching stomach. She was ten days late, and she had never, ever, been late before.

One time. Just one time, she'd made a mistake. As wretched and guilty and ashamed as she'd felt the next morning, she never once thought she might be pregnant. A shudder started at the crown of her head and shook her body so violently the water in the steaming tub rippled and curled.

Stupid. How could she have done such a stupid, stupid thing? Lilibet Springer, who was in control of her destiny, who was going to be a lawyer, who was going to take her mother out of this hellhole, was pregnant. Just like Donetta and other high school friends, she'd been caught.

Too scared to even cry, she prayed softly, her voice sounding shaky and hollow in the small, empty room.

"Is this meant to be, Lord? Is this what you want of me? Help me to know."

But she didn't listen for an answer, didn't need God to tell her that she already loved the life within her, and that Cle would make a good father, and that a Hutton grandchild would have the safest life in the valley. The knowledge should have brought joy, but it didn't. Heart heavy, she sank lower until the water hit her chin and her hair floated around her.

All her dreams crushed in a moment of weakness, a moment of childhood love turned sour. How ironic that she should acknowledge her deep love for Black in the same moment she'd conceived Cle's child.

"Dear God, help me to be strong. . . ." A single, desperate sob escaped as she tried to finish her prayer. "And help Black to understand."

Chapter 18

The first of September dawned on the mountain with crisp air and vivid colors. A jay fussed high in a paw paw tree. Squirrels chattered, and a fawn skirted the clearing she'd just crossed. They were as nothing to Lilibet. Until this moment, she'd always arrived at the glen with anticipation and joy. Now, feeling an actual drag to her feet, she approached her favorite place with dread. Would Black be waiting for her? She hoped so. She didn't think she had the courage to wait for him. The last time she'd seen him, three weeks ago, they'd driven to Charleston to have dinner and see *Rear Window*. He'd wanted it to be a special evening. He was leaving to visit manufacturing firms in New York and California to study new production methods they were using for television and other electronic components. They had talked about how the business was a new challenge for him, a new frontier, and how it presented opportunities for improving living conditions for the people of West Virginia.

He'd been upset with her when they parted, unhappy that she still hadn't told Cle she was going to law school, and that Black had become an important part of her life. He was mystified, unaccustomed to the uncertainty he sensed in Lilibet. He told her when he returned he expected to see her packing for law school, and that he'd drive her to Morgantown himself to make sure she got there.

She stuck her chin up in the air and arrived at the glen with a determined glint in her eye. Nothing would defeat her. Not this. Not anything.

Black was there, standing between the saplings, looking out at the gorge. His powerful shoulders blocked a portion of the morning light pouring into the glen. He turned to face her and, even across the distance that separated them, his eyes burned into hers. This is what she'd lost. Swept by a wave of despair, she swayed and leaned against the nearest tree for support.

A slow grin formed on his face as he strode toward her. "My secretary thinks I'm crazy. She picked me up at the airport in Charleston this morning and, accustomed to my manic work habits, was prepared to work through the day and night. Two hours later I got your call and left everything on my desk."

She stared at him, not able to say a word. She was committing to memory every feature of his face, the arrogant tilt of his head, the sensual grace of his walk, the smokiness of his voice.

"I'm sorry—" she began, but he quickly shushed her.

He reached for her and pulled her against him. "Don't say anything. Just let me look at you. Do you know how happy I was to hear your voice? From the moment I landed my hand itched to pick up the phone and call you. Every time I called from California, Marm said you were out. What have you been doing? No, don't answer . . . I don't want to know anything except that you're here in my arms."

He brushed her lips with his and a rush of heat hit both of them. He whispered in her ear, "Umm, you taste good. You're habit-forming, Elizabeth. I missed you every agonizing second."

A little longer. She would stay in his arms just a little while longer. He felt so good. So big and strong and sure of himself. She had the comforting feeling that Black could fix anything, heal anything, make any hurt go away. She allowed herself a kiss on the warm skin she could reach just below his ear. She inhaled deeply, willing herself to remember the fresh, healthy male scent that was Black. Oh, dear lord, but this is exactly what she needed to forget.

She pushed herself away from him.

"Started packing yet? Three years from now . . ."

She held up her hand to stay him. "Please, Black, stop. I'm not going."

"What do you mean? Of course, you are. I'm going to be there when you graduate."

"No." She took a deep, shaky breath. "I'm marrying Cle next month."

An awesome stillness swept his body as her words echoed in the glen.

"No."

"Yes. I'm pregnant, Black."

A crazy quilt of pain, betrayal, and monumental disbelief leapt into his face and eyes.

He took her by her upper arms and held them tight. She could feel his rage though the heat of his hands as they fused to her arms, and she was almost afraid of him.

"How could you let yourself be trapped that way?" he demanded savagely.

"I haven't been trapped. I love Cle."

"The way you love me?"

"No. I . . ." Her eyes fell away from his.

He shook her. "Look at me! Do you love me?"

"Yes," she screamed at him. "Do you love me?"

He released her and turned sharply to walk away from her, but she heard him say, "Yes, more than you know. Jesus, what have you done?"

He came back to her, his face rigid with pain.

"How did it happen?" he asked, his jaw set so hard he could barely get the words out.

"It just . . . happened." She told him about Joe Carpozzoli, the funeral, the dance, and Cle's crying. "I felt sorry for him. Cle needs me."

"Maternal feelings for him? My God, Lilibet, you can't go around mothering the world. You can't take care of Cle. He has to learn to take care of himself. Some people walk around with their umbilical cords in their hand looking for someone to plug into. That's Cle."

"It isn't. He's good and kind . . ."

This time it was his turn to interrupt her.

"Stop. You're making me sick. I didn't realize how much they'd gotten to you. Pappy's played an intricate game of cat's cradle with you. He's played on your loyalty and your sense of honor until you're blind to the truth."

"Cle will take good care of me," she said defiantly.

"Is that what you want . . . to be taken care of? You can take care of yourself."

"My family—"

"Is that what this is all about? Gratitude to the Huttons for all they've done for your family? You don't owe anyone anything—you certainly don't owe them your soul! That belongs to God. We honor others by reaching for the best in ourselves and expecting them to do the same. You don't owe Cle or the Huttons a damn thing!"

Bit by painful bit, she was disintegrating inside.

She stretched out a hand to plead for his understanding, a groping gesture she was unused to performing. "Black, please, you have to understand. Cle loves me. He has always assumed we would be married. He's been so good to me. I can't hurt him. He needs me. You don't."

"You don't marry someone because they need you. You choose a life mate because your souls come together . . . because they belong together. We are already part of each other, you and I. We don't even have to come together to know this." As he said it she knew it was true, but it was too late for them.

She held herself rigid, trying desperately to control her turbulent emotions. She must not let go, must not fall into his arms to be comforted, to ask forgiveness. Her child needed its father. Cle would be a good father.

"That kind of love will grow between Cle and me."

"No! No, it won't." He grabbed her and kissed her harshly, and her knees went weak at the nearness of him. He released her mouth but held her tight, the tendons in his throat taut with fury. "That kind of love will never grow between you because Cle isn't whole as you and I are whole, Elizabeth. It's two wholes coming together that explode, that generate energy, that make music, that create light. It's a connecting."

"Black, please."

"Are you asking me to understand, to forgive? Well, I won't. You'll never connect with Cle. You'll never have the kind of love with Cle you deserve," he threatened, as if putting a curse on her. "Never!"

Something inside her broke, and the anguish, like

splinters of glass, pierced every part of her. She'd expected to receive his blessing but knew now that she wouldn't. Did he hate her? With great care and deliberation she swept into a pile what remained of herself, praying she would find the glue later to put her soul back together. A coldness crept from her feet up to her chest. She shrugged off his hands and stepped away from him.

"Do you hate me?"

He took a moment to reply, his eyes surveying her face as if to memorize her features as she'd memorized his. Then the familiar stoicism returned to his face and his eyes became shuttered.

"I could never hate you."

She reached toward him. "Friends?"

He rejected her hand. "I'm afraid that would be too painful for me. Goodbye, Elizabeth."

She caught the sob threatening to break from her frozen chest and, holding her head high, turned to walk from the glen.

Black closed his eyes when she walked away. He'd known the second she'd entered the glen that something was wrong. The stricken look on her face told him everything, but he'd tried to hold it off, had chattered and rattled on like an old lady. He was afraid to open his eyes now for fear of seeing his life's blood red on the moss-covered ground around him. His jugular vein, his wrists, his heart had burst open and the blood was surely gushing in a flood at his feet. He opened his eyes. She was gone . . . and he was still alive.

Suffering the furies of the damned, he sat heavily on the same log he'd rested on the day he'd given her the painting lesson. The thought of Lilibet in Cle's bed made him physically ill. He fought the nausea building in his throat, and spat hard, but couldn't rid himself of the bitter taste of defeat and irrevocable mistakes.

"I blamed her . . . but it's me—it's my fault," he said to the empty glen.

Face it, Brady. You let the most precious part of your life go because you were afraid you'd be tied, shackled, denied free will. He'd let escape the one person who

could have truly freed him—and who could have made
the freedom worth living.

The torment of loss, of knowing he would never share
anything with her again, was unbearable. The keening began deep in his soul, and built slowly until it became a
full-throated snarl. In his rage and despair, he had turned
to the primal screams of the forest to voice his pain. He
rose to his feet as it became a banshee wail and grew and
grew until the sound was a part of him and a part of the
mountain. The scream that tore from his soul reverberated
back and forth and around the mountain.

Halfway to Uncle East's cabin, Lilibet stopped in her
tracks, the hair on the back of her neck rising at the
sound. Dear Lord, what was it? Could it be Black's cougar, Cat? Fear of the big cat made her look swiftly around
her. There was nothing. The harrowing scream was almost human, broadcasting excruciating pain, as if someone were beating their breast in a requiem of unbelievable
sadness. The fearful sound struck terror to her heart and
she put her hands over her ears but it was impossible to
shut out. She began to run but the tortured wail followed,
licking at the corners of her heart, soul, and mind.

She arrived at the cabin breathless and exhausted, tears
streaming down her cheeks. Uncle East was waiting for
her. One look at the pain on his face confirmed the terrible suspicion that it was Black's keening that tore at her.
Would Uncle East turn away from her because of the decision she'd made, because of the wounds she'd inflicted?

She stood at the bottom of the steps and looked up into
his anguished face. He came down the steps and gathered
her into his withered, wise old arms He held her as the
sound circled around and around them. Lilibet's body
shivered continuously at the excruciating pain in the now
strident peals.

They stood there silently, the old man with his protecting arms around the young woman, until the sound lessened and finally stopped. His healing hand stroked her
head soothingly until the tears and the shaking stopped.

He tilted her chin up so he could see her face.

"Knowing you both as I do, it isn't difficult to imagine

what has just happened. He will heal, Elizabeth. So will you."

"I've hurt you, too, Uncle East," she said, her voice cracking. "I'm so sorry."

"Don't be sorry. When you or Black hurt, I will hurt. Love doesn't always bring joy, Elizabeth. You've made a decision you obviously felt was the right one. Both of you will learn to live with it."

"I'm marrying Cle Hutton, Uncle East. I'm carrying his child . . . and the Hutton family has provided for my family. I . . ." She couldn't go on.

"I won't ask if you love Cle, I would only caution you to remember that love is not a currency, not something to be used for barter. I love you for what you are, not for what you bring to me. When you need me, I'll be here."

She departed soon after with promises to visit before winter set in.

Uncle East tamped fresh tobacco in his beautiful pipe and sat in his rocker to wait for his grandson.

Dusk had fallen when Black climbed the three shallow steps to the porch. He was naked except for his leather thong and moccasins. His body was dusty, and scratched here and there, his muscular chest heaving from his exertions. East figured he'd gone to the cave, changed into his Shawnee apparel, and had just finished a punishing three-hour run. Black leaned over and kissed his grandfather's brow then sat silently on the top step, leaning against the railing post.

He gazed out over the fast purpling, gold-shot sky while his grandfather inspected him like a mother bear inspects a returning cub. Only Grandfather East would detect the faint ravages of torment that remained on his grandson's handsome, noble face. It was dark before either one of them spoke.

"Cat race with you?"

"Yes."

"Who won?"

"I did—for the first time. I needed a victory because I allowed fortune to cheat me of something I wanted more than anything."

"Kierkegaard said, 'To cheat oneself out of love is the

most terrible deception. It is an eternal loss for which there is no reparation, either in time or eternity'."

"There will be reparation for me. No longer will I hold back. I'll take what's mine from now on." He paused. "I came back to the valley because of Elizabeth, to establish a business that would take care of us. I wanted to prove to her that I was more than the wild boy she'd met on the mountain. Now I will go and do what I've always wanted. I'm going into the air force, Grandfather. I want to fly."

Grandfather East's heart broke at the bitter anger in Black's voice. Had all the wisdom and love in his upbringing been for naught? Had Black learned to hate? He shivered at the force of hate a man like Black could generate. He remembered again the angry five-year-old child shaking his fist at the mine workers who carried his father's body home. He remembered how the anger and grimness had transposed into love as Black learned to live with nature and heal animals.

"You've made great progress with Brady Electronics. Don't make the same mistake I did, Black. Don't desert the people who've come to trust and rely on you."

"I've trained my people well. In the meantime, I need to fly high and free for a while."

In the midst of the great sadness and worry Uncle East felt for his grandson, he searched for and found his faith. It might take a heap of living, but he speculated that eventually Black would again rely on the values he'd learned as a child. He prayed that the anger and hurt hadn't broken the passionate heart beyond repair.

A month later in the Springer house on Big Ugly Creek, Dr. Mabel Turner, known as "Miss Mabel" in Yancey, stepped back to survey her handiwork. Her velvet brown eyes, cornered with fragile crow's-feet, filled with happy satisfaction. She sighed and smiled at Lilibet who stood before her in her wedding gown.

"You are the most beautiful bride I have ever seen, my darling. I know every mother thinks that, but I truly do believe it. In my heart you're the daughter I never had.

Thank you for allowing me to help you select your gown."

Lilibet kissed her cheek. "Thank you for coming here to help me dress, and for being so kind and gracious to my parents."

Miss Mabel ran her hands over her hips, smoothing out any wrinkles her elegant, navy blue taffeta dress suit might have incurred while she was kneeling in front of Lilibet. Her silver-streaked auburn hair was coifed in a graceful French twist, perfect for the tiny net-covered cocktail hat she would soon perch on her head. A small frown marred her smooth forehead.

"Lilibet, you were right when you insisted on getting dressed here in your own home. Pappy should never have made such a to-do about wanting you to leave for the church from the Hutton house. I'm proud of you. Don't ever let him bamboozle you."

"I think he's ashamed of where I live, Miss Mabel . . . which is rather amusing since this is one of his camps. Don't worry, Pappy may be a power to be reckoned with, but I'm strong, too."

Mabel smiled, but silently, she wondered if the girl would be strong enough. The Huttons had already hog-tied poor Lilibet, and she didn't even know it.

Shaking off her concerns, she patted Lilibet's hand and said, "You'll grow even tougher as the years go by. You have the grit of your mountain forefathers in you, and don't ever forget it."

She looked at her watch. "Where did your mother go? We have to leave for Yancey shortly."

"She went to search for more galax leaves for my bouquet."

"It's a lovely, lovely bouquet your mother and sister made for you." She laughed. "I loved the look of dismay on Pappy's face when you told him Marm and Margot were arranging your bouquet."

"Marm's good with flowers, and it was the only thing she could afford to give me."

At that moment Marm opened the door, her arms filled with waxy, dark green leaves. She gasped when she saw Lilibet. The gown, a gift from Miss Mabel, was magnificent. The duchess silk-satin had a full skirt and chapel train strewn with silver and pearl calla lilies. The cap-sleeved, scoop-necked bodice was overlaid with organza and elongated to emphasize Lilibet's slim waist. She wore simple pearl earrings and a single strand of pearls, gifts from Cle. On her arm was an elaborate pearl, diamond, and platinum bracelet from Pappy. Lilibet stood quietly while Marm oohed and awed.

Miss Mabel reached for the crown of seed pearls waiting on the bed. "Mrs. Springer, we're ready for you to help Lilibet with her headpiece."

"Oh, my . . . well, I have to put these leaves . . . then I have to wash my hands . . . I'll be right back."

Margot came in to be inspected while they waited for Marm. She and all of Lilibet's attendants wore floor-length dresses in autumn jewel colors. Margot was the maid of honor and her dress was a deep sapphire blue. She pirouetted rather awkwardly for them, her cane tapping lightly on the worn linoleum, and they clapped their hands in approval. Her cheeks flushed with excitement. Lilibet thought she'd never seen her look so pretty.

Marm returned, struggling into her own gown of gold lace. Pappy Hutton had bought all the gowns except Lilibet's, but Miss Mabel had insisted on helping with the selections. Miss Mabel was the only person Lilibet had ever known, besides Belle, who talked back to Pappy Hutton.

Miss Mabel zipped the back of Marm's dress and patted her hair into place. "I believe you need a bit of makeup, Mrs. Springer."

Marm glanced fearfully toward the kitchen where the men were gathered. "My husband doesn't allow me to wear makeup, Miss Mabel."

"This is a special day and what he doesn't know won't hurt him. Sit down in front of the vanity there and we'll fix you right up."

Margot shut and locked the door while Miss Mabel applied a touch of eye shadow, rouge, and lipstick to Marm's faded face. When she was finished Marm beamed with joy. Lilibet caught her breath—she'd never seen such joy on her mother's face.

"It's time now, Mrs. Springer."

Marm reached reverently for the regal crown of seed pearls and placed it gently on Lilibet's head. It rested in the middle of feathery platinum curls that Miss Mabel had brushed to the top of Lilibet's head, leaving a few strands to wisp softly about her face. Miss Mabel handed Marm hairpins to secure the headpiece. Then they brought forward the cascade of filmy white veil and let it fall gracefully over Lilibet's face and down to her feet.

Tears welled in Marm's eyes.

"You put Queen Elizabeth to shame, Lilibet," she murmured. She wiped her eyes. "I've spread sheets in the truck to protect your gown. Your daddy don't understand why you wouldn't accept Pappy Hutton's offer of a limousine, but I think I do."

"Thanks, Marm." Lilibet kissed her mother. "Let's go."

The junkyard was filled with neighbors and fellow mine worker friends of Roy Springer's—people Pappy Hutton said couldn't come to the wedding. Miss Mabel had made certain there was something for them to eat as they waited for Lilibet to emerge from the house. They'd socialized all morning, exchanging camp gossip, and marveling about the wedding. They sat on upended bathtubs and broken sofas, perched on the hoods of wrecked cars, and ate chicken drumsticks and potato salad. Lilibet, in the house all morning and unaware of what was going on, was surprised at the crowd waiting for her when she stepped out onto the porch. For a brief moment there was silence as they stared solemnly at her and she stared back at them.

She dropped the skirt she'd hoisted with both hands to keep from sweeping the grime-covered porch and waved to them. There was a general murmur of approval and they smiled and waved back. They made way for her as she maneuvered carefully through the yard with Miss Mabel and Marm coming behind her to hold up her train. Lilibet knew somehow that the crowd wanted to stretch out a hand and touch her to see if she was real. For one impish moment, she wished that they would. A picture of herself arriving at the church in a grimy, fingered, chicken-grease spotted gown, and of the horror on Pappy

Hutton's face, gave her a flash of amusement and satisfaction. She needed some humor. She'd held close to herself all morning, not allowing anyone to see her mounting
anguish.

She heard whispered comments.

"Atta way, Lilibet. Yer doin' yer mam and daddy
proud."

"Good luck, Lilibet. Wish my dotter'd been as smart as
you."

"Give Pappy Hutton what fer, Lilibet!"

"Don't fergit us. Come back and visit."

The tightness squeezing her heart loosened a moment
as she realized she was giving the camp people a moment of glory and happiness, something to remember and
talk about for weeks to come.

Roy Springer had washed and shined up his truck as
well as he could. He helped Lilibet into the sheet-covered
cab, and Marm and Miss Mabel arranged her skirts so
they wouldn't wrinkle. Roy put the truck in gear and they
rode off down the rutted road through the middle of Big
Ugly Creek, Lilibet waving to the people on their
porches. Marm, Margot, Aunt Roo, and Uncle Bub followed behind in Miss Mabel's Mercedes sedan.

She was happy she was riding to the church in her daddy's coal truck. She hated Big Ugly Creek and everything
it represented, but she'd never been ashamed of it. She'd
never been ashamed of her family, or who she was and
where she came from, and she never would be.

Miss Mabel, driving the Mercedes, saw Lilibet's head
tilt back proudly. The incongruity of the beautiful, pristine bride riding with pride through the dirty coal camp in
her father's beat-up truck struck her as hilarious. She
laughed and murmured to herself, "Hold onto your
britches, Pappy Hutton. I don't think you really know the
package you've just bought."

In the stone vestibule of the Episcopal Church of the
Good Shepherd, Clarice, Donetta, and Sally Kay crowded
around Lilibet. Lilibet would have been happy with just
Margot and Clarice attending her, but she knew Donetta
would be hurt if she wasn't asked, and the Huttons had

insisted on Sally Kay. Pappy said they were having the
biggest wedding Yancey had ever seen and she was to
have as many bridesmaids as possible. Donetta's face was
lit with excitement, Sally Kay's pinched with envy, and
Clarice's drawn with boredom she was trying to hide for
Lilibet's sake. Their rich burgundy-colored dresses
matched the scoop-necked style of Margot's. Their arms
were filled with gold marigolds and galax leaves. Donetta
and Sally Kay's inane chatter drifted in and out of her
ears. Trying to think of anything other than the ceremony
to be conducted in the next half hour, Lilibet watched as,
across the vestibule, Pappy and Miss Mabel exchanged
some words. She wondered what they were talking about.

"I don't know how you pulled the puppet strings on
this one, Pappy, but as usual you got what you wanted—
only this time you may have gotten more than you bar-
gained for."

"You did a fine job with her, Mabel."

"I didn't do it for you. I did it for Lilibet." She paused
for a moment and stared him straight in the eye. Then she
said in a fierce whisper, "Don't destroy her, Pappy. I
know you're going to use her, but for God's sakes, don't
destroy her. If you do you'll have me to deal with!"

Pappy reached out and ran a dry finger slowly down
her jawline, from her ear to her chin. An amused smile
stretched his thin lips. "Aside from the fact that you were
sensational in bed, Mabel, I loved your grit and fire.
Don't threaten me. You know better."

"I'm the only person you haven't conquered, Pappy. I
had to get away from here to achieve it, but I did. Poor
Clada . . . she never saw the real you until it was too
late."

He clucked and shook his head back and forth. "Now,
now, Mabel. I accepted that you were my equal a long
time ago and we've been friends. You don't mean to tell
me this wedding is going to tear down a friendship."

"Oh, no, I'll be around old *'friend'* . . . to make sure
you're not taking advantage of Lilibet."

The organ music swelled and they left each other to
take their seats in the sanctuary.

* * *

As the chords of "The Wedding March" filled the church, Lilibet and her bridesmaids moved closer to the arched entrance, Roy Springer hanging back until the last minute. He was a jumble of nerves.

Donetta was squeezing her arm and chattering in loud whispers. Lilibet wished she'd be quiet. "The Lord has seen fit to bless thee, Lilibet. Look! The man sitting behind Pappy, that's the governor—and next to him are Senator Yeager and that other United States senator whose name I can't remember. And the fat lady with the round purple hat—she's that rich oil guy's wife, Winthrop. Praise the Lord!"

Sally Kay gave Donetta a withering look but had to add her own two cents. "I bet the flowers cost the Huttons a pretty penny. I've never seen such lavish decorations, and I hear the reception will be the party of the year. Too bad your parents couldn t have helped some, Lilibet. I know that makes you feel bad, but don't worry, that quaint bouquet your mother made you is real nice and—"

"Shut up, Sally Kay," Clarice said, and gave her a little shove toward the red-carpeted aisle. "It's time for you to move out."

Everything flowed in slow motion as Lilibet waited and watched her sister and friends walk toward the altar. Was this really happening? or was this a cruel dream? Her body began a fine, uncontrollable quaking and her eyes blurred. The colors in the dresses of her bridesmaids, the heads of the people waiting in the crowded pews, the flower-bedecked windows and chancel, all seemed surreal, hazy and wavering in various shades of yellow light. She stared fixedly at her feet, praying the unreal sensations would disappear.

Her father took her arm and she looked up at him with dread, knowing it was time to walk down the aisle. Through the haze she saw him smile. Automatically, she smiled back, fighting to breathe normally. He cocked his head back proudly, and she experienced a brief moment of triumph; although for now, there would be no law school, Marm, Margot, and Daddy would have the first security they had ever known, and her child would have its father. Somehow, some way, she would accomplish her dream of practicing law.

All of a sudden she felt bought and sold. Trapped, Black had said. No! *Don't think of Black.* Don't think of his strength, of his green eyes that always seemed to read her soul. Don't think of the bitter anguish on his beautiful face, or the wretched lines of pain around his sensual mouth. A sob tore at her throat, and she tripped on her gown. Her father, giving her a worried look, brought her up sharply.

Don't think of Black. Accept this. Now! Think of the happiness she saw in her mother, think of the pride she saw in her father, think of . . . she saw Cle now, blindingly handsome in his cutaway, and Sam standing so serious beside him. Cle's eyes adored her and her heart fluttered briefly the way it used to—but was it from affection or fear? And was that an expression of relief on his face? She wondered why.

She recited the words of the ceremony. Only as she said "I do" did she awaken, for as surely as if he'd really been there, the cry of the cougar echoed through her soul until it shattered her heart.

PART THREE

WINTER 1966

Chapter 19

The President of the United States, Thomas Hay Lodge, cocked his head to better hear the voice of his dinner partner, the beautiful Lilibet Hutton. Although the speeches she made for her husband were delivered with forthright passion and riveting prose, her normal speaking voice had been schooled to delicate, lilting tones. All of Washington knew Lilibet was a favorite of the President's. Few congressmen and their wives were invited to the White House on a regular basis, but the Huttons, with only eight years seniority, were frequent guests.

Entranced by a clogging exhibition she'd performed six years ago during his inaugural celebration, the fun-loving president had asked Lilibet to waltz with him at one of the formal balls later in the evening. Protocol said the President need only dance with a guest for a few minutes before changing partners, but President Lodge had spent his entire allotted time at Union Station with Lilibet Hutton. They'd been fast friends ever since. The President, like everyone who knew Lilibet, felt better about himself and the world after he spent time with her.

Lilibet's warm violet eyes never left the President's face, her attention rapt and sincere; he knew she was truly listening, unlike the general Washington crowd who never looked at one another when they talked. Afraid they might miss collaring someone more important, they directed their voice to you but their eyes darted about, searching for their next target. Lilibet possessed the rare ability to really hear what you were saying and to hone in directly on what you were feeling. Her understanding of the problems you carried and her gentle encouragement had bolstered many a flagging spirit.

"Cledith's campaign is going well, Mr. President, and his opposition is minimal," said Lilibet. "Thank you for the offer to come to West Virginia and campaign for him, but I really don't think we'll need you. Your schedule is exhausting as it is. I'm sure you don't have the time."

"For you, I'd make the time, Lilibet." For you, not for Cle, he thought cynically. "Are you positive you don't need me? I thought Cle was getting in over his head when he announced his campaign for the Senate. Thought he ought to spend a few more years in the house. Pappy must have been pushing the hell out of him."

Lilibet merely smiled and turned to answer a question from the white-jacketed waiter. A good Washington wife, the President thought. Keeps her personal life to herself. She was Cledith Hutton's best campaign weapon. Cle and Pappy Hutton knew this and took the utmost advantage of her charm, beauty, and brilliance. She was elegance personified—besides being the only natural blonde in the room, he thought with a wicked grin. She'd avoided the current bouffant-with-bangs rage, wearing her hair in a style that was short and simple but stunning. She wore a floor-length, white silk pleated skirt, topped with a white sweater delicately beaded with crystals and seed pearls. The crystals on her sweater, and the exquisite diamonds in her small ears, danced with reflected light from the chandeliers, contributing to her already luminous appearance.

Actually, it didn't take much smarts to know why Cle was running. Pappy was power hungry. His money and the young Huttons were his ticket to higher echelons.

"Mr. President, I—"

"Lilibet, I've asked you time and again to call me Tom."

"And I do, when it's only you and me and Maisie, but this is a state dinner."

"Who the hell cares? I insist."

"Yes, sir, Mr. Lodge, sir." She saluted him and her lilting laughter lifted above the quiet conversation.

He loved it when she laughed. It was only then that the tiny traces of tragedy vanished from her face. Only those who knew her well would notice the fragile lines about her eyes and mouth that told of many private hours of suffering.

"What were you about to say before I interrupted you?" he asked.

"I was about to say that I've changed my mind. I'm going to subject you to a grueling tour through our raped coal valleys. When you see our once beautiful streams running yellow and red with acid drainage from the mines, devoid of any aquatic life. you'll help me push through the Environmental Reclamation Bill."

Had she forgotten his two trips to West Virginia three years ago for the funerals? "Are you going to bug me about that damned bill again? You've got the whole House in an uproar."

She laughed again.

"How else am I going to get anything done?"

It was true. She did Cledith Hutton's work for him, but so subtly and smoothly that his constituents didn't know. Even without her hard-won law degree, earned with night courses at Georgetown University, Lilibet would have been a formidable opponent. Cle did the glad-handing, the party going, the myriad of glitzy publicity opportunities as they occurred, but everyone on the hill knew it was Lilibet Hutton who actually wrote the bills, who worked with the interns and research assistants and made sure i's were dotted and t's crossed. Lilibet's intelligent grasp of the issues, which meant so much to her, and her tireless lobbying behind the scenes, were what got the job done.

"The Harrison Easterling Foundation has poured a lot of money into our rescue missions," she continued, "restoring our land and helping keep our people alive, but it's not nearly enough. We have almost two million acres covered with waste from the mines. Some of the culm heaps have been smoldering for decades. The stench is nauseating. People have to live—" She stopped abruptly when she noticed the amused gleam in his eyes.

"Let me see," he mused, "Is this the ninth or tenth time I've heard this speech?"

She laughed. "But if you saw it ..." She halted suddenly, pain filling her face for a fleeting moment. "Of

course, you have seen it. You were kind enough to come
to Daddy's funeral, and . . . that same awful year . . . you
came to Collins's."

He placed his hand over hers and held it firmly until he
saw he regain her composure. He knew she didn't like
talking about the death of her only son, so he smoothly
resumed the conversation.

"Yes, but I'll come again, and I'll sign the damn bill if
you can get it to me."

"I will, sir, I will," she promised. She had her work cut
out for her. The ERB should have passed the last session
but never got to his desk, and he had a suspicion that
someone was sabotaging the bill Lilibet had worked on
for four years. Seeing her radiant face, he made a mental
note to have one of his spies do some digging—he would
do anything to see Lilibet's face light up with happiness.
Hell, men had started wars for a lot less. Besides, he considered it an excellent bill and they desperately needed to
restore the ravaged, depleted coal fields. Private funding
from the Ford Foundation and the Harrison Foundation
could do only so much.

The French Ambassador to the United States, Henri
Monteux, who was seated to the right of Lilibet, sought
her attention and the President reluctantly let her go. Before he turned to the Finance Minister from Egypt, seated
on his left, he made a quick appraisal of the room, taking
note of which tables seemed the most animated, which
seemed tense, and who was holding sway at each. Nothing escaped his discerning political eye.

His darling wife, Maisie Lodge, sat at an adjacent table. With her usual kindness, Maisie had seated all the
malcontents at her table; she was a wonder at keeping
peace. She'd also requested Congressman Cledith Hutton's presence.

He and Maisie considered Cle Hutton a charming, en-
tertaining lightweight. Hutton always made Maisie laugh,
so he was a good counterpoint to the sour faces around
her, but the President knew Maisie had another, ulterior
motive for seating Cle next to her. She monitored his
drinking, keeping him so busy laughing and talking that
he didn't have time to get sloshed. Maisie, with her New

England determination, was going to make sure Lilibet did not have another embarrassing evening at the White House. From the looks of it, though, Maisie was fighting a losing battle this evening. Alcohol was never served in excess at the White House, so Cle must have been pretty well tanked when he arrived, because his eyes were beginning to glaze over. Sometimes you could excuse the overindulgence of alcohol if there was a compassionate reason, but Cle had been a boozer long before the death of his son.

He heard Lilibet ask Henri Monteux if she could practice her French with him, and marveled at her refreshing honesty. Most of the women in the room would have been embarrassed to admit they couldn't speak French fluently. Eight years in Washington rubbing elbows with powerful people from all over the world, dining with royalty, and helping make the laws of a nation had put a dazzling finish on Lilibet Hutton but had not spoiled her. She remained the mountain waif he'd first seen at his inauguration, endlessly interested in everything around her.

The President wanted to speak with her again but saw that she and Henri were engrossed in their conversation. He turned with regret to the stern-faced Egyptian Minister who sat on his other side.

A Marine Corp aide made his way through the tables and waited at attention at the President's side. Thomas Hay Lodge cut short his dialogue with the Finance Minister. The young aides had standing instructions not to disturb the President or his guests unless it was an emergency.

"Yes, Lieutenant Rankin, what is it?"

The marine leaned down to whisper in the President's ear.

The President nodded and said, "Thank you. I'll take care of it."

A phone call for Lilibet from Pappy Hutton. The man had incredible balls, but even he wouldn't disturb a state dinner at the White House without good reason. The thought of more trouble for Lilibet seemed incredible. He touched her arm to gain her attention.

"Lilibet, there's a phone call for you from Pappy. Lieutenant Rankin will escort you to the library. Let me know if you need me."

Lilibet's face blanched for a moment, but she stood, smiling, and followed the marine through the Gold Room.

Conversation stopped as she passed each table of elegantly clad guests, and a silence grew in the room. She smiled brilliantly, nodding to acquaintances, and took the time to exchange a few words with the British Ambassador who was a special friend. Thomas Hay Lodge smiled a small private smile, and exchanged a significant glance with his wife, Maisie. They regarded Lilibet as the daughter they'd never had, and they were proud of her poise under fire.

Lilibet hurried through the marbled halls, empty except for the marine guards stationed here and there. Her heart pounding with fear, she made her way swiftly down the broad staircase to the library, her white silk skirt floating soundlessly behind her. What now? Was it Marm or Margot? Fat Sis? Dear God, it couldn't be Genie. The laughing image of Collins's twin filled her mind. Fate wouldn't be that cruel.

Her hand trembled as she picked up the receiver.

"Yes, Pappy."

"Lilibet, you get Cledith and come home to Yancey right now. Clarice has been arrested for prostitution. She's in county jail."

Relief rushed through her, then anger at Clarice, then worry. Clarice had finally lost control.

"There's nothing we can do, Pappy. You own the sheriff and everyone else. Get her out. Then get her the psychiatric help I've told you she needed."

"She won't accept my bail money and . . ." His voice broke for an infinitesimal second, and her heart beat faster. She'd never known Pappy to show any emotion except when Collins died. "There's something else. Genie's real sick. She wants you."

"Dear God, why didn't you tell me right away? What's the matter with her?"

A drumbeat of fear tapped hard in her temple, incessantly driving away all rational thought. Its loudness almost drowned out the sound of Pappy's tense voice.

"It's pneumonia. It came on real fast. She's in Yancey County Hospital."

"We'll be right there, Pappy."

Twenty minutes later, Lilibet and Cle sat in the rear of the chauffeur-driven limousine Pappy provided for their use when they were in Washington.

Cle patted Lilibet's knee. "I'm sure it's just a bad cold. You know how protective Pappy is about Genie. Sam's arranged a charter flight for us. He's at the house, so we're going there first to pick him up."

Lilibet couldn't reply. She was sick with worry. Pappy hadn't told her about Genie right away because he was scared. Pappy was never scared.

"I'm more concerned about Clarice," Cle continued. "Jesus H. Christ! What has Clarice gotten herself into now? Lilibet, you have *got* to talk some sense into her."

"It's a little late for talk, Cle."

"Dammit to hell! Why would she do something like this in the middle of the campaign? She knows how important it is—she could at least try to stay out of trouble. Sam said she arrived in Yancey last week for her semiannual 'fuck-Mike Crisp-all-over-the-county' routine. Tom Tee called Sam and told him he saw Clarice and Mike fucking on a roadside picnic table, for Christ's sake! Why doesn't she stay in Europe with the jet set, and just swim nude in a few more fountains like she did last year? Besides, I thought she was having a fling with Black Brady. Saw a picture of them together in the *Post* last month."

"Clarice told me they were good friends and that was all," murmured Lilibet. "Cle, I don't want the press to know about Genie's illness. They won't give us a minute's peace."

"Why not, Lilibet? Wouldn't the sympathy thing gloss over the bad publicity about Clarice?"

Red anger filled her, the actual color brimming her brain, spilling over into her eyes. For a moment, the dark car was filled with the color. She fought it. Her hands formed into fists, the nails biting into her palms. *Don't give way. You have no time for anger.*

Cle's lack of concern about his daughter while he fretted about the effect of his sister's notoriety on his campaign shouldn't have shocked her. She thought she'd grown accustomed to his shallowness long ago.

Lilibet knew something was eating away at Clarice. She immersed herself in the notorious activities of the continental set she ran with, and then would come home for a short period to play with Mike Crisp. During her Yancey stays, Lilibet sensed an urgency building in her sister-in-law, but Clarice would leave in a big hurry before they'd had a chance to talk about it. The pattern had repeated itself for years. She seemed driven, almost possessed.

Cle leaned forward, his elbows resting on his knees, and dropped his head to his hands in despair.

"Dammit, Lilibet. Why did this have to happen to me? The campaign was going so well."

"We're ahead in the polls and I'll make sure we stay that way," said Lilibet coldly. "Genie needs us right now, so forget about the campaign. Sit up, Cle. We're pulling up to the house and there's a crowd of reporters."

Cle sat up and put a brilliant smile on his handsome face. He'd had years of practice in hiding any signs of heavy drinking, so he emerged from the car with assurance, pulling himself erect. His face was set in the proper blend of serious concern for his sister's problems, with just a small, sweet vulnerable smile for the voters. He reached in to help Lilibet out of the limousine and flashbulbs flashed on and off frantically.

Cledith and Lilibet Hutton's honeymoon with the press had never ended. Cameras followed their golden heads everywhere, recording the rise of this couple from the coal fields to intimacy with the power-makers in Washington. Cle loved it. He was happiest when the press was with him. Lilibet hated it and tried to avoid reporters and cameras whenever possible. Her quiet dignity and obvious distaste for blatant publicity intrigued the press. The more she avoided them, the more they sought her out.

This was a happy night for the Washington press corps.

A scandal in the Hutton family! Juicy grist for the news-paper mill for at least six months. maybe longer. Like mad dogs salivating at the mouth, they smelled a full-fledged scandal involving the Huttons. The last time the Huttons hit the front page for anything other than politics was three years ago when their seven-year-old son, Collins, was killed.

The nation would never forget the poignant front-page photograph of a black-clad Lilibet Hutton emerging from the funeral services, her grief-stricken husband supporting her, their close friend and family attorney, Sam Adkins, on her other side. Hardened reporters got tears in their eyes when they relayed the story of how Congressman Hutton and his son, on their way home from the Yancey Country Club one rainy Saturday evening, were side-swiped by a hit-and-run driver. Congressman Hutton had struggled to gain control of his car but found it impossible on the slick, curving mountain road. The car impacted in a high-banked gully near the highway. Congressman Hutton escaped with scratches, but his son, Collins, was dead on arrival at Yancey Valley Hospital.

Tonight, questions and comments were hurled at them as they pressed through the anxious phalanx of reporters outside their Georgetown home.

"Congressman, how long has your sister been soliciting?"

"Mrs. Hutton, how will this affect the campaign?"

"Congressman, the *Times* has it from reliable sources that your sister is a 'madam', that she runs a whorehouse in Yancey. Is that true?"

"Mrs. Hutton, have you spoken with Pappy Hutton? What does President Lodge think of all this? Weren't you with the President this evening?"

"Congressman, look this way . . . we need a picture for *The Charleston Gazette*."

Cle turned, waved, and smiled, although of course he'd abandoned his usual campaign grin for a sad sort of smile.

The questions filling the air were giving Lilibet a head-ache. Her stomach muscles clenched nervously and she willed herself to relax. *You've been through much worse,*

Lilibet, you'll get through this. You've got to get to Genie. Keep smiling. They were almost to the door. There were only the television cameras to battle through. Relief spread through her as the front door opened and the formidable bulk of Sam Adkins stepped out onto the old-brick stoop. Ignoring the cameras, she focused on Sam. Thank God he was here. He had always been there for her, but the last three years she had needed his strong, reassuring presence constantly. She saw him say something to the television cameraman, and the man retreated a few steps.

Dear Sam.

"Hey, Congressman, did you know you've got a new opponent in the Senate race?"

The question, thrown from the back of the crowd, stopped Cle in his tracks. He searched out the reporter and found him. "Hi, Jim. How ya doin'? What new opponent are you talking about?"

"Black Brady. It just came over the wires."

Lilibet stumbled and a cameraman reached out to break her fall.

"Who?" asked Cle in disbelief.

"Black Brady. You know, the millionaire who owns those BEC plants. Isn't your sister a buddy of his?"

Lilibet's vision blurred, but she knew Sam was there. She brushed aside a microphone thrust in her face and stepped blindly into Sam's arms. He swept her protectively into the haven of her Georgetown home.

"Everything's okay. I'm here. Get a few things together and we'll be in Yancey in no time," he whispered in her ear.

If wishes were airplanes, Lilibet thought, I'd be back in my comfy bedroom in Georgetown, with Genie in my arms. The drone of the small plane's engines tuned out the whispered conversation between Sam and Cle. She didn't want to hear it anyway. She would have enough to deal with when they got to Yancey.

She pulled her camel cashmere coat closer around her, and tucked her feet up under her to keep them warm. The poorly heated DC-3 did little to dispel her shivering. It seemed as if she hadn't really been warm since the night three years ago when Collins died. A single warm tear trailed down her cold cheek. She was glad the cabin was dark, for she didn't want Cle and Sam to see her face.

She'd imposed an unspoken law on her family and friends—no one was allowed to speak of Collins when she was around. But if they could see her now, they'd know whom she was thinking about and try to console her. She didn't want consolation. She wanted only to hug her misery to herself silently, privately. It was the only way she could keep him with her. When good things happened, the grief worsened because Collins wasn't there to share them. When bad times came, like now, she wondered if she could bear it anymore. The grief she was sure she'd buried deep within her welled up fresh and raw. Her only consolation, her only joy and reason for living now, was Genie.

How Collins and Genie had loved these late-night flights back and forth to Yancey! The blackness of the night with its parade of lights from small towns passing beneath them had delighted him. Together, they'd learned identifying features of each, noting the lights from a ballpark, or a shopping center, or a railroad station. Collins had a good memory. Like his father, he remembered names and faces easily. He would have been a good politician, but he'd wanted to run his grandfather's mines when he grew up, a notion nurtured and encouraged by his doting grandfather.

The irony of it all. Two years of instructing Cle and guiding him patiently through the intricate negotiations of mining had convinced Pappy that Cle had no head for business. Staring him in the face, however, was the perfect politician, which suited Pappy even better. Seeing Cle's boredom with the mines and his magic with a crowd, Pappy pushed him into politics sooner than he'd planned. After all, Cle's charm with people and his love of the limelight made him a natural. Who better to take care of all of Pappy's political machinations? Besides, Pappy had Collins to run the mines when he was old enough. Cle won his first congressional race at age twenty-five and here they were, eight years later, running for the Senate.

Cle's irritated voice cut through her reverie. "Goddammit, Sam, give me another beer."

"Can't ol' buddy. We're landing in fifteen minutes. You gotta be stone cold sober. The press doesn't know about Genie, but they sure as hell know about Clarice. One whiff of beer breath and the press will be all over you like flies on dog shit. Go brush your teeth and gargle some Listerine."

Lilibet smiled in the dark. Sam could handle Cle better than anyone. He would need major handling if they were going up against Black.

Black.

No. She had enough to think about. She hadn't put Collins to rest yet. His blue eyes, young and trusting, gazed at her through the black night outside the small plane window, and behind him floated an image of Genie . . . gasping for breath. No! The "knowing" never lied. She'd learned to trust it. Her own breath came in short gasps and she loosened her coat collar, knowing she was breathing for Genie. *I'm coming, Genie. Hold on, sweetheart. Please. I love you.* She saw a hand caress Genie's forehead and knew Marm was taking care of her namesake. But Genie needed her mother. *She needs me.*

The lights of Charleston twinkled through the night and the pilot told them to fasten their seat belts. She thought of the Bette Davis line, "Fasten your seat belts, boys, it's going to be a bumpy ride." Appropriate words for the months ahead.

Pappy Hutton's helicopter, a line for line copy of Black Brady's newest one, sat on the runway, waiting to take them on the bumpy journey across the mountains to Yancey.

Chapter 20

Lilibet slipped her hand beneath the oxygen tent and took Genie's hand gently in her own. Her once laughing, active child lay still and pale. She ached to hold her in her arms.

"Doctor, may I hold her for a few minutes?"

"Certainly, Mrs. Hutton."

"Make it quick, Lilibet. She needs all the oxygen she can get," Pappy said. His thumbs hooked in a silver-threaded brocade vest, Pappy sat in a corner trying to seem unconcerned, but his face was as pale as Genie's.

Lilibet gathered the limp body in her arms and gave Pappy a withering look.

Tucking the damp, golden head under her chin, she held the precious body next to hers and rocked back and forth, humming a lullaby. Regina Clarice Hutton. The beloved twin of Collins. Named for Marm, at Lilibet's insistence and to Pappy's dismay. Always smaller than Collins, her ten-year-old-body was light and fragile. She'd tried so hard to keep up with her brother, chasing after him, swimming until she was exhausted, playing ball ineptly but with great spirit. Collins always watched out for her, made sure she was included in all that he did, and Genie assumed the universe existed because Collins Hutton needed a place to live. They enjoyed the special, spiritual closeness that many twins did. In precarious health since her birth, Collins's death had almost destroyed Genie.

"How did she get so sick so fast?" she asked. Dear God, she'd left her only three days ago. Genie had wanted to spend a few days with her friends in Yancey before going back to school in Washington.

Fat Sis, sitting next to Pappy, her lacquered gray hair all askew over her forehead, answered.

"She had the sniffles, but we didn't think it was anything to worry about. Donetta's Jane Etta invited her to a slumber party. Four or five little girls were there and they stayed up all night. Genie was exhausted when she got home, coughing, sneezing. She read most of the day. I got up around midnight to check on her and she wasn't in her bed." Fat Sis sighed, her voice trembling. "We found her down by the river, passed out."

Lilibet rocked her child, trying to keep the anger from her voice. "Why, in God's name, would she go out of the house in the middle of a freezing night?"

Fat Sis tried to speak, but couldn't. Pappy said, "She'd lost Collins's baseball cap—your old Reds' cap. You know she sleeps—"

"Yes, I know she sleeps with it," returned Lilibet angrily, then caught herself. *Don't blame Pappy and Fat Sis. They love her, too.* Her voice broke as she asked, "Did she find it?"

"Yes. It's there someplace beneath the sheets," said Pappy quietly.

Lilibet felt beneath the pristine white sheets and found the faded, crumpled red cap. She brushed her lips across the frayed surface, then rooted it between her breasts and Genie's chest so that together the two of them held the cap safely next to their hearts.

"What's being done for her?" asked Cle. He stood next to Lilibet with his hand on her head.

"Penicillin, and the best of the newest drugs," said the doctor. "Give it a couple of days. She'll be fine. She should go back to bed now, Mrs. Hutton."

Reluctantly, Lilibet placed her daughter back beneath the plastic tent and brought the sheets up under her chin.

"Where's Marm?"

"I made her go home to rest for a while," said Fat Sis.

For the hundredth time, Lilibet thanked God she'd been able to move Marm into the empty house next door to Anna Adkins after Daddy died. Marm had wasted away to a bag of bones while she'd nursed him through the last years of his "black lung" disease. Lilibet bought the house with money she'd saved from the salary paid to her by Cle, and from legal consulting she did in the rare spare time she had to herself. Marm and Margot loved living in town and it was convenient for Lilibet to keep an eye on them.

Pappy cleared his throat and came to replace Cle at her side. "Lilibet, you're going to have to go get Clarice out of jail."

Pappy stood tall and demanding, his wintry blue eyes staring into hers. She stood to face him, toe to toe.

"No, Pappy, I'm not. My responsibility is here right now."

"Clarice won't let anyone near her. Says she wants you to come and get her. She won't accept my bail money, screams at, kicks, and scratches every deputy who comes near her."

The doctor put his arm around her shoulder. "It's okay, Mrs. Hutton. Regina is stable now. Her breathing has improved since you held her. Go to the courthouse, then come back here."

She closed her eyes, drew a deep breath, and let it out slowly.

"All right, let's go."

A weak, watery-blue dawn crept over the mountains as they pulled up to the Yancey County Courthouse. The town square was filled with newspaper reporters and curious onlookers. Burly off-duty state troopers, hired by Pappy, tried to keep a semblance of order but the crowd was growing unruly. One of the guards opened the Cadillac door for Lilibet. Sam and the trooper helped the Huttons push their way through the milling throng.

"Don't worry, Cle, this ain't gonna hurt nothin'. We're behind you," someone yelled.

"Well, I ain't," another voice called. "Hope that yellow-haired slut serves some time."

"Yeh, about time someone in the Hutton family got arrested for something . . . murder would be more like it." The last comment was muttered by someone nearby and not meant to be heard, but was carried by a trick of the wind directly to the ears of the passing family. Lilibet's heart thudded against her ribs. Were they referring to Cle and Collins?

Pappy had arrived before them. In the anteroom of the jail, he yelled at the sheriff. "I don't care if that self-righteous prig president of the Ladies Guild from church did see them with her own eyes. You should never have brought Clarice in here, Hager."

"Mrs. Bailey was screaming at me to arrest Clarice, and Clarice was sticking her wrists out for the cuffs, screaming at me, too, daring me. It was in the courthouse square in broad daylight. I had no choice, Pappy."

"For the last time, let me see her immediately."

"Simmer down, Pappy. Clarice says she wants to see Miz Lilibet and Mr. Brady, and that's all."

"Hager, you hillbilly dolt, you know nothing about running a jail. I'll have your badge for this. Besides, what the hell does Black Brady have to do with anything?"

Lilibet wondered the same thing as Pappy's irate voice followed her down the frigid, institutional-gray corridor. The sickening, oversweet antiseptic smell of Pine Sol seeped deep through the pores of her skin, making her already nervous digestive system queasy. Her journey through the cell-flanked passage behind the key-clanking guard brought acrid memories of her visit to Eugene in the prison at Moundsville. Much to her relief, he'd been caught running moonshine for the MacDonalds and was spending ten years in the state penitentiary. Unfortunately, the MacDonald brothers were free, and the mountain grapevine rumored they were busy brewing up their poison in a still hidden somewhere up-country.

"Hey, hon, you goin' to a ball or somethin'?" The wisecrack came from a prisoner leaning against his bars, leering at her. "Save the last dance for me, toots. I'll show you a real good time."

"Shut up, Bubba. This here's a lady."

She glanced down at her long, white silk skirt, bedraggled and mud-spattered now. Somewhere, in the middle of the long night and this interminable morning, she'd forgotten that she still wore the skirt and crystal-beaded sweater she'd donned for the evening at the White House. Had it just been last evening? It seemed like forever. She shoved her fists down into the pockets of her warm coat and prayed for this morning to be over soon.

The guard stopped, unlocked the door to a small, windowless room and ushered her inside. At least it wasn't a cell with bars, she thought.

Clarice, restlessly pacing the close confines, enveloped her in a close embrace. Her hair hadn't been washed or brushed for days, and the bilious-green, prison-issued smock was too large for her and hung off one shoulder, exposing a bra strap. Lilibet held her tight and they said nothing for a few moments. She could feel Clarice's quick, almost panicked breathing.

Finally, Clarice's voice came in a little girl's whisper. "I'm sorry, Lilibet. I know I've gone too far this time."

"What happened?"

"Mike was mad at me, so I got back at him by luring Mayor Browning out to Ruby's. We got drunk and ended up in the bushes in front of the courthouse. That old bat Martha Bailey saw us." She giggled. "Actually, it was kind of funny."

Lilibet sighed and drew away from her old friend.

"It isn't funny, Clarice. Mayor Browning's family has been humiliated; he will be kicked out of an office he has held for twenty years; and you have debased yourself. This isn't fun and games. I really wish you would get some counseling."

"Why? Because I like to get drunk and fuck around a bit? Don't be a such prude, Lilibet."

"You're losing control."

Clarice shrugged and tossed her head.

"My precious brother must be worried about the bad publicity. Tough! He's got you. I have no one. I need the fun."

"You have me."

"I know." Clarice's mask of indifference fell and her face broke into lines of wretched misery. Her voice small, she said, "Just love me, Lilibet. That's one reason I wanted you to come ... you never judge me. Neither does Black."

Long ago, Lilibet had become accustomed to hiding any reaction to Black's name.

Clarice's face resumed its familiar lighthearted, yet taunting expression. She smiled wryly as she took note of the silk skirt and evening sweater. "Take you away from some fun?"

"Sure did. I was having a tête-à-tête with one of my favorite guys at the White House."

Clarice laughed, a dry laugh devoid of humor or happiness. "Sorry. I seem to have a special talent for screwing up the lives of those I love best."

Lilibet's heart plummeted. Clarice had never talked in such negative terms about herself. Her arrogant, "I'll do what I want to, damn the rest of the world and what they think" attitude, had carried her through several critical points in her life. No matter that her attitude was usually the wrong approach, it had worked for Clarice. Now she was teetering between defiance and dejection.

"Clarice, that's not true."

Clarice held up her hand to stop any further comment. "Don't worry. I'm the same tough broad I've always been. I cried last night, but then I thought of you and your incredible strength when Collins died, and how you held us all together—even Pappy. We're a rotten bunch, Lilibet. We don't deserve you."

A key sounded in the lock. Black Brady walked in, brisk and impatient. "Is this your newest version of 'Clarice's Escapade of the Month'? If it is, I don't like it."

Within Lilibet an unnatural stillness fell, then exploded like thunder in her ears and she was suddenly dizzy. The roaring grew until she was deaf and she closed her eyes, willing away the dizziness. In disbelief she opened them to watch the scene unfolding in front of her, the sound of their voices tinny, as if coming from a great distance.

Clarice, laughing with pure joy, flung herself into his arms. "Oh, Jesus, it's good to see you, Black. I knew you'd come. The BEC office in Paris said they would locate you."

"They did, immediately, but they said you'd been arrested for murder, not prostitution. That's why I came." He carefully inspected her face, running his thumb along her chin line. "What's going on?"

"I knew you wouldn't come if I didn't make it sound serious. Please don't be angry with me, Black, lambkin."

He undid the fingers that were worming beneath the crisp collar of his white dress shirt and stepped away from her. "I am angry, Clarice. I don't have time to run around the world rescuing you. Your behavior is reprehensible. You don't need me here. You're in Yancey with family."

Lilibet couldn't see Black's eyes, but she could see Clarice's and they were brimming with adoration and passion. The lust in her eyes filled the small confines of the room with a primitive female desire so strong it shimmered like heat waves. A stab of unwarranted anger hit Lilibet, shocking her. She couldn't remember when she'd been so angry, and she felt her face flush with embarrassment. Smothering in the stifling heat of Clarice's passion, and shaking with burning anger, Lilibet hurriedly turned to leave. Clarice's voice and her own curiosity stopped her.

"I don't care if you are angry with me. You're here. That's all I wanted." Clarice cuddled close to Black and slipped her hand beneath the lapel of his charcoal gray, custom-made suit. She played with his regimental striped tie and looked up at him, her eyes half closed. "Where were you—on one of those mountains you're always climbing in Tibet?"

"No. I had just left Charleston and was headed for New York."

"Oh, too bad. I kept you from sin city. I took Lilibet away from the White House! How do you like them apples?" Incredibly, a tinge of pride at all the havoc she'd created surfaced in Clarice's voice, and Lilibet knew Clarice had taken advantage of the whole incident to gain attention from her and Black.

Black looked at Lilibet for the first time and, for an endless moment the world spun crazily off its axis and she with it. The roller-coaster ride of her misbehaving heart stopped her breath. All the years of ignoring news accounts of Black, of avoiding any event where he might be, of blocking out the emotion his name evoked, crashed around her in ruins.

His eyes swept over her, registering nothing but polite interest. "Yes, I see. How are you, Lilibet?"

Marshaling her tongue, her vocal chords, and the little air remaining in her lungs, she managed to reply steadily, "Fine, Black. Why don't you tell Clarice what you were doing in Charleston?"

Whatever possessed her to say such a snippy thing?

Shards of silver ice radiated in his green eyes. Their gaze held for a painful moment. She could feel a crack in her carefully constructed defenses, as if a dam were ready to break, its water begging to be set free. She could feel her bottom lip tremble a fraction. She steadied her lip and sucked in her breath. Please don't look at me like that, Black. Go away. *I don't want to feel this way again.*

He turned back to Clarice, caressed her shoulder, and gave her a quick peck on the forehead. "I was in Charleston announcing my candidacy for the United States Senate."

"Against, Cle? But why, Black?"

"You never want to talk about politics and serious things. Do you think now is the time to start, Clarice?"

"Not really. Tell me later. I just want to get out of here."

"I've paid your bail," said Black, "and I'm taking you home."

"But I want to go with you."

"You can't."

"Excuse me," Lilibet said. "Clarice, I have to get back to the hospital and Genie."

Black turned to her, a look of concern on his face. "I'm sorry. I heard about your daughter. I hope—"

"She's going to be fine," Lilibet interrupted and hurried out, anxious to be free of the tiny, imprisoning area, and the uncomfortable emotional heat generated by herself and Clarice. Remembering Black's dislike of confinement or bonds of any kind, and his passionate love of freedom, she wondered how much longer he would endure the small, windowless room. Only the love of a friend—or a lover—would draw him even close to a jail.

She sagged weakly against the closed door, and heard

Clarice ask, "How long can you stay, Black? In Yancey? Please, can't you stay awhile?"

The abject begging in Clarice's voice tore at Lilibet. Clarice was obviously, blatantly, in love with Black. Did he feel the same way? He was certainly affectionate with her. How long had this been going on? And what business was it of Lilibet's anyway? Sick with guilty desire, terrifying jealousy, and confusion, she was plagued by questions as she raced down the cold corridor calling for the guard, ignoring the curious comments that came from the cells she passed.

Chapter 21

Sam slammed the door shut on the newest Hutton Cadillac, and made sure it was locked. "Drive carefully, Lilibet. Wish I was going with you, but having Marm along will be nice."

"It's also nice knowing Genie's well and safe with Miss Mabel in Washington. I have to go to Belleville, Sam. Cle really needs the support of the town council. They insist Pappy has influenced his vote, and that Pappy is sandbagging my ... Cle's Environmental Reclamation Bill. They're ready to endorse Black. I may be able to turn the tide before the debate tomorrow. Take care of Cle."

Sam glanced at the motel where Cle was still sleeping, and then at Lilibet. A look of sympathetic understanding passed between them. "I will. He hasn't had anything to drink for a month. He's just tired. I'll wake him soon as you leave. We've got that meeting at the elementary school at noon."

Three months ago, Genie's illness and Clarice's arrest had set Cle on a drinking binge they'd had difficulty hiding from the press and public. Genie's recovery had been slow but she seemed fine now, and nothing made her happier than being with Miss Mabel. Clarice's arrest had remained a lurid sensation for months but had not affected the campaign to any significant degree, much to everyone's relief.

"Thank God, Clarice has been busy with the campaign."

"Yeh, working for the enemy camp. She won't even spy for us," Sam said with a benevolent grin. "She's hellbent on working for Brady. Can't believe that neither you nor Cle could convince her not to work for him. But, at least Brady keeps her sober, which is something none of the rest of us has been able to do."

Lilibet shrugged her shoulders. Clarice's desertion was still a bitter pill to swallow. Cle's commanding lead in the polls had dwindled to a few percentage points and Lilibet was determined to hold those points. Cle did everything right—his smile, his handshake, his direct gaze, his baby kissing, his inestimable charm—but support for Black was building steadily and surely.

Sam bent and gave her a quick kiss on the cheek, and she pulled out of the motel parking lot.

"Thank you for inviting me to come along, Lilibet," said Marm. "I've never been to Tug Fork or Belleville."

"You're good company, Marm. Sometimes these trips can be lonely." Her mother was a comfortable companion. She didn't say much, but enjoyed every small thing.

Campaigning for the United States House of Representatives had not prepared Lilibet for this statewide Senate race. Every day brought a new motel room with its tiny slivers of soap, a strip of sanitized paper across the toilet seat, and a worn chenille spread on the bed. The gravy-drenched chicken banquets, the rallys in the rain or hot sun, the quick-paced walk through the center of town to shake hands, all became a blur after a while. But the faces, ah, she loved the faces and she remembered many of them. The faces and the issues kept her going.

The two-hour drive to Belleville took them through one of southern West Virginia's most beautiful valleys. The woods glistened with a mist of light-silver spring rain, and peeping through the budding green trees they could see the first of the shy, pink dogwood blooming beneath the protection of its taller compatriots. Lilibet took her time, mindful of the wet roads, enjoying the signs of fresh, erupting renewal of life they passed. She rolled her window down and inhaled the earthy fragrance of spring. The rain had rinsed away the last of winter and the air held a precocious, dewy fragrance.

Ahead loomed one of her favorite mountains and a landmark for regular drivers of this route. Nature, with its odd caprices, had shaped the peaks, trees, and hillocks of the summit in the shape of Mickey Mouse. She explained this to Marm and told her to look for the mountain's two perfectly rounded ears.

"How odd, Marm. We should be seeing Mickey Mouse by now, but it's been a while since I came this route. Maybe I'm wrong about the location. They must be visible around the next turn."

She jammed on her brakes and stopped in the middle of the road.

In utter shock, she stared up at a shorn, tattered mountainside. The ears were gone. In their place were two huge, ugly white gashes. A strip-mine operator had slashed his excavations across miles of once green mountainside. His hill mined out, he'd gone to the surface and robbed what was left of the age-old edifice.

"Damn!"

"Lilibet. How ugly. Who would do such a thing?"

"A greedy mine operator who acquired what we call 'broad form deeds'." This was typical of what she was fighting and she shook with anger. "Many operators have acquired mineral rights under so-called 'broad form deeds,' which allows them to do any amount of damage to get to the coal, even though they might not own the land. Only a few mountains remain legally protected by their owners."

She drove on, squeezing the wheel tightly, wishing it were the throat of the greedy destroyer who'd stolen the beauty and dignity of the mountain.

"Thank God, Pappy hasn't resorted to strip mining yet. He's mined out much of the land he owns around Yancey, but he's moved his operations farther north. He's tried for years to buy the rights to Catawba and its sister mountain, Aracoma, but the absentee owner has bound the mineral rights tight," she explained to Marm. "They can't be touched no matter how many lawyers Pappy uses or shenanigans he pulls."

Lucky for Uncle East with his secluded cabin on top of Catawba, she thought. She hadn't seen Uncle East for three years, but she didn't want to think of the last time she'd seen him.

She swerved to avoid a wide rut in the center of the

road. Another evidence of mine operator neglect, she thought in disgust. They extracted all the coal and left no pillars to support the surface. Only wood timbers supported the mine roof after the coal was gone. The result was mine roofs tumbling into man-made caverns. The surface cracked and heaved and paved roads split wide open.

To take her mind off her frustration, she flipped on the car radio and found "The Sounds of Silence" by Simon and Garfunkel. She hummed along softly and Marm joined in. Lilibet gave her a happy glance. Marm was a different person since Dad died and she'd been living in town. She was safe and so was Margot, even though Margot complained about driving Lilibet's old car, and not having enough money for clothes. Well, she'd done her best. At least Marm was content.

She thought about the people she would talk with in Belleville. The rallies and town meetings always went well when she did the advance work; besides she was uncomfortable around Cle much of the time. She'd tried to shake off the unwanted feelings but couldn't.

Rotating red lights ahead slowed her approach into Belleville. A state trooper halted her progress.

"Sorry, ma'am, there's been an accident up ahead. We have no way to reroute traffic unless you want to turn round and go back up yonder twenty miles to the Mud Flat turn-off."

"How long will the wait be, Officer?"

"Shouldn't be more'n a half hour. Get in line behind the Ford pickup."

Lilibet pulled up behind the truck. There were only three vehicles in front of her so she could see the accident clearly—although she wished she couldn't. It was a simple fender-bender, but the flashing red lights and their spinning reflection on the wet pavement brought sharp-edged images of three years ago. She lowered her eyes and studied her fingernails but the pain-wracked images kept coming. She closed her eyes and they were worse, coming in segments like stills from an old movie. Tiny beads of perspiration broke out on her brow and she shivered. Lost in her private hell, she was startled when

Marm's gentle, work-worn hand closed around the trembling fist in her lap.

" 'Twas a day like this, wasn't it, darlin'? You've never talked about it. Don't you think it's time?"

"I don't think I can, Marm."

"Yes, you can, and you'll feel better for it."

With shaking hand, she turned off the ignition switch and watched the windshield wipers settle in place. The interior of the car was silent now, but they could hear the drip, drip of the rain on the hood.

She took a deep breath and said, "Maybe you're right. I'll try."

Marm held her hand tight.

"It was a day like today, only raining harder," she began shakily. "Genie was practicing the piano, and Sam and I were playing checkers in the library when the sheriff called. He said Cle and Collins had been in an accident and somebody must come. Sam wanted to go by himself, but Pappy and I insisted we should go, too. Sam drove."

She remembered the apprehensive silence in the car, she in the passenger seat, Pappy in the back. The rain had come down harder on that day and the windshield wipers swished back and forth, swirling water on and off the glass, and blurring her vision as they approached Deadman's Curve.

"There were lots of highway patrol cars, the lights on them spinning red. At first, that's all I could see. Then I saw Cle. He was sitting by the side of the road, his head hanging between his knees, his arms limp at his sides. He was soaking wet, and his shirt was torn, but I knew right away he was okay. I thought Collins was probably just out of sight."

She couldn't voice what she'd seen next for the pain of it was unbearable. In the center of the rain-slick, glass-strewn road, lay a bedraggled, crushed Cincinnati Reds' baseball cap, the one that Collins had appropriated from her when he was five years old. It was then that she'd known.

"I walked toward Cle in a kind of trance, Marm. It's burned into my brain now, but then it was all like a newsreel in slow motion. Behind Cle, over the top of the hill,

I saw a trooper's helmet, and then the rest of him came in view, and . . ." Her voice broke but she forced herself to continue. "In his arms he carried a small, blood-caked form. He carried Collins so tenderly, Marm."

She remembered with hellish clarity the huge tears flooding the trooper's ruddy, time-wizened face as he walked to her through an absence of sound and a suspension of color, time, or movement. With utmost care he placed in her arms his precious burden, the inert body of her son. Sam stood behind her, holding her firmly by the shoulders.

"He put Collins in my arms. Have you ever felt the life go out of a child, Marm? I felt Collins's life leave him as I held him, and it was then that life stopped for me, too. When you feel the energy—the energy that contained the warmth, the laughter, the love, the dreams—when you feel it leave and you're left with a vacant husk, nothing left, the finality is inexplicable hell." She heaved a dry sob and Marm squeezed her hand harder. Lilibet struggled on. "For one awful moment, I wanted to shake his body, to will the breath back into it. I even swore at God and told him to stop teasing me like this."

Marm hugged her. "Cry, honey-child. Can't you cry, child? You're so strong—maybe too strong."

Marm's arms around her brought the tears to the back of her eyes but they wouldn't surface. The lonely pain wrapped itself around her as it always did, trapping her, keeping her prisoner emotionally and physically.

"I'm afraid for the tears to come, Marm. Afraid that after the tears, I'll be so empty I won't want to live." She bit her lip. "Sometimes I feel like Humpty Dumpty—like if I cry, I'll never be able to put all the shattered pieces of me back together again."

"Cle doesn't seem to have trouble crying," said Marm. Cle. She had to tell Marm the truth about Cle.

Cle, slumped on the ground by the side of the wreckage-strewn road, had finally looked at her, his bloodshot, red-rimmed eyes begging her to forgive him. The thick fog of alcohol fumes that eddied around him had nauseated her. His slurred words slammed her like a fist in the ribs that she could feel to this day.

"Oh, yes, Cle can cry. He's great at crying. Cle looked at me and said ... 'I'm so sorry, Lilibet. So damn sorry. Din't mean ... a thing ... tried, but I din't see the damn curve'." She took a shuddering breath. "He was drunk, Marm—stinking, rotten drunk."

"No," Marm protested.

"Yes. Cle was drunk. But I didn't have time to worry about him or what it all meant at the time. I sat square in the middle of the road and hugged Collins to me. I rocked him, and sang lullabies to him like I did when he was a baby, the ones you taught me." She'd keened and mewed like an injured kitten, trying to exorcise the unbelievable pain. "Finally, Sam lifted both of us in his arms and put us in an ambulance. I don't remember anything after that until I woke up the next morning in my bedroom at Hutton house and you were there."

Marm soothed her arm and said, "I wish I could carry the pain for you, that I could make it all better, make it go away. When you hurt, I hurt." She hesitated a moment, afraid to ask the question hovering on her lips. "Lilibet, how come they said it was a hit-and-run driver? How come Cle wasn't arrested?"

"With Sam's help, Pappy bribed the state troopers and the hospital personnel, so Cle was never charged with vehicular homicide as he should have been." Bitter anger surfaced in her voice, and her jaws ached from the effort of holding back a scream of rage. "Cle's made so many journalist friends, the press accepted without question his story of a sideswipe by a hit-and-run driver."

"That's horrible, but I know you wouldn't lie to me, child."

"Cle's not what you think he is, Marm. He fooled me for a long time. I guess I let myself be fooled."

She'd discovered after a few short years of living with Cle that the golden young god she'd married was really a gilded, empty vessel of a boy. What she'd thought was self-confidence was really bravado concealing a weak and fear-filled personality. So the love turned to mothering as she tried to protect Cle and his image. Then came the shattering realization that Cle's bravado, and his fears covered an innate selfishness—a manipulating selfishness, dedicated to making the world around him serve his needs. But she'd made a commitment before God and her parents, which she intended to honor. Also, she'd had her children to consider. They needed their father. So she busied herself with Collins and Genie, and the vital legislation she and Cle were working on in Washington, and made her marriage work.

There was little love left. She loved him as she would a brother or a longtime friend. Their sexual encounters came further and further apart, and were less and less satisfying. The last time they'd had sexual intercourse Cle had labored over her, his perspiration dropping on her as his tears had the first time they'd made love and the twins had been conceived. For years there had been no joy, only a mechanical coupling that Marm said was natural when a man and woman had been married awhile. Lilibet didn't like to believe Marm, but supposed it must be true.

The children were her center, and nearly filled the hollow hunger that had gnawed at her since she'd lost her innocence. Worse than anything, she supposed, was the fact that she didn't miss Cle at all when they were apart—in fact, was relieved when he wasn't around. But she accepted this as her lot in life, remembering with wonder her naive, youthful assumption that she, unlike Marm, would be safe and happy always. Collins's death and Cle's part in it forever changed her uncharacteristic placid acceptance.

"Six months after the funeral, after the shock had worn away, I gathered the strength and energy to leave Cle. When I told him he cried. It's funny, I never saw Cle cry until the summer we graduated from college, but after that he . . . anyway, he asked me for a week away, just the two of us, where he could make an attempt at reconciliation. Do you remember when we went to the Virgin Islands?"

Marm nodded.

"We rented a beachside cottage. It was beautiful and peaceful and I listened to him and tried to be fair. Eventually we decided to give it another try." Cle's tears had flowed freely during those sun-drenched, planter's punch days. He'd made passionate love to her and told her how much he loved her and needed her, and she'd realized his grief was as heavy as hers. "But in the end I stayed because of Genie, not because of Cle. Pappy has made sure I will never divorce Cle."

"What do you mean, child?"

"Pappy swore that if I left, I would never see Genie again. They would win custody of her and turn her against me. He said he would pay to have people swear I'd committed adultery and would have pictures doctored, and records faked, that would prove I was an unfit mother."

So she had submerged her fury at Cle's careless disregard for Collins's life and had stayed because she couldn't lose Genie, and once again, Cle needed her. Since then, to retain her dignity and her sense of balance, she had dedicated herself to the bills in Congress that were so crucial to West Virginia.

Handling her grief for Collins, and helping Cle and Genie manage theirs, had taken a vast amount of her emotional resources the last three years, but as busy as she was, no matter how she filled her days, nothing had dimmed the pain. This campaign was helping though. The sharp edges of grief were dulling and blurring, and although deep inside the grief resided like an unwelcome guest, the fight against Cle for the Senate seat kept her so busy she was able to put aside her pain for whole days at a time.

The trooper tapped on her dripping window and she lowered it.

"You can move on now, ma'am. It'll be slow though. Lots of traffic today. People coming in for the political debate tomorrow." He leaned down and peered at her. "Say, ain't you Lilibet Hutton? Gee, sorry, Miz Hutton. I'd have tried to get you out of here if I'd a known it was you."

"That's all right. See you tomorrow?"

"Yes, ma'am! I'll be there."

Lilibet entered the backstage area of the Belleville High School auditorium. Marm had offered to come with

her, but Lilibet knew she wanted to watch the color television at the motel.

As she explored the wings, stepping over ropes and
drops, she reviewed her unsuccessful visit with the town
council. For some reason she could not fathom, they insisted Pappy Hutton was sabotaging the Environmental
Reclamation Bill. Why on earth would they think Pappy
would want to defeat his own son's bill? They were polite
and kind, said they were looking forward to the debate tomorrow, thanked her for bringing it to Belleville because
it had generated weekend business for them, but they
would not divulge the source of their information or endorse Cle.

School was out for Easter vacation, so they brought her
over here, unlocked the building, turned on the lights,
showed her how to work the spotlights in the auditorium,
then left her alone, telling her they would see her at the
debate tomorrow. Early in the campaign they would have
remained to fawn over her, making sure she remembered
their names and all the favors they could do for Cle. Was
it this damnable rumor about the ERB that was making
them lose percentage points, or was it the efficiency of
Black's campaign? Because of constant coaching from
Lilibet, Cle was sure of his stand on the issues. The same
issues were important in Black's speeches, which wasn't
surprising since she and Black had always been passionate about the land, and the people of southern West Virginia. In the beginning, Black's stand on repairing land
damaged by careless, greedy mine owners had fallen on
deaf ears, and had hurt him. But he had begun to make
inroads, and Pappy had finally humored Lilibet, allowing
her to insert a few mild references to the Environmental
Reclamation Bill in Cle's speeches. Cle halfheartedly
spoke the words she wrote for him, but Black delivered
impassioned speeches about the "beloved mountains of
the state, and the wildlife, and the rivers." Lilibet knew
most voters didn't care about trees, rivers, and animals,
but she hoped they were learning they wouldn't have any
jobs if the land about them wasn't cared for.

Black's stand on the Vietnamese War had also hurt him
in the beginning. He'd spent two years there, flying

fighter jets, and had returned to the U.S. outspoken in his stand against the war. The uncaring attitude of the American public toward Vietnam veterans ignited a vitriolic response from Black. Pappy refused to let Lilibet even address the volatile subject, but maybe Black was hitting a nerve with some people.

What was missing in their campaign? Why were they losing points? She'd had an opportunity to observe the candidates together only once. While Cle's smile flashed like an automatic flash on a camera. Black's smile came infrequently but encompassed you. While Cle winked and smiled, Black seemed distant, but he listened intently and when he spoke it was magic.

Avoiding Black on the campaign trail had become a game with her. Though their trails crisscrossed now and again, she always managed to be in the opposite end of whatever county or city they found themselves. Her anger at his entrance into the race had not abated. This was Cle's race, his seat, but she was honest enough with herself to admit that she thought of it as her own. Black had never been interested in politics before. Why didn't he just keep making money and playing around the universe?

She found the light board with all its levers and switches and worked with it a bit. Seemed simple enough. She brought up the house lights and walked onstage to look at the color of the backdrop. This was the first debate of the campaign and it would be televised. Six years ago, the televised presidential debates between Thomas Hay Lodge and Robert Tate had ushered in a new era in political campaigning. The candidates found the airtime expensive but essential.

The backdrop was dark blue. Cle should wear a light blue dress shirt and conservative maroon tie, she decided.

With a start, she realized someone was in the auditorium with her. How long had they been watching her, and who was it?

She didn't have to ask. She knew who it was. The power of his presence shimmered toward her like heat lightning on a summer day. She turned around and found Black sitting in an aisle seat nine rows back.

With his head leaning against the seat's back, his hands
linked across his chest, his long legs crossed at the ankle
and protruding into the aisle, Black was the picture of
ease and leisure. The look in his mesmerizing green eyes
was unreadable but, like a spotlight, they pinned her center stage.

"Backdrop to your liking, madam?"

"What are you doing here?"

"You should know better than anyone that I always
scout the terrain before entering."

"I didn't know you did your own advance work."

"Always," he said, continuing to stare at her.

His steady gaze gave her a moment of disquiet and she
groped for a neutral subject.

"How is Uncle East?"

"He's eighty-seven years old. He's fragile. You'd know
that if you took the time to visit."

Black's statement revived a sense of guilt she'd carried
with her since Collins's funeral. "I'm sorry. He came to
my son's funeral. He hugged me for a moment and then
disappeared. Everyone was in such a daze . . . no one paid
any attention or asked who he was. It was difficult for me
to climb the mountain later . . . I've been so busy."

He let an uncomfortable silence settle between them.
How could she tell him she was afraid to face Uncle
East's unconditional love, his piercing wisdom, afraid he
would see clear through to the deterioration of her soul?

"How did he know—about Collins, I mean? He has no
radio or newspaper."

"I told him."

She was afraid to ask where he'd been in his worldly
adventures, or how he'd communicated with his grandfather. She didn't want to know too much of Black and his
personal life. In Black's case, knowledge was seductive
and she knew she could be pulled all too easily under his
spell.

He hadn't moved an inch nor cracked a smile, and a
baffling agitation grew in her. She decided to try a little
humor to break the tension.

"Still playing Indian?" She forced a smile.

"Once a year . . . on the first of September."

"Oh, I suppose because the mountains are so lovely then."

"No," he said. "The first of September is an anniversary of treachery and betrayal."

Their last time in the glen together, twelve years ago, came to her full force and she trembled at the residual anger in his voice after all this time. She ignored his remark. Irritated with her trembling, and angry herself now, she walked across the stage toward him.

"Why did you enter this race, Black? You certainly don't need the money, *or* the power, *or* the attention," she said, tension shaking her voice.

He watched her as she descended the proscenium steps and came up the aisle. When she reached him, he unfolded his tall form and stood up, loosening his tie as he did so. Hesitant to stand so close to him, given the havoc he wreaked on her senses, she retreated a step. Her hand flew self-consciously to the collar of her yellow silk shirt, then she dropped it and shoved it into the pocket of her twill pants.

"What's the matter, Lilibet? Afraid of me?"

"Don't be ridiculous. We're old friends aren't we?"

"Are we?"

"You didn't answer *my* question, Black. Why did you enter this race?"

"To right some lost causes," he said.

A charged illumination seemed to outline Black's body. He had what people called presence, was one of those beings who walked into a room and without saying a word, or making a gesture, mandated the air about him. Caught in the energy that rippled around him, Lilibet valiantly fought the tug of its current. Her brain raced in circles, incapable of another word or comment to keep the conversation going. His gaze never wavered from her face and her heart began skipping beats until it careened crazily.

Lilibet wanted to make an acerbic comment, but it died on her lips. A thick silence, charged with high voltage, throbbed between them. Lilibet wanted to look away, but couldn't. Neither could she think. It was as if the world around them had stopped spinning, leaving her rooted in time and space with nothing but Black's fine-tuned, tension-strung body in front of her. Yet his face revealed nothing. His finely drawn mouth, with its slight but sensual fullness so capable of inducing mindless passion, was immobile ... until his gaze left her face and traveled with blatant pleasure down her body.

Taking in every inch of her, not rudely but with appreciation, she felt his eyes touch her body as keenly as if he'd brushed her shoulders, her breasts, her belly, with his fingers ... or his lips. His green gaze lingered a moment on the buckle of the leather belt that circled her slim waist, as if he'd like to undo it, then returned to her face. The hunger in his eyes was raw and fathomless. So maybe he didn't hate her ... or was the hunger simply the physical urge of a man accustomed to claiming any woman he wanted? She tore her eyes away from his and dropped them to the bronzed column of his throat, looking warm and inviting against the blue of his loosened shirt collar. She reached to touch the sweet hollow at the base. . . .

"Black? Where are you?" Clarice's voice rang through the doors at the rear of the auditorium. "Oh, there you are. I've been looking all over this podunk school. Holy shit, even Yancey High had signs to tell you where the auditorium was."

She walked down the aisle toward them.

Lilibet, shaken out of the spell Black had cast over her, grabbed the back of a seat and held on while she fought to regain her equilibrium. She stuck the fingers of her other hand in a back pocket and stood rigid, hoping her flush of embarrassment wasn't evident.

Clarice continued her acid commentary about "hicksville Belleville" as she approached them. The tight periwinkle blue sweater she wore matched the blue of her eyes and was tucked into form-fitting white jeans. When she reached Black she put her arm through the crook of his elbow and leaned against him, giving his arm a miniature massage with her breasts. She glowed up at him.

"Hi, darling."

He smiled at her. "Hello, bad girl. What mischief have you been into today?"

"Nothing, really, Black. I've been behaving like I promised. I delivered all of those fliers, and made arrangements with the Belleville radio station to run those thirty-second spots."

"Good."

The musky scent of female territorial rights emanated from Clarice like the aroma of baked bread. She looked at Lilibet with friendliness but the "hands off, this is mine" sign was as clear as if she'd hung it around Black's neck. Lilibet felt like the proverbial third hand in a cribbage game.

"Hi, Lilibet. Hope everything is okay with my twin, but we're going to beat the holy hell out of you, you know."

"Clarice, it would be nice if you'd call Fat Sis, or Pappy once in a while," said Lilibet. "You know you broke his heart when you went to work for Black's campaign."

Clarice's face grew cold and rigid and she drew even closer to Black. "I called Fat Sis this morning, but Pappy doesn't care about anything but himself, Lilibet. I can't believe after all these years you're still dancing to the strings he pulls."

"That's not fair—"

Clarice interrupted. "Oh, I know you're onto his game and maybe even Cle's, but your blind loyalty—"

"That's enough, Clarice," Black said in a firm voice.

"I have to go," said Lilibet. "I have to call Genie, and I'm expecting a call from Cle. We're coming at you with both barrels loaded tomorrow, Black, but best of luck to you."

Automatically, she stuck out her hand to shake his, as she would when she wished anyone good luck. The touch of his warm, firm clasp caused a small earthquake within her. She hastily tried to retrieve her hand but he held it a moment, two fingers slipping beneath the edge of the sleeve that circled her wrist.

"Thank you, Lilibet. We'll see you tomorrow evening," he said, and released her hand.

The West Virginia senatorial race was an important race nationally because its outcome affected the teetering balance of power in the Senate. Television cameras and commentators from the three major networks had situated themselves early, blocking the awed but irritated view of the locals. Lilibet worked the room efficiently, soothing the frustrations of those who couldn't see, entreating the visiting press to show some kindness, remembering names, laughing at jokes, and sending aides backstage with last-minute notes for Cle. The lights dimmed and the debate moderator walked onstage with Cle and Black.

Weak with relief, Lilibet leaned against the wall at the rear of the auditorium. There was nothing more she could do. Early in the campaign she'd learned that coaching Cle from the sidelines confused him. Now she tried to relax, knowing his success or failure was out of her hands. She observed him critically for a moment, and was satisfied. He looked the perfect candidate: polished blond hair, a glowing smile, impeccably dressed in navy blue blazer and maroon tie.

Cle had won the toss and gave the first answer. With religious intensity she trained her gaze on Cle, but when it was Black's turn for rebuttal she couldn't avoid looking at him any longer. She heard him say something about "flood hazards because of denuded land in narrow river valleys," and then gave up, as all the thoughts that had circled in her brain since their encounter yesterday came forward full force.

If she were going to color him a color it would be black—not the black of evil, but the black of hard-rock strength and tensile steel, with lustrous reflections, and mysterious shadows here and there. Heat rose in her chest with the memory of her misbehaving hand yesterday, and its impulsive urge to feel the hollow at the base of his tanned throat.

The words—and the points Cle and Black were accumulating, or losing—were a blur to her. She'd known since yesterday that she was in trouble. Black Brady's hypnotizing effect on her had shaken her to her roots. She was a married woman, for heaven's sakes, and even had she wanted to pursue her obvious attraction to Black, there was Clarice to consider. They were having an affair and Clarice was in love with him. Flushing hot with the memory of Black's fingers on her wrist, she stood away from the wall, forcing herself to concentrate on the debate.

Like lightning, the reason for Black's climb in the polls struck her. It was as if she'd been wearing someone else's eyeglasses and had just removed them. Had she been so concerned with winning that she'd blinded herself to what was so blatant? Yes.

Cle wasn't ringing true. Cle told his listeners what they wanted to hear and meant none of it. Black meant what he said. The people were reacting to the intrinsic worth they saw in each man. What would happen when they reached the voting booth? Would they vote for the man, or the company defender they saw in Cle?

She sagged back against the wall. They had to win. She had nothing if they lost. Deep within her she knew Black was the superior candidate, but her need to win and her entrenched protectiveness of Cle battled with her honesty.

Applause jerked her from her thoughts. The debate was over. Questions were being shouted by the press. Sam slipped through the swinging doors and stood beside her. She took refuge in his solid, reassuring form.

Sam leaned down to say quietly, "Let's get Cle away from here before they ask him something he can't answer."

Backstage they found the confrontation they'd long been dreading.

Cle, red in the face, shouted at Black. "You're an absentee citizen, Brady. You haven't really lived in West Virginia in years."

"It's none of your business, Hutton, but I'm here more than you know."

"You don't belong here."

"Tell me, Hutton, do you know what a paw paw tree looks like, or where the peregrine flies, or the name of the highest peak in this state? Do you know where the Shawnee hunted, where the last chestnut stands?"

"The people of this state want jobs, not a nature lesson."

"They do need jobs, and I don't see you or your father doing anything to improve their lot," Black replied coolly. "The only people in this state who live decently are Brady Electronics workers."

"You baby your BEC employees, Brady."

"No, I treat them like human beings."

"You treating my sister like a human being, Brady? You keeping her happy, fucking her?"

A chorus of gasps came from the campaign workers surrounding the two. Cle was losing his temper, and the first sign of fury showed on Black's face. Lilibet grabbed Sam's arm, and the two of them moved forward to bring an end to the acrid exchange.

"Your sister needs help, Cle Hutton, and she doesn't deserve the ugly comment you just made," Black said.

Sam put his arm around Cle's shoulders and patted him on the back, while Lilibet put her hand on Black's arm to forestall any more words.

Cle and Black glared at each other.

Sam said, "Come on you two, let's finish the evening like gentlemen. Shake hands."

They both ignored Sam.

Cle, noticing Lilibet's hand on Black's arm, said, "One more thing, Brady. Stay away from my wife."

They all saw Black's body stiffen like a bowstring. Lilibet felt it. With every ounce of control she possessed, Lilibet casually removed her hand from Black's arm.

"Are you threatening me? Don't." Black hissed between clenched teeth. "I wouldn't resort to stealing another man's wife. I take only what's mine."

He stalked out.

Chapter 22

"Cle's going to win, isn't he, Sam?" asked Margot, a nuance of worry in her voice.

He smiled down at her. She was light as a feather in his arms, her limp scarcely noticeable as they danced.

"Sure he is, little one."

"You don't have to be so condescending with me, Sam. I know all about the problems with the campaign. For the first time in my sister's life, she seems to have run into a force she can't conquer, namely Black Brady."

"Don't worry about Brady. We're going to win."

He wished again that he could give up his obsession with Lilibet and marry Margot. She was pretty, soft, and easy to be around. He recognized her corroding jealousy of Lilibet, but no one was perfect. Lord, if anyone could understand envy it was himself.

"Look, Sam, there's Black now. God, can you believe the gall of him, appearing here?"

"Margot, the governor's annual Fourth of July celebration has always been neutral ground during any election year."

"Yes, but the governor's endorsed Cle."

Yeh, thought Sam, but only after Pappy greased his palm with fifty thousand green ones.

"Doesn't make any difference," he said to Margot. "The United Mine Workers originated this statewide winging fifty years ago so the members could meet all the candidates for office. The UMW isn't much involved now but this picnic has taken on a life of its own through the years."

"Oh, I love all of this, Sam."

He looked around the vast tent erected on the banks of

the Kanawha River in Charleston. It was a festive sight.
He loved it also, but he was well acquainted with the rotten shadow work here, the money passing hands, and the
deals being made. He'd engineered much of the back-
room intrigue himself. But he would let Margot keep her
illusions.

"I love it, too, Margot."

The "non-era" band, with its bland music, and the
wooden floor they danced on, were at one end of the
gaily decorated enclosure. At the other end was a fiddling
band, and a caller instructing a group of square dancers.
In between, artisans from all over the state had set up
their wares, displaying West Virginia-made quilts, watercolors, carved wooden toys, and jams and jellies. Outside
the rolled-up sides of the red, white, and blue tent, mountain games drew enthusiastic participants, and a crowd of
people settled themselves in chairs before a stage where
bagpipers prepared for a concert. Chartered buses had
brought in campaign volunteers from all over the state.
Candidates for various offices moved among the crowd
shaking hands, the Hutton and Brady supporters warily
skirting one another.

"But you have all the excitement of Washington. I only
have lil' ol' West Virginia."

"Margot Springer, you should be ashamed of yourself.
You've visited Cle and Lilibet frequently in Washington."

"I know. I'm just hinting for an invitation from you.
Lilibet and Cle will be even busier when he's a senator."

Irritated with the suggestive whine in her voice, he
whirled her around quickly and grinned gamely. "You've
got it. After the election, I'll make sure just the two of us
have a Washington weekend. Okay?"

Her smile brightened and he breathed a sigh of relief.
He hated to hear Margot whine. He hated to hear anyone
whine. But when Margot whined it was worse, for then
every whit of the voice that reminded him at times of
Lilibet disappeared. *Change the subject, Sam. Aha. Cle.*

"Do you see Cle?" he asked her.

"No."

He knew that was a lie. Margot always knew where
Cle was. Her eyes followed him like the flitting tail on a

kite. She was comfortable with Sam, and probably had an idea she'd like to marry him, but she worshiped Cle.

"But I see Pappy and your mom dancing," Margot said. He stiffened. "Yeh, so do I."

Sam was sure Pappy was unaware he and Margot were in the vicinity. The arm that circled his mother's back was stretched, so Pappy could get his hand situated comfortably on her breast. Methodically he massaged Anna's ample breast while they danced, arrogantly confident no one could detect his dirty little deed. His mother's face was pink but she didn't pull away from Pappy. Sam hoped Margot couldn't see. However, she'd worked for Anna for years now, and if she hadn't guessed about his mother's affair with Pappy Hutton then she was worse than dense.

Sam was thirteen years old when he walked in on Pappy and Anna one afternoon after school three years after his father's death. Face red and chest heaving, he'd retreated, running from the house like the hounds of hell were after him. Nothing had ever been said; he'd never mentioned it, nor had his mother, or Pappy. Pappy never came to the house again but Sam knew they met somewhere. With a child's prescience, he knew his mother had been coerced or blackmailed, and he knew why. Pappy had threatened to fire Anna from her lucrative job, and he'd promised a bright future for Sam if Anna would let him diddle her once in a while. Anna and Sam had pretended for years that Sam had no knowledge of her affair with Pappy.

His teenage hatred for Pappy, and disgust for his mother, were put aside as he reluctantly took advantage of the privileges his mother's affair had gained for him. He could never let her think her vulgar sacrifice had been in vain. He'd kept meticulous records of the money spent on him and later, when he'd earned his own hefty bank account, he paid back every cent. Problem was, his mother had become addicted to the furtive excitement Pappy created in her humdrum life. She'd become as obsessed with Pappy as Sam was with Lilibet. Obsession was a sickness in the Adkins family. It had killed his father.

The secret sin Anna Adkins bore was the nerve center of her life. She guarded it zealously, frightened someone would discover the sordid physical mating she thrived on, yet unable to give Pappy up. Pappy knew it and drew his own sick enjoyment from the knowledge.

The familiar angry churning began in his stomach and he pulled his gaze away. He could scarcely look at them anymore.

"Oh look, there's Cle, dancing with Sally Kay," said Margot.

Sam watched as Cle and Sally Kay danced by, Sally Kay batting her false eyelashes at Cle as if they were in high school again. Her bouffant pageboy bounced with each step they took. Her husband, a shoe salesman at Sears, stood on the sidelines glowering at the two of them. Christ! That's all we need—a confrontation between Cle and a two-bit shoe salesman, and right here under the governor's nose, thought Sam. *He's supposed to be shaking hands near the quilting booth like we told him to. The fool. He doesn't deserve Lilibet . . . but you've always known that, haven't you, Sam?*

He fought his fury, but his teeth clamped together so fiercely a pain shot to the crown of his head.

"Sam," Margot said with concern. "There's blood coming from the corner of your mouth. Did you bite your cheek?"

Sam said nothing as Margot retrieved a hanky from her pocket and solicitously wiped away the trickle of telltale blood.

"Cle, honey, you haven't lost your smoothness. You're a better dancer than you were in high school," said Sally Kay.

"Is that the only thing I'm better at, sweetness?" He glanced around and then slipped his tongue into her ear. She giggled.

"Oh, no, honey pie, you've improved in other areas too. Last night was scrumptious."

Cle knew he'd had too much to drink but he was handling it well, and besides, he deserved some fun. Everyone expected him to be this superhuman person who didn't really exist. It was easy to be a leader in Yancey because everyone knew him and the Hutton name so they assumed he knew what he was doing. They adored him. But in Washington, the responsibility of making important decisions was too much for him. Thank God for Lilibet. Where was she? There she was, over by the toy booth talking with Miss Mabel. He slipped his hand down and squeezed Sally Kay's butt. Umm, he couldn't wait to get more of that, later maybe . . . if he could get rid of her hick of a husband for a while.

"Cle, the fiddler is turning up for the cloggers. You don't suppose Lilibet is going to embarrass us all, do you?"

"Doesn't embarrass me, Sally Kay. She hasn't clogged since the President's inauguration six years ago. Might be fun for her."

It *did* embarrass him but he'd never admit it to Sally Kay. When Lilibet danced her joy and lust for living radiated to everyone in the vicinity. He liked the envious looks he received from other men, but he hated what they must be imagining. Lilibet was a Hutton, and she would be bedded only by him. He endured the attention she garnered because the mountain people loved the clogging, and they loved Lilibet, which meant more votes for him.

"The nerve of Clarice!" said Sally Kay. "She's prancing around here like she owns the place. Been hanging on the governor's arm, and swigging beer from the barrels. Honest to God, you'd think the whole state didn't know she'd been arrested for turning tricks, and then she brings you more bad news by working for Black's campaign."

Cle eyed his twin with distaste. He was a bit high but Clarice was fast on her way to inebriation.

"Yeh, but there are times I'm glad Clarice is working for Brady."

"Are they having an affair, Cle?" Sally Kay looked at him, her eyes bright with rabid interest. "I mean, Black scares me to death . . . but nothing scares Clarice and she's always with him."

The music stopped and Cle pushed her toward the bar.

"Do dogs bark, do fat babies fart? Sure they're screwing. Clarice has been horny for Brady since the first

time she saw him at Ruby's the summer after high school.
She followed him around for years hoping to catch him in
a weak moment. Don't know when it happened but I'm
positive he's been layin' it to her. I love my twin, but
she's an animal. Come to think of it. I've heard he may
have screwed with animals before. They say he could
fuck a cougar if he had a mind to."

"Jesus, Cle, you're not serious "

He shrugged his shoulders. 'Who knows? He and
Clarice have some sort of weird relationship. He's bailed
her out of pokeys from Nice to Nigeria."

Sally Kay sipped a Tom Collins, and licked her lips
daintily. She listened with fascination to this story of people who lived in a world she knew she hadn't the courage
to enter.

"Why does he rescue her from all the scrapes she gets
into?"

Cle ran a finger around under the thin strap of Sally
Kay's chartreuse sundress.

"Use to be Sam's job, but Black was always in the vicinity, so he inherited it. I suppose he takes care of her
out of some noble idea of watching out for a fellow West
Virginian—besides if hot pussy is readily available, any
man would be a fool not to use it. Right, Sally Kay, my
best girlfriend?" He put his finger in his mouth, licked it
thoroughly, then wiped it around the edge of Sally Kay's
pink lipsticked lips.

"That's right, Cle, honey," she said, and pursed her
mouth to blow him a kiss.

Lilibet saw Cle play with Sally Kay's mouth. She
sighed wearily. Would he never grow up?

"When are you going to give it up, Lilibet?" asked
Miss Mabel.

"Give what up? The election? You know I hate a defeat. We're going to win."

"I didn't mean the election," said Miss Mabel, her
voice ripe with meaning.

"I haven't the slightest idea what you're talking about."

A young girl, dressed in a skirt afloat with crinolines,

and black patent shoes with taps hurried over to stand breathlessly in front of Lilibet.

"Excuse me for botherin' you, Miz Hutton and Dr. Turner, but we was wonderin' if Miz Hutton would dance with us. We would sure be honored if she would." Her pretty young face was flushed with smiles and excitement.

"Well, I don't think . . ."

"Hey, yeh, Mom, you haven't danced in a long time," said Genie. "Do it!"

Lilibet smiled down at Genie, sitting on the ground at her feet, chocolate ice cream dripping off her chin. Clogging was the last thing Lilibet felt like doing, but she couldn't refuse the honest entreaty and respect on the young dancer's face, or the excited plea in Genie's eyes.

"Sure. I'd love to," Lilibet said. She gave Miss Mabel and Genie a kiss, and told them she would see them later.

Relieved she'd dodged the perceptive comments she'd sensed the older woman was about to voice, she followed the young girl to a backstage area where they found a pair of shoes to fit her. She tossed her shade hat aside and pulled on the borrowed patent leathers.

The toe-tapping rhythm of the fiddlers caught her ears as she tied the bow on her shoes and her heart lifted a fraction. Whisked on stage with the rest of the dancers, she soon found herself lost in the timeworn, venerable cadence of the mountains. If her feet felt a bit leaden in the beginning, and her knees a bit unyielding in her brain's request for more energy, she ignored them and forged on determinedly, until she reached the far horizon of forgetfulness.

Tears stung Mabel Turner's eyes as she watched Lilibet's valiant effort to regain the joyous movement of life that had been so easy for her in earlier years. The Hutton family's selfishness, the loss of Collins, concern for Clarice, and the weight of the campaign on her shoulders had sapped Lilibet of her vibrancy. The very essence of her personality that Mabel had thought would help sustain Lilibet through the years, might be the very one defeating her. Determination. Determination to make her

marriage work, determination to carry out her marriage
vows, determination to win.

There's a time to quit, my child. she cried out silently
to the nimble, quick-stepping figure on the stage. The
skirt of Lilibet's delphinium blue sundress whirled happily, giving lie to the heaviness in her heart. *There's a
time to say, I've given it my best, I accept what you are
but this isn't me and I'm not one of you, and walk away.*
But, Mabel sighed, Lilibet must learn for herself.

A quiet, husky voice interrupted her anguished
thoughts.

"How do you do? You must be Regina Hutton."

Black Brady had crouched to the ground and was intro-
ducing himself to Genie.

"Yep, 'cept they call me Genie." She stuck out her
hand as she'd been taught to do, and he took the sticky
chocolate mess and shook it. "You're Black Brady."

"That's right. You have your mother's eyes," he replied.

"That's what people tell me. Uh, I'm sorry that my
dad's going to beat you, but . . ."

Mabel could tell she was searching for something to
say to make Black feel better.

"But?" he asked with a smile.

"I like the picture you painted of that mountain place
that's in my mom's private sitting room in Washington."

Mabel saw Black swallow hard. "Thank you," he said,
and tugged gently on her blond ponytail.

He stood up and introduced himself to Mabel, then
stood quietly next to her, his eyes trained on the dancing
blue figure on the stage. The man fascinated her. Always
had. She'd never met him but she'd read in the *Wall
Street Journal* of his quest for excellence, his demand
that his employees give of their best. In return they were
treated like royalty. Racier tabloids reported Brady's
quest for adventure and excitement Here was a man who
lived to the hilt, daring life to rob him of any succulent
bite he might care to savor. If she were thirty years younger, she'd have been happy to savor it with him. She
hadn't told Lilibet yet, but she wasn't going to vote for
Cle. She was going to vote for Black Brady.

"Do you suppose the joy has been amputated permanently?" he asked her, his eyes never leaving Lilibet's whirling form, and she knew immediately what he meant.

"Do you?" she returned his question.

He didn't answer for a moment and she studied his face. The touch of grim bitterness about his sensual mouth surprised her. He didn't seem to be the sort of man who would have any regrets, and yet it was there, as surely as if she'd etched it there herself. Understanding flooded her in a rush as she remembered the watercolor that hung in a hallowed place in Lilibet's private sitting room in Georgetown. She realized his perception of Lilibet's loss of joy could only come from someone who'd loved her once. Black Brady had loved Lilibet once. Did he still?

"Do I think the joy is still there . . . the honest, pure, giving joy that could take your breath away?" Black turned to look directly into Mabel's eyes and gooseflesh rose on her arms at the fierceness in his eyes. "Jesus, I hope so. They're destroying her."

"Yes," Mabel replied, lifting her patrician eyebrows, a challenge in her eyes.

He gave her an odd smile, tilted his head in a respectful nod, and walked away.

Alone, and grateful for the quiet, cool place she'd found beneath a willow tree near the fast-flowing Kanawha River, Lilibet hoped she'd have a few moments of peace. The tree's long, drooping branches shielded her safely from the prying eyes of the crowd behind her over the crest of the hill.

She fanned her hot face with her battered, white straw hat. Her hair clung to her face in wet ringlets. For the first time in years she was afraid. The clogging should have revived her old sense of herself, should have relieved the weariness she'd detected creeping among her thoughts and actions. Fear. She hated fear. Fear could defeat you. An involuntary shudder racked her body. She held herself stiff with apprehension. *You're losing it, Lilibet. No.* She tried to relax but her body shook spasmodically, and she couldn't stop it. *You're just tired,* she told herself desperately. Thank God no one could see her. It would stop in a moment . . . wouldn't it? Was she going to faint?

"Come to me, Elizabeth."

Her heart flipped, then beat at a furious pace. Had she sensed he would come? Had she summoned him by the sheer force of her need? She didn't know or care—she only knew she was glad he was there.

She turned around and took one step into Black's arms. They closed around her as if she'd never been gone. He held her tight and sure, hugging her face against his neck. Washed with relief and longing, she clung to him. For a long time he simply held her as her trembling body fought to calm itself. Then, keeping her close to him with one big hand pressed against her waist, he stroked her damp golden curls.

"Shh, shh, you're fine, you're doing fine," he soothed into her ear.

"Black, I'm falling apart."

"No, you're not. Not you. You're going to make it. Genie is beautiful. She has your eyes."

"Yes."

She knew he was dangerous, but she didn't care. His kind words, the unyielding strength of his body, undid her. She shook uncontrollably, wishing the tears would come, and he held her with all his might, letting her know he was there if she needed him, but granting her that choice. He stroked and soothed her body until the tremors lessened and disappeared. Finally, he took her chin and raised her face to his. His mouth captured hers in a soft, reassuring kiss and she sighed with pleasure and kissed him back. His lips and tongue, hot and searching, demanded more, as a hungry man asks for food long denied. She gave into the pressure of his savage mouth and a warm, sweet tingling spiraled deep within her. *Oh, God, I want this so much, please forgive me. Is this so wrong?*

With aching tenderness, he kissed away the hot tears that surfaced but wouldn't fall, then took her face and held it with both his hands to stare at her as if he couldn't look long enough. She'd dreamed of the hollow at the base of his throat; now she touched it gently with her fingers. It was warm, and sweet, and smooth, and tan, and the pulse beat was sure and strong. She stood on tiptoes to kiss it, and she felt him tremble. He caught her to him again and held her face tight against his shoulder for a moment, then his lips nuzzled her ear. She licked his neck and loved the tinge of saltiness, the taste of Black. Again, she joined her mouth with his, and with every heartbeat he drew her deeper and deeper into the racy excitement of his mouth. With each supple stroke of his tongue, a faint corresponding cry came from the back of her throat, and then she felt the iron-stiffness of his erection surge against her stomach. A flush of joy such as she'd never experienced before ripped through her. With surprise, she felt a hot, velvet wetness seep from her and into her cotton panties. *Oh, God. Wonderful bliss.*

With the little willpower she retained, she pushed herself away from him and looked up at him with a hesitant smile. "You don't hate me?"

"I hated you. Not anymore," he said softly.

She loved his face with her eyes.

"We can't stay here, Black. We can't do this."

"Why not?"

"You know why?"

"Explain it to me."

"Don't do this to me, Black."

The quaking started again but he brought her softly back into the shelter of his arms. Somewhere, above on the tent grounds, someone called her name.

She pushed away from him again.

"We're going to beat you. I'm going to win, you know," she said, laughing up into his eyes.

He laughed with her, caught her chin to place one more swift kiss on her sweet mouth, and said, "I know you're going to try your damnedest, my darling."

She tore herself from his arms, picked up her forgotten straw hat from the ground and ran to see who needed her.

He didn't hate her. He didn't hate her. The phrase sang in her heart as she ran up the incline that crested the river. What difference did it make? He had Clarice. But the knowledge that Black didn't hate her had lightened her step, and her feet flew as she ran to the large communications trailer on the tent grounds. Automatically, she searched for Genie as she ran and spotted her learning dance steps from one of the cloggers.

Campaign aides manning phones in the trailer looked at her with awe and she knew who was on the phone. One of them indicated the headset she was to use and she sat down while they waited with bated breath.

"Hello."

"Mrs. Hutton, the White House is calling."

"Yes."

Thomas Hay Lodge's pleasing, resonate voice came over the line. "Lilibet?"

"Yes, sir?"

"Are you alone?"

"No, sir. Should I be?"

"For this conversation, yes."

She asked the people in the trailer if they would leave for a while and they scurried to do so.

"Okay," she said into the phone with a smile. "What state secret are you about to divulge?"

"Chin up on this one, kiddo. Grab hold of whatever's near and don't let go." He hesitated for a moment, then plunged into the news he obviously hated to tell her. "Pappy Hutton has been sandbagging your Environmental Reclamation Bill. He pays his flunkie congressmen to assure you of their vote, and then to vote against you when the bill comes before the house."

Lilibet was unable to speak for a moment and the President was silent while the extent of the betrayal sunk in. She drew a deep, trembling breath and asked, "How long has this been going on?"

"Since the very beginning. If your bill is passed it will cost him millions to clean up the damage he's left behind. He's been working strip mine operations under a different name. Most recently a place near Belleville called Mountain Ears, or Mickey Mouse, or something of that nature."

Shaking with anger she said, "How stupid I've been. I knew the ERB would cost him but I thought he had an ounce of decency in him. He told me he liked the bill because Collins would have liked it. Does Cle know?"

He hesitated a fraction. "I don't know. My spies have proof about Pappy but nothing on Cle."

"Let me think a minute," she said.

Finally, she said, "Tom, will there be an investigation?"

"Yes, but not until after the election. We need more proof before filing charges, and neither party wants a scandal right now. Fortunately, most of the offending congressmen are 'lame duck.' "

"Good, because I want to win this election. It's too bad the filing date is past or I would run myself, but I can handle Cle after he's in the Senate. I'm going to come down on Pappy and his cohorts so hard, they'll never know what hit them."

She stepped from the trailer a different person than when she entered. The chill that had taken residence in her bones when Collins died was defrosting. Frozen in shock and grief for three years now, the melting heat of her rage felt righteous and invigorating.

Did Cle know? She didn't want to know the answer yet. She'd learned enough from Pappy Hutton to know when to keep her cards close to her chest, and when to play them. She would beat Pappy at his own game.

Chapter 23

Pappy Hutton pressed the buzzer on his intercom.

"Anna, bring me a cup of coffee with some brandy. I'm celebrating this morning."

Anna bustled in with his coffee, a smile on her plump, pleasant face. "It's a beautiful September morning, isn't it, Mr. Hutton?"

He didn't answer, but peered at her over the cup of steaming coffee. "Lock the door."

Her face pinkened. "Mr. Hutton . . . I—it's early . . ."

"Don't worry, Anna, you're not going to have to lift your skirts for me this morning. I just don't want any interruptions for a few minutes."

She locked the door and came to sit by his desk with her stenographer's pad.

"It's taken me years but I've finally found out who owns Catawba and Aracoma. The great and noble Harrison Easterling Foundation. God save me from the do-gooders," said Pappy sarcastically. "Brady is on the board. We're going to initiate a discrediting campaign against the foundation. After all, my dear, they've caused years of deprivation and poverty by not allowing that land to be mined. The miners who're sitting up in those hollows with their thumbs up their asses, moaning because they don't have any work, are going to love hating the foundation and Black Brady. Less votes for Black, more for Cle. What do you think?"

Always uncomfortable when he discussed an immoral issue with her, Anna cleared her throat and smiled weakly. She knew how long he'd seethed in frustration over his thwarted efforts to gain control of the lush, untouched land that lay between Yancey and Matterhorn.

She didn't want to make him angry. She was afraid of him when he was angry. Her smile grew broader and fixed. "Sounds fine."

"Good." Pappy got up and walked over to select a cigar from the humidor on the sideboard. "Lilibet been around the office lately?"

"Well, no, sir, no more than usual. She visits Margot sometimes, but Lilibet is so busy. She really should get a rest. She looks terrible and . . ."

Pappy waved his hand at her, indicating he didn't want to hear any unnecessary drivel. She shut up.

"You haven't seen her going through the new file drawers in the security room?"

"No, sir, but she does have a key."

He blew a plume of pungent smoke in front of him, and thought for a moment. "Have the locks changed . . . and call Tom Tee Frye. Tell him I want to see him."

Cledith Hutton Campaign Headquarters, next to Carpozzoli's on the square, was frantic with activity. Enormous posters imprinted with Cle's smiling face plastered the walls. Glancing at the grinning poster looming over her desk, for one panicky moment Lilibet felt smothered. She drew a deep breath and took another drink of cold, rancid coffee. She'd rather be in Washington with Genie, and yearned for a quiet moment of her own. The titanic struggle to stay ahead of Black in the polls, and her secretive efforts to unearth proof of Pappy's double-dealing were wearing her down. Don't blame it all on the campaign, she told herself. *You haven't had a moment to yourself in years. You've accommodated everyone but yourself, permitting their absorption of your time and interest.* She admonished herself for the selfish thought, but every time she thought of Pappy's betrayal, she wished she had an extra leg to kick herself for being so gullible.

Clarice had returned to the Hutton house early this morning. *Delivered* to the house was more like it. Black's top aide, an old flying buddy, had arrived at dawn with a drunken Clarice in his arms. With abject apologies, he'd said Black thought Clarice needed sobering up and home was the best place for her. On questioning from Lilibet, he'd divulged that Clarice had been with Black in the panhandle when Pappy Hutton called to demand she leave Black's campaign and come home. She'd promptly gotten herself soused and Black hadn't the time to nurse her through this one.

"You mean this has happened before?" Lilibet had whispered, trying not to wake the rest of the sleeping household.

"Yes, and Black takes good care of her, but he said she needs healthy food and her own bed, not the sort of thing she'd get on the campaign trail."

He left, saying they would call later to check on Clarice. Lilibet had helped an incoherent Clarice to bed, put Fat Sis in charge of her, and fled to headquarters in a fit of exasperation . . . and jealousy.

Hours later, she was still chastising herself. Jealous of a drunk? Really, Lilibet! But she was. Jealous of Black's caring for Clarice. She could see his tanned hand soothing Clarice's brow, tucking the covers beneath her chin, slipping beneath the sheets to warm . . . *No! Stop this. They are not your concern. This campaign and Cle are your concern.* The magical stolen moment with Black under the willow tree two months ago seemed like a dream, a guilty but poignant dream

She gulped down a few bits of the pizza Tony had sent over, made a phone call, and signed some papers.

"Jane Etta," she called to a young aide passing by, "please bring me a cup of hot coffee."

Jane Etta Frye, Tom Tee and Donetta's oldest child, brought her coffee.

"You've been here since six o'clock this morning, Miz Hutton. It's almost eight now and you haven't stopped all day. You should go home and get some rest."

Lilibet smiled fondly at the pretty sixteen-year-old. It was a mystery how Tom Tee and Donetta had ever produced anything as sweet and sincere as Jane Etta. She'd spent her entire summer vacation working as a volunteer here in the campaign office.

"Thank you for worrying about me, sweetheart, but I'm fine. You're looking especially pretty this evening."

"Thank you. I have a date later. Did you notice my new diamond ear studs? Daddy gave them to me this morning."

"They're lovely," Lilibet often wondered how Tom Tee could afford the expensive jewelry he gave to Jane Etta and her mother. He'd been the manager at Murphy's Five and Ten for ten years, but she knew the salary wasn't commensurate with his spending habits. She had a strong suspicion Tom Tee was on Pappy's under-the-table payroll.

"Mr. Adkins called," said Jane Etta, reading from a sheaf of messages in her hand. "He and Congressman Hutton are in Peach Fork. They said to tell you the speech went well last night, and they would be home late tomorrow. Oh, and there's a message for you to call a number in Matterhorn. A nice lady, wouldn't leave her name but said it was important."

"Thank you." Curious about the woman in Matterhorn, she lifted the receiver and dialed the number.

A woman answered and Lilibet said, "Hello, this is Lilibet Hutton in Yancey returning your call."

"Lilibet, this is Laura Brady. It's nice to hear your voice after all these years."

"How wonderful to hear from you, Mrs. Brady. Does your son know you're consorting with the enemy?"

Laura Brady laughed. "Somehow, I don't think Black thinks of you as an enemy. Yes, he knows I'm calling. We wanted to tell you that my father has passed away."

"Oh, oh no," cried Lilibet. Her sorrow was hard and immediate. Tears welled and a bony, hard to swallow knot formed in her throat. Softly, she said, "I'm so sorry, Mrs. Brady."

"Don't be, Lilibet. He went as he wanted to, as he'd planned to."

"Dear God, what do you mean?"

Laura Brady hesitated. "I think he would like to tell you that. I know you're terribly busy, but do you suppose you could visit the cabin at some point? He left something there for you."

There was no hesitation for Lilibet. She'd known she

would go to the cabin the moment she'd heard of Uncle East's death. Five years had passed since she'd last visited him. When the twins were born she'd had little extra time, and when they'd grown old enough to go with her, she'd felt it was unfair to ask them to keep the secret of Uncle East's existence. She'd managed one or two trips a year, until the last five years when the politicking got so hectic . . . and then Collins's death. Her mind dizzied, refusing to accept the fact that she'd never see Uncle East again, never feel his healing embrace, his warm words of wisdom.

When light broke in the morning, she would be on her way up the mountain.

"Lilibet, will you be able to visit the cabin anytime soon?" Laura Brady asked again.

Her throat rigid with intense emotion, she choked out, "Yes. I'll go as soon as possible."

"Good. I don't need to know when you're going, but it would be nice to talk with you when you return."

"I'll look forward to that," said Lilibet. They exchanged a few pleasantries and said goodbye.

The world had suddenly become a flat and dreary orb of meaninglessness. There was no longer anything to look forward to. Lilibet stared into space and gripped the metal edge of her desk until her hands were numb. How selfish she was. All those years she'd meant to go visit . . . there was always something more important to do. But there was nothing as important as Uncle East, no matter what her excuses were. Now he was gone. Amid her enveloping sorrow she felt a deep shame. Finger, by painful finger, she undid her death grip on the edge of the desk. Her hands dropped useless to her lap. She massaged them the best she could.

She glanced around to see if anyone had noticed her distress. The volunteer at the desk next to hers watched her curiously, but most were busy at their phones. She shakily straightened her papers and notes and pretended to yawn.

"I'm going to call it a day," she said. She called a volunteer miner to her desk. "Billy Hank, I'm taking the en-

tire day off tomorrow. I have some errands to run in
Charleston. You're in charge until Sam gets back."

"Sure, Miz Hutton. About time you took time off. Buy
yerself somethin' purty."

Chapter 24

Lilibet stepped into the clearing. A silk-gray dawn, painted with streamers of pale pink, filled the meadow around Uncle East's cabin. She'd left Yancey before light, using a flashlight and foot-sure memories to guide her up the once familiar path. Looking neither left nor right, she approached the cabin with a silence bordering on reverence. She focused on the rocking chairs sitting empty on the porch. Or were they empty? She could have sworn Uncle East's favorite chair rocked rhythmically in the cool, still morning air.

Not a sound could be heard in the clearing. It was as if the birds, the animals, the grass, and trees were holding their breath with expectation, waiting for her arrival. She found she was holding her own breath and let it out slowly as she mounted the steps to the porch. The chair stopped moving. Had it truly been rocking? She gave it a gentle push and it rocked, empty, but happily.

The interior of the cabin was the same: gracious and beautiful in its simplicity, with a faint scent of dried wildflowers and fresh evergreens. It was here she'd first learned that elegance didn't mean the moneyed garishness of the Hutton house. Elegance was the creative alignment of color and fabric and comfort, suited to please the eye and the user. She circled the sitting room, touching every table, book, and cupboard as she went. On the mellow old chestnut table lay a thick envelope with her name on it. With a trembling hand, she picked it up and sat in the cushioned chair next to the fireplace.

Her eyes closed, she recalled the lessons Uncle East had given her on centering herself. They had stood her in good stead on many occasions but she hadn't meditated since Collins died. Now she willed herself to relax, release, and let the silence enter her soul. Slowly, a modicum of peace settled within her—the first real peace she'd experienced in years. She opened her eyes to read the contents of the envelope.

Expecting a simple letter from Uncle East, she was astonished when several documents fell into her lap. She ignored them and picked up the letter. The crackling of the white sheet of paper sounded loud in the peaceful silence of the cabin.

Dear Elizabeth,
    The time has come for me to travel on. I have loved and learned to the highest realms of my desires on this earth. I have achieved what I came to achieve and now must go to other places and endeavors.

    Do you remember the conversation we had about "human beings forgetting they were more spirit than they are physical?" I have sensed your distress about Collins. I understand why you have not been to see me, but if you had come I would have reminded you of our conversation. It is time for you to let him go. Collins has been with me since his departure, is with me now, and is helping me prepare for the journey he has already taken. Before you read the next page of this letter, please go into the stillness and know both of us are with you.

She dropped the pages and let the solitude, the cool quiet, and the aura of love in the cabin settle into her spirit. With a certainty as solid as the floor beneath her, she felt a rough, gnarled old hand cover her right one, and her left was patted reassuringly by a small, soft hand she knew so well. She held to their touch for a moment, then her heart quickened and tears of release welled and spilled onto her cheeks. She wiped her eyes. A whisper of their presence remained with her, and the miracle of their caress would never leave her. Even if it never occurred again, she would know Collins and Uncle East were always with her.

"Thank you, Uncle East."

She picked up the second page of the letter.

Black will explain me and my angry journey to the mountain many years ago. He will also tell you how I left. It's really not important, but knowing you and your curiosity, you will want to know.

I am leaving you the cabin and Catawba Mountain. Black will have Aracoma. He has something to show you on Aracoma. Laura will receive the fortune I seem to have accrued during my time here.

I leave you with one more thing. Even though you never spoke to me of your hunger that is never satisfied, I know you possess it and I understand it. It is only because you were once filled, Elizabeth, that you now recognize you are empty. Once, when time began, you were filled. You will be again. Follow your heart, Elizabeth, no matter the cost or the odds. Follow your heart and be filled.

And now, to paraphrase Walt Whitman on old age and dying ... I have grown and spread myself, and prepare to pour "myself grandly into the Great Sea."

Always,
Uncle East

Like a child, she clutched the pages happily to her breast.

"Thank you, Uncle East, for giving me what I needed most, a return to my roots, and the assurance of yours and Collins's continued presence." The sound of her voice startled her, and with a smile she realized it was the first time she'd talked out loud to herself in ages.

"But you must have been a bit loco in your last days. The mountain belongs to the Harrison Easterling Foundation. I found that out recently while snooping through Pappy's papers. Thank you for the generous gesture, though. I'll pretend it's mine."

Curious about the other papers in the envelope, she ruffled through them. Her eyes widened in surprise as she recognized official deeds and documents transferring the ownership of Catawba Mountain from the Harrison Easterling Foundation to her, Lilibet Springer Hutton. She gazed out the large window overlooking the mountains, trying to remember what she knew about Harrison Easterling. Grannie Springer had told her the story of the famous millionaire who'd vanished in the early part of the century. Newspapers and magazines sometimes ran stories on unsolved mysteries and the tale of Harrison Easterling was always included. What connection did Uncle East have with the HEF?

"Uncle 'East' . . . Is 'East' short for Easterling? . . . he must have arrived here about the time of the disappearance. If that's so, Uncle East, you sure fooled me. Once, I remember wondering about your expensive pipe, but I figured Black or Laura must have given it to you."

The weariness in her bones and soul had begun to lift the moment she entered the clearing. The letter from Uncle East, the meditation, the wondrous knowledge that Collins and Uncle East were with her, had all lifted her heart a notch higher. Now, accepting the idea that this cabin where she had spent so many happy moments was actually hers, she explored its nooks and crannies with a long-dormant buoyancy. Drawn to the sleeping area where she had never been, she ran her hand lovingly over the red and green patchwork quilt on the twig willow bed, and picked up the polished briarwood pipe from the side table to sniff its rich, savory smokiness. Resting on the deep-set windowsill was his dulcimer. She plucked a string. The resulting ping was the awakening signal Uncle East's world waited for.

Bluebirds called back and forth to one another, their musical notes blending with the flutelike sounds of the wood thrushes. The whispering breeze of the pine carried the buzz of bees working to capture the last of the summer pollen, and the chatter of squirrels scurrying to fill their lodge with a winter's supply of nuts. Lilibet raised a window, then opened the cabin door to better hear the symphony she had evoked with the ping of the dulcimer. The mountaintop was telling her they knew who she was and they approved of the caretaker Uncle East had left behind.

She sat on the porch as she had so many times, listening, her feet on the top step, her back resting against the post railing. She half expected Raffles to emerge from beneath the steps but he didn't. Idly, she wondered where he was, and the new coon dogs Uncle East had purchased a few years ago. Judy was long gone, given a proper woodland burial at the ripe old age of ten.

Contentment filled her and she waited, for she knew he was coming, had sensed it the moment the symphony had begun. Black would be here soon.

Black stood for a moment in the shadow of an elderberry tree at the edge of the clearing, taking the opportunity to observe Lilibet at leisure. In her faded jeans and the oversized man's shirt she'd knotted at the waist, she looked like the teenager he'd rescued on the mountain trail sixteen years ago. But even at this distance, he could see how pale she was, and so thin she was almost translucent.

They had moved in similar but not the same circles in recent years, and he'd avoided any cultural or political affair that he knew Lilibet would be attending. Deliberately, he'd sought a fast, adventuresome—some would say thrill-seeking—crowd to run with. On the few occasions they'd arrived at the same social function, Black had assiduously kept a low profile, staying in the background and taking the opportunity to observe her as he did now. His chameleon ability to disappear into a tree line, or heavy brush in the forest, worked to his advantage when he wanted to dissolve into woodwork, or wallpaper, or fluted marble columns. Lilibet never knew he was there. The lovely women he escorted at those times, were always mystified at the change in his personality, and irritated at their inevitably short stay at the party.

He thought now of the precious moments he'd held Lilibet in his arms by the river in Charleston. Her fragile body had clung to his like an exhausted swimmer to a lifebuoy. He'd wanted to lift her in his arms and carry her away to a never-never land where no one would ever intrude, disturb, or trouble them—where they could just *be,* and where he could love away all her hurts and griefs.

"You can come out now, Black."

He smiled as he entered the clearing and crossed to her. "Forgot about your 'knowing.' "

"No you didn't. With your talent for blending into the scenery, you just figured it would be a while before I knew you were there."

"How long have I been here?" He bantered with her a bit, trying to contain the huge joy growing in his heart at the thought of the two of them alone here at last.

"I've known you were coming for the last half hour. I have to confess though, I'm not sure how long you've been standing beneath the elderberry tree."

"Long enough to know you look perfectly at home here." He paused, raising his eyebrows to give her a questioning look. "I'm hoping we can put aside the campaign for a while."

"We can," she replied with a note of relief.

"You've been avoiding me."

"Yes, except for the time by the river in Charleston. You were there when I needed someone . . . it seemed so natural, but it never should have—" She broke off and he let an uncomfortable silence stretch between them. Her hands, usually composed, fiddled nervously with the knot of her shirt.

"Clarice sober yet?" Was that annoyance he saw cross her face?

"Clarice is fine," she said stiffly. "It took Fat Sis all day to dry her out. I certainly wasn't going to nurse her."

Black, pleased with the spark of spunk he heard in her indignation, was careful with his next words.

"She needs help, Lilibet. More than I can give her."

"Well, you've certainly changed. I can remember when you showed no tolerance for people who overindulged."

"There was a lot I wouldn't tolerate in those days. Let's just say the years have mellowed me. And you, Lilibet, what have the years done to you?"

"I don't want to talk about me. I want to talk about Uncle East. Black, I'm so sorry he's gone. He was my lodestar, my guiding light. When things went wrong, I would think of Uncle East and feel better right away. You must feel terrible."

"Miss him, yes—always will. Feel bad, no. Grandfather lived and died the way he wanted, and not many people can do that."

"This place won't be the same without him, and I can't believe it belongs to me. I feel awful about not coming to see him. I thought about him every day but . . ."

He sat down beside her and took her hand in his. She started to retrieve it but then let it rest in his, and the gesture filled him with hope. He wanted to take her in his arms and breathe the fresh fragrance of her hair, feel her hips against his, but for now he forced himself to be content with her hand. It was a promise, a beginning to the end of the emptiness of years without her. He had chased himself around the world and back, trying to escape the lovely face engraved indelibly on his heart and mind. Finally, in a brutal confrontation with himself in a lonely hotel room in France, he knew he would have no peace until he came back for her.

"You mustn't feel that way. Grandfather understood. You were the first person he thought of when he decided to leave. He said he knew you would feel guilty and that you mustn't. He said you were going through a growth passage, and when you emerged on the other side he wanted you to have the mountain to come to for refuge."

"Black, is it possible . . . was he Harrison Easterling?"

"Yes, he helped develop the first practical photoelectric cell in 1904 and was also instrumental in the manufacture of vacuum tubes, which became essential in electrical equipment. Grandfather's own particular genius was adapting inventions for practical use, and setting up factories that could produce them efficiently for the mass market."

"Why did he leave it all and disappear?"

Black knew she was sincerely interested in his grandfather's story, and needed her curiosity assuaged. She deserved to know. but he also knew that, like himself, she needed to keep talking so that she could regain control of her emotions. They were both struggling with a poignant loss, but they were also fending off the physical sensations that surged between them. They needed time to balance themselves, so he talked on, quietly and calmly.

"Grandfather hated incompetency and inefficiency. He believed we should give the best of ourselves at all times, and if we did so, using the individual gifts God issues to each of us, we would solve many of the ills of mankind. He hired only those who shared his beliefs."

Black told her of the year when his grandfather's troubles began. In 1907, a radical union called the Industrial Workers of the World, labeled "Wobblies," infiltrated his company. It was a front for communists dedicated to overthrowing the capitalist system, and Harrison Easterling hated the insidious discontent they sowed among his well-treated labor force.

"The labor situation grew intolerable everywhere. Grandfather's products were suffering. In 1909, my mother, Laura, was born and his beloved wife Felice died during the birth because of an incompetent doctor. Grandfather went wild with grief. In the end, he decided he didn't want to be part of a world that tolerated less than excellence. He gave his best workers a year's severance pay, fired the rest of them, turned the power off in his plants, locked the doors, and disappeared."

Intrigued, Lilibet asked, "How did the Harrison Easterling Foundation come into being?"

"He set up a trust fund for my mother and several employees who'd been with him since the beginning. Once a year he met with the attorney he'd left in charge, made a few adjustments in his investments, and returned to the mountain. The by-products of his inventions, and several other patents he'd applied for, grew and multiplied. With his permission, the principals involved—my mother and the others—decided to form the foundation, which they run."

"Did he ever regret his decision?"

"Yes. Later, he felt he should have remained with his employees and fought the system, but by that time he was addicted to this place, and had found a peace beyond anything he'd ever known."

"How did he die? Was it an accident?"

"No. I'll show you later."

"Black, neither you nor your mother will tell me how he died. It must have been a traumatic and painful death, something difficult for you to talk about, something you don't want me to hear, but I'll have to know sooner or later. Please, tell me. I'm a pretty strong lady, you know."

"You don't have to tell me how strong you are . . . but please put your curiosity at rest. There's a time and place for everything."

Smiling at the frown of frustration on her face, he watched her draw a deep breath and compose herself. They sat quietly for a few moments.

"Isn't life odd sometimes, Black? Look what happened because Uncle East wanted peace in his life. The Harrison Easterling Foundation has helped thousands of people, more than he ever imagined. And he was the seed, the source."

She stood up, stretched her arms over her head, and yawned. She covered her mouth with her hand and smiled in embarrassment. "Sorry. I got up so early to get here, I forgot breakfast . . . I need a little nourishment and I'll be fine in no time."

He laughed. "Your appetite hasn't changed, I see."

"Let's raid Uncle East's ice house," she said, a mischievous twinkle in her eyes.

"It's your ice house now, but it's empty. I cleaned it out. But I know where you can satisfy that grumbling stomach. Let's go." He grabbed her hand and pulled her through the meadow and into the forest.

She jerked her hand from his.

"Where are we going? I don't feel like waiting while you catch a fish with your bare hands, and I have it on the best authority that the nearest diner is a hundred miles away."

The sight of her angelic face filled with righteous indignation was more than he could resist. Thank God there was still some of the spunky child in the sorrow-worn woman. He quickly kissed her lips, then placed a butterfly kiss on the tiny brown beauty mark near the corner of her mouth. Her bottom lip trembled and she stepped away from him. "Don't do that again, Black."

"Tell me you didn't like it. I've known since you came into my arms under the willow tree that you still want me. Your body told me all I needed to know, Elizabeth."

"I . . . don't call me Elizabeth, and don't kiss me again. Please."

He ran his thumb gently along her delicate jawline.

"I'll call you Elizabeth whenever I want, but I won't kiss you again. Not now, anyway. We have a few miles to travel. For once in your life, follow my advice. Your tummy and your questions will be satisfied. Okay?"

"Okay. I'm ready for adventure, Captain Bligh. No more mutiny."

An hour later, they traversed the barren, flat-rock summit known as Christmas Ridge. One towering evergreen dominated the sparse landscape. Lilibet's breath was coming in short gasps. The high altitude, and years of less rigorous exercise were taking their toll. Far ahead, Black moved relentlessly on and she eyed his broad back with building resentment.

"Hey," she called through cupped hands. "Could we rest a minute?"

"It's not much farther. Just beyond Christmas Tree. You need toughening up."

"You really are Captain Bligh!" she grumbled.

Cool September wind swept across the barren ridge, making Lilibet's eyes water and blowing her hair into a mass of tangles, but she struggled to catch up with him.

Black stopped at the base of the mammoth tree and waited for her.

"This is where Grandfather died."

Mystified, she brushed the hair from her eyes and asked, "What was he doing here?"

Silently, Black pointed to a fifteen-foot-high wooden platform on stilts. A fallen ladder lay on the ground nearby.

"Grandfather built himself a bier. From the condition of the dried and preserved saplings he used to build it, I'd say he'd been planning his departure since last fall."

Lilibet remembered the dignified death ritual of the early Indian tribes.

"Do you mean he came here by himself, climbed up there, pushed the ladder away, and then lay down to die?"

"Yes." A liquid brightness in Black's eyes revealed his grief, but Lilibet could also see his immense pride in the grace of his grandfather's last earthly act.

"I think I understand why . . . for Uncle East, not being

able to take care of himself would have been unbearable, and he would have hated living in Matterhorn with your mother."

"Yes, and he liked the idea of controlling his own destiny. He knew only parts of it are ours to control, but he used those parts to the fullest, and left the rest up to God. He often said he didn't believe in suicide, but considered this ancient Indian rite of the aged and infirmed, performed only when the person and body are useless, a dignified departure blessed with God's consent."

"I'm not sure I understand . . . was he in pain?"

"No. The aging body, when it's had enough living, begins to eat and drink less. Concerned loved ones force food on their elders when they should be left alone."

"Are you saying Uncle East starved himself?"

"Not really, not at first. He noticed he was requiring less food and realized he wasn't enjoying what he was eating. He knew his body was saying it was time to go. That's probably when he began to gather and preserve the saplings. The Indians of this region considered the red cedar the most sacred of all trees, and that is what he used. He built the bier while he still had strength. Then, one day he came here, climbed up, probably meditated, and lay down to pass over."

"But the birds and animals, didn't they . . . pick at him, bother him?"

"They seem to know what's happening and respect the passing over of humans. Some say there's a holy light that suffuses the body for days before and days after it dies, warding off animals and such. I also think Cat sat beneath the bier guarding him."

Tears rolled freely down Black's cheeks. Lilibet had never seen him cry before and the sight of the tears on his tanned face wrenched the breath from her. She moved to embrace him but he motioned her away.

"No! If you touch me now, I won't let you go."

Her arms dropped, helpless and empty.

"When did you find him?" she asked softly.

"I checked on him once a month, so I was here the middle of July. He was thin but happy and content, and divulged nothing of his plan. He must have come here shortly after that. I found him a week ago. A letter for me, and one for my mother, were on the table with yours. Mine, among other things, explained what he had done and where to find him. His body was in perfect condition, brown from the sun, preserved and dried like a hickory nut. There was a wonderful expression of peace on his face."

"Was Cat here?"

"No. I haven't seen Cat for several years. But I found her dried spoor under the bier."

"I'd like to visit his grave, Black."

He hesitated, pain twisting his usually inscrutable face.

"His ashes are scattered on the mountain. The hardest thing I had to do was . . . incinerate his body." His voice shook. "I could have buried it, but he would have hated that, or I could have left it here until it disintegrated, turned to dust . . . but I pass by here to and from—" He paused a moment. "I didn't think I could bear that."

She reached out for him but he walked away from her and stood for a long while looking over the vast mountain vista. She knew he was gathering himself together, so she sank limply on a flat boulder nearby and tried to do the same. She meditated and then said a prayer of farewell to Uncle East. When she opened her eyes, Black sat on the ground in front of her, smiling.

"You must be famished by now. Ready to eat?"

"You bet."

"We're going to cross the gap to Aracoma. Come with me—and don't ask questions."

Chapter 25

Lilibet couldn't believe her eyes. A stunning house rose above her where it shouldn't be. A barely discernible walking path led up the last summit to the house, but there was no driveway, no road. She stopped, rubbed her eyes, and looked again. It was still there, an amazing blend of nature's beauty and man's ingenuity wrought in gray stone and silvered cedar. She wasn't dreaming. Built to complement its surroundings, it was an integral part of the cliff itself, rising harmoniously, each level flowing into the ledge on which it sat. Not a tree had been disturbed or uprooted. The oaks and evergreens nestling close by anchored the house in space.

Black turned around to motion her forward and laughed at the disbelief in her eyes. "Yes, it's a house and it's mine."

"Black, I know you're talented, but even you can't produce a house out of thin air."

"It took me five years of helicoptering men, machinery, and supplies up here. It's unreachable except by helicopter, or the path we just took from Grandfather's cabin. Like it?"

"Like it? It's magnificent."

"Good. Wait till you see the interior."

As they climbed the remaining incline, Raffles and the coon dogs ran to welcome them. After petting the animals, Black led her across a granite terrace and they entered the house through a massive wooden door carved with intricate American Indian figures.

The structural purity of the house was even more evident inside. A massive expanse of glass looked out on infinite blue sky and far mountaintops, and she caught her breath at the floating sensation created by the openness. Cantilevered into space, the house was an aerie, a proper nest for a man who loved to fly, who loved his freedom.

Stark white walls were a dramatic background for the modular but comfortable furniture in white, silver blues, and emerald greens. Ample topaz pillows supplied splashes of warmth throughout, as did huge copper urns filled with imaginative arrangements of dried wheat sheaves and fresh mountain greenery. A soaring stone fireplace filled the opposite side of the dramatic expanse.

In awe, she tiptoed through the spacious living room, afraid the room would tilt with her weight and spill her into the vast space beneath it. She touched the glass, and the heat of the noon sun warmed her fingers.

"Well?"

Entranced, caught up in the drama of the house, she whirled at the sound of Black's voice.

"I love it. How can you ever leave here?"

"It's difficult sometimes, but the world has to be lived in and reckoned with. This is where I come when I need reenergizing. It's not quite finished."

"Not finished? Oh, Black, it's perfect."

"Almost. Come, and enter my kitchen, said the lecherous chef to the starving beauty."

She laughed and followed him into the efficient, streamlined, stainless steel kitchen. Steering clear of conversation about the campaign, or Clarice, they chatted while Lilibet whipped them up fluffy omelets, and baked flaky biscuits, which they smothered with butter and honey. They caught up on the years, Black telling her of the glaciers he'd scaled, his love for the electronic components industry he'd spawned, the madcap countess he'd almost married, and his mother's newfound career in conducting the affairs of the Harrison Easterling Foundation. She told him of the happy days with Collins, of the struggle to get her law degree at night school, and the bills she had pending in Congress. As they cleaned up and put away the last dish, she glanced at him rather shyly.

"Black, could I see the rest of the house before I leave?"

"I brought you here to see it. I wanted your approval."

A mischievous gleam sparkled in his green eyes. "I lied about Grandfather's storehouse. It's filled with food."

"You mean I didn't have to cross a mountain and a half for an omelet and biscuits?" she asked, laughing.

"Disappointed?"

"No. I wouldn't have missed this for the world."

With obvious pride, he showed her the music room with its acoustic walls and gleaming black grand piano, and the guest bedrooms, each room climbing a level with the rise of each corresponding mountain ledge.

Black's bedroom was on the top ledge. Shades of midnight, sky blue, and softer hues of blue had been used on the floor and the few pieces of angular steel-framed furniture. An expanse of glass created the same feeling of floating and space as it did in the living room. In the center was a large, square, puritan-white bed on a midnight blue pedestal. A suggestion of softness came from many pillows of various shapes and sizes heaped in a cascading pile on the downy surface. Overhead a skylight let in the bright September sky.

Black pushed a button near the bed and louvered shades covered the skylight, making the room shady and cool. "For sunny afternoons," he explained.

"Ingenious . . . marvelous."

"Ala-ka-zam," he said, pushing another button.

Lilibet gasped as the entire ceiling parted and they stood with the sky for a roof, the sounds of birdcalls and breezes flowing in and around them.

"For romantic nights."

Her enchantment with Black's aerie crumbled.

"Oh, has Clarice been here?"

Maroon colored his stern face for a flash. The look he gave her was unreadable. He jabbed another button and the ceiling closed, the louvers covered the skylight, and the room was cast in mellow shades of twilight.

"The house tour is over," he said coolly. He ripped his white T-shirt off over his head and headed toward doors off to the side. "I need a shower after hiking all morning. You're welcome to any of the guest baths if you'd like to do the same. Wander at your leisure."

Embarrassed that she'd asked the question and shaken

by his change in attitude, Lilibet left the room. Why had she asked such a stupid question? It was none of her business if Clarice had been here.

A door, partially ajar and adjacent to Black's room, drew her. She pushed it open to find a small, warm library, three of its walls lined floor to ceiling with books. The fourth, a wall of glass, looked into the jade heart of the forest. Deep-cushioned wing chairs with footstools were at either end of the fireplace. She knew immediately that he spent a lot of time here.

A strobe light illuminated a single, large painting hung on the stacked gray stone wall above the fireplace.

Her hand flew to her mouth in shock.

The painting was of her in the glen. He'd captured the glen in summer twilight in prisms of pearly lavender and rose, the verdant trees patterned in pale moss jades and silver purples. The landscape was the background for the gossamer figure seated next to the pond. A gauzy gown of white hinted seductively at the creamy body beneath it, intimated a suggestive triangular shadow at the apex of her legs, and boldly displayed the salmon peaks of her breasts. Her face and hair were incandescent, a shimmering aureole illuminated her platinum hair, and golden light leapt from her violet eyes.

In shivering wonder, she gazed at herself portrayed as a goddess of the woodlands. It was the most intensely beautiful, sensuously romantic painting she'd ever seen.

All the old feelings for Black, the suppressed longings she'd kept so rigidly in control, tore lose and raged around inside of her, squeezing her heart until it hurt.

"No, Black," she whispered.

Why did you come back to the valley, back into my life? She'd given him up for Collins and Genie, the only honest points of love in her increasingly bleak existence. Her life wasn't happy—contentment would always be out of reach—but she'd finally managed to accept her lot . . . until now.

A door in the wall of books opened and Black walked in, toweling his hair dry, another white towel tucked around his naked torso. He glared at her for one tense moment, then tossed his towel into a chair and advanced toward her.

"So ... you've seen it. The door should have been locked but I'm unaccustomed to having guests."

He hooked a finger in the waistband of her jeans and pulled her toward him. The wet towel circling his hips dampened her shirt. His lips were set, rigid with anger. He was still furious about the Clarice remark ... and was he angry she'd found the painting? A tremor of fear mixed with desire shook her.

"Why did you come back, Black?" she asked in a desperate whisper. "I know it wasn't just because you were concerned about strip mining. If you came back because you finally forgave me, it's too late."

"Is it?"

Still holding her at the waistband he ran his free hand casually, almost arrogantly, across her breast and watched the nipples tighten and thrust through her shirt.

"Don't do this, Black."

Looking into her eyes, he ignored her plea and continued rubbing sensually at the now aching peaks, daring her to stop him.

"I came back because I'm tired of running," he said in his smoky voice. "Living on the edge has lost its challenge. I'm truly alive only when I'm here ... and when I'm with you."

She choked off an anguished moan as the tension in her swelling breasts became almost unbearable. She gathered what resistance she had left and pushed away from him.

He pulled her back, his arms iron tight around her shaking form. He whispered in her ear, "You are the ultimate challenge, Elizabeth."

He laved her ear with his talented tongue, surely, softly, sensually taking his time. The crisp, black hair on his firm chest rubbed hot and alive against her chin. She fought the urge to lift her hand and feel them with her fingers. Her skin was sensitive and burning to the touch, her clothes suddenly too constricting where the fabric touched. Desire pooled in her stomach and melted down into her loins. Her knees gave way. To keep from sinking to the floor, she embraced him ... and knew a blinding moment of having arrived home.

"Black, we shouldn't, we can't do this," she managed to whisper.

"Yes, my darling, we should, we can. I didn't know this would happen when I brought you here today. I was willing to wait for as long as it took. But we won't let this go—not this time. I swore once if I ever had you in my arms again, I'd never let you go." He breathed the words in an undertone as he brushed her face with butterfly kisses. "I didn't know the battle would last this long or be this terrible, but I won't retreat now—when it's almost won."

Raw lust mounted swiftly in Black. After years of urgent need for her, his body cried out for consummation. But he had mastered control and denial, and though stretched to the breaking point, he was determined to prevail in this situation, seducing her until she begged him to enter her. He felt his erection growing beneath the towel. With iron will he held it semihard. He didn't want her to bolt when she realized the savageness of his craving for her.

He stilled the wild beating of his heart as he nuzzled his nose in her hair, and kissed the sweet skin on her neck. God, she felt wonderful—silky, fragrant, warm. He unbuttoned her shirt. A small sob escaped her as he kissed the soft swell of each breast. Carefully, so as not to frighten her, he tugged the shirt from her jeans and removed her bra, kissing her shoulders as he did so. He kissed her mouth and her lips parted to let the kiss deepen. She moved against him, sighing, and her lips moved over his anxiously. Lacerated with need for her, he swung her up into his arms and carried her to his bedroom. Kneeling, he laid her gently on the large bed. She clung to him, her arms fast around his neck.

"It's okay. Let go of me, Elizabeth. I want to look at you."

She released him and he stood up, reveling in the sight of her on his bed. The endless, tortured nights of imagining her in Cle's arms were gone. She was here where she belonged. Her creamy skin glowed in the late afternoon twilight and her platinum hair curled sensuously around her face. Her violet eyes were hidden by long-lashed lids.

"Open your eyes and look at me, Elizabeth," he said, almost afraid of what her eyes would reveal.

Flecked with gold, her eyes held a touch of fear, but also fierce abandon and excitement, and his heart leapt with joy.

Lilibet wouldn't take her eyes off of him, standing so tall and savage above her. Would he see that she was afraid, afraid of what they were about to unleash?

"Remove your clothes, Elizabeth," he ordered.

She numbly unbuttoned the jeans and struggled out of them, kicking them away from her while he watched. Lightly, he ran one hand over her breasts, her stomach, and the springy, curly center of her sex. She hurt from yearning for him. The lingering brush of his fingers on her body stirred unbearable anguish and her knees jerked up in reaction. He took her bent knees in his hands and held them apart.

"Have you ever touched yourself?" he asked hoarsely.

She couldn't speak, and shook her head back and forth.

"Give me your hand, Elizabeth. Learn to love the sensual part of yourself."

With one of his fingers he inserted her finger between the swollen lips of her sex. She closed her eyes, and moaned softly as he moved her finger in and out. In the recesses of her lust-fogged mind, Lilibet wondered why she had ever denied herself this pleasure. She heard him talking to her in low tones. What was he saying?

"Pleasure yourself; I want you to feel the softness and wonder within you." He extracted his finger but hers continued its new discovery. "Keep going, Elizabeth, don't stop."

She felt the creamy wetness of her own desire and knew what he wanted to feel. Then, with wild surprise, she felt strong contractions hugging her finger, arousing all of her with warm movement, and she cried out in wonder.

"That was just a promise," Black said softly. "To-gether, we're going to share something much greater be-cause we'll be giving all of ourselves to each other. I've dreamed about this—about awakening your body to joy beyond your imagination. And I've never wanted anything so much as to see you discover this with me. Open your eyes, Elizabeth, and look at me."

She forced her pleasure-weighted eyes open and saw Black still standing above her, the towel gone, his muscled body taut with tension. His green eyes glittered. A vein in his neck rose and fell, beating erratically. His male member stood erect, engorged and pulsing, and she remembered the sight of him on the river rafting trip and how she'd compared him to a stallion in heat.

He held her gaze.

"There hasn't been a second in the past twelve years that I haven't ached for you," he said, "but I will not take you unless you want me. Do you want me, Elizabeth?"

Black held his breath waiting for her answer.

"Yes."

Black knelt beside her and lowered his dark head to her flat stomach covering it with moist kisses, his tongue flicking in and out, tantalizing the nerve endings in her hips and thighs. He suckled her breasts hungrily, pulling her nipples deep into his mouth. *My God, I'm going to die with need for her.* He couldn't get enough of her breasts, her mouth, and the hot sweetness of her femaleness.

Lilibet had never known such exquisite agony. With each pull of his lips, teeth, and tongue on her breasts she felt a corresponding knifelike throb in her vulva. The desire for him was excruciating, heavy, hot and almost more than she could bear. Her nipples, inside his mouth, were taut with painful wanting. Gently, he traced the lush, triangular patch of golden curls and slipped his supple hand between her thighs. She caught her breath as he caressed the soft, inner flesh of her thighs until his fingers found her tender core. They worked sensuous miracles and she felt herself growing ... harder. Yes, harder. The small nubbin he manipulated was engorged and felt ready to burst.

Her breathing fast and fevered, she covered his chest with kisses, pulled at his arms to hold her tighter, and bit at his lips and ears. Frantically, she kissed the hollow at

the base of his throat, the hollow she'd dreamed about
and had ached to touch. *Please take me, Black, please. I
can't stand this any longer. Make me one with you. I want
to feel it, know it, give myself to you.*

Black found himself in a sexual frenzy he had never
before experienced. Mounting her, he spread her legs
with his hands, then braced himself above her with both
arms. He tested the quivering wetness of her and then entered once slowly, then out again. She was hot, creamy,
tight, and utterly delectable.

With a guttural, triumphant cry, he thrust himself into
her. She clung to his shoulders, her nails biting into their
tanned smoothness. She cried out with pleasure, at the
glory of Black within her, a satisfaction she'd never
known. His huge, hot hardness filled her over and over
again, and though her body cried for release, she wanted
this to never end.

Wildly, with burning, mindless passion, they consumed
each other time and again, commanding fate to make up
for all the cheated years.

Through a maddening haze, she heard him say, "Come
with me, darling, come with me. Please. Now!"

They were up and over in a world of flashing colors
and exhilarating release and abandon. He thundered into
her, emptying himself once, and then again. Above her,
she heard him scream like the cougar, the keening primitive and exalted. His explosion filled her with the essence of Black himself and she knew a quick second of
sorrow that much of it overflowed and spilled onto her
thighs. She wanted to keep it all within her, precious and
safe. The muscles of her vagina contracted over and over
again, and she experienced another, shattering, blissful
climax. Dear God, let this never end.

Dazed, he lowered himself to lay gently on top of her,
still nestled within her. Slowly, he moved back and forth
once more, giving them both time to come down from
where they had been, and giving him time to adjust to the
gut-wrenching tenderness he felt for her. For a long,
lovely moment he rested on her, then carefully lifted himself off and on to the bed. They lay side by side holding
hands, their breathing calming down, peace settling softly

in the recesses of their minds and bodies, a delicious languor enveloping them.

But then, because he couldn't bear to be so close and yet not closer, he brought her tight against him, reveling in the feel of her fragile form against his hard one. He caught a corner of the cover and wrapped it protectively around them. She turned and folded her body spoon-fashion into his, her buttocks fitting cozily against his thighs.

They lay for a while in the clean blue space of the room and sky, exhausted and satisfied for the moment. The absolute rightness of what had just occurred between them had shattered them both. The exaltation of discovery, of complete recognition and correspondence with a similar soul, was startling and almost fearfully exhilarating. This was beyond special, beyond words—there was no explaining how they felt.

Lilibet marveled at the miracle they'd just experienced. She'd never known such bliss existed. She loved this quiet time with him, and the way his even breathing tickled her ear. Such a small thing, yet the intimacy of it made her feel they'd been together forever and would always be. She wouldn't, couldn't think about Cle, not now, not yet.

Black kissed her ear, then whispered into it.

"Thank you, Elizabeth. I knew it would be like this. I've known it since the parking lot at Ruby's."

"Black, I had no idea. For the first time in my life, I'm not hungry for anything—food, feelings, sustenance of any kind. I've always had an emptiness. It's gone now and I . . . feel complete. You did that."

"No, we did it together." She felt him smiling against her cheek. "Something else is now complete."

"What's that?"

"The house. When I said it wasn't finished, this is what I meant. Brady's Lair has just been blessed. I built it for you. I came back for you."

"What about Clarice?"

He sputtered, and she thought he was angry again, but then she knew he was laughing. He turned her over and took her chin in his hand. "Listen to me. I have never slept with Clarice, have never made love to her in any form or fashion—and never had a desire to. Clarice has never been here. This house is sacred, meant only for you and me. Clarice is a wounded puppy. I take care of her when I can. How could I help it? She was everywhere I went."

"She's in love with you."

"Not love, darling. Obsession is more like it. She's an alcoholic and needs professional help. Let's not talk about Clarice. Let's talk about you."

"Must we?"

"It's time you let it all out. I've watched you, Elizabeth. Watched you waltz with the President in a beautiful white dress . . . one of your dreams accomplished, only I wanted to be the man you were laughing with."

"You saw me the evening of the French Society Ball?"

"Yes. I've observed you several times. That's the reason I finally came back to claim you. Each time I saw you, the sorrow was etched deeper into your face, and the misery in your eyes was more than I could bear. But I came back for selfish reasons, too. Everything seemed empty without you. The intrigue and challenge I found in surpassing others in the electronics industry lost its edge, and the sailing, climbing, and exploring that I once found so exciting became dull, meaningless. Your face, your voice, your laughter met me at every turn. I knew I needed you to make it all worthwhile."

"Black, what a beautiful thing to say. Thank you." She kissed him and sighed. "I'm sorry you saw my misery. I didn't think I was that transparent."

"Only to me."

She sighed.

"Well, you're correct. I'm drained, never nourished. They're all so thirsty and I seem to be the one to give them drink. I'm unhappy, but that's all right. Genie keeps me going. I can handle it."

She told him of all the years of Cle's faithlessness, of Pappy's double dealings, of Fat Sis's increasing reliance on her, of Clarice's gradual descent into lust-ridden hell, of Margot's hidden resentments. In the end, she told him the true story of the tragedy that had taken Collins's life—the drunken, selfish, thoughtless afternoon that had sniffed out a promising life, and robbed her of her only son. And for the first time, she revealed the guilt she carried for allowing Collins to ride with Cle.

When she told him of Pappy's threat to take Genie from her if she told the truth or left Cle, Black swore savagely, and held her tightly to him. The last of her words were muffled in his shoulder. A dry sob shook her.

"Have you cried? In all this time, have you really cried about Collins, my brave mountain sprite?"

"Not since that day."

"Cry, sweetheart," he whispered into her hair. "Cry. You're safe with me now."

And she did. He held her shaking frame as gut-wrenching sobs erupted from deep within her. She cried in self-pity, in anger, in resentment, in sorrow, and finally, with relief.

Slowly, softly, after the last sob had left her, he made gentle love to her, willing the force of his feelings to heal her.

Afterward, weak but utterly satisfied, she lifted her head and gave him a silly smile. "There's something you should know. I use the birth control pill, and have since it first came out. When I realized the kind of man I'd married, I wanted no more children."

"Twelve years ago, I was careful about beginning another life inside of you," Black said, "but I have to be honest with you—this time I would be elated to know my seed grew within you."

Exaltation flamed through her. Black wanted all of her. He wanted to share himself and his life with her and a child. Wild happiness fired and grew to fill every corner of her body and soul. She covered his face with kisses and held to his shoulders for a moment, indulging in the fantasy. Then she turned her face away from his on the pillow, accepting the depressing, drenching reality of her marriage to Cle. She and Cle had a history together that involved years of shared joys and shared tragedies, people and family, vows and promises.

"How wonderful that would be." She paused, hesitant to continue. "But, Black, I must go back. I have a cam-

paign to finish. I can't leave Cle in the middle of the
campaign for many reasons."

Black shot out of bed, glowering at her, the sheet hanging half on, half off him.

"You're going back?" he asked incredulously.

She glared back at him with defiance.

"Black, think of the scandal if I stayed with you. Not
only would it hurt both campaigns, but it would devastate
Marm, and—Sam, and the others. Cle isn't a bad person,
Black, he's just . . . weak. Actually, we make a good
team. He attracts the votes and I get the work done. I also
want to get the upper hand on Pappy, and make sure
Clarice gets into therapy. More than anything, I have to
figure out a way to keep Genie."

"I understand why you need to finish the campaign, but
come with me, work in my camp. You belong with me,"
he said impatiently. "I'm a powerful man now, Elizabeth.
I can make sure Pappy doesn't take Genie from you. I
thought I could wait, be patient until you recognized how
futile your blind loyalty is. But now that I've had you,
tasted you, been filled by the love that we share, I can't
let you go. I will not let you go back."

She stood now, nude, and magnificent in her anger.

"I will! You can't stop me."

"Are you saying that even after what happened between us this afternoon, you're still going to let them
suck the life out of you. You're not divorcing Cle?"

"I can't—not yet . . ." How could she explain that her
inbred sense of honor demanded she straighten out her
life with the Huttons before she left them? How could she
explain her fear of Pappy and his threat to take Genie
from her? Black had asked her once if she was afraid of
Pappy. She had denied it, but she *was* afraid. "I want to
win the seat for Cle. I want to leave things better than I
found them. Cle will need—"

His voice cold as ice, Black interrupted her. "Don't
fool yourself, Elizabeth. If you think Cle can function as
a United States Senator without you, you're wrong. And
if you think you're going to give me Cle's leftovers, coming to me only when you have time, you are badly mis-
taken."

"That's not what I meant. I haven't slept with Cle in a year and I never will again. Please, understand—"

"Tell me the truth," he said harshly. "Did you sleep with me hoping I'd bow out of the race, or at least let up on the campaigning so you could win?"

"My God! You would believe that of me?"

"At this point, Mrs. Hutton, I don't know what to believe. I do know you have just said you wouldn't carry a child of mine, and you wouldn't divorce the fool you're married to."

His cold anger and cruel words hurt more than the thought of leaving him. She gripped his shoulders in desperation.

"Black, please listen to me. I will leave Cle, but I must leave him honorably, and I have to be careful because of Genie. I have to leave Cle with something to cling to, something that will make him more of a person. He *is* Genie's father. I've been as guilty as anyone else in catering to him all these years. After it's all over, after I've done my best to give him an anchor, to give Genie a father she can be proud of, then you and I can be together. It's what I want more than anything."

With heavy resignation, he saw she sincerely believed what she said. After all, her ability to see only the best in others, to finish what she'd started, and to feel a responsibility for the welfare of others no matter how badly they'd treated her, was one of the reasons he loved her.

He brought her close to him and sighed into her hair. "All right, my poor, misguided darling. I want you to know that I'll be a great father. I'll take good care of Genie and love her as you do. Forgive my anger and the terrible things I just said. I don't like this at all, but I understand that you feel you must finish something begun long ago."

Not wanting to tell her his anger hid a wrenching fear that he would lose her, he kissed her forehead tenderly.

"But, be warned," he continued, "I'm still going to do my damnedest to defeat Cle. What will you do if I win, Elizabeth?"

"I will accept that I've done my best to do the right thing, and I will come to you, Black."

Black didn't like it, he didn't like any of it. He wanted her by his side now and forever. A sense of urgency swept over him, so strong it almost choked him. He held her tight, hating the knowledge that he had to let her go.

"It's late, Black. I'll be missed I must go."

As he released her, a brutal forboding took root within him. The feeling that they were being swept toward tragic events over which he had no control shook him to the core. With every fiber of his being he wanted to keep her with him, but it was not his right to keep her from what she clearly felt was her mission.

"Elizabeth, I will not come for you again. When you know the cord between you and Cle is severed completely, then you come to me."

The ride home in Black's helicopter through the star-studded night was sheer torture for Lilibet. Black sat in frozen silence, working the controls automatically, the old inscrutable expression on his proud face.

Neither of them spoke.

His last words resonated through her ears, drumming through her brain and body. She'd promised she would come back to him . . . but she also knew there were no guarantees in this crazy world, and the mere thought of not being with Black again struck terror to her soul. She realized now that her love for Black could no longer be denied. Living a life without his love was tantamount to committing a sin, for it was an all-knowing, all-encompassing, yet liberating love of body and spirit.

She held herself abnormally still, afraid if she moved or opened her mouth she would go over the edge, or have a nervous breakdown, all those things people talked about when they'd come to the end of their strength. An absurd picture of herself tearing knobs from the instrument panel and beating at the glass around them horrified her.

Hold still. Hold on. Hold still. Only the slight rise and fall of her chest indicated life remained within her.

Chapter 26

The day before the election was chilly, raw, and gray with rain. The Rainbow Diner was warm, but almost empty; Pappy Hutton's cadre of followers and the breakfast regulars had cleared out. Eulonie Bevins wiped away spilled egg yoke and toast crumbs from a red plastic tablecloth. While she worked she watched the table up front where Lilibet Hutton sat with Sam Adkins and Jane Etta Frye. She suspected they were going over last-minute details of this crucial day.

Eulonie worried a molar with her tongue, feeling for a bit of bacon. Miz Hutton looks real sick. She's so tired she's near dead, thought Eulonie. Ought'n be out in this awful weather—tired as she is, she'll catch her death. *Should I tell her?* It will only burden her more.

Eulonie Bevins loved Lilibet Hutton. Lilibet had always made an effort to talk to her, had always treated her with kindness, when no one else would. She always asked about Eulonie's health, made sure her fatherless children had a nice Christmas, had hired a tutor to teach her to read, and given her books that opened a new world for her. She'd even visited Eulonie's small house in the hollow to make sure they had enough fuel in the winter. Lilibet Hutton was the most decent and honest person Eulonie had ever known.

Her searching tongue worked harder as she struggled with her decision. Should she tell Miz Hutton what she knew? Not the worst of it, but the information that would make a difference in the election. She thought Miz Hutton would want to know. The other stuff, about the murders, she couldn't even begin to think of telling those things. They would kill her. She wouldn't put it past them to cut her tongue out if they found out she'd told Miz Hutton *anything*. She didn't care if they did cut her tongue out. *I'm ugly anyway*. But she did care about dying.

Sam Adkins paid the bill, and left the diner with Jane Etta. Miz Hutton lowered her head into her hands for a moment and sighed. Eulonie eased her way up front, wiping tables as she went.

"Howdy, Miz Hutton. How about another cup of coffee?"

"Howdy, Eulonie. Sure, I'd love another cup. I'm going to need all the caffeine I can get today."

As Eulonie poured the coffee, she looked back to check Pappy Hutton's regular corner. It was empty, and the only other customers were on the other side of the restaurant.

Eulonie cleared her throat. "Miz Hutton, I've got some dirty stuff to tell you. I'd 'preciate it a whole lot if you'd pretend we's jest havin' a regular conversation."

Startled for a moment, Lilibet composed her face and smiled up at Eulonie. "Sure."

"You know, they think because I'm ugly I must be deaf and dumb. They talk in front of me. Oh, they whisper and such, but I hear." She gave the room a furtive scan. "They's sellin' votes, Miz Hutton. Pappy's buyin' the miners' votes for ten dollars and a pint of whiskey."

"I knew some of it went on, Eulonie, but I've been so careful to make sure we get honest poll workers."

"This ain't some little operation. They's bringin' in illegal voters from out of state, hidin' them up in the hollers, then bringin' them in with fake voters cards."

Lilibet's wan face turned whiter. Her hand shook as she raised the coffee cup to her lips. "I believe you, Eulonie, but if I'm going to do anything about it, I need proof."

"Yes, ma'am. Try way up any of the hollers goin' out toward where you use to live at Big Ugly. I gotta go."

She scuttled off toward the kitchen. Lilibet left the diner with a determined set to her chin.

Lilibet slammed the library door behind her. She stood in the hallway dripping and shivering. Neither Pappy nor Cle had had the courtesy or the concern to ask her to re-

move her wet coat and boots. The ornate cuckoo clock
Fat Sis had brought back from Germany chimed five
bells. She could hear Belle banging pots and pans in the
kitchen. The smell of pot roast and potatoes filtered
through the house. She realized this was one of those moments you remember forever.

A moment of decision.

She closed her eyes and saw again the daring look in
Pappy's eyes, the arrogant twist of his mouth. "So what,
Lilibet! You've spent the day snooping and spying. Yes,
we've imported voters. We always do, but we needed
more this time. Your friend, Brady, gave us a real run for
our money. What are you going to do about it? Tell everyone your charming, loving husband is a crook? I don't
think so. You've always been a loyal part of the team,
Lilibet. Don't make waves or you'll be sorry."

Cle had said, "Lilibet, I knew nothing of this. I swear."

But one look at his face told her he not only knew, but
approved. Oh, Cle would have kept his hands clean,
looked the other way, but he knew.

Gripping the handrail, she pulled herself up the stairs
and into the bedroom. She removed her wet coat, shook
it, then took great care in hanging it to dry in the adjoining bathroom. She then removed her boots and meticu-
lously scraped the mud from them into the bathtub. She
knew she was being silly—just delaying what she knew
she must do.

She took a hot shower, and the water streaming over
her body stripped away years of pretense and denial.
She'd thought she could wait until after the election to
leave, to escape the poison in this family, but she would
not be a party to the monumental dishonesty that was taking place at this very moment. She would not be an ac-
complice to the mockery Pappy made of the law-making
process in Washington. All these years she'd excused
Cle's weaknesses as just the immaturity of a good man;
she'd closed her eyes to his unfaithfulness; she'd even
put up with his drinking because she thought he was so
miserable about Collins's death. She'd kept herself sane
by believing none of Pappy's or Cle's machinations could

besmirch her own soul, or threaten the ideals she held so dear.

But she'd been wrong. By staying with the Huttons, she'd lost some of herself. She'd tried so hard, and held on so long ... but she knew it was the end. The end of a marriage, the end of a dream. Cledith Hutton was not a fit man to hold office, or be a father to her chid, and not even the most determined will could make it so.

She rubbed herself dry with a thick, white towel, wrapped it around her, and returned to the bedroom.

The only glimmer of joy or hope in all this misery was the thought of Black. Thank god he was back. She would see him soon. The image of his face brought a lift to her heart, and gave her the courage to head for the telephone next to her bed.

"Hey, man, why would Lilibet call a press conference seven o'clock, election eve? The polls open in twelve hours. Can't tell me it's nothing but another campaign ploy. She's the smartest of the lot."

The reporter sucked a heavy drag off the last of his cigarette and threw it on the butt-strewn floor. The barnlike room at the Sons of Italy Hall, where Yancey's community dances were held, had been converted into a press room. Television cameramen jockeyed for better vantage points in the noisy, smoke-filled room.

"Thing that interests me," said his buddy, "is Pappy and the rest of them didn't know anything about a press conference when I talked with Sam Adkins this afternoon. This seems to be Lilibet Hutton's show."

"Shut up. Here she comes."

A silence, made up of respect and also fascinated curiosity, descended on the room as Lilibet Hutton made her way to the microphone. She wore a dark navy wool suit, the tailored cadet jacket trimmed with crested gold buttons. She'd never looked more beautiful, or more vulnerable. She was alone.

"Ladies and gentlemen of the press. I have an announcement to make. No one wanted to win this election more than I did ... so this announcement is painful and embarrassing. I am resigning as manager of my husband's campaign for several reason. First, the rumors and innuendoes about money laundering in the Harrison Easterling Foundation are being fed to you through Hutton Mining, and they are false. The foundation, chaired by Black Brady's mother, Laura Brady, is an honest organization of inestimable value to the state of West Virginia. Secondly, I have proof that my father-in-law, Pappy Hutton, was ready to buy this election. Not only is he paying miners within the state for votes, but he has also imported miners from other states. I also have information that his influence on votes in Congress defeated environmental issues that would have been beneficial to the state of West Virginia."

Turmoil broke in the room as reporters and cameramen moved in for questions and close-ups.

"How can you prove Pappy Hutton is buying votes, Mrs. Hutton?"

"Take a trip up any of the hollows between here and Big Ugly. You'll find tent camps with imported voters in every one of them."

"How do you know Pappy is behind it? What about the candidate, your husband, Cledith?"

"I have seen Pappy in the tent camps with my own eyes. I asked my husband if he knew anything about the vote buying, and the influence peddling in Congress and he swears he does not."

"Why isn't he with you tonight?"

Lilibet's chin jutted out defiantly. "Frankly, he doesn't approve of what I'm doing."

"Are you telling people not to vote for your husband?"

"The people have to make up their own minds. They will have to take the information I have given them and decide for themselves."

"Are you voting for your husband, Mrs. Hutton?"

They saw her visibly whiten and clutch the podium in front of her.

"No."

Bedlam broke loose.

Lilibet tried to answer the questions thrown at her, tried to control what was left of the press conference, but it was impossible. She felt someone standing at her side and looked up to find Sam.

He smiled at her, and took her arm. "Ready to go?"

"Yes. You might lose your job, Sam, but thanks for rescuing me."

They walked away from the podium and out a back door, the press's continued questions screaming in their ears.

Black Brady campaign workers in Matterhorn watched the television in delighted disbelief.

"Are you voting for your husband, Mrs. Hutton?"

"No."

They jumped, cheered, and thumped one another on the back, and turned to Black for his reaction. The candidate sat with his arms folded across his chest, staring at the television, his face set and grim. They watched in astonished silence as he rose from his chair, grabbed his jacket, threw it over his shoulder, and left the room.

Black halted halfway down the hall. The monumental urge to get to Lilibet—to shield her and take her away from the whole mess—had to be controlled. His appearance at her side could be disastrous for everyone . . . and he'd told her he'd never come for her again. She had to come to him. Fine beads of perspiration broke out on his brow as he battled with himself, and finally collapsed sideways to lean futilely against the wall.

Sam held her elbow and ran interference through the crowd that pressed around them. Hecklers booed and hissed at Lilibet. "How lucky can a man get having you for a wife? Traitor!"

"Hey, slut, you're as bad as your sister-in-law."

Sam turned around and glared threateningly at the man who'd made the last remark. "Don't listen to them, Lilibet."

"Well, it's definitely a Hutton crowd, isn't it, Sam? I should have known better. I should have driven to Charleston and made the announcement."

On Main Street, the crowd started pushing and shoving. Tony Carpozzoli opened his door and beckoned to them. Sam shoved Lilibet through the door and Tony locked it behind them.

"You sit down right here, Lilibet," said Tony. He motioned her to a booth. "Those animals. They got no right to even speak to you. I'll get you and Sam some beer and chili. Nice, eh?"

"Thanks, Tony. That would be great," said Sam.

Lilibet curled up in a corner of the booth, almost in a fetal position. Sam sat down next to her and tried to take her in his arms, but she would have none of it. She shook her head. He got up and sat across the table.

"Pappy said to tell you not to come home."

"Why doesn't that surprise me? What did Cle say?"

"I think Cle is still in a state of shock. He's said nothing."

"I'm going to Marm's. I own that house and they can't keep me out of there. Miss Mabel went to Washington so she could fly down here with Genie tomorrow. I called her before the press conference and told her to keep Genie in Washington no matter what Pappy says."

"Lilibet, does this mean you're going to divorce Cle?"

"Yes. I've known I would leave after the campaign, win or lose."

Sam swallowed hard and reached to take her hand.

"You know I'm here for you, whatever you decide. I want to be a part of your life. I lo—"

Distressed by the hope in his big brown eyes, and the adoring look on his face, she held up her hand to stop him. "Don't say it, Sam. I can't talk of love, or leavings, or marriages, or anything right now. I've been so busy all day tracking down leads and following rumors, I haven't had time to think of tonight's consequences."

"Lilibet," said Sam, his voice soft and warm, "I think you know I've waited for you, waited until you saw the mistake you made. I . . ." He hesitated.

Gathering what was left of her waning courage on this fateful evening, Lilibet seized the moment and covered his hand with both of hers. "Sam, you're the best friend I've ever had. There was a time, after Collins died, when I imagined we might end up together, but I know now that I love you as I would a brother, and I always have. Nothing has ever, or will ever change that."

"But, Lilibet, that's enough to start with. I'm willing to settle for that."

She had to tell him. "Sam, I love Black Brady. The day after tomorrow, I will call him and tell him I'm coming to him. But, please, Sam, I beg you not to tell Pappy."

Disbelief, then livid anger flashed in his eyes. Gone as quickly as it came, his face settled into a stonelike mask. She shivered, suddenly afraid of Sam—but that was silly. She'd always trusted him. Then he smiled and his face softened into the familiar warmth and geniality that were his trademark.

"Well, I almost made a fool of myself, didn't I? I wish you and Brady all the best. That's all I've ever wanted for you, Lilibet . . . the best."

Lilibet squeezed his hand affectionately, relieved the news of her and Black was now in the open.

"Sam, I'm so angry with myself for not seeing some of these things about Pappy sooner. Did you know, Sam? You take care of much of Pappy's dealings."

"Not his dirty stuff. He wants to keep me pure. He's got to have someone who looks squeaky clean in Washington. Who told you, Lilibet, who's been talking to you?"

"The information about the influence peddling in Washington came to me from a reliable source and I've been investigating it since July. Someone else told me recently about the massive vote buying here in the state."

"Who?"

"Can't tell you, Sam."

"I should know who told you, Lilibet. It would be safer if I could talk to this person and find out all they know. Then we won't be in for any rude surprises later."

"Sorry, Sam, can't do it."

"You can trust me," he said, insistent.

"I know I can. Maybe someday I'll tell you. Years from now when we're old and gray." She tried to smile.

Tony brought the beer and chili and they were quiet while they ate. Hecklers still hung around outside, pounding on the window and swearing at Tony for sheltering Lilibet and Sam. Tony pulled a green shade down over the door and windows.

"Can we use the back entrance when we're ready to leave, Tony?"

"Sure, Sam. Lilibet, you ever need help you come to me."

Marm's house was warm and cozy. The two of them sat on the sofa in front of the television, eating popcorn and watching the returns. How nice to feel safe and cared for, even for a little while, thought Lilibet.

"I can't believe the race is so close, Lilibet," said Marm. "I thought Black would win easily after you held that press conference."

"We have a few more hours before all the precincts are in. Anything could happen. Black's been out of touch with the people of West Virginia for a long time—and no matter how crooked Pappy is, he owns a lot of people."

Marm patted her hand. "I'm proud of what you done, honey. I'm scared of the Huttons. There was a time when I didn't think we could exist without them, but you done the right thing. We've got each other and Genie."

"Where's Margot? She's been gone all afternoon."

A look of distress filled Marm's face.

"Hope you don't mind, Lilibet. She's at Hutton campaign headquarters. We had an argument. She says you're crazy, and she's going to lose her job if she don't get over there and kiss ass." Marm covered her mouth in embarrassment. "Sorry, you know I don't like you girls talking that way, but that's what she said."

"Don't worry about it, Marm."

Marm was talking, and the television droned on, reciting returns from all over the state and county. Lilibet fought to stay awake, but the emotional exhaustion of the last few months did her in. Marm shook her awake at midnight.

"Lilibet, Lilibet, wake up honey. You'll want to see this." Marm handed her a cup of coffee.

In a stupor, she stared at the television and saw Cle raising his hands over his head, waving *V* for victory.

Next to him were Clarice and Fat Sis. Sam stood in the background. Someone had been wise enough to advise Pappy to stay at home. The screen flashed to Black giving a concession speech, and then back to the Hutton victory celebration. All the helpless souls Pappy had bought through the years had stayed with him and voted for Cle. Afraid of losing what little security they possessed, they'd willingly ignored the truth and clung to their corrupt savior.

Abraham Lincoln was wrong, she thought. You *could* fool most of the people most of the time . . . and she'd contributed to the masquerade until yesterday. Because of her stubborn will to win, and her misguided sense of loyalty to Cle, she'd helped elect to the United States Senate the weak son of an evil, manipulative man.

Nauseated with self-disgust, she covered her mouth and ran to the bathroom to vomit.

She woke up the next morning to find Marm placing a cold cloth on her hot forehead. She tried to sit up but fell back with a groan.

"Lay still, child. You've been burning up with a fever and then shaking with chills all night long. You got yourself a good case of the flu."

"I've got to make a phone call, Marm."

"Later. You're exhausted, Lilibet. All the stress and strain of the campaign wore down your resistance. And you got soaked when you was going in and out of those hollers looking for those illegal voters. Here, drink some orange juice."

She tried to drink from the glass Marm held to her lips but finally pushed it away, her hands shaking. "Please, Marm, I have to make a phone call."

"Okay, if you insist. I'll help you downstairs to the telephone."

With Marm's arm supporting her they made their way to the bedroom door, where Lilibet's knees gave way and she sank weakly to the floor. Her head whirled dizzily and she was sick to her stomach. She could hear Marm saying Sam was on his way over with the doctor. She didn't want the doctor. She wanted Black. Wavering in and out of a gray fog, Lilibet tried to tell Marm she wanted Black, but she fainted before she could say the words.

Chapter 27

White walls, white sheets, soft rubber-soled shoes padding around an antiseptic room. An endless hum of fuzzy sounds. Lilibet knew she was in the hospital, but try as she might, she couldn't keep her eyes open long enough to focus on anything or anyone. She knew Marm was holding her hand and talking to her but she couldn't reply. Every effort she made to open her mouth and speak was lost in the struggle to breathe.

"It's all right, darlin'. Whatever you been trying to tell me is not near as important as you getting well. Relax and let the drugs help you rest. Doctor says you got pneumonia and you have to be very quiet."

Marm's soothing hand moved up and down Lilibet's listless arm. The loving hand was cool against the heat of her skin.

Marm's voice went on. "Sam left strict orders that you're not to be disturbed or have visitors—not even Margot or Clarice. He took the phone out of the room, too, even posted a guard at the door. Said he didn't want any nosy reporters snoopin' around. I'm glad—selfish, too, I guess. It's nice having you all to myself."

Was it today, tomorrow, or the next day? An unfamiliar male voice spoke to Marm. "She needs complete rest and isolation, Mrs. Springer. Sam was right to take these precautions. Your daughter wore herself out—almost ruined her health during that campaign. But she'll be just fine in a few weeks."

Her hearing was distorted, fading in and out, smooth, then ragged and torn, like her breathing. Were Sam and Marm arguing?

"Sam, I know Lilibet trusts you, but I got to say that I think you done the wrong thing."

"I'm sorry, Mrs. Springer, I guess I'm going to have to tell you the truth. Cledith went on a drinking binge at Ruby's after the election. We tried to sober him up at home but he kept slipping out of the house. To dry him out, we had to send him off to a secured clinic. Since Lilibet was ill, too, we issued the press release saying the two of them were sequestered away in a secluded mountain cabin, trying to patch up their marriage."

"You also said it might be called 'a second honeymoon'. Lilibet will be furious. You shouldn't have done it."

Lilibet managed to murmur a squeaky whisper. "Don't . . . wrong."

"Love Jesus, she said something."

"Please, Marm . . . find Bl—"

Sam's voice spoke swiftly. "She's trying to tell you it's all right. But she shouldn't be talking or thrashing about like this. Call the doctor, Mrs. Springer. I'll stay here with her."

Sam's big hands held her shoulders and smoothed her sweaty hair. His dry lips kissed her hot cheek, then moved to her lips, pressing a furtive kiss there. "Shh, darling. Let me take care of you. The doctor's going to give you another shot to make sure you rest quietly. I've made sure no one will bother you here. Not Cle, not anyone."

Soft, padded shoes again, Marm, the doctor. Sam moving away, a prick in her arm. Sam ordering everyone, even Marm, to leave the room. She knew quick fear and then oblivion.

Sam moved to the window, his jaw set as he stared out into the grim November evening.

"You'll stay here with me, my darling. We'll keep you sedated until my sources say Brady has left the country," he murmured to himself.

He went back and sat next to her bed in the chair he'd appropriated for himself. He lifted her hand and reverently kissed each finger, unable to keep himself from sucking just a bit on each one.

* * *

In a few moments of clarity, when she struggled up from the drugged state they'd reduced her to, Lilibet realized she was being oversedated, probably on Pappy's orders. She began to stash away the pills given to her by the solicitous nurses. She turned them under her tongue until the nurses left, and then spit the pills out, tucking them beneath the mattress until they could be tossed into the wastebasket. When she was able, she convinced Marm of the truth, and Marm began to help her, secreting the pills out of the hospital to throw away. Slowly, but surely, she regained her strength, and despite Sam's protests, convinced the doctors she was fully recovered.

Two weeks later, weak but determined, she left the hospital with Marm. For a week, the two of them stuck to the healthy regimen Lilibet had worked out for herself. Lots of Marm's hot vegetable soup, hearty chicken and dumplings, and long brisk walks in the afternoon sun. The press, discovering her alone, and Cle back in residence at the Hutton house, pestered her with questions about the supposed 'second honeymoon.' Her standard statement was given in terse, no-nonsense terms. "Senator Hutton and I have separated and a divorce is pending. Any further information you will have to obtain from Senator Hutton. Please don't bother me anymore."

Finally, after their questions remained unanswered, the cadre of reporters dwindled until she was left alone.

Black seemed to have vanished from the face of the earth. Lilibet had phoned and cabled every BEC office in the world, to no avail. She'd talked to the Harrison Easterling Foundation, insisting they must know the whereabouts of Black and Laura Brady. After the fifteenth telephone call to Black's administrative assistant, a sympathetic secretary told her Black had gone into seclusion for a while and had left instructions he was not to be disturbed under any circumstances.

Dark despair filled her when Marm said, "Black was very visible right after the election. He made himself graciously available to the press and the public, and offered his assistance to Cle on any legislation where he could be of help. Lordy me, Lilibet, if I'd known it was Black you were trying to tell me about, I'd a sure called him. Funny thing was, he disappeared right after Sam put out that press release about you and Cle having a second honeymoon."

Had Sam kept her from Black on purpose? She tried to believe that he hadn't, but as the days went by and the facts kept presenting themselves so logically, she knew that Sam had deliberately kept everyone from her, most importantly, Black.

Anger and despair almost overwhelmed her, threatening to undermine her hard-fought battle to regain her health. With fierce determination, she lifted her spirits by reminding herself that Black would have to surface sometime, and when he did she would convince him the story of her and Cle and the supposed "second honeymoon" was just that—a fabricated story.

Next week was Thanksgiving. The one bright spot in her existence was the knowledge that Genie would be home and spending the holiday with her, Marm, and Margot. The custody battle had already begun. Her lawyer had played on Pappy's shrewd manipulation of public opinion, telling him that Genie should spend Thanksgiving with both parents. She would stay with her mother until seven in the evening, then go to the Huttons for the remainder of the night.

Privately, Pappy had told Lilibet it would be the last holiday Genie would ever spend with her.

Chapter 28

Lilibet and Genie pushed open the back door to the Hutton kitchen, letting in a cloud of icy morning air. Belle gave them a big smile. The spicy aroma of pumpkin pies and boiling cranberries filled the friendly room.

"Lordy, it's good to see you all, Mrs. Hutton." She gave Genie a big hug. "I've sure been missing you around here. Wish you were going to be here for Thanksgiving dinner today."

"I've missed you, too, Belle. Thanks for calling to let me know Pappy's out of the house for a while. We came to pick up the portrait."

Belle basted the turkey, the steam rising to mist her cheeks. She shoved the turkey back in the oven and wiped her hands on her apron. Sorrow lined her warm face as she looked at Lilibet.

"Fat Sis told me to phone you. She and Pappy are at the country club for the morning."

"Where is Cle?"

"Not sure. He disappeared 'bout an hour ago. He disappears a lot these days," Belle said, a frown creasing her brow. She glanced at Genie who was listening intently. "Genie, girl, you go into the pantry; you'll find some of those cherry-filled cookies you like. Pack some up for your Grandmother Springer."

"Gee, thanks, Belle. I dream of those when I'm in Washington."

Genie disappeared into the huge pantry off the kitchen and Belle said, "Cle thinks you're bluffing about divorcing him. Believe me, you're better off without him. Stick to your guns, Mrs. Hutton."

"I am. Is Clarice here?"

"In the library with Sam."

"Then I came at the right time. I want to talk to her about the clinic I found in Switzerland. From all my research and all the people I've talked to, it seems to have the best record for treating alcoholism."

"If you think you're going to convince Clarice to admit herself for hospitalization, you're just whistlin' Dixie. You'd have to hog-tie her first. It's nine o'clock in the morning and she's already lit higher than a Christmas tree," Belle curled her lip in disgust. "Besides, I wouldn't be worrying about any of them anymore. They're a sorry lot and you've been taking care of them long enough. They is wrong the way they been treating you, Mrs. Hutton. Don't you let them have Genie."

"Believe me, I don't intend to."

"They is bloodsuckers, Mrs. Hutton, takers not givers." Belle lowered her voice. "Pappy is evil. You be careful."

Lilibet smiled. "Don't worry, Belle. I can take care of myself. They're not going to murder me or anything. Sam would tell me if I was in any danger."

Belle glared at her. "You heard what I said. Sam's part of the family. I didn't like it one bit when he kept the news of your sickness from everyone. Wasn't right."

Lilibet hugged her. "Where is the portrait?"

"I wrapped it in flannel and plastic. It's leaning against the wall in the library."

Genie reappeared, carrying a brown sack filled with cookies, crumbs around her pink lips.

"Genie, love, stay with Belle. I'll just be a minute."

"Okay, Mom."

As she walked through the somber dining room, Lilibet flashbacked to the first summer she'd dined here with the Huttons, and the way Pappy had grilled her on unions and politics. Well, she thought grimly, when the congressional inquiry begins after Christmas, Pappy will be the recipient of the grillings. She could derive satisfaction from that if nothing else. But the satisfaction was tinged with sadness. They'd had good times here, all of them. After the children came, it had been even better. Parties and laughter and excitement about politics . . . in the beginning. No matter what happened from now on, she knew this family life was broken. She would never live here again. She hadn't felt safe since the press conference. Pappy's retribution for her betrayal would come, of that she was sure. The manner in which he exacted his revenge was what frightened her, like waiting for the other shoe to drop, or the next drip of water from a leaking faucet in the middle of the night.

She stopped short of the library door when she heard Clarice's voice, drunken but taut with tension.

"Pappy will get Genie, you know."

"He'll have a hard time throwing mud on Lilibet."

Lilibet faded against the wall outside the door and listened.

Clarice whooped with laughter. "Don't be ridiculous, Sam. If my dear, sweet father is capable of committing murder, he'll stop at nothing in a custody case."

"I don't want to talk about this."

"Why, because you're afraid, Sam? Are you, Sam? Are you afraid?" Clarice taunted him.

"Shut up, Clarice. We promised we would never talk of this again."

"We were fifteen then, Sam. Maybe if I'd talked about it more since then, I wouldn't be the lush I am today."

"Sober up, Clarice."

"No, Goddammit. Look at my mother up there smiling down at us so beautiful and kind. No wonder Cledith won't look at the painting. It's all her fault, Sam. All of this."

Sam sighed wearily. "Aren't you forgetting that my father was a major player?"

"Oh, your father was like a lamb to the slaughter. She was beautiful and Pappy mistreated her, and your father was her knight in shining armor. He was going to rescue her from her misery. I could always figure out the mornings your dad would be coming because Mama would sing and primp. I would pretend to be sick and stay home from school."

"You've already told me all this."

"Did I tell you that I hid under the bed twice while he was laying it to her? God, they could get it on. That's when I heard them talking about running away together."

"Must we talk of this, Clarice?" Sam asked. Lilibet could hear the pain in his voice.

"Still want to fuck me, Sam? That's when I told you, remember, when you were fumbling around with that big dick of yours?" Clarice laughed hysterically.

"How could I forget? You really know how to deflate a hard-on. You asked me if I was as good at fucking as my father was. You couldn't wait to tell me the whole story, could you?"

"I had to talk to someone. I'd been holding it in since I was ten years old. I tried to tell Cle and he didn't want to hear it."

Lilibet heard liquid sloshing into a glass. Someone was pouring a drink. She'd eavesdropped enough. Embarrassed, her heart jumping erratically at what she'd just heard, she decided to announce her presence before they could continue. Clarice's next words stopped her in her tracks.

"Shit, Sam. Don't you ever look at me and hate me? I mean, hell, my father murdered your father."

Lilibet was sure they could hear the thudding of her alarmed heart. Her impulse was to run away as far and as fast as she could, but she knew she had to know the rest of it.

"No, I don't hate you. We're the victims, Clarice. My father told me if anything ever happened to him, I should look to Pappy Hutton. But it was hard for a child of ten to believe 'the great white father,' Pappy Hutton, would harm anyone. By the time I was fifteen, and you told me about the affair, I figured that was the reason Pappy was screwing my mother—to get back at your mother and my father. I accepted that crazy logic for a while."

"Yeh, but Sam, I think God or Satan—don't know which—meant for us to know. It was right after I told you about the affair that the five-year memorial service was held for the miners in that accident."

"And someone said it was a shame they hadn't been able to find my dad's body . . . the only one they couldn't find. My mother never told me they didn't find Dad," Sam reflected bitterly.

Clarice's voice fell and Lilibet strained to hear the

words. "Shit, Sam. That was the worst. Both of us raking through that spooky abandoned mine Eulonie told us about, and finding your dad's skeleton. I mean, Jesus, Sam, it's still there . . . I mean the bones, and his leather jacket—"

Clarice's voice rose to a high hysterical pitch and Lilibet heard a slap. She jumped. It was hard to breathe.

There was a short silence and then Clarice said, "Ooh, I liked that, Sam. Do it again and then let's fuck on the sofa."

"Shut up, Clarice."

"Whoops, forgot. You're saving it for Lilibet, aren't you? 'Cept I know 'bout those lil ol' trips you and Cle make to the whorehouses here and in Washington, and the girls you bring in for him on the campaign trips. You like 'em, too, don't you, Sam? I think Lilibet knows about Cle. Wonder what she'd think if she knew you and Cle like to share his whores?"

Sam's voice was cold and dripping with venom as he said to Clarice, "If she finds out, I'll know who told her. So she better not find out. Understand, Clarice?"

"Ah, come on, Sam, just one little tumble on the sofa?"

"Go take a cold shower! Lilibet is coming to pick up the twins' portrait."

Lilibet's inclination was to flee the house as fast as possible, but she had to have the painting. It was the only portrait she had of Collins. If she didn't take it now, she might never have another chance. She walked quickly away, grateful for the thick shag carpet that muffled her footsteps. Halfway down the hall she turned around, and whistling an aimless tune headed back toward the library. She put a smile on her face as she entered.

"Happy Thanksgiving, one and all."

Clarice, a red mark across her cheek, a glass of rich, amber Virginia bourbon in her hand, stood by the window, staring out. She swayed, spilling her drink as she turned around to greet Lilibet. "Well, if it isn't Senator Hutton's wife. They sure did a number on Black, didn't they, ol' friend? Seen him lately? I can't find him anywhere."

"Clarice, go upstairs and take a shower like I told you. Here, Lilibet, let me take your coat."

"No, Sam. I can't stay. I just came to pick up the painting, and a few clothes I need for winter."

"I'll put the picture in your car while you get your clothes. Maybe you can talk Clarice into going upstairs with you," said Sam. He picked up the large painting and left.

"Leave me alone, just leave me alone," said Clarice and sank into Pappy's chair by the fireplace.

"Trust me, I'd be happy to," said Lilibet with relief.

She ran up the stairs and burst into the spacious bedroom she'd shared with Cle.

Cle's naked buttocks flashed white as he cursed and flipped off the woman he was screwing. "Goddammit, can't I have any privacy . . . son of a bitch, Lilibet!"

In shocked disbelief, Lilibet watched as Margot's face emerged from beneath Cle's shoulder, a gleam of triumph in her eyes. Lilibet's sheerest lavender nightgown lay discarded at the foot of the bed.

She couldn't breathe. It felt like a mule had kicked her in the stomach with both hooves. Like the time she'd fallen from the Paw Paw tree at Big Ugly—no air. She groped for the door frame and couldn't find it. She heard Margot laugh and Cle telling her to shut up. In a watery haze, Lilibet saw Cle put on his robe and come toward her.

She slammed the door in his face and ran down the hall, almost tripping down the stairs in her haste to get away. The house, no matter how tacky or overdone or filled with sorrow, had always been a symbol of security for her. Now she thought she would smother with anxiety before she escaped the heavy, sinister atmosphere seeping from its walls. Cle was calling after her but she could hear nothing except a whining buzz in her ears, like a dentist's drill, and she could barely see through the red haze of her anger. What a fool. What an utter, utter fool she'd been.

Trying to control her panic, she called for Genie and reached her car as Sam closed the trunk.

"I think it will be fine . . . Lilibet, what's the matter? You're shaking."

Belle came out of the house with Genie. "Sam, you've got a phone call."

"Where have you been, Mom? You said a minute, and it's been longer than that."

"Bet your mom was talking with your aunt Clarice and Sam in the library. Have a nice Thanksgiving," Belle said, then waved and returned to the house.

Sam took her arm. "Lilibet, how long have you been here?"

"Why, I just arrived, Sam. You were there when I came into the library." She fought to keep her voice level and calm.

"From what Belle said, you've been here longer than five minutes."

"Genie, get in the car. Really, Sam. What difference does it make anyway?" She shook his hand off her arm and reached for the door handle.

He pulled her around to look at him, holding her arms in a vise grip. "How long have you been in the house? Answer me!"

"Stop this, Sam. What is the matter with you?"

"I read you like a book, Lilibet. Something's wrong."

She looked through the closed car windows. Genie was eating cookies and reading one of the books she always carried with her.

Under her breath, she said to Sam, "I just found Cle in bed with Margot! Does that satisfy your morbid curiosity?"

For a moment, relief spread over his face, but he didn't let go of her. "Damn, I'm sorry you found out about that, but you've filed for divorce. Why do you care?"

"I knew Cle played around, Sam. but it hurts like hell to know he's using my own sister. How low and insensitive can he get? From the look in her eyes, she's been hoping for this for a long time. God knows how long it's been going on. Let go of me, Sam!"

His hands tightened on her arms and he studied her face keenly. "You're more than angry, you're frightened. Did you hear me and Clarice talking in the library?"

She tried to keep the horrible knowledge out of her eyes, tried to keep her chin from shaking, her heart from pounding. Jerking her arms from his big hands, she climbed into the car.

"I haven't the slightest idea what you are talking about! Marm has Thanksgiving dinner ready. Tell Margot we'll be disappointed if she doesn't come home for Thanksgiving dinner. She and I can talk later."

Forcing herself to drive sedately away, in the rearview mirror she watched Sam hurry toward the house. Did Sam know she'd heard him and Clarice?

The steering wheel was cold beneath her palsied hands. The engine sputtered as her shaking knees jerked her heel and toe up and down on the accelerator.

"Something matter with the car, Mom?"

"No, honey. Just the engine warming up in this cold weather."

She crossed Tow River Bridge into Yancey and headed toward Main Street. In retrospect, the scene with Cle and Margot shouldn't have been so shocking. It had served to thaw the numb fear that had set in as she'd stood and listened outside the library. Pappy was a murderer. She had to think.

An odd clicking sound penetrated her fear-fogged mind. Her teeth were chattering, not with cold but with alarm. She clamped her jaws together tightly but it hurt, so she let go and felt her chin begin to quake again. Should she go to the sheriff right now, or wait until she'd figured it all out? Instinct told her to drive on past the ugly, yellow brick jail.

Her first consideration had to be Genie and Marm. All hell would break loose when she revealed what she'd just heard. Knowing how slow the wheels of justice ground, it might be months before justice prevailed and Pappy was punished. In the meantime, he would make sure she suffered hideously. He would rip Genie away from her, and make life a living hell for Marm.

The cabin. It was hers now. She would take them to the cabin. It was early in the day. She could probably arrive back in the valley and put things into action before it was time for Genie to arrive at the Hutton's that evening. Before any alarm bells rang to alert Pappy . . . or Sam.

* * *

The climb up the mountain had been slow going. Marm was pretty tough, but Genie's little legs had tired easily. They stopped frequently so she could rest, and toward the top took turns carrying her. Marm understood the urgency of the trip, but for Genie's sake they tried to paint it as a grand adventure. She and Marm had packed supplies, and Lilibet made sure they had sufficient firewood before she left to return to the valley.

Back in Yancey, she realized she couldn't go to Marm's house. Anna Adkins lived next door. Main Street was empty, thank God. The holiday. She passed Carpozzoli's and saw a dim light coming from the rear. Yes. Tony had said she should come to him if she ever needed anything. The restaurant was closed for the day but maybe Tony was there.

She drove around and parked in the rear alley. The smell of fresh made coffee welcomed her as she stepped from the car. Cinching the belt of her camel coat tighter around her, she approached Tony's rear door with hope.

"Tony, are you here?" The calm sound of her voice amazed her.

Tony's head popped from around the shiny steel pizza oven, a surprised but delighted expression lighting his face.

"Why sure, Lilibet. Come in. Why aren't you home with your family?"

"Just needed a place to be quiet for a minute . . . we have a lot of company and you know how it is with big family dinners." She hated to lie, but it was the only excuse she could think of.

"Sure do. Came down here for the same reason. I love my grandchildren but sometimes they drive me up the wall. You get some coffee and sit awhile."

"Thanks, Tony. Uh, if anyone calls for me, I'm not here . . . okay?"

"You got it."

Coffee cup in hand, she settled with relief into a comfy back booth. Tony pulled the green shades down over the front so no one would see her here. They wouldn't know where she was unless they checked the alley and saw her car.

The frantic climb up and down the mountain had given her time to think. She mulled over her options. She dismissed Cle and Margot. They weren't important anymore. For Clarice she felt deep sorrow. Clarice needed more help than even Black had imagined.

It was Sam who made her sick to the stomach. Sam had always been her best friend, her protector, her port in a storm. Sam loved her and wanted her. She'd been ready to dismiss her anger at his sequestering her in the hospital, attributing his acts to overprotectiveness. She'd seen the hope in his eyes when she told him of Margot and Cle—hope that now that she knew the final ugly truth about Cle, and Black Brady had removed himself from the scene, Lilibet would come to Sam.

Dear Lord. Sam and Clarice, and probably Cle, have known for years about the murder. Knowing Cle and Clarice, she could understand why they didn't report it, but Sam . . . Pappy murdered his father! Underneath his capable, kind, all-caring demeanor there had to be a seething cauldron of hate and bitterness. Suddenly, she was more afraid of Sam than she was of Pappy. She saw now his subtle control of Cle and Clarice, and thus his power against Pappy.

Her immediate concern was getting her information about the murder of Sam Adkins, Sr., to the proper authorities before Pappy got to her.

Pappy Hutton owned everyone in West Virginia, from the governor right down to the sheriff. Except for two people.

Black Brady and Dr. Mabel Turner.

Forget about Black. Even if she'd wanted to ask Black for help, she couldn't. She racked her brain again for any smidgen of knowledge she may have missed as to his whereabouts. Was he at Brady's Lair? If there were phones in Black's aerie she hadn't seen them. She hadn't the time to search for him anyway. Her plan to journey the world in search of him had been thrust into fast-forward motion. Tears pressured her eyes but she resisted the urge to let them flow. Black, who loved so ardently and hated so passionately, must be shattered right now. Did he hate her again? She didn't think so. He was a bigger man than that. Imagining her and Cle reconciled, Black must be struggling with powerful emotions. She prayed for the chance to hold him in her arms again and tell him the truth. For one precious moment she allowed herself to remember the feel of his arms around her, the tease of his tongue on hers, his teeth around her nipple, the warmth and safety she felt when she was with him. The coffee cup clattered as she lowered it shakily to its saucer.

Miss Mabel would know what to do.

"Tony, do you have some change? I need to make a call from your phone."

"Sure. You welcome to use my private phone."

"No, thank you. I'll go up front and use the public pay phone."

She removed her earring and dialed Miss Mabel's number in Morgantown. It rang over and over again but there was no answer. Of course, Miss Mabel must be spending Thanksgiving here in Yancey with her brother, Judge Turner. She retrieved her nickel and dialed Judge Turner's residence outside of Yancey. No answer. They've gone on one of Miss Mabel's famous trips. Don't panic, Lilibet.

Tony brought her more coffee.

She took a drink, then rested her forehead against the phone. Think. Weak with fear, she allowed herself a moment to sit and take another sip of coffee. She could feel Tony watching her now. He would start asking questions any moment.

Eulonie. Eulonie Bevins knew something. She'd surely heard more than what she'd told Lilibet about the vote buying.

The nickel scratched noisily across the metal surface of the phone as she tried, with a shaking hand, to insert it in the slot. Go in, dammit. There. Thank God.

Eulonie's West Virginian drawl echoed in the receiver.

"Eulonie, this is Lilibet Hutton. Sorry to disturb you on your day off . . . but I need to ask you some questions."

"Yes, ma'am."

"Eulonie, do you have more information about Pappy Hutton that you'd be willing to tell me?"

Silence.

Lilibet tried again. "I think you might know something about Sam Adkins, Senior. If you do, you know you can trust me."

"Please, Miz Hutton, I don't know nothin'."

"I think you know a lot, Eulonie. I know you're scared. So am I. But together we can put Pappy Hutton where he belongs. In prison for a very long time."

"Dear gussie, Miz Hutton," whispered Eulonie into the phone. "Don't say such things."

"I don't have time to talk anymore. I have to locate my friend, Doctor Turner, Judge Turner's sister. She can help us."

The phone was ringing in Tony's kitchen. She heard him answer it. He called to her.

"I have to hang up," Lilibet said to Eulonie. "Don't be afraid. I'll talk to you later."

Tony was hurrying toward her, a worried look on his face.

"Tony," she said. Giving a little laugh, she casually re-attached her earring. "Is that call for me? Thought I told you not to let anyone know I was here."

"Sorry, Lilibet, but it was Donetta. She's volunteering at the hospital today. Said Deputy Hager saw your Cadillac in the alley. There's been a terrible accident, Lilibet. It's Miss Mabel. She's hurt real bad, and she's been asking for you."

At first Lilibet thought this was a ploy of Tom Tee's to find out where she was, but the look on Tony's face, and the sorrow in his voice convinced her he'd believed Donetta. Besides, Donetta wouldn't be a part of anything underhanded. You're getting paranoid, she thought. You're not even positive Sam knows you heard him and Clarice, and if he knows, you're not sure he told anyone.

She checked her watch. She had another hour before Genie was supposed to arrive at the Huttons.

Miss Mabel needed her.

She thanked Tony, wrapped her coat around her and ran to her car.

* * *

Tom Tee was waiting for her in the Yancey County Hospital parking lot.

He grabbed her by the arm and said, "Let's go. The doctor says Miss Mabel's gonna die."

They headed toward the Emergency Room entrance, but before they reached the broad swinging doors, Tom Tee shoved her into an anteroom off to the right. She caught a whiff of the chloroform even before he removed the bottle from his pocket. She turned to knee him in the crotch. Too late. The cloth tickled her nose. She spun into space.

Chapter 29

The sickeningly sweet chloroform burned and curdled her dry mouth. She pursed her cracked lips and tried to spit, but couldn't. Be thankful for small favors, Lilibet. At least they didn't gag her. *They figured you'd be so deep in this wretched mine, no one would hear if you screamed.* With a feeling of despair, she realized they were right. Between waking up and falling back into a stupor, she'd screamed to no avail. She was fully awake now and would scream no more. It was useless. Her time was better spent thinking about how she could get out of here.

Keeping her mind busy kept at bay the sheer terror she'd experienced when she'd regained consciousness and realized where she was. The deathly silence of the pitch-black mine cast her directly into the nightmare she'd had since she was a child, provoked when Eugene had deserted her in a cruel game of hide-and-seek. Lost and terrified, it had been hours before she'd fainted and Eugene had had mercy and carried her out. But this was no nightmare and there was no one to rescue her.

"Cowards." Her croaking voice startled her.

They were cowards. Tom Tee, and whoever helped bring her here, they were cowards. They hadn't the courage to kill her outright, or the decency. They'd left her to starve. This way they would never see the last look on her face, or hear her last words, or know whether she died in pain, or when she died. They would try to pretend it never happened ... but she'd make damn sure she haunted their nightmares, and every waking hour too. At least she knew Marm and Genie were safe.

She lifted her chin from her chest and pain exploded

through her head. She didn't need hands to know there was a lump the size of a lemon at the back of her skull. The coffee she drank at Tony's lay sour in her stomach, and she ached with hunger. How did you do it, Uncle East? How did you starve yourself to death?

"Black said Uncle East's body was ready to die. Obviously, mine isn't."

It hurt her throat when she talked, but talking helped her stay awake. They'd taken her coat, and her wool skirt was bunched up around her bottom. She was freezing. If she went to sleep, she might freeze to death.

She had no idea how long she'd been here. She'd driven into the hospital parking area about six in the evening. From the way she felt, she figured it must be past midnight. It's always past midnight in the mines, she reminded herself.

The thin, twisted cord binding her wrists and ankles cut and chaffed her skin. Her arms burned. They had pulled her arms and hands tight behind her. Warm blood trickled from her wrists down into her stiff, clawed hands and dripped off her fingers. The warmth of her own blood felt good in the frigid, motionless air, but she was careful not to aggravate the skin anymore. The scurrying of rats was the only sound she'd detected. If they smelled her blood, they would be on her in no time.

She shuddered.

No, by God, I'm not going to starve to death, or die of pneumonia, or rat bites. I'm not going to die here. I'm not!

Whistling and talking would keep her awake, and it might keep the rats away, too.

She forced a weak whistle through her parched lips. She tried "Born Free" and it sounded pretty good. Gathering air in her lungs, she tried again with "Strangers in the Night." The effort exhausted her. Was there enough air in here? Add suffocation to the list, Lilibet. No. The rats were here. They needed air, too, so the oxygen must be okay.

Something soft brushed her cheek. Heart racing, she caught the panicked scream that curdled in her throat. Were they still here, tormenting her?

Voice shaking, she said, "Tom Tee? If you're here, say so, you coward."

Nothing. No movement or sound. Suddenly she realized she'd be happy to see even Tom Tee.

"Tom, are you here?" she asked, a note of hope in her voice. She was smarter than Tom Tee. She could talk him into taking her out of here, into letting her go. "Tom Tee?"

A faint, high-pitched squeaking sound startled her, and then she knew what was with her. Bats. Her heart beat so fast she was afraid she would lose consciousness again. She hated bats even worse than rats. They flew at you, and tangled in your hair. They bit and drew blood.

Don't be ridiculous, Lilibet. Vampire bats exist only in South America.

Uncle East hadn't taught her much about bats. They were night creatures, and she and Uncle East hadn't camped out many nights. She tried to assure herself that bats were simply nice little furry mammals who happened to have wings. She remembered helping Genie with a school report about bats. They liked to eat insects or small amphibians, not humans.

The high-pitched sound came again. Shuddering, she forced herself to ignore it.

She was losing feeling in her feet. Her loafers were gone, too. Move, move, move.

A rat, its paws cool and scaly, investigated her bare leg and then settled its rough fur on her thigh, the long tail swishing against her knee. All rational thought and self-control left her. She screamed, the pain in her throat knifing through her head, and jerked her legs as hard as she could. The rat squealed and scurried away while her scream ricocheted back and forth in the claustrophobic black space. The high-pitched squeaking stopped.

Stop this. Pull yourself together or you'll never get out of here alive.

She moved her legs again, wiggling her toes, trying to get the feeling back. They began to prickle and smart.

"Come on, Lilibet. Move. You're beginning to see better. Become a cat. Figure out the few shapes you sense around you."

Jerking her knees up and down, she felt a prickling sensation returning to her toes. Good. She tried swiveling on her bottom. It worked. She felt insecure away from the rock wall that had supported her back, but she would find it again. At least she knew now she could maneuver herself. A brave rat nipped at the sleeve of her blouse. She groaned in fear and jerked her elbow away from his sharp teeth.

Digging her heels into the thick sediment of gritty coal dust, she hunched forward a few more inches, searching around with her toes. Nothing. Why would there be? She had a sense of being deep in the bowels of the earth. No one had been here in years. But still she squirmed and searched. There. What was that? A long, smoothish object. Felt enameled in some places, splintered near the middle. A knob on the end . . . on both ends. There were more of them—whatever they were.

"Feels like, feels like, come on Lilibet . . . remember the blind man game you played when you were a child. Remember your sensation-and-touch-lessons with Uncle East. Concentrate."

Bones. They were bones. A skeleton. Dear God. Were these the bones of Sam Adkins, Sr.? Had they brought her to the same place? Why not? No one but Sam and Clarice had discovered the bones in twenty-five years, and then only at a hint from Eulonie. Pappy would assume this was a safe place to discard unwanted people. Horrified at her find, her stomach heaved.

Don't be ridiculous. They are the bones of an animal. Surely they are the bones of an animal. For a moment she thought about searching for a human skull, but then put the notion aside. These were not human bones—maybe they weren't bones at all. *You're imagining things, Lilibet.*

Shoving the bones, or whatever they were, to the side, she fought back her nausea.

"No. You will not get sick, Lilibet Springer. Look for something, anything."

She squirmed around, making her area of maneuverability larger. Her feet found a loose mound of cloth, and with great relief she recognized her coat. They had hurriedly dumped the coat when they'd dumped her.

Slowly, painfully, her bound, bloody hands explored through the powder, searching for a forgotten tool, a sharp piece of coal or rock, anything.

There. A rail track. Buried beneath three inches of silt and grit, the ancient rail line was still there. Her fingers kept searching. She found a bolt connecting two rail sections, but it wasn't sharp enough. Inching her way along, she finally found what she was searching for: a small piece of metal rail, still attached to the main rail, but torn and ripped . . . and sharp.

A rat nosed at her toe and she kicked at it, losing her hold on the precious section of sharpness. She groped again, her stiff fingers delving deeper, praying. There it was. Carefully, she worked to scoop away the grit around the jagged metal until it was clear.

Painfully, she began to saw at the cord that bound her wrists behind her back. Awkwardly scraping cord back and forth across the jagged piece of metal, she prayed this would work. Sometimes she would miss the mark and the broken edges cut her wrists instead of the rope. Already bleeding and aching, she used the fresh pain to keep her going.

After what seemed like hours, she had made little progress and was exhausted. She moved and hunched her way back to lean against the wall for a moment.

"I'll just rest awhile." She fought the sleep but it came anyway.

"Wake up, Elizabeth. Wake up. Get back to work."

She jerked awake. "Is that you, Uncle East?"

At first worried she was losing her sanity, she soon relaxed in the comforting presence she sensed with her.

She worked her way back to the rail and began to saw at the cord again.

Eulonie Bevins flipped bacon on the griddle and glanced to the front of the diner. Early morning light filtered weakly through the filmy windows. First customer hadn't come in yet. Thank you, Jesus. Would give her time to think. She picked up the newspaper and read it again.

LILIBET HUTTON SEARCH FUTILE

said the bold headlines.

The search for Lilibet Springer Hutton, estranged wife of United States Senator Cledith Hutton, widened today. The disappearance of Mrs. Hutton and her daughter and mother on Thanksgiving Day has sparked a massive three-day hunt by the National Guard and local officials that has yielded nothing. Family and friends are mystified, saying Mrs. Hutton was in good spirits and good health, as were her daughter and mother. Fearing foul play, Pappy Hutton said that though he and his daughter-in-law had recently had a difference of opinion, he has vowed he will find her and prosecute to the fullest extent persons having anything to do with her disappearance.

Black Brady, chairman of the board of BEC Industries, entered the picture yesterday, coming forth to volunteer the use of his helicopter fleet. Brady made numerous sweeps across the mountains but found nothing. Brady himself has now disappeared, but his pilots and crews continue to hunt for the lovely Mrs. Hutton and her family.

Eulonie put the paper down and poured herself a cup of fresh coffee. Fear flickered in her eyes. Her tongue worried with her molar, her scarred face twisting in concentration.

Her hand shook as she downed the last of the coffee. She removed her apron, folded it neatly, and walked into the owner's cubbyhole.

"Mr. MacGinnes, I'm takin' a few days off."

Her boss looked at her in shock. In thirty years, except for a sick day here and there, Eulonie Bevins had never had a day off.

"Are you sick? You can't just walk out. The breakfast crowd will be—"

Incredulous, he watched as she shoved her arms into her moth-eaten coat, picked up her worn, red plastic handbag and marched out.

Lilibet looked behind her into the cave where she'd spent the night. High on the mountainside and camouflaged with brush and rocks, the small cavity had been her refuge after her escape from the mine late yesterday afternoon. By her reckoning, the cave was several miles from the mine. If Tom Tee or Pappy were looking for her, it was probably safer inside than out here in the sun, but it was cold where she sat on the ledge and she craved the sunlight. The sun befriended her, burning bright and sure, and she bathed in the glorious sunbeams, their rich, yellow warmth seeping into the marrow of her bones. Nothing had ever felt so wonderful.

She tried not to close her eyes because doing so called forth the terror-filled hours of sawing on the cords around her wrists and ankles, and then crawling along rusted railway tracks through endless miles of tunnel. She'd finally found an inclined passage that led upward to a deck, and then another passage, and another, always upward, crawling through some spaces barely large enough to squeeze through. Uncle East and his friend, Black Eagle, had kept her going. They would let her rest, then would nudge her awake and push her on again until she found her way to the entrance of the mine and out into the blessed light.

She knew she must move and put more distance between herself and the abandoned mine, but she lingered. There was a creek close by and she hated to leave its security. She'd slaked her terrible thirst several times during the night, and cleansed the worst of the filth from her body. Her hands were cut, her fingernails ripped to the quick and still encrusted with dried blood and coal grit. Her legs and feet were in the same condition.

At least she wasn't as light-headed from hunger as she'd been when she discovered the dry cave. She smothered the coals of her fire, and with her teeth, stripped the last bit of squirrel meat off a small bone.

"Thank you, Uncle East, for getting me this far. I have a feeling I'm on my own now." She laughed weakly.

"Pappy has no idea I can survive up here—besides, I'm sure he thinks I'm dead. Tom Tee wouldn't tell him that he didn't have the guts to kill me. The joke's on Pappy, right?"

Problem was, she had no idea where she was.

She tried to look for landmarks. She knew the shapes, names, and locations of most of the mountains in southern West Virginia. When she was a child she thought they were funny. Chimney Stack Mountain was, of course, a mountaintop that looked like a stacked chimney, and Caped Man Pass was a gorge that looked like a man with a cape, and so forth.

But nothing she could see looked familiar. *Just start walking, Lilibet. Put one foot in front of the other.*

"Which direction?" she queried herself.

She turned to the left, but it didn't feel right. She started forward. No. When she stepped to the right, the back of her neck prickled.

Thank you.

She gathered her torn coat about her and started off.

Four hours later, she'd lost the sun to grim November clouds. But when she'd awakened at dawn that morning she'd estimated the time and set her battered watch. It said twelve thirty . . . of what day, she had no idea. She finished a rocky climb up a cliff and rounded a bend in the mountainside. A glacial wind gusted and tore at her but she clung tenaciously to a boulder.

"Be my friend, old man mountain," she whispered, as she searched across the gorge. "Let me rest here while I look for something I recognize."

Winter had set in. The trees, denuded of leaves, stretched their scraggly arms to an empty, dismal gray sky. Only the green of the evergreens dotted the peaks and valleys stretching before her. The mountains were not friendly in winter, the landscape daunting and forbidding.

Her heart skipped a beat. Is that Devil's Peak?

Yes. The back side. Catawba Mountain and the cabin were a two-day trip to the north.

Black stood outside Cat's cave with a frown on his face. Impervious to the cold, he'd stripped to the basics:

a skintight leather jerkin, breeches, and moccasins. On one hip rested a sheathed knife, on the other the latest in ground-to-air communication transmitters. A grim smile relaxed his clenched jaws for a brief moment. Lilibet would get a kick out of his clothes . . . if he could ever find her—if she was still alive. He clamped his teeth until his jaws ached. He refused to even consider the possibility that she wasn't alive.

Mabel Turner had tracked him down in Austria to tell him of Lilibet's disappearance. He was skiing there with his mother, and licking his wounds. Not only had he lost the election, but he'd lost Lilibet, the real reason he'd returned to West Virginia. He was not accustomed to losing, and the taste of it was bitter. The irony of it all was that neither he nor Cle should have been candidates or victors. Lilibet should have been the one who won. He'd lost the election and Lilibet.

He'd waited a week for her to call or come to him as he'd told her she must. He'd come back to claim her twice. When she left him the second time, they both knew he wouldn't come for her again. So when the press announcement of a reconciliation between Senator and Mrs. Hutton was released, it had been more than he could bear. All things considered, he should have kidnapped her and escaped across the world somewhere. Wouldn't that have generated some headlines, he thought wryly.

He'd left West Virginia for his chalet in Austria, the closest thing he knew to heaven, except for Brady's Lair. He'd not been able to face returning to Brady's Lair since he flew Lilibet away from there in September.

Finding Marm and Genie at the cabin had lifted his spirits for a while. He had taken them to his mother in Matterhorn and notified Miss Mabel in Morgantown.

Cat, where are you? I need you. I've searched every inch of Catawba and Aracoma. Can't find Lilibet or you. If she was still living, Cat was twenty years old and slowing down a bit. No dammit, I would have known if Cat died. I would have known if Lilibet died. Deep in my soul, I would have known.

For the first time in his life he was lonely, but he ignored the alien feeling, and buried it along with the

gnawing fear of finding Lilibet too late. For he *would*
find her, if it took him forever, he would find her. And,
by God, when he did, he would give her no choice, he'd
keep her by his side forever.

He studied the pewter-colored winter sky. It was going
to snow. Wherever you are, my darling, take shelter.

There were other mountains to search, and abandoned
mines honeycombed everywhere.

He detached the transmitter from its cradle and spoke
quietly into it. "Anything, Jake?"

"No, sir. We're in the northeast sector now, sir."

"See that the men get food and rest, but don't let up,
Jake."

"No, sir. Good luck, sir."

With stark resolve evident in the set of his face and his
lean body, Black Brady disappeared into the tree line.

Devil's Peak was behind her now. Time to rest. She
settled on a decaying chestnut log. Trying to warm her
frozen feet, she buried them ankle-deep in dry leaves on
the ground before her. Her breath misted in front of her.
Rummaging in the pocket of her coat she found hickory
nuts she'd saved, and wild cherries. Breakfast had been a
rotting paw paw.

It hadn't been too bad—tasted like overripe banana.
She sucked on the big round seed of the cherry while she
studied the mountain terrain ahead of her.

The curlicue of rocks near the peak told her it was the
south side of Catawba. One more day. She could make
it. She was light-headed and weak but she could make it.
She had to. She had to make sure Pappy Hutton was arrested and punished. It was the image of herself testifying
against him that spurred her on.

What an utter fool she'd been.

She'd let herself be lulled by all the security and safety
provided by the Huttons. *Talk about dishonesty, Lilibet,
face it. Your fear that your children wouldn't be provided
for, and your demand for a secure existence for Marm
and Margot, got you into this mess. You knew you could
take care of your family but you wanted to be sure. Not
enough faith in yourself, Mrs. Hutton? Right.*

Like a miser approaching his safety deposit vault, she'd been drawn into what she thought was a stronghold, but which in reality was an entrapment, and her nurturing nature kept her there; a crutch for Cle, a listener and only friend for Clarice, and a pair of strong shoulders for Fat Sis. *But my, my, my, Lilibet, it was your desire to outlast or outdo Pappy that really did you in, wasn't it?* Her desire to win, to be the best, was simply that . . . *her* desire, not Cle's. Wanting to be a lawyer, and a United States Senator was really her dream, not Cle's. Pappy played her like a violin. He knew she'd get Cle where he wanted him.

Thankful for the warmth of her grit-ladened coat, she buried her hands in the pockets. Come on, Lilibet, stand up.

Forcing herself off the log, she stepped out. One foot in front of the other, that's all it takes to keep going. She raised her eyes to the curlicue rocks on Catawba and started forward.

Eulonie Bevins wandered about the dusty, littered bus station for a while. She'd never been out of Yancey County, and here she was in a strange town hundreds of miles away from Yancey. Afraid to ask strangers questions, she finally departed the drafty building and began to walk up and down the hilly streets of Morgantown, the college town she'd traveled to.

The muscles in her calves were giving out. She sat down on a slatted bench and looked again at the address she'd written on a scrap of paper. She'd have to gather her gumption and ask someone.

A young man with an armload of books came to sit on the bus bench next to her.

She cleared her throat and held the scrap of paper before his eyes. " 'Scuse me, sir, but could you tell me where this house is. I'm lookin' for Miss Mab . . . Dr. Mabel Turner."

"Sure. She lives two blocks away. Follow this street, turn left at the traffic light. Dr. Turner's house is the big house at the top of the hill."

"Thank you."

Fifteen minutes later, Eulonie took a deep, nervous breath, clutched her big handbag tight to her chest, and walked up the flagstone path to Dr. Mabel Turner's house.

Lilibet estimated she must be halfway up the south side of Catawba. It was terrain she'd never traveled before. The going was slow and arduous. Her feet were bleeding and she rested frequently, so she wasn't making the progress she'd hoped. The weeks in the hospital and the debilitating hours in the mine were contributing to her weakness. But she kept going, cursing Pappy Hutton with each breath and every painful step.

She caught a bush and pulled herself up another incline.

What was that? She stopped to listen.

The murmur of voices? Yes. Oh, dear God, thank you. *Must be someone camping.*

She pushed on excitedly. Other noises came to her. *Sounded like metal rattling, maybe buckets. Close by.*

A thicket of rhododendron hid the activity. She started to call out to warn them of her approach, but the smell of sour mash stopped her. She stooped to peer through the scraggly brush and what she saw stopped her heart.

Giant pots stood bubbling before a jerry-rigged contraption she knew was a still. Quickly, she backed away from the thicket.

"Well, well, well, girlie. Come to visit us?"

At the sound of Jud MacDonald's voice, she whirled around and found him standing ten feet behind her.

"Hey, Virg, look who's here!" called Jud to his brother.

Virgil MacDonald emerged from the woods on her left. He stopped and stared at her in amazement. Then a slow, lecherous grin crawled across his gap-toothed face.

"Well, if it ain't the fancy Lilibet Hutton? You been missin' us mountain boys, honey?"

"We can't let her leave, Virg."

"Nope, that's true. But we been taught to show company a good time. Right, Jud? So the three of us is gonna have some fun first. You'll be glad you come to visit, Lilibet."

Her only avenue of escape was between Jud and the thicket. She calculated her chances of making it past him. She had no choice. Virgil ambled toward her, and so did Jud. *Come on, Jud ... a little more space between you and the thicket and I might make it.*

"Cat got your tongue, Lilibet?" Virgil sneered. She could smell the urine, whiskey, and body odor from across the clearing. For the first time in her life Lilibet felt true horror. Her mouth sucked in upon itself and she took a shuddering breath. *One more step, Jud.*

She swung around and took off. Jud made a grab for her but missed.

Adrenaline fueled her wasted body and she ran like her feet had wings. She raced into the thicket, jumping over boulders, and around trees and bushes. With her heart in her parched mouth, she ran for her life, for she knew with dead certainty that Virgil and Jud would rape her before they killed her.

She knew she couldn't outlast them, but maybe she could find a place to hide. As she ran, she searched frantically for a cave, gap, gully, large tree—anything to wedge herself into. Nothing. They were too close now anyway ... they would see wherever she tried to hide herself.

They were gaining. The smell of them permeated the frosty air about her. A snowflake drifted lazily in front of her. Than another. Her lungs burned, demanding air. Her legs ached and her knees grew watery with each leap she took. Disoriented, her heart laboring, she had no idea in which direction she ran. Was she heading toward the cabin or away?

A hand grabbed at the tail of her coat and yanked her backward. She fell and scrambled madly to her feet, but was yanked down again by the grunting filthy pig. It was Virgil. She pulled and scraped and inched her way along the ground away from him, her broken fingernails scratching futilely against the frozen earth. He laughed and, like a dog on a leash, let her scurry on her knees while he held her by the coat.

Tired of playing with her, his animal lust mounting, Virgil jerked her hard toward him. He turned her over beneath him, his grubby, whiskered face inches away from hers. Panting with heated excitement, he pushed the coat away from her chest and ran his hands roughly over her breasts.

"Waited a long time for this, Lilibet. This time you ain't gonna get away. You a grown-up married lady now, so you oughta be real good at fuckin'."

"Hurry, Virg. I want some, too."

"Sorry Jud's in such a hurry, honey. It's been a while since we had any pussy. We been up here makin' shine for a long time."

Virgil shoved her wool skirt up and tore away her silk panties. She bucked and clawed with the little strength she had left. Jud unbuckled his belt and unzipped his trousers, exposing himself to her, then he knelt to hold her while Virgil did the same.

Snowflakes melted on her face. Are they really snowflakes? How beautiful, she thought deliriously. Virgil fell on her, all of his weight resting on her as he fumbled with himself.

I'll think about the snowflakes.

Chapter 30

Two hundred pounds of savage orange pounced on Virgil's back.

Virgil screamed as the big cat's claws penetrated his thick flannel shirt and dug into his flesh. He flailed his arms about, trying to get a hold on the animal, but she yanked him off Lilibet and played him like a ball of yarn. His scream of terror was cut short as Cat broke Virgil's neck with one twist of her powerful jaws.

At first sight of the cougar, Jud let go of Lilibet and scrambled up the mountainside. With elegant but lethal ease, Cat caught him. Jud kicked and punched at the cougar. He wet his pants and whimpered as she toyed with him, prolonging the kill. First she tore off an ear, then ripped a gash across his cheek, then nibbled on his fingers. One sinewy paw on his chest secured him to the ground while she snapped his wrist in two. She went for his throat then and severed his jugular. Jud's blood arced high over the clearing, then dripped soundlessly from brown, leafless trees to coat the frozen earth. He bled to death in seconds.

Cat lifted her head and cried. The high, mournful keening lifted above the trees and valleys and became a roar of triumph and retribution.

Miles away, Black heard the cry. His heart lifted in momentary joy. Whatever else happened this day, he knew Cat was alive. He headed toward the sound as it ululated across the mountains and soon found her tracks. He picked up his pace and ran like the deer he'd raced when he was a boy.

An hour later he entered the clearing.

Even Black—with the awful sights he'd witnessed dur-

ing the Vietnam War, despite the vivid memories of the
cruelties he'd seen in nature and animals—even Black
could not believe the savagery, and yet peaceful poignancy of the scene he came upon.

Absolute stillness lay over the crazy quilt of bloody red
carnage and fresh white snow.

Jud MacDonald lay torn and tossed in a bush, var-
nished with his own blood. Virgil lay dead near Cat, his
chest on the ground, his bearded face angled awkwardly
toward the sky.

Cat lay with both paws protectively across Lilibet's inert form, licking and cleaning Lilibet's wounds, her furry
body shielding the smaller, vulnerable one from the
lightly falling snow. Her tail swished disdainfully back
and forth across Virgil MacDonald's body. Lilibet had
fainted, or withdrawn to a safe place of her own making.
Black knew not which, but he knew she was breathing.
Tiny puffs of mist formed over her mouth as her warm
breath hit the winter air.

The rush of gladness he experienced when he first realized she was alive brought him to his knees in thankful
relief.

"Thank you, Heavenly Father."

Rising shakily to his feet, he walked cautiously toward
Lilibet and Cat, unsure of Cat's reception. Cat looked up
from her gentle cleansing of Lilibet's hands. She'd known
he was there all along but only now did she acknowledge
his presence. She looked at him as if to say "It's about
time you got here." There was something else he sensed
about Cat. An attitude of accomplishment, a long-
forgotten wrong finally righted. Yes. He'd often thought
the MacDonald clan responsible for the massacre of Cat's
family. The smile on her feline face told him he was correct.

He knelt beside the two of them.

"So, old girl. You got 'em good, heh?"

Cat went back to her licking. "You're going to have to
let me touch Lilibet, you know. I know you're happy and
you want to take care of her, but it's my turn now."

Slowly, he extended his hand to rub the top of Cat's
head. She contemplated him with her gold-green eyes and

purred, a warm, humming rumble from deep within her chest. She rose on all fours and stood for a guarded moment squarely straddling Lilibet, then stepped daintily away, clearing space for Black.

With quick expertise, Black ran his hands over Lilibet's body. No broken bones. No bleeding from the mouth. Didn't seem to be any internal injuries. But she was emaciated, scratched and bruised, caked with coal dust and dirt. He could tell she'd been tied because of the rope burns around her lacerated wrists and ankles. She was blue with cold.

He fingered her matted hair, and tears flooded his angry face.

He took the transmitter from his hip.

"Jake, scramble this." He waited a few seconds.

"Okay, boss."

"I've found her. Tell no one! Until I'm sure who's responsible and have the proof to make it stick, she's not safe anywhere. I have two or three suspects I'm damn sure were involved, but I need to make sure Lilibet is safe first. We'll take her to the Lair."

"Gotcha."

"This clearing isn't large enough for you to land. The forest here is as thick as some of the stuff we saw in Nam. You'll have to lower a litter and bring her up. Hurry, Jake. The snow's beginning to stick and . . ." his voice broke a fraction, ". . . and Mrs. Hutton needs attention fast."

"Right. Give me your vector."

Black told him where they were and replaced the transmitter.

Black did then what he'd been aching to do since he'd first entered the clearing. He knelt and kissed Lilibet on the lips, gathering her carefully into his arms. Gently, he carried her away from the bloody forms of Jud and Virgil MacDonald and sat with his back against a large oak tree. With infinite tenderness, he covered her filthy face with kisses and, crooning a soft song, rocked her like a baby.

Cat returned and lay beside them. Her velvety purring blended with Black's croon until the gully was filled with a lullaby of love.

* * *

For five days, while father sky embellished mother earth with a deep mantle of snow. Black nursed Lilibet. High in his lair, just the two of them safe and secure in the midst of the crown of whiteness that surrounded them, he bathed her, spread healing ointments on her wounds, and force-fed her with nourishing broths. He massaged and exercised her arms and legs, using all the skills taught him by his grandfathers and newer techniques picked up in Vietnam. She was recovering physically. The bruises were disappearing, the cuts scabbing over, the rope burns fading. Her color was good. The translucent blue had been replaced by a faint pinkness in her cheeks.

It was her mind that wouldn't come back. He didn't blame her. Who would want to live in the world she'd barely escaped? Thank God for Cat But he was worried. If Lilibet didn't open her eyes and respond soon, he would have to take her off the mountain and find the best psychiatric care available.

He sighed and got up from where he'd been sitting by the bed staring at her. She wore his warm, navy-blue flannel robe. Her platinum-gold hair had been washed and brushed till it shone and curled around her peaceful face like a halo. Even if he weren't madly in love with her, he'd think she was one of the most beautiful women he'd ever seen. Her inner essence shone through even in this placid, inert state in which she existed. He leaned over and kissed her forehead.

"I love you, Elizabeth." Why hadn't he told her he loved her when she was here before? Afraid to reveal the depth of his feelings? Probably. *How stupid, Black. Is anything more important than this?*

He tucked the covers about her neck, and reluctantly left to use his radio transmitter and conduct business he'd neglected for a week. When he'd finished, he checked on her again, then built a roaring fire in the huge fireplace in the living room.

He poured himself a snifter of cognac and sat in a leather recliner. Not yet twilight, the huge expanse of glass around him held a scenic sight he ordinarily would have feasted upon. Stretching before him were infinite miles of mountains swaddled in a pillowy comforter of virgin snow. The fading purple hues of twilight cast an ethereal misty-blue sheen over the vast whiteness. A once-in-a-lifetime scene of enchantment, but unendurably lonely unless shared with Elizabeth.

The coon dogs lay quiet by the fire. Raffles was hiding. Cat had established herself on the ledge directly above Elizabeth's room, and hadn't left except to catch small game for food.

Elizabeth ... yes, he would call her Elizabeth from now on. The child Lilibet would always exist within her but the queenly, noble woman was truly Elizabeth. No matter what anyone else called her, she was Elizabeth to him as she had been to Grandfather. Come back to me, Elizabeth, he prayed.

Neither the fire, nor the brandy, nor the hauntingly lovely scenery helped lighten his desperate mood. He paced back and forth, and for the sixteenth time that evening climbed the stairs to check on Elizabeth. Her breathing was calm and even.

Tormented by his worry and his longing for her, and wracked with recriminations for things undone and unsaid, he paced like a madman next to her bed.

Music. Maybe music would help.

The music room was unlit except for moonlight illuminating the grand piano and Black left it that way, liking the way the moonlight lifted the reflection off the snow and carried it into the dark room. He rippled a few chords to limber his fingers. There was no hesitation about the music he wanted to play. It was a Gershwin night. And though she couldn't hear, he would play to Elizabeth.

Remembering Lilibet as a teenager, he started with "Liza," the strong, happy notes flowing and climbing ecstatically. He moved into "But Not for Me," lilting and lonely, then segued into the slower, more wistful and plaintive "Embraceable You." Easily then, with technical expertise and an emotional understanding of the piece, he played "Rhapsody in Blue." Lost in the pain, and in the glory of his love for her, Black let himself go. The dramatic melody, sometimes haunting, sometimes joyful, crashed and soared over the muffled winter forest.

* * *

Hazy and distant at first, the music penetrated the far recesses of the safe dreamland to which Lilibet had retreated. Luring and entreating her, the serenade drew her to the door of consciousness and then tugged her across the threshold. When she opened her eyes, she knew immediately where she was and questioned neither why nor how. She only knew the rightness of it. Black had opened the louvers on the glass ceiling and she looked into a satin-black sky sparkling with a million stars. The beauty of the house as it blended into the forest and mountains around it, and the knowledge that Black had built it for her, lured her into a complete awakening. Brady's Lair was a symbol of Black's understanding and knowledge of what they shared. Beyond anything she had ever known, she knew she belonged here, and she began to know the depth of his love for her.

Slowly, she sat up, not sure how she would feel. A bit light-headed, very hungry, but surprisingly strong. She ran her hands lovingly over Black's soft robe, then inspected her hands and feet. The bruises were yellowing and fading, and the lacerations healing nicely, blessings she could attribute to Black's healing skills. For a moment she remembered her last moments beneath Virgil MacDonald but then shut them out. Later, she would deal with that terror and how she had gotten here.

Swinging her legs over the side of the bed, she tentatively explored the floor with her feet and decided she was strong enough to stand up. She stretched and yawned, amazed at her strength. Black had taken excellent care of her.

Drawn toward the symphony ringing throughout the house, she tightened the tie on the flannel robe and padded toward the music room. As she passed the small library, she glanced in to see her portrait still illuminated, the rest of the room dark.

She entered the music room, walked to the center and stopped, transfixed by the enchantment of the glass-walled room, the night, the melody, and the man with his back to her who played such soulful music. She felt as if they were suspended in time, floating in the speckled space over the white plains and peaks beneath them. A corona of starlight and snow luster lit the room, outlining Black with its iridescence. His head bent, his strong hands and arms moving over the keys, he was lost in the passages of his rhapsody. He finished with a dramatic crescendo Gershwin would have loved, and then slipped into the melancholy "Someone to Watch Over Me."

Every poignant note of the refrain filtered into her body and housed itself in her soul. Incredulous, she heard Black's loneliness ... this strong, self-confident, worldly-wise man, accustomed to solving other's problems and conquering vistas unknown to most men, was lonely ... for her. As his music permeated her very being the back of her neck prickled, and the tingling ran down her spine. His loneliness matched her hunger. She realized now what the "knowing" had tried to tell her the first time she'd heard Black play at Ruby's so many years ago.

"I love you, Black," she whispered.

His keen hearing picked up the whisper and his hands faltered on the keys.

Black stopped, one hand gripping the edge of the piano, the other falling to his lap. He was afraid to turn around, afraid even now, that she would see the joy in his face at the sound of her voice.

"You shouldn't be out of bed," he said, his low voice filled with emotion.

He felt her hands on his shoulders and caught both of them in his.

"I'm fine. Really, I am. Besides, how could I sleep with all the noise you were making?"

They both laughed a little.

"It was so beautiful, Black. I could listen to you play forever."

Exactly what I'm hoping, my darling, he thought to himself.

Able to look at her now without breaking into tears of relief or joy, Black turned around and inspected her critically. "Are you sure you're okay?"

"Positive." She pirouetted away from him, and then curtsied. "All due to your excellent care. I could use a snack, though."

He roared with laughter and, holding her around the waist, whirled her around the starlit room. "If you're hungry, you're back to normal."

"Black, please . . . you're making me dizzy."

Instantly contrite, he picked her up like a child in his arms, kissed her on the cheek and said, "I'm sorry, darling. It's just so wonderful hearing you speak, seeing the pink in your cheeks, knowing you're hungry. I have a huge fire going in the living room. I'm going to put you in front of it in a comfy easy chair while I fix your dinner."

While they ate savory chicken soup, buttered corn bread, and crisp green salad, Black answered her endless questions of how he'd found her, and how they'd transported her here. He told her he'd discovered Marm and Genie happily toasting marshmallows in the cabin fireplace, and that they were now in Matterhorn with his mother. She told him of all that had happened: the conversation she'd overheard between Clarice and Sam, Margot and Cle, Tom Tee and the coal mine, her tortuous trek through the woods. Afraid to ask the awful question that had haunted her since awakening, she left it till the very last.

"Black, you know I passed out when Virgil . . . is there a possibility—did he . . . ?"

Sitting at her feet on the thick Navajo rug before the fire, Black reached for her hand and kissed it. "Did he rape you? No, sweetheart. No. Cat got to you in time. But just to make sure, when my mother brought supplies the first day, she also brought a nurse she could trust. You're fine, thank God. She also informed your mother and Doctor Turner that you were safe with me."

A great relief settled in her and she sat back to enjoy her cup of hot tea. "I wondered how you conjured up the delicious soup and corn bread," she teased. "Your mom, of course."

Concern crossed her face as she had another thought.

"Black, I have no idea how long I was in the mine. How long have I been here?"

"You've been here five days. You disappeared from Yancey two weeks ago."

"Dear God, Black!" She set down her cup with a click. "I have to get back. I've got to start things rolling against Pappy. People have to know about him and the evil things he's done all these years, to Sam's father, and me, and the illegal strip mining, and the votes he bought in Washington. . . ."

She tried to get up from the recliner but Black gently pushed her down. She couldn't understand why Black was sitting there so calmly smiling at her . . . Black who was almost maniacal about injustices.

"What's the matter with you? He and Tom Tee, and maybe even Sam, tried to murder me. I thought you'd be wanting to hang them from the first tree."

"I did, and still do. I have satisfying visions of slicing Pappy right down the middle, gutting him, and then feeding his insides to Cat. Fortunately, he was nowhere nearby when I found you, or that's what I would have done. I will extract my own revenge from Pappy in my own time, in my own way." She shivered, knowing from the tone of his voice that he meant every word he said. "My first priority was making sure you were safe and well."

"But now we have to go and make sure the whole world knows about Pappy."

He restrained her again.

"You are my prisoner, milady. You can't leave here until I say so."

"But, Black, there are things to be taken care of."

"*You* have to be taken care of. For once in your life you're going to be pampered and loved and spoiled as you deserve to be."

She sighed. "Sounds delicious, but—"

He placed a finger across her lips to shush her, then gently rubbed her bottom lip as he talked to her.

"I have a radio transmitter here, and yesterday I received great news. Pappy Hutton and Tom Tee Frye have been arrested and are being held without bond for the moment."

Mystified, Lilibet asked, "How did that happen? I know Marm doesn't have that kind of courage, and your mother and your helicopter pilot don't have proof."

A big smile spread across Black's face, his white teeth gleaming in the flickering firelight

"Eulonie Bevins."

"Eulonie Bevins?" asked Lilibet, still confused.

"She took a bus to Morgantown, found Doctor Turner and told her everything she knew about Pappy. Doctor Turner called the President, and between the two of them they made sure Pappy had handcuffs on him in no time."

Lilibet laughed in delight and whacked the arm of the chair with exuberance. "God, I wish I could have been there to see the look on Pappy's smug face."

"Unfortunately, I think you'll be seeing plenty of Pappy and the rest of them. The next few months, and maybe years, will be filled with testifying and trials, many of which you will be a major part."

"I don't care. I can't wait. It's time for Pappy to reap all the evil he's sown, to know what it feels like to be powerless," she said eagerly, but then worry chased the look of delight from her violet eyes. "But Clarice might crack under all this strain, Black. She says she hates Pappy, but they were very close. They have a rapport no one else in the family enjoys."

Black took her hand in his and kissed it softly. "Clarice had a nervous breakdown when you disappeared, sweetheart. Pappy kept her restrained in her room. When the federal marshals came to arrest Pappy, Doctor Turner was with them. She took Clarice to Switzerland to the clinic you suggested."

"Thank God! She'll finally get some help."

"How do you feel about Cle and Margot?"

"They deserve each other, Black." A shadow crossed her face. "I don't think I'll see much of them in the courtroom though. Poor Margot. Cle will amuse himself with her until he gets bored and then find someone else."

"Elizabeth, I've done some investigating on my own, and have had some excellent detectives and attorneys working on this for months, ever since I announced I was running for public office. I sensed there was a lot of double-dealing going on. What I'm trying to tell you is . . . you may have to testify against Cle, and Sam, too. Are you up to that?"

"Yes, I hate it, but I'm facing it. I faced it as I was fighting my way through the woods to get to Catawba. With Cle, it doesn't surprise me. In Sam's case it breaks my heart." She stopped a moment, searching for the right words. "I let Pappy bully me with his threat to take Genie. She was the only thing I had left. All those years, I followed a childhood notion of security for myself and my family . . . when all the time my safety and security were within me. I had only to have faith in myself and God. When I acknowledged that, I fell to my knees beside a barren sycamore tree and I felt so damn good, I didn't care if I died right there and then. I knew Marm would take care of Genie. There was only one more thing I wanted to do before I died."

Black took her tiniest toe in his mouth and sucked on it, then went on to the next one.

"What was that?" he asked between sucks and kisses of the pink toes.

"I wanted to find you."

Black's dark head moved up her leg and his lips found the ticklish sensitive spot on her knee.

"Come down here and tell me why," he said as he brought her into his arms and onto the rug next to him.

Leisurely, he unknotted the tie that held his thick robe around her and opened it to spread his hand flatly across her bare belly. He leaned on one elbow and stared at her while his fingers moved seductively in the hollows of her hipbones. Speechless, she couldn't say another word as he created magic on her yearning body. She wanted to see all of him and stayed her hand for a moment while she pulled his sweater over his head, exposing the expanse of his tanned shoulders gleaming in the firelight.

Lowering his dark head, he whispered in her ear, "I went crazy when I couldn't find you. You are the center of my existence, the reason I live. I want so desperately to be inside of you."

He yanked off his jeans and she could already feel the hard thrust of his arousal against her thigh. He placed his hand between her thighs and finding the dark, gold velvet he was searching for, inserted one, then gently two fingers to pleasure her. His sensual lips moved seductively over her body. Starting at her throat, his tongue trailed kisses down to her breasts, circling one and then the other, over and over again. She shuddered with pleasure, and raised her head to kiss and nip at his ears, his shoulders, whatever she could reach. He shook his head, "No. Later. Don't move."

He took each nipple into his mouth and sucked deeply into his throat, and each tug on her breast brought a small cry from the back of her throat. She gripped his arms, wishing he would let her kiss him, caress him, but he forced her to lie still while he tortured her with exquisite seductiveness. His mouth left her breasts and traveled unhurriedly down to her waist, then to her curly mound, kissing and blowing the softness there. When his tongue touched the warmth between her thighs, she jumped with surprise and exquisite agony. His fingers left her, leaving her empty until his dark head settled between her legs and his tongue entered the sultry, salty moistness there.

His tongue moved in and out, in and out, sucking the honey hungrily, and creating spasms of pleasure that lifted her body from the floor. He held her down while she bucked and cried out.

"Please, Black, please."

He withdrew his tongue and raised his head to move back up her body, finally reaching her mouth, his mouth demanding and searching; she tasted herself on his lips.

He lifted himself from her, breathing hard.

"Touch me, Elizabeth."

Without hesitation she reached for his thick arousal, shocked by the hot satin sheath. She watched his face as she moved her fingers up and down the rigid, silky smoothness. He closed his eyes and groaned in sweet agony. "That's right, sweetheart," he murmured roughly. "Softly now. That's all yours, my darling, it belongs to you."

She sobbed and he moved quickly then. He braced himself over her and drove his shaft into her, groaning with pleasure and the promise of what was to come. She rose to meet him but he held her hips, demanding she lie still. The exquisite agony and ache of wanting him, raged through her like a volcano until finally she screamed for him to release her.

Mercifully, he let her hips rise to meet the slam of his. They hammered against each other in mindless, primal ecstasy, searching for the release only the other could give. The airy room, suspended in space, held only the sound of the popping fire and the hungering moans of two people reaching for the stars together. Lilibet cried out for Black again and again.

"Now, my darling, go over with me," he rasped in her ear.

Both of them shook in endless spasms of joy until Black exploded into Lilibet. His shout of triumph met her cry of victory; his seed filling and spilling over her, molding and holding them together in the ultimate release.

They clung selfishly to each other, knowing they had experienced again the completeness of two similar souls in search of each other. Lilibet felt cherished but not possessed. Black felt anchored but not imprisoned.

He brought her down softly, carefully, kissing her ear, nuzzling her collarbone, caressing her breasts. When he eventually, tenderly pulled out of her she sighed happily. The knowledge that she could soon have Black within her again gave her a ringing joy and satisfaction.

"Black?"

"Umm?"

"You hated me for a while, didn't you?"

He chuckled, then he wrapped her close to him and kissed her hair.

"For a short time, I was consumed with hatred and bitterness, but my love for you was stronger. When I let the love conquer the hate, I began to watch you and then to wait for you as, underneath, I always had. I love you even more now than I did then," he said softly.

"Tell me again, please."

"I love you, Elizabeth Springer. Will you please be my wife, my companion, the mother of my children, my one for all time?"

She toyed with his hair for a moment, pretending to

think about it. "Will you mind when I run for the Senate against Cle?"

"Mind?" he demanded indignantly. "What the hell do you mean? I've been sitting here planning your campaign for the last few days. I'm going to be your campaign manager."

Lilibet laughed. "I think this country is going to have its first pregnant United States Senator."

Epilogue

SPRING 1972

Chapter 31

She'd left Brady's Lair before dawn, wanting to reach the cabin in time to see the sunrise. The children called this her "alone" place. She and Black had shown them the secret glen. It was their favorite spot for picnics. But the cabin was hers to come to for rest and renewal. The family was welcome only when invited, and she'd invited them this morning. They would be here soon.

When the Senate was in recess, the Brady family often came to the mountain for long weekends. They toured different areas of West Virginia throughout the year, holding town meetings and keeping in touch with the concerns of the citizens. Lilibet had been in office for four months and had already become a popular public servant. The ultimate destination on these trips was always the mountains.

A black-capped chickadee settled on the back of the rocker next to Lilibet. The rocker tilted back, then moved lazily back and forth.

"Hi," Lilibet said softly, and smiled. "Thought you might be with me this morning, Uncle East. It must remind you, as it does me, of the spring I met Black, and graduated from high school. We've done a lot of living and learning since then. But I think you suspected some of what was to come."

She marveled again at the intricacies of fate, the interwoven threads that influenced lives and relationships.

Cle resigned from office three years ago. The scandal of Pappy's murder and graft conviction was more than he could handle. Pappy was serving a life sentence in the state penitentiary in Moundsville. Tom Tee was there, too, serving a life term for kidnapping. The court had

never been able to find concrete proof that Cle had
knowledge of his father's crimes, so he'd never been in-
dicted. After his resignation, the governor, still one of
Pappy's lackeys, had appointed a political crony to Cle's
seat. Lilibet defeated the appointee in the last election.

Sam disappeared right before the trials began. The rumor mill said Pappy had Sam murdered so he couldn't
tell all he knew. Lilibet didn't think so. Sam was smarter
than Pappy, and angrier—and his hatred was boundless.
She was sure he was alive and well somewhere in South
America or Europe. Black never said anything but she
knew he was tracking Sam down. Knowing her husband,
he would find Sam one day—and she didn't care to spec-
ulate on what would happen when he did.

Margot had gone back to school for a teaching degree.
She lived with Marm and taught second grade at Yancey
Elementary.

"Hey, Mom, hope you've had enough 'alone time',
cause here we are."

Genie's light, teasing banter interrupted her thoughts.
She caught her breath as she watched her daughter cross
the meadow. *Dear God, she's not much younger than I
was that spring ... and she looks like me, except she's
taller. Please, God, make it easier for her than it was for
me.* She grinned ruefully, knowing that wasn't possible—
that Genie had her own lessons to learn.

Behind Genie, Black unloaded Black, Jr. from his
backpack and set him on the ground. The three-year-old's
tan legs flashed in the sunlight as he ran excitedly toward
his mother. Black caught up with Genie and put his arm
around her shoulders as they followed Blackie at a more
sedate pace.

The tiny movement in her distended belly amused her.
She was six months' pregnant and the newcomer already
recognized the presence of its family. She ran a soothing
hand over the bulge beneath her bulky white sweater.

"Aunt Clarice called from Paris. She's coming home
next week with her new husband," called Genie.

It was Clarice's fourth husband in as many years, but
she seemed happy enough.

"And guess what, Mom?" Genie continued. "The supply helicopter brought the morning newspaper, and you made the headlines again."

Genie waved the newspaper in the air.

"What did they call me this time? A militant environmental witch?"

They all laughed. Blackie reached the porch, refused help with the steps, and climbed into his mother's lap for a big hug and kiss.

"No, the 'Battling Brady', a female storm trooper fighting polluters. Do you think you're going to do any good, Mom?"

"It's a new cause, Genie, and people have to be educated. But, yes, someday we'll see progress." She brushed the black hair out of her son's eyes.

Black kissed her on the cheek and whispered "I love you" in her ear. He handed her the paper and pointed out an article in the bottom right-hand corner.

She read it while Genie took Blackie into the cabin for a snack, and Black settled on the top step, his head against the post.

HUTTON FILES FOR BANKRUPTCY

read the lead

Cle Hutton, who has been handling Hutton Mining affairs while his father is in prison, has filed for bankruptcy and gone into seclusion at the Hutton homestead in Yancey with his second wife, Sally Kay. According to bank officials, Hutton made some bad investments and needed cash to cover operating expenses for the company. Hutton was counting on the bank to roll over his notes. He discovered the notes had been bought up by a blind trust that demanded immediate payment. Unable to come up with the money, the former senator had to declare bankruptcy. Further investigation by this reporter revealed there is nothing left of the once powerful Hutton empire. Unconfirmed sources say the Harrison Easterling Foundation and BEC control the blind trust that owns the Hutton notes, but repeated phone calls to BEC offices have been ignored.

She looked at Black. He was staring out over the mountains in the distance. Silver glanced through his shining mane of raven hair, and curving furrows framed his sensual mouth. Her heart still raced when he touched her. In all thoughts and spirit, they were one.

"Well?" she asked.

He smiled savagely.

"No comment, Senator Brady."